Ma
Sur
Jam
boo
of i
Her
bee
He

THE LIFE

THE LIFE

A NOVEL

MALCOLM KNOX

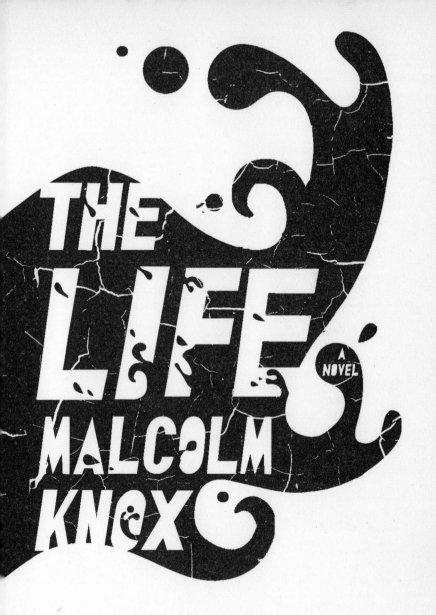

ALLEN&UNWIN

First published in Great Britain in 2011

This paperback edition published in 2012

Allen & Unwin
c/o Atlantic Books
Ormond House
26–27 Boswell Street
London WC1N 3JZ
Phone: 020 7269 1610
Fax: 020 7430 0916
Email: UK@allenandunwin.com
Web: www.atlantic-books.co.uk

A CIP catalogue record for this book is available from the British Library.

ISBN 978 1 74237 761 2

Printed in Italy by Grafica Veneta

10 9 8 7 6 5 4 3 2 1

For Lyn Tranter

DAWN PATROL

He sleeps with the radio on, all-night news services.

BBC World Service, Deutsche Welle Radio, National Public Radio, news in pulses, markets, terror, earthquake, war, numbers, old voices, waves of words cart him through the night. He is dark but his dreams speak from daytime.

He likes the radio even when he is asleep.

Most of all when he is asleep.

· From the word sea he fishes his up time, no alarm clock needed, early riser, alarm set inside him—

Now: Here he comes this man—

All in how you get up, all in how you plant the feet . . .

Paddle paddle paddle and *push, Go* . . .

He levers his fat legs, knee-free tubes, hairy calves off the horizontal and *up* . . .

. . . plants his feet perfect:

. . . standing up and on his way . . .

Out of bed. Feet land in his thoughts

in his thongs

sore big toe, stubbed black last fifty years, stubbed by the land.

Up out of his room, wash hands, past Mo's room, seventy-five-year-old ladies don't sleep good, sleep with their eyes open, their ears open.

Turning a blind eye: her genius. Mo's blind eye, 20/20.

Feels his way down the hall.

This place, this home unit: he had nightmares they'd of looked like this box him and Mo live in: blond brick, two bedrooms in a row of identikits built to confuse, who knows how the oldies find their way home from the dining hall.

Galley kitchen, bathroom with rails, bedrooms with rails, tidy garden, concrete steps. With a rail.

He is living in a retirement village. The Great One living in a retirement village.

Depends what you mean

by retirement eh.

Snug two-bed unit with rails. Rails aren't even metal, they're white plastic. Wouldn't hold him up if he fell on them. Diagonal security grilles on all the windows, all the doors, the screens. They've buggered up his diagonals, his lines he lives by, diagonals and perpendiculars, buggered up by security grilles, brown aluminium, every edge doing him wrong—

Yeah this is where he's living.

Depends what you mean

by living.

THE BI FRICKEN OGRAPHER

Yeah and so then this day you come in the kitchen and Mo sitting there with her and it's a bird, and you see Mo hates her cos Mo's blue pouchy pebbles are bright with charm but dull too, eyes like used Christmas glitter, and she's serving Arnott's Assorted and real leaf tea and acting like the bird's here to marry her boy.

How you know Mo hates the BFO:

Her bright friendly eyes: if looks could kill.

'Who are you?'

The Great Man just come in from a walk to the milk bar. Pine-lime Splice and Burger Rings. Morning tea. Got asked for an autograph. Told the grom I wasn't Dennis Keith, though people pick me for him all the time.

How's about ya do his autograph and be him anyway, the kid's gone.

And why would I want to do that? I've gone. *I wouldn't want to be him even if I was him, so why would I want to be him when I'm not?*

He's a legend, the kid goes.

Yeah, I go. *Like King Arthur.*

You are him eh.

Nah, some other kid come up drag his mate away. *DK died yonks back.*

'I'm from *Surfer*,' this bird goes. 'The mag.'

We're sitting at the melamine kitchen table in the retirement home unit. I am fifty-eight years old and eighteen stone. I am Dennis Keith, still sort of.

'Right,' I go. '*Surfer*.'

Girl looks at Mo. Mo looks at her biscuits.

'Not *Surfing*?' I go. Sitting in the middle of the kitchen at the end of the melamine table from the old house, DK's last sea anchor.

'No,' the girl almost laughs, nervy. 'Not *Surfing*. *Surfer*. Why, has *Surfing* got you lined up for a feature interview as well?'

Get up wash hands in the kitchen sink. You don't like the diagonals of this sink.

Grunt: 'Have *you* got me lined up for an interview?'

Have you, interview? Vyou, intervyou? Stop it DK wash your hands siddown.

Mo just squats there like Buddha her end of the melamine table and explains. How I should remember, *Surfer* called and called and begged and begged, it's the thirtieth anniversary of the Straight Talk Tyres, the famous day of days, and they know DK don't give interviews but they begged and begged and when all was lost they begged again . . .

'What's in it for us?' I drop in on her

yeah as if I'd remember and she knows that

Mo knows the score: we don't give our story away. We say no polite: no thanks. Then they ask again we don't say it polite. Keeps things simpler. In the early days back in them late eighties when people was starting up all that *Where Is DK Now?*, I wasn't available to say no. I was 'incapacitated', she meant to say, except what she said was, I was 'decapitated'. When they come knocking—them magazines, biographers, movie scouts, so-called TV producers—Mo tell them 'speak to our solicitors'. Then she give them a solicitor which don't exist. That sent the right message sent it real well.

Their image: The Great DK, this big mysto figure: enigmatic, elusive. For a little while they dig that. But when the little while got long they stopped digging it. You weren't an enigma, you were just unreliable. No good for film. Mercurial: good. Compulsive liar: bad. Like if you'd just had a Tarax to drink, right in front of them, you'd swear you'd had a Fanta. Your own amusement, pulling their legs. Pulling their legs right off, like insects. You saw an interview with this movie guy who been on your tail a while, had copped one of Mo's 'solicitor' letters.

Not an enigma as such, this guy said about you. *More like a dickhead.*

By the middle nineties they stop asking.

These days nobody asks. They know our stance. We don't want Hollywood or such to exploit us, our story. We ain't interested. We're permanently decapitated.

Not that they're asking.

Now out of nowhere this bird, this magazine.

'Not a brass razoo for our story,' Mo goes. 'But they're kindly paying us five hundred for the tea and bickies.'

Money's on the table. Ten of them puke-coloured ones. I give a shrug. Mo's money. Mo takes care of the coin. Mo's broken thirty years of silence and let in this girl she doesn't like. Strange but who am I to go against my Mo.

Sometimes when they asked me to sign a contract or an autograph I do it in this magic ink pen I got from a magic set, which the ink fade out and disappear five minutes after I signed. I never hung round to see their faces when they found out, but got cacks to imagine.

'So.'

Fussing round the kitchen pretending I'm doing stuff, fixing food or cleaning up but just fussing round really, putting off sitting down with her. Got the aviators pressed down hard on the nose. Wash hands again.

I sneak-peek the bird. She's sunburnt, used to be brown hair now pineapple yellow. Plain face but honest. Meaty round shoulders. Pineapple shoulders. She surfs. About twenty. Or thirty. Or forty. How would I know females. Poor kid realise she's not gunna make a living from surfing so the back door is work for the industry or write for mags and surf as much as she can, same diff in the end, industry pays for everything, calling the tune and paying the piper, and five hundred so we can't complain eh.

In a bikini under her yellow sponsor T-shirt and cut-off jeans. So there she is

My biographer/My oh my/my bi/my buy/My bi dog walker/My bi log roller/Bugger, spit it out DK. Can't do it.

'So you're my Bi Fricken Ographer.'

Sneak-peek the awe. Brown eyes, an ore of awe. White rings of awe round black and brown donuts. She's trying to hide it, be cool girl, be cool with DK. Many moons ago The Great Man get jack of the awe.

'Just cos you're a pretty young bird don't think you're gunna crack me.'

And she likes me straight-up eh I called her pretty and nobody ever calls this pineapple-shoulder girl pretty: strong yeah, tough yeah, determined yeah, but never pretty. Gritty not pretty. She's nuggety and tough and determined but not so nuggety and tough and determined she can't be flattered by an eighteen-stone moustached aviator-wearing cap-wearing fifty-eight-year-old lives with his Mo in a two-bed unit in a retirement village and will never have a conversation with her when his eyes aren't on the horizon, checking the waves, the waves, half the time forgetting what he's saying or been asked. That will be every conversation she ever has with him: he's not there. He wants her to know that now. But he can still colour her up.

Mo sitting there, hating the girl. Mo her poor old face stretched into her hospitality smile.

Copied from something she saw on the box.

But she's the one let this BFO in. For five hundred. Things must be tight.

He gives her more razzing, this BFO. Does his Weird Ole DK the crazy bones legend. Oh she might crack him yeah.

'Why don't you both go for a walk,' Mo cuts in all cheery like you're shy lovebirds. 'It's walk time anyway, Den. Go on.'

Clock the clock. Eleven thirty. No choice. It's walk time.

Down the hill. In my kingdom. Marine Parade. Centre of the surfing universe, Billabong and Globe and Rip Curl and Quiksilver and Roxy and who knows what, greatest concentration of breaks in the known world, greatest concentration of rip-off merchants and sunglasses salesmen and the streets of gold brick lay down their red carpet every day The Great DK come down for his constitutional.

Don't say much just taking in the sights.

'This where you've always lived?' she goes.

I take her two more blocks before I speak.

'Live in the tube. Always did. Yeah.'

'In the tube, right.'

'The ones wondering what I was doing when I wasn't in the tube, they made up stories about me.'

'Made up stories.'

'They couldn't handle me. I left it all in the water. And so but they needed more from me, so they made up their stories. The myths. The Great DK. The Legend. All bull. Here. This place. Where it all began. But didn't really.'

The DK guided tour: take her down Rainbow Bay, palm trees and grassy verges and concrete canyons of holiday units. Streets you follow, streets you avoid, you're on automatic. She wants to go left at the bottle shop but a certain corner got its own forcefield and you head off other way. The kerb gutter's been done over with crazy paving. Agave trees everywhere, remind me of me: sharp leaves, roots stripped bare, public display, what you see is what he's got.

The boulder at the mouth of the path between the car park and Snapper Rocks. Locals' boulder. Used to be The Pit. Used to be spraypainted with a locals' warning.

Now spraypainted:

DK LIVES

She sees me back home. Hand on me elbow work me up the steps. Cos I won't grab that rail . . .

Her questions she won't ask about the unit, the retirement village.

The diagonal security grilles buggerising me diagonals. Plastic rails on the steps, plastic rails in the bathroom, plastic rails in the shower.

Never, Dennis, never grab your rails, first rule of . . .

BFO don't ask him nothing about The House, so he doesn't hate her. Let her back next time.

Day me and Mo moved into this unit was the day I started waking up at three in the morning and riding to The Other Side.

WATER FRONTAGE

He can't remember being a kook. Fifty years ago. Or maybe he never was. Maybe he just turned up one day and . . . yeah . . .

Every night he's out there. Every morning two hours before dawn. Nobody sees him. He tries not to see himself, lumbering fat old kook.

Goes out there every night or

or morning yeah that black cold hour too late for night too early for dawn.

Hour when the cops come drag you off.

Out in the dark his chopper in the garage with the Daihatsu Charades and Toyota Camrys and Mazda 3s and Hyundais them safe little toy cars, then yeah this one Sandman panel van sprayed purple and orange . . .

Grabs his chopper by the throat walks it up the driveway, rode it when he was twelve years old and eight stone, rides it now he's fifty-eight and eighteen.

Never lost this one. Never loses nothing.

His fat legs, knee-free tubes fold round the wheels and he's off in the dark out the gates, away, he's out, busted free, breakout! Thongs pump through the retirement roads and roundabouts, his mouth opens and shuts round each cross street, he's on his highway and zips through shops and past servo and on causeway and out of town, out of here, over the river and now his nostrils open to the night-time stink of onshore salt and mangroves and frogs, life at last, he can smell frogs and it's deeper than dark, the darkest dark where nobody won't never see him . . .

The lights of town a long way behind, The Great One doesn't throw no shadow in the shadows, big blob on a pushbike in his sleeping T-shirt and his sleeping boardshorts and his thongs, and he's off scot-free

yeah.

MALCOLM KNOX

He homes in on the stick hidden in trees, the stick in the sticks. The nest.

Parks the Malvern Star, leans it in the scrub and pulls out stick.

Moonlight on fibreglass.

A bird scoots.

Tinkle behind him as the chopper falls on a root.

Yeah but

but what he hears is tomorrow's swell through the scrub over the dune, through the sea grass, over the dune down the path across the open stretch, up the channel . . .

He's here. On The Other Side. Where no-one come.

Only way he can do it. Only way he can get them off his tail, stop them watching.

The way it has to be, has to be, whatever will be, no—

He will make it what it will be.

Yeah . . .

But he can't be watched.

Steps into the ink.

Creatures blindness fear.

No:

memories.

Paddles into yesterdays.

Makes ripples with his hands and sees Hawaii, North Shore, Sunset, waves the same no matter how big or small.

Or like Lisa said: you see waves you see music . . .

Beneath him the board half sinks, poor old stick wondering what's it done wrong to end up here under an eighteen-stone kook.

Puts his fat hands under his big round boobs, should get a bra, wonder the boys don't wolf-whistle him down the beach, or maybe they do.

Maybe they do yeah.

Pushes up to sit and for a sec thinks he's got it at last, but nah not this time, over we go, a wobble and a check and over we go . . .

Can't even sit on his board in the water. Can't balance: glug, not even a splash.

Weeks of nights he spends paddling trying to sit up but over he goes. Brings him to tears.

Stick squirts out towards the bank. He wades over, bungs it under his chest paddles back in water so shallow his toes scrape on the slimy bottom . . .

Stretch his mind he can see Sunset, Pipe in the ripples he makes when he falls off his board . . .

But DK you're not even in the sea. The sea would bring real waves, knock him down and for good, drowner waves for a drowner on his drowner fricken board. Should be going out on a learner board in little learner waves on a bright clean sparkly day like all them learners.

Worse than death.

Not even in the sea. He's in the lagoon. In the dark. In the night. Over The Other Side. Over the causeway. Out of town. Away from the curse, away from the whispers, away from the dead. In the morning.

Tears.

Nobody sees him cept the one he's trying to kid.

Alone where nobody can see him thrashing and falling and inviting all the bad back in, opening the door, all the bad and the waste, death and the waste, murder and the waste, waste and the waste . . .

He is waste.

Collects itself up like bluebottles on the high-tide line, and the high-tide line is that seventy-five-year-old lady back there, only one who knows, right now lying awake in her bed wondering can she still pretend when he gets back to wake up and not know, pretend they had a normal night sleep and now for breakfast she make his muesli, like she made it since the year dot, he's hungry as usual, surfers are always hungry and he's no exception and when the surfing went away the hunger didn't . . .

She'll ask has he done his greens and his whites and his blues, same questions every day, her blind eye 20/20, her pretending she isn't the only one who knows . . .

. . . yeah . . .

She knows.

She's the high-tide line it collects round:

His Mo.

Do anything for him.

•

Back into town. In the unit, wash hands, creep past Mo's room. His bed has a deep dent in it like a trench or a burrow. When he climbs back in the salt has dried on him.

Radio's still on.

DAY AT THE RACES

This other day three days later:

She's waiting for us when Mo brings me home from the shops. We been at the mall I sit at the playground eating a pine-lime Splice while Mo done the supermarket. I get to push the trolley back to the Sandman.

Home sweet plastic rails, diagonal grilles. DK wash hands in the kitchen sink and make a burst for the melamine table.

BFO waiting on the doorstep. DK carves straight past her.

BFO lets me Mo fix her a cup of tea, bag this time, then straight into it *Surfer* or *Surfing* must be on her case, deadlines and whatnot. Asks me why I give it away.

'Eh?'

'Why did you give it away?'

I tell her I haven't given nothing away.

'They reckon I've give it away but I never did, thing is they're scared of me, they wanna drive me off the world tour, they know I'd still beat em all but they got agendas . . .'

From behind me face I can see the way she's looking at me. The size of me. The shape of me. The sweat on me. The cripple shuffle out Mo's Sandman panel van sprayed purple and orange. The welcoming handshake like laying something dead and boned in her hand: gag toy, silicon turd. She doesn't know is it polite to laugh, ever, and let me know she's in on the joke, or more polite to pretend I'm to be took serious.

She doesn't laugh. She looks at me quiet and solemn.

So I tell her to laugh. About my conspiracy theories she just lapped up.

'It's a joke, Joyce.'

She shakes her head.

'My name's not Joyce.'

Females! I dunno and never will that's for sure.

She keeps on searching me like she's guessed something. Like it isn't as laughable as everyone, most of all me, the DK I'm giving her at any rate, makes out.

Or maybe I'm thinking wishful.

I tell her straight: 'No point you talking to me.'

'Why?'

'Story's already written. Old-time legend, burnt out, disappeared, haunts the scene like a ghost, but gets up for one last wave, one last Big Tuesday—'

'It was Big Wednesday.'

'Yeah?' Put two fingers up either side the pads of me aviators, scratch me nose, glasses moving up and down so she nearly gets a glimpse of The Great Man's eyes. 'You sure? I thought it was Thursday.' *Tuesday/ Wednesday/Turdsday.*

Now she smiles. Reckons I'm having her on.

It's all on the record: greatest surfer on the planet, the pothead, the smackhead, the manic genius, the sick bastard, the schizo, the flame-out, the yeah but it's

'You've already wrote it,' I tell her. 'You already know it. But you don't know nothing. Jigsaw with too many missing pieces, too many pieces look same as other pieces.'

Love jigsaws, do them all time day and night, or did in the old house.

'I'm ninety-nine parts urban myth. It's all there. It's all here.'

Well yeah . . . but no!

DK's signature line.

The girl in the fibreglass:

DK's moment in time.

'Story's all wrote,' I go on. 'Legend, epic. I'm Morrison, Hendrix, Joplin, Moon. Done gone died young left a good-looking corpse.'

'But you didn't die.'

Yeah nor did Jagger. Jiggery jaggery/Jig jags and zig zags/I done zigs and zags between me zigs and me zags/Yeah! Go DK you rule!

'Makes you so sure?' I go.

I'm both rolled into one: the dead legend who gets to watch the rest of the movie.

But from the exit aisle.

'Remember the sign on that rock,' I go.

'DK lives?'

'Yeah right think about it.'

She thinks about it. Nothing.

Give her a hand.

'Why'd they write **DK LIVES** if he's still alive?'

I don't give her eye contact. She never catches me. She doesn't stop trying but it's just the ruddy don't know for

keep the aviators pressed down on her.

While she's interviewing me or whatever it is she's doing to me I get the panics and up I go, bust out of some sentence—hers or mine doesn't matter—and go in my bedroom and shut the door on her. Won't come out till she's gone.

I know what she's thinking out there.

One afternoon we go in this pub. She tries to take me out to the beer garden scope the waves but there's people there and I don't like those.

Next to the beer garden is this surf shop. Two world champions—two!—young enough to be DK's grand kids!—at this surf shop one of them owns—owns!—gracing the world signing their gear, but when they clock DK in the beer garden they come over and chat, cool but not so cool they can hide their awe, and DK makes sure the BFO sees it tucked in behind jokes and grins. World champs don't even see the BFO.

'Hey DK sizey out there today,' first world champ goes, nodding at Snapper over DK's shoulder. DK doesn't follow his look. *DK Today/ DK Today/Like that. Idea for new TV show.*

Second world champ comes out, gives a general Hawaiian horn hand. 'Got a few this morning. Fully sick DK.'

BFO looking at me. Me looking anywhere but. Her. Them.

I'll give them *sizey*.

I'll give them *fully sick*.

World champ asks DK, 'Ya goin for a paddle this arvo?' A running gag. Running gag. Keeps on running like these kids run, building up its fitness so one day it can be a real gag.

'Not this arvo son,' I go, 'I wouldn't want to take all yer waves.'

'Yeah good onya. Later, DK.'

And the BFO's not up to this not up to it at all, not one bit. Shaking in her thongs. Not cos she's a girl. I don't give a stuff about that. It's cos I'm her hero. And them world champs is her heroes. And I'm their hero. So I'm her hero times two, hero squared.

Them hot new kids don't have time for no rumours.

For them the DK name can never be bad.

No jail time, no dead birds in fibreglass.

Cos DK is the best there ever was and that rubs everything else out.

When she goes off to buy two schooners I slip off in the scungy TAB. I couldn't give a fart about racing never have, but it's empty at least.

She come back. She goes, to make conversation, 'What's your tip in this one?'

It's dogs. Roddy was into dogs. Said when them in the know didn't want it to win, they give it two litres of milk before the race and it couldn't run for nuts. No dope test for milk. No jockey to blame. Nice system, dogs.

'The white one,' I go.

The BFO squints at the screen. They're all white or faded. Dodgy TV set. *Dodgy doggy.* Stop DK.

'With the tablecloth on,' I go to help out.

The one with the red and white check jacket or shirt or suit or whatever it is they call that thing the dishlickers wear.

She puts down ten bucks.

It come in.

Next race she goes: 'Which one this time?'

'The white one,' I go. 'With the tablecloth on.'

She puts down ten bucks.

It come in.

Next race she goes: 'Which one this time?'

'The white one,' I go. 'With the tablecloth on.'

She puts down ten bucks.

It come in.

She thinks I'm some kind of mystic see the future and that and she's right I am, I was, DK = pure genius. Genius for seeing what's coming next. I can read the undercurrents start paddling so I'm in the take-off spot before anyone else, I can read the very bloody ocean itself . . .

I'm two hundred up when I put my hand out. First time I've seen her fighting with herself. I get a giggle: she isn't such a brown nose that two hundred bucks don't mean something to her. She don't want to give it to me but then she thinks she got to. She's better off than I am. But reckons if she give it to me that easy I won't respect her now, never mind tomorrow morning eh.

She looks at me like I'm having her on.

'Give,' I nod.

I take it all and my Bi Fricken Ographer is spewing. She tries to force herself to be nice but can't. Me pissing meself. Here she is sitting on a three-foot offshore day in a dark stinking TAB in a pub when we could be out at least scoping waves, or better still me scoping and her out surfing, and instead I've took what thirty bucks? off her, plus one-seventy in profits, insult to injury.

'You know,' she goes, 'I wasn't sure if you'd like going down past the surf shops and the waves and the guys and everything, I mean, anymore.'

I don't say nothing.

'It must make you . . . miserable, I guess I thought. To see guys like that all out there, doing it, living the life that you . . .'

She give up trying to be nice now.

From the pub's bottle-o I get her to buy the most expensive bottle of wine with my money.

Then I remember I don't like wine. Never dug alcohol. Haven't took one sip of the schooner of beer she got me.

Do your research girl. The Great DK never drunk.

I mean drank.

And yeah the look she gives me outside the bottle-o it's not she's in a mood it's it slipped out she couldn't stop it it's
yeah she
so what's she doing here if
hates me guts eh.
Me own BFO hates me fricken guts.

•

MALCOLM KNOX

We walk out the pub with this forty-buck bottle of plonk and me with one-sixty in my pocket and the BFO she's eh what's not to love?

She dumps me without a word at Mo's, says she has to go for a wave.

Says it to drive in the knife she lined up in my back with that talk about me being miserable seeing surf shops and kids surfing

says it thinkingly.

Gets her money's worth yeah.

I go in give the wine bottle to Mo. She goes all gooey and soft and give me a kiss on me old noggin, then turns all suspicious, like—'Where did you get this?' Then gooey and sweet again. Can't remember me ever giving her something on her not-birthday, not-Xmas. Ladies like gifts. It means a lot to her.

Even though Mo doesn't drink ether. I mean *either.*

MO DON'T DRINK NEITHER

A big old lady Mo is, genuine big and genuine old, everyday cotton floral print house dresses balloon out like shrouds/*like clouds*/like mushroom clouds over the stalks of her legs still fine and slim and not a vein in them, she lets them show, legs like Rod's, surfer legs, lolly legs . . .

She's got a stack of different dresses and they're all the same. House dress floral print in pale blue, in pale pink, in pale green, in pale yellow, in pale grey, in pale blue, in pale pink, in pale green, in pale yellow.

Mo was always the big flower folding me in, called me her little bee hiding in her petals. But before she was big she must of been small and yeah but she doesn't like to talk about it, 'hardscrabble' is her word, dunno what it means but I know what it means, hardscrabble, her lot, sixth of twelve, country town but in one them streets of country towns like streets of the suburbs of the cities, houses butted against each other: chainlink fence, cracked concrete drive, fibro garage, buffalo grass lawn, fibro cladding, lino floors, fibro walls, terry towelling bedspreads, reek of damp and mothballs.

Chainlink, cracked concrete, fibro, buffalo grass, fibro, lino, fibro, terry towelling, damp and mothballs.

They was Catholics and her parents thirsty ones, her dad a driver her mum a womb. The 'walking womb-dead' Mo calls her. They guzzled and grizzled. Mo tried to grow up fighting versus eleven other mouths. Parents too thirsty to step in and umpire. Mo grew up fast, or slow, hard to tell she says.

Chainlink, cracked concrete, fibro, buffalo grass, fibro, lino, fibro, terry towelling, damp and mothballs.

They fought for something to eat something to wear, was always someone fighting you and someone pally with you but never the same one, so she said, a crew of twelve but not a crew or a team at all, every man jack for themself, and mother and father too thirsty for words and off to the races Saturday and home drunk to drink some more. Thirsty work, being Mo's parents.

Amazing bit was, she said, her mum and dad loved each other and enjoyed each other's company, preferred each other over the twelve. She wondered why they had nippers at all. They had a true romance. When they shot through on the spree they shot through together left the eldest nippers to look after the rest. To fight and fight and gang up and backstab and lie and it was nasty and brutal, Mo always says, nasty and brutal, shaking her head, not the time to go into the details, not now it's so long ago, not even back when it wasn't so long ago

yeah nasty and brutal.

Chainlink, cracked concrete, fibro, buffalo grass, fibro, lino, fibro, terry towelling, damp and mothballs.

They bring her up to not know nothing about nothing except how to fight to get to the end of the day, get food in her tum and a corner to sleep in. She had this sister who didn't like mash potato, snuck it in scrapes under the edge of the table when no one's looking. After the meal's over Mo creeps back in the kitchen and under the table and picks off potato dried hard as clay. Chips! Hard days eh.

She sure didn't know nothing about boys and what boys done with girls, and this from a girl with four brothers, but four brothers meant seven sisters and when there's seven sisters it's the sisters rule, the brothers aren't boys, they're just terrors and fighters like rats. Not boys.

So she didn't know what boys done. With girls. *To.*

She won't talk no more. Maybe the BFO'll crack her open on the details. The girls home, the nuns, the running away. The rest of it.

Chainlink, cracked concrete, fibro, buffalo grass, fibro, lino, fibro, terry towelling, damp and mothballs.

And screaming. Someone always screaming at the top of their voice. *Keep your voice down to a scream*, Mo used to scream at me and Rod. We thought it was funny. She was funny.

How'd she get to stay funny after all that? That *hardscrabble*? But she was. She tease us and kid us and pull off our bedspreads in the morning sing out, *Hands off cocks and put on socks! Wakey wakey, hands off snakey!*

How'd she do that?

She never took a drop of alcohol that's for sure. Or I never saw her. Said she had an allergy.

She never did no exercise neither. Said she had a bone in her leg.

I tried alcohol but it didn't agree with me neither. It disagreed with me. I disagreed with it. We agreed to disagree, drink and DK, kept each other at arms length.

What Mo said about drink: *We agree to disagree.*

She stayed funny among all that cracked concrete, fibro and buffalo grass. And the stink of tinned meat cooking in a saucepan of boiling water. How they knew it was dinner time.

Or at least, she made me and Rod laugh.

The BFO'll ask me about them rumours went round and round in my heyday: DK a foundling. How he been living on the beach, the rocks eh, till Mo picked him up—tough, yeah. Rumours. How DK's real dad, this rumour Rod himself started up as a joke when we was trying to raise coin to send me to Hawaii, was Duke Kahanamoku (yeah, the resemblance is amazing if you take away the colour of me skin and eyes and hair . . .).

I'll tell the BFO she better ask Mo, and this is a good answer to protect me and protect Mo, cos if there's one person the BFO is more scared of than me it's my Mo, and the nicer Mo is to the girl the scareder the girl is of Mo, so if there's anything I don't want to talk about I'll say to the BFO, 'Girl, you're gunna have to ask Mrs Keith on that one.' It's as good as *Well yeah . . . but no!*

Better. Cos she's not gunna ask.

ALL LINED UP

I nick out in the dead of night the dead of morning, the hour when the cops come raiding. They raid me now they won't find me there. But they haven't raided me since me thirties, the eighties, so fat load of good it's doing me. I wish they could raid me now, wish I could of said back then, *Come back in twenty-five years boys.*

I get it all lined up: Ride in on a wave of radio words, legs over the bed, past Mo's room out the diagonal grille door, down the steps (don't touch the rail!), in the garage, past the oldies' cars, *Oldsmobiles* yeah, out through the shrubs and toy roundabouts, over the causeway, stink of frogs and mangroves, pedal my chopper to my bush, down chopper, pick up stick, wade in the lagoon and

and water's warm as soup left to go cold. The phosphorus lights up to greet me, fairy lights.

Can sit on my board now. Wobbles but holds. I'm not tea-bagging. Can hold my head high. The nose points up out of the water like a great big prong and it hits me how dickly the whole thing always was.

Never hit me at the time but

but yeah

how it always was. How it never was.

I didn't realise.

Must of been obvious to everyone else but. The way I sat. Big nose at ten o'clock while every other kept his down under the water . . .

But I can sit up on the damn thing, flap round big meaty paws scare them mangrove birds into the air.

Least you can still scare someone.

Get the stick back in the bush, meself back onto me chopper, back onto the track, back on the road, back over the bridge, back through the sleeping streets, back in the sleeping house, back in me sleeping trench.

Radio still on.

And it's still dark.

WHAT'S THIS THEN

Then the morning when the BFO is already here and she's with Mo
and they're having a cup of instant coffee and *laughing*.

Real laughing.

Long time since that.

I come in the kitchen in sleeping T-shirt and sleeping boardies and
aviators. They look up at me like I'm just this feller who lives there
who's got up out of bed.

Not like I'm *me*, and yeah they're laughing.

I say nothing. Get my muesli into the bowl, fill it with milk, sit
me end of the melamine table. Starving.

Every day same big bowl of muesli, same brand filled with milk.
It's not there, I go nuts.

They didn't have that brand in Hawaii . . .

Mo telling her about Joe.

Joe Blow, Mo's bloke, Rod's dad. Joe was a racing identity, a tinker,
a tailor, a soldier, a travelling salesman, a colourful character.

Joe give her a home.

Joe always creeping off from it.

Joe no good to anyone, cept when he come home he get her up
the duff again.

'Could of been more,' Mo says, 'he got me duffed every year after
Roddy but they wouldn't take.'

The last ones standing, Rod and Mo. Yeah and DK don't forget DK.

Laughing like a pair of old girlfriends:

She's telling the BFO:

'Everyone wanted me to get rid of Joe. Give Joe Blow the throw!
Like an advert jingle it was. But you know what? I couldn't get rid of
him cos he was never around to get rid of!'

What they're laughing at.

MALCOLM KNOX

And then she goes Joe liked her pregnant cos he liked the look of her, you know, and she cups her hands round the chest of her house dress round the pale green floral print and I'm sick to me stomach and the BFO giggles behind her hand, and now I know as I mow down my muesli that they've forgot I'm here at all, I can't believe it, the BFO must of put something in Mo's instant coffee get her yammering away like this, I'm embarrassed and disgusted and I get up and take my muesli and try to find somewhere else to eat it but the unit this hellhouse is too small and I don't like anywhere else can't sit anywhere else but my end of the melamine table and so yeah, I sit back down to listen to this girlie talk about how *hardscrabble* Mo's married life was moving from one place to the next, every year up the duff, Joe off doing his whatsit wherever he was, not *being got rid of*, denying her the pleasure, all round the countryside, and she's getting pregnant in boats, on the dinette of a caravan, in a raging thunderstorm, none of them taking but, and lucky too cos she's got her boy Roddy and never enough to feed him with . . .

. . . yeah . . .

She worked. She worked in pubs. She worked in laundries. She worked behind the desk of a SP bookie counting his money. She worked doing typing for a mayor. She always worked. When she needed someone look after Roddy she dump him on her friends, always the same:

Chainlink, cracked concrete, fibro, buffalo grass, fibro, lino, fibro, terry towelling, damp and mothballs.

She tried going back to live with her mother and her father but they were still all tied up in each other they were lovers, they still drunk and drunk and shot through on the spree together, they were old ones now pickled in drink, but pickled together, together, no room for their sixth and her nipper.

Their grandson.

No room for Rod, no time for Roddy.

So Mo gone back to Joe. Or back to the place where he'd find her when he come back. On again with the Mo-Joe Blow show.

This is where my muesli is done and I walk out the house, and the BFO doesn't even notice I'm gone.

. . . yeah . . .

I go for a walk round town, *my* town. All the park benches been replaced by wooden seats shaped like surfboards. Everything round here that could be shaped like a surfboard, is. Signs, plaques, letterboxes, outdoor showers, even windows: all the same shape, like the place has some kind of surfboard-sickness on the brain. Seems the only things that aren't shaped like surfboards anymore are surfboards.

I go for a walk to *my* milk bar. Don't need to say, don't need to pay. Pine-lime Splice and a bottle of orange Tarax. Ta, Bob.

'No worries, DK.'

'No worries, Bob.'

I don't mind this new Bob. They've changed over the years, folk who own my milk bar, changed too fast for me, but the first one was Bob back when I was a grom, and I can't keep up so whoever they is they's all Bob to me.

Two groms and this bird ask me for an autograph.

I do me usual. Low growl like a mangy mongrel—

'What's that mean?'

Smaller of the grommets holding out a bit of newspaper, today's paper that is, and a Bic biro.

'Like, can you sign this Mr Keith?'

I look at it like he's asking me to do the Su Fricken Doku. I look at him but he can't know that; my trusty mirror aviators on.

The same aviators I had when . . .

'Sign? What's sign?'

Low mongrel growl. How cranky old dogs get.

He nods holding his nerve. They can hold their nerve with this fat old man they can hold their nerve looking over the falls of an eight-foot face sucking up behind Snapper . . .

I draw breath waiting . . .

The bird steps forward and I think she's gunna say 'Please? Pretty please with sugar on top?'

But instead she lifts up her singlet. Just like that. She got a bikini on. With her thumb she points to the brown V on her chestbone . . .

. . . yeah . . .

The Enigmatic Legend, the King of the Point, The Man, The Great Man, drops their Bic biro on the cracked concrete footpath.

Chainlink, cracked concrete, fibro, buffalo grass, fibro, lino, fibro, terry towelling, damp and mothballs . . .

'Me Splice's melting,' I go.

They watch me waddle off. No laughter no laughing no giggling. Grom's getting mad at the bird.

They aren't seeing his royal fatness wobble up the hill. Me knee-free tubes lopsided.

He's going off at her for cruelling their chances.

'No respect! You gotta have respect!'

His barking at her, last thing I hear.

I love the youth of today. They don't know a fricken thing and if they were told it they'd turn their back on it. Cos they know everything already. The rumours about Lisa belong to their parents and cos they belong to their parents the rumours is just that, bullshit to the kids.

I love them kids.

THE QUESTION

Except for the fricken BFO who's set up camp at the red melamine table with Mo when I get home and now they've got buttered slices of white bread, a plate of wet iceberg lettuce leaves, slices of tomato, processed cheese, chicken loaf, Peck's Anchovette Paste, help yourselves ladies, sure, be my guest, don't mind me

and the thing is they

I wash hands, plonk down at the head of the table, the man of the house, The Man of the Point, the Legend, the King, the one three kids are down there now in the break telling stories about, new stories about King Dennis The First down the bush telegraph, the surf telegraph, the coconut wireless, up the coast on the salt breeze, all of them talking about me, about me, about me . . .

And I'm listening to my Mo on about herself:

'Ah the sixties. Not much fun them years, not much "Sixties" happening for the Keith family.'

'When Joe left us without the keys to whatever house we was living in and we stayed in the Salvos hostel for six weeks till he showed up again.'

'When we had no rent money and live in a fishing shack on The Other Side, dirt floor, no electricity, no stove, no running water.'

'When Joe turned up late at Rod's christening and the priest sang out, "What's the name of the nipper?" and Joe's meant to say, "Rodney Brian Keith", but instead he forgot the nipper had a middle name and he sang out, "His name's Rodney Keith, isn't it!" so that my boy gets christened "Rodney Keith Keith".'

'When we was living in the country and Joe's trapping roos and Rod put kero on the open fire and singed all his hair off. In hospital—'

—loads of hospital stories—Rod with meningitis, Rod with hepatitis, Rod with an infected tooth, and Mo, Mo had to go in a lot for herself, with mysteries, mysteries, always mysteries that left them in some stranger's home for a few weeks Rod fighting with their kids till it all got too rough and Mo come out in the nick of time—

Rod causing trouble with a capital T—

When Rod sconed some kid with a hammer.

When Rod scalped some kid with a crowbar.

When Rod flayed some kid with a sander.

When Rod got some kid with the back of a knife.

When Rod pushed the bar heater onto a kid.

When Rod pushed a kid off a high fence and that kid got mauled by the neighbour's standard poodle.

When her and Rod live in a caravan in someone's backyard.

When they live in someone's granny flat. (Chainlink, cracked concrete, fibro, buffalo grass, fibro, lino, fibro, terry towelling, damp and mothballs . . .)

When they pitched a tent in someone's backyard and live in that.

When it blew away.

When Mo give up and left Rod at an orphanage, a Catholic boys' home, just like she been at one years earlier, and when she realised she'd went full circle, orphanage to orphanage, shot through on to shooting through, nuns to priests, she raced back and took her boy out of there and the paperwork took her best part of the day but it taught her a lesson, taught her the final lesson, and this is when she scrounged up the deposit—Whack!—bang down on a house.

The House.

Bang, she smack her hand on this very melamine table, here it is, a deposit, on a house, and it happened to be fifteen minutes' walk or four minutes' ride on a chopper from the finest point break on the east coast and finest point break in the known fricken universe. You ask me.

Bang. Down goes the deposit.

Her and Rod got the house. The House.

Rod didn't know nothing about nothing. When he asked Mo did they own the house now she said, *We're all in debt to the bank, we owe all our money to the bank now,* and Rod didn't get it, he couldn't sleep he was so scared, he had nightmares about pipes and factories and darkness and noise, factory noise, cos he thought she owed so much coin she never pay it back and they'll come take the house away.

And then young Rodney Keith Keith discovered that point break and stopped thinking about the bank.

And he discovered someone else for a change.

When her and Rod move to the seaside, the Gold Coast, the coast of gold, the salt air up their nostrils, allowed at last to go to the pound and get what Rod always wanted which was a dog, and the dog she got him was this beagle cross called Sam . . .

And Mo worked peeling and veining prawns.

And Rod collecting bottles from the beach rubbish bins to trade in for twopence each, making ten bob on a good day which he'd then take to the butcher and buy a bag of bones for Mo to make a week's soup with . . .

And . . .

And . . .

And . . .

When . . .

When . . .

When . . .

The BFO come all this way to listen to my life story and instead what she's getting is Mo and Rod. I'm hardly even in it. I'm the King of the Point, The Man, the Legend, the Enigma, and the BFO isn't even listening to me or asking me ONE SINGLE QUESTION . . .

But she is. I catch the sly flash of white under her black eyelash, not so much awe now she's over the awe, and I can see, I see, how she reckons she's setting me up, bringing me to the boil, where I'll be so jack of listening to Mo on and on about herself and Rod and their flaming *hardscrabble* that . . .

How brain damaged you think I am girl?

The BFO, trying to make me jealous.

Instead she gets me upset.

I lock meself in me room.

When she come back the next day I don't come out.

Mo has to keep her entertained.

When she come back the next day I don't come out.

Mo has to keep her entertained.

When she come back the next day I don't come out.

She gets tired of Mo.

And that's what makes me real upset.

BFO's mistake: kidding herself she has an open mind, that her story isn't already wrote.

What makes me upset?

When she goes:

'So Mrs Keith there's this bit you've skipped over.'

And you can hear a pin drop but it's not a pin, it's the BFO's heart.

Through the wall between my bedroom and the kitchen I hear Mo scratch round and save the day.

'Ah then love, you mean Shangrila.'

QUEENSLANDER!

. . . yeah no, don't want her to get me started on The House, I start I won't finish, and that wouldn't be fair on me would it.

Every inch. Every square cubic inchlet of The House I knew
nah *know*.

It was a QUEENSLANDER House, I remember the word. Me first memory. Even though I was a Queenslander I never heard there was houses with the same name. QUEENSLANDER. And it has a name on a plaque by the front door: *Shangrila*. Mo said Shangrila is Chinese for This Is It We're Set.

The QUEENSLANDER was wooden on stilts with lattices downstairs round the stilts and big airy rooms with fans and a sleepout veranda surround the kitchen and heaven on twelve sticks. It was half a house really, this boarding house that been down on Kirra beach and the owner had sawed it in half and put one half on a truck and send it up the hill. Cos it was a boarding house it had lots of tiny crooked rooms upstairs and down. Mo didn't like them but Rod thought it was a ripper all them rooms nobody needed, scuttled through like a rat, like a dirty little possum, every square inch. Eventually Mo begin knocking out a few walls with her bare hands to make bigger rooms to live in.

In the backyard there's banana trees and rubber trees and palms and big tropical flowers, hibiscus and whatnot.

Shangrila didn't have no views of the beach. It had a view of the neighbour's house but that was also a QUEENSLANDER so nobody didn't mind.

It had a view of the cemetery over the back fence.

Sam loved the QUEENSLANDER except being a beagle he was always following his nose first asking questions later. Mo built this big wire fence round the backyard but Sam dig a hole under it. Her and Rod filled in the holes and Sam get his nose under the gate and push the latch up and get the thing open and he's off, down the road, sniffing foxes or whatnot. Her and Rod called him Houdini.

It was like he didn't want to be with them.

But then he gets tired of wandering and plonk himself someone's front doorstep and they read the phone number on his tag and he had a name, Samuel J. Keith, and then the phone call and it's Christmas all over again.

Cemetery wasn't strictly Catholic or Jehovah's Witnesses or whatever, it was allsorts. Buddhist, Hare Krishna, Church of England, you name it. Only place on the Gold Coast where all them minorities could go and be left in peace. Dunno where they come from, there wasn't none at the local school cept for a couple of Chinese, they must of been trucked in from all over south Queensland. They all had separate sections, like it mattered to the Hindus to give the Muslims a wide berth even if they was all pushing up the same daisies.

Sam got off on rooting round the gravestones and mausoleums. Thought he'd died and went to heaven. Why he was always pulling the Harry Houdini under the back fence: he liked sniffing among them zombies.

Sam and Rod was always in that cemetery. Played chasings and hide-and-seek and always laughing and clowning round. Played in there at night heaps. At first it was a bit scary and Rod creep the crap out of the mourners who come in there by jumping out behind a tombstone. But laughing and horsing about was his way of getting over the spookiness. The louder he was, the less chance the undead had to come crawling up his spine. Sometimes people'd shoo him away there was a funeral or whatnot going on, but Mo said he brought new life to the graveyard. It was filled up with mango and avocado and banana trees and them coloured flowers, hibiscus and frangipani and that. Pretty nice place if you weren't dead. Great view of the ocean if you can stand up to see it.

And so yeah it was one night Sam barking his head off in the graveyard. Mo says her and Rod come running, they think Sam's scoped some zombie or what have you.

'So me and Rod creep out there, it's twilight hour, not dark but not light,' she goes, Mo to the BFO this is, 'and I've got a torch. We're creeping so light me knees are knocking. Sam's growling away at this little stone crypt, you know, bone house thingy, and Sam's no growler I'm telling ya, so it's strange all right. He's off his rocker. There's a doorway half open. Rod's whimpering behind me, saying "Don't go Mo, it's zombies in there." And then so I go first with the torch and poke it through the doorway and I see something move and I scream the top of me lungs. There's a pair of eyes shining in the torchlight. I turn to Rod and say, "Don't worry love, it's a possum. Go back to the house." But I know it's not a possum and so does Roddy. Me hands are shaking like a leaf. I say: "Hello?" And the eyes move towards me. I'm ready to run when I feel a hand on me back. I jump a mile in the air, but it's only Rod. He hasn't gone nowhere. He's rooted to the spot. "What is it, love?" I go. And Rod's looking at the eyes. He can see better than me. Or he recognises. And he goes: "It's him, Mo." "Who?" I say. "It's him. The sea urchin." "The what?" And Rod starts pissing himself. Hard to tell if he's laughing cos it's funny or it's a reaction to the nerves. "I seen him down the beach," he goes. "I tried kicking shit out of him but he run away. He lives in The Pit." "Eh?" I go. "What you on about? What Pit?" And Roddy just starts laughing, not nasty but kindly, like, and moves past me into the entrance of the bone house and goes: "Come on, matey, come out here!" And I look back into the bone house and I can't describe it, how filthy he was, how shrivelled and pathetic and frightened, he was feral, you know? People use the word feral but they don't know what it means, or they wouldn't use it anymore if they saw a kid like this. Feral. He was an animal. He couldn't talk, only grunt. But when Roddy calls him, like he's calling a pet animal, the dirty little thing shuffles out half cripple half sideways. He won't look at me. He looks at Rod or Rod's ear and there's something in the pair of them, I can't put it in words love, but you knew something was up, something like . . . yeah nah, I dunno, but they're in cahoots eh, I can just see it all in that look of theirs, he come out of the bone house and that's it, I remember telling meself, this is us, this is our family, me and Roddy and Sam and this little sea urchin thingy, is it a boy, is it a mar fricken supial, Lord knows. I know I'm meant to find out whose he is and that, and do the paperwork and what have you, he must be someone's eh, but this other little voice is telling me he's mine. That's what he is. He's *mine*.'

Love for the first time. First love. I can sit in any spot of that House and I have me diagonals and me perpendiculars all lined up. Window casements to doorframes. Doorframes to chair legs. Chair legs to mouse holes. Mouse holes to bedheads. Any room of The House, I had all me lines worked out.

I knew exactly where it was safe to tread and where not
yeah love.

No more chainlink, cracked concrete, fibro, buffalo grass, fibro, lino, fibro, terry towelling, damp and mothballs. No more for her no more for Rod. No more for me.

The House was the end of Joe, the beginning of DK.

That House was the first place Joe wanted to settle down and stay with Mo and Rod. Once he seen it. Joe dug QUEENSLANDERS too. He dug the sea air. Dug the beach, a few minutes away. Began to dig Mo again.

But then he sees me, huddled in a corner, can't speak.

Joe didn't dig the sea urchin.

'What's this?' he goes.

Mo tells him I'm her foster kid.

'Where from?' Joe goes.

'Business is it of yours?'

'You've had another?' goes Joe, jumping to the wrong conclusion as always. 'Whose the fuck is he?'

And then it's on, young and old.

She'd have none of it yeah getting up the duff and all that getting the crud beaten out of her. With Joe it was either kick him out or let him get her all pear shaped again.

She was peeling and veining prawns, typing, counting money, then working at the hospital, not even a nurse, not trained, she was kind of an orderly, poo carrier.

But still that was better than having Joe around.

She give Joe Blow the throw.

He didn't go quiet. Made a racket and went to hit her but she started screaming blue bloody murder and so did me and Roddy, not on our Mo you don't, and so we're hoeing into him yeah, and maybe this is the first thing I ever remember, I'm only five or something and it's me and Rod going to work on this Joe, Mo helping us, we're a team right, and the thing about QUEENSLANDERS is the neighbours know pretty much all of what's going on and Joe's sober enough to figure out it was better to take the hint than be drug off by the boys in blue.

Mo heard he went out west, inland to work the races and married some bird out there. Mo didn't care. Well shot of him.

Full name Joseph. *Joseph Bloseph.*

Mo sit us down, me and her and Rod and Sam, and she goes, *Well yous lot it's just us now, and that's the way it's always gunna be, just us, me and yous, and I promise yous that yous are my whole life, won't be nothing else for me, yous my whole life yous lot. Okay? So don't let me down!*

Sure she was joking. She didn't mean Sam. Didn't mean Rod really. Reckon Rod reminded her too much of the dreaded Mr Blow.

What she meant when she said her *whole life* was, she meant Yours Truly. Her boy Den.

Was that night I woke up with the nightmare, went in her room, stood at the end of her bed.

Mo?

Huge mountain in there, tuft of brown hair at the pillow. She didn't say nothing.

Mo I had a bad dream.

Still didn't say nothing. For a second I thought she was dead and I started to cry. Soft swallows like I'm choking on milk. I take a step towards her and the mountain stirs and a big fat white arm, the underside white and wobbly like a raw oyster, it comes up.

Moey? I'm shivering there, it's not cold but.

Still didn't say nothing. I'm looking at her arm which is up like one of them boom gates.

So I got in under it and but

yeah and it

you can't say

yeah a big flower folding me in, her little bee hiding in her petals.

•

'You had to take him to the children's services?'

Mo's had enough of this questioning now.

'Course, love, course. The children's services.'

She's getting up and cleaning the kitchen all of a sudden.

'And where was he from? Whose was he?'

'Ah love, me back's giving me hell today, all that sitting and talking, women's pains eh.'

'You adopted him or fostered him? There's a bit of difference in—'

'Listen love, I'll tell you all about it tomorrow, right? Tomorrow? Me head's splitting open and I've got a million chores to do. And Den'll be getting hungry.'

DECAPITATED

And so here's how I get shot of the old BFO: I offer full cooperation.

She's perched in front of me in the kitchen, drinking Mo's tea and eating Mo's Vo Vos. She come in from a surf or so she reckons. Big round brown plate of a face, eyes the green of afternoon sea. Hanging off DK's every word.

And so I cut back on her:

'Where ya staying? In a motel or what?'

She nods, eyes on her notebook.

'Lonely there?'

She shrugs her pineapple shoulders in a way tells me I've hit the nail. What is it with these birds? Why's it they have to wreck themself trying to fight it out in the blokes' world? Sure they can win, but winning kills em. Kills em of loneliness. Cos blokes isn't worth mixing with, blokes isn't worth beating. Specially surfers.

'No place for a lady,' I go respectfully.

'Salright.' Short. She doesn't want me getting personal on her. Like she's behind that one-way glass stuff. Wants it like she can see me but I can't see her.

'Carn,' I go. 'Don't ya come and stay with me and Mo? I give ya full open access. Save some coin. Get out of that lonely motel yer in. Come sleep on the fold-out. Can have me twenty-four seven.'

This old man, he played twenty-four seven, he played knick-knack on my devon/on my heaven/on my Kevin . . . Bugger it get your feet between them diagonals Den and oh no here come the parade of them you have known . . .

She looks up at me with eyes big as her shoulders, like she's got everything she wished for but it scares the pants off her.

Then shakes her head slow.

'I can't do that, Dennis.'

. . . Kevin Levin/Devon Nevin/Steve Neave/Merle Thurle . . .

'Don Conn,' I go. *Lisa/Lisa McGeeza/Exmire Sexwire . . .*

The BFO giving me a funny look. Her brown face white as a sheet and that. Her fear more real than yours.

I push the aviators back up me nose. 'How come? We won't bite.' *Thanks love. Got me out of a pickle there.*

'Um, I'll think about it,' she goes in this way that says she's already thought about it, thought it right through.

And so that day's the last I see of her for a while. She checks out of the motel too.

I outsmarted her again. Pure natural genius.

See—that's how I find out:

She does know.

SECOND LOVE

Mo get her sense of humour back when Joe get the throw. But also she meant what she said. Never looked at another bloke. Never had another friend when you think of it. It was all us and her yeah
    nah *me* and her.
    Poor old Mo she put all her eggs in this one basket and before long must of thought Rod keep turning up like a bad penny she couldn't get shot of.
    Strange thing when your Mo don't really like her own boy so much. Even to us, the Keiths, where strange was normal, even to us we got it deep down how she was with Rod and it was strange.

How do I remember why I was there when they found me eh. I was too little. I was five or what have you, how do I know. They said I live on the rocks at the point, under the surf club and in the bone house, but don't ask me love, I don't remember nothing. DK was rubbish dumped illegally. There's signs telling you you can't do that.

Joe kicked it a few years later, when we was teenagers. Rod asked Mo can we go to the funeral somewhere in outback Queensland (no way was she letting them bring him home to lie behind our back fence; she'd had enough of him looking over her shoulder and down her front when he was alive). But Rod wanted to go to the funeral. Joe was his dad and that after all.
    'Nah,' she goes. 'I don't know him.'
    'Even send flowers?'
    'Nah,' she goes. 'I don't know him.'
    Real edge in our family.
    Rod took years to forgive her.
    I didn't give a fart. Joe wasn't my dad was he.

MALCOLM KNOX

Mo tried to make us work. Good luck to her! We go round scrounging glass bottles from rubbish bins and all over the place. You get twopence refund. I couldn't be buggered. Then Rod come up with this idea. He was the ideas man Roddy: more efficient if you go straight to the source and raid them crates of lemonade and Coke behind the shops *before* they send them out, or bust into the milkman's truck, swipe some bottles, drink them and score the refunds later. So we go swiping them and but Mo caught us cos so she banned that racket and put Rod on hard labour. She pulled strings and got Rod this job at the hospital for a while: cleaning up poo. Scrubbing dunnies. Nepotism isn't it, the way people can get jobs for their kids.

Me I ended up with the easy work, this paper run before school, up at four, on me brand-new chopper I got for my tenth birthday, delivering papers round town. Not too bad in the end. I was an early bird anyway and

yeah the beach

had a good arm. Used to aim at their flowering plants. Rolled-up paper like a spear . . .

Sam run along beside me, no lead or nothing. He just wanted to run.

Coolangatta wasn't big but it was all on hills, paper run good exercise for me lolly legs with the big tray of papers on the back of me chopper, and I get to the top of Greenmount Hill and look down on the dawn patrol, the surfers out with first light, little dots of them on Rainbow Bay up Snapper Rocks down Coolie Beach to Kirra. Only ones in town up that early was fishermen, surfers, garbos and yours truly.

Never got out of the habit. Didn't have clock radios then just knew when to wake up.

Long way down the hill, on the grey pink morning glass. Surfers eh. Mo dug them figurines in a model shop, would of collected them if she had any coin, and these board riders from a distance were like them. Trim waves on their longboards, big wooden planks like doors, I stood on my chopper on that hill dreamboating so long I was always late to finish my paper run and late for school

•

yeah, I watched

them old-time surfers, they went the way the wave took them. Trimmed a smooth line from peak to shoulder, one direction only, strolling up and down their boards dropping their knees into a half a turn, hang five hang ten, cruisy, pretty, like drops of water sliding down a windowpane.

And when they jumped off you wouldn't even know the wave been ridden.

The wave was the thing not the surfer.

Like flies on a horse's arse, along for the ride.

You watched the waves and turned your face to look along the headlands: the pull-offs and car parks and overlooks.

Always there was cars parked, nose to the break, engines running—

Always a man inside—

Watching—

Just this one man per car, maybe having a smoke or just concentrating—

Watching—

Like you.

It was that important yeah.

Late fifties. Everyone knew everyone else, the Goldie a string of small country towns back then, and soon me and Rod at the public school was known as the ragtag nippers of Mrs Keith the lady peeled prawns at the fisho and carted poo at the hospital. Nice lady well respected best prawn peeler and poo carter there was, you need your prawns peeled and your poo carted, Mrs Keith's your lady, and all them other parents did their bit taking up the slack so we weren't left alone in the afternoons or with no mates or no lunch or no afternoon tea. I don't remember but there must have been a fair effort to keep us out of strife and

and yeah they thought me and Rod was brothers, both Mo's boys, why wouldn't they.

I knew I was adopted but.

Cos every time we had a blue Rod gets purple in the face and shouts at me: 'Yeah ya little scumbag, yer *adopted*.'

Rod tells everyone at school I'm adopted, but nobody believes him, they all think that's just Rod being Rod.

•

MALCOLM KNOX

Mo was always home for breakfast and dinner. Breakfast a huge bowl of muesli and milk. Dinner always meat: chuck steak, shanks, bone marrow, offcuts, offal, didn't matter, once in a while a real T-bone or lamb chump chops. Always meat. We was starving. She always says she found me hungry and I never changed. Once I got my hands on a bunch of stale spring rolls they were throwing out from the milk bar down on Marine Parade, Bob's it was called. I scarfed twelve of them. When I get home Mo asked me why I stunk of grease and dim sim.

Scored twelve spring rolls, Mo.

And what ya do with them?

I knew she didn't like them so there was no harm saying:

Ate them.

She looked at me a while like she didn't know to believe me or not.

You save any for Roddy?

I shook my head.

Mo sort of trying not to grin.

So, I said to break the silence. *What's for tea then?*

And when it was over I was still hungry so I have another bowl of muesli and milk and then a loaf of sliced bread spread with butter and Vegemite and peanut butter and lemon curd. Roddy had a big tank too. Mo always made sure I got a bit more than Rod, but it's not what you get it's how you use it, and with Rod you could see where it went, it all went into his big chest, big arms, big thighs, while for me I just had hollow legs, dunno where it all went cos I ate and ate but took my own sweet time with the growing part of the bargain.

Then if it was dark me and Rod fly out in the cemetery with Sam, play hide-and-seek or spot-the-zombie.

My first schoolteacher was Mr Turner who got called Mr Turnip which was a saviour for me because I was sitting in class going *Turner/Sterner/Burner/Churner/Learner* and even *Nurnur-ne-Nurnur* and would call him whichever one was in my head at the time he asked me a question, like my brain was a pokie machine and it was random the way the words spun round and where they stopped. It was only just starting to happen back in those days, not happening much at all really, just now and then, but when it did it got me into trouble, like when Mr Turner picked me out for one of his questions and I went, *Um, I don't know, Werner Furner!*

Once I could focus on *Turnip* I was in the clear.

But he was a good one and president of the clubbies, the surf lifesaving club down at Rainbow. He got me and Rod enrolled in the juniors, the Nippers, and he come and get us Sunday mornings, me only morning with no paper run and Rod's with no poo carting, and walk us down the club.

Flag races, tug-o-war, wading, boards, pillow fight, three-legged races, sprints, mouth-to-mouth . . .

Mo said I grew in the water, I was a mermaid man. When I got cut or hurt I always healed quick. Mo said it was cos I was the son of a starfish. Sea Monkey. Just add water.

Swim classes in the ocean baths at Snapper Rocks, the porpoise pool out on the end of Rainbow Bay. Sharky Jack Evans aka The Man of the Sea kept his dolphins there, you can swim with them and everything till the council made The Man of the Sea move the whole show to his Jack Evans Porpoise Pool and Sharkatarium over the hill behind D-Bah. Me and Rod swim in them pools, mucked about on the inner tubes and chuck huge bombs throwing ourself off the rock ledge in the deep end one knee tucked up under the chin and the other stuck straight out. Made tidal waves, scared hell out of the swimming lessons. Then we go to that suicide hole in the lava rocks on the edge of the pool, hurl ourself in when a swell was coming, duck in behind the rocks it poured over us like a waterfall. You weren't nobody till you done the suicide hole.

I never needed to learn to swim. Mo said I already could. Was born with it. *Don't need teaching*, she said to Mr Turnip, *just throw him in and let him go*. Pure natural genius.

Can't say I took to the discipline of being a junior clubbie but. You get loads of privileges being a junior clubbie. Like the privilege of going to the shops buy ice creams for the older blokes, or the privilege of digging a huge deep hole in the sand for them while they lower the level on their keg of a Sunday afternoon, then let yourself get pushed in while they rained beer, wee and chunder on you for their amusement. That was how they initiated you and if you really really wanted to be a clubbie you put up with your privileges

yeah nah them clubbies

me and Rod didn't. Me and Rod didn't go much for the clubbies or their rules full stop. They took themself and their patrol duties too serious. We couldn't get that worked up about it. When we were on patrol me and Rod chuck jellyfish at the girls to scare them and yell out SHARK when they're doing their wading. Only I wasn't that scary because I'd get all spun out in my pokie machine head and call out BARK or LARK or DARK or MARK and nobody paid any attention or got scared at all, so Roddy generally took over the yelling part of it until Mo caught him and then so she bundled him back off to the hospital for a few hours hard labour.

Neither of me or Rod got into the flags and the sprints or for that matter any of the sandplay. What we dug was staring out past the mob of Nippers to the point, Snapper Rocks, where men on their big long logs were slicing up the lines of water breaking across the bay.

Must of watched them waves for years before I rode them. Must of sat in the classroom fly-catching driving poor old Mr Turnip mad with my inattention, just watching them, watching them, for years before I rode them.

Second love. After The House:

How the lines formed up outside the bay and marched in like an army. I counted numbers. How sets come in threes, three waves per set, three sets per sequence, three swells a month, like there was some god or lord out there, some gawd, who could only count up to the magic number, three. Third wave in a set was always the biggest. And the third wave in the third set—the ninth wave—biggest of the lot. I work this out from my classroom window. You can't knock a good education eh.

Offshore wind was good, onshore not so good. Offshore combed the lines up like ripples of ladies' hair in one of them setting eggs they have. When they got big they stand up and feather and keep standing up right till they met the sandbank, then the wind keep holding them up so they broke from the inside and just kept peeling, walling up out to the shoulder

yeah

how do you know that Den?

Just do eh

onshore wind made them crumble all over the shop, and plenty of days back then it was the least bit onshore there be nobody out, not a sausage.

Late fifties they were lucky bastards, choosy and all.

And but see there's just something about the shape of a beach: the green headland, the black rocks, the yellow sand, the sea which is blue or grey or green or even red and every shade in between, and the foam which is white, and the way they're all just *set up* like that, like it's this perfect arrangement of nature.

What I mean is, everything you can ever want is there in that setup of green bush, black rock, yellow sand, blue water and white foam. I get mad with happy stomach butterflies thinking about it.

I could see how the take-off near the rocks was the tricky part of the wave and none of them log riders dare paddle where it stood up vertical right behind the black granite. Instead they sit out wide, on the shoulder, where the take-off was more level, wait till the peak of the wave had already broken and then paddle into it, their legs cycling round in the air like they were riding invisible bikes, and then they're up, crabbing up and down the board, drawing their lines up the face, down the face, up the face, down the face, slow and easy, always pointing the nose out at the fat shoulder of the wave, up the coast to Kirra.

We knew these men the local butchers, plumbers, chippies, teachers, police, shopkeepers. Don Conn was one. Kevin Levin. Ted Thurle, whose missus was Merle. Sometimes their boys surfed too but they were also working men, apprentice butchers and whatnot. There was no surfie bum culture back then, the late fifties early sixties on the Goldie, not that I was aware of anyway. These were the working men of our town and this was what they done on their mornings, their afternoons, their weekends, whenever it was glassy or offshore, this was the priority, get out there and go dancing with them waves.

So many went to waste too. Waves.

Drove me mad.

Me and Rod weren't no good as clubbies. Had to wear dick-stickers and clubbie caps. With our long hair we looked like nongs. We had the longest hair in the school, which was beaut there it showed the teachers couldn't rule us, but once we was wearing them little lifesaver string caps, the hair halfway down our backs just looked stupid.

Tourists come to drown at Greenmount and I'd of let them. If they get in trouble and I had to swim out to them I wouldn't wait for a lull between sets to bring them in, like the clubbies did. I swim them into the gnarliest section so we both get belted on the sandbank.

No point saving them without teaching them a lesson too. Scare the hair off them so they won't go in the water no more, ever. Prevention's better than cure eh.

Me and Roddy had to do one patrol a month. We were so useless they picked out small days for us, no rips, no dangers. On big days when there was any threat of a tourist getting washed out they put us on suntan oil duty. Ladies shell five shillings to be sprayed with suntan oil. Rod sell the suntan oil for profit and fill them cans with cooking oil he pinched from hospital. Not that they knew.

Least I hoped it was cooking oil.

Only reason to put up with the patrol was you got a hot shower and a locker in the clubhouse. Sell your soul for a hot shower and a locker. So you more or less set up camp there all summer. Me and Rod grew scales. Lived there
on the sand in the water on the sand in the water.

When we didn't want to do patrol Rod come up with this third guy, 'Sam Johnson'. We put down his name to do our patrol for us. For a few weeks them dumb clubbies really thought Sam Johnson was watching the tourists while me and Rod went walkabout. They never figured out Sam Johnson was our ruddy beagle.

Rod made up the Johnson bit. Sam didn't really have a middle name.

You was allowed dogs on the beach them days. Sam hung out with us, first beagle in the world trained so he wouldn't run away. Sat there with a big smile and tongue hanging out and as long as we give him water and ice cream he wouldn't go for people's fish and chips.

I won all the swimming races even though I was such a weed. Something about water smoothed me out. Clumsy bugger on land, fish out of water, gasping for air.

In the water I was genius, pure genius.

•

Bloke called Gary Trounson had a surfboard hire stall on the beach just down from the club. Sixpence an hour on a Surfoplane, ninepence on a polystyrene Coolite funboard, shilling on a nine-six logger. Swell get up, me and Rod go missing from patrol cos we've nicked a couple of Surfoplanes to throw about in the shore break. They were white and slippery, cheap as buggery. Surfoplanes were surfmats: no fins to steer, just rubber handles to hang onto while you fly down a wave.

The other thing they were good for was, Gary let local companies paint their names on the Surfoplanes for adverts. So when they were propped up on the hire racks the Surfoplanes also told you useful information like

COME NAKED TO COOLANGATTA, BILL STAFFORD WILL DRESS YOU

or

ROTHWELLS COOLANGATTA FOR YOUR BEACH WEAR.

Big money in adverts, big coin.

Soon Gary Trounson had us working for him. Drag the loggers down from his shop to the stall, take the Coolites, take the surf skis, take the Surfoplanes and blow them up with the air pumps, then chalk numbers on them so he can keep track.

We put up a sign saying 'Back in Ten Minutes'. Served us well that sign. We stick it up and pinched boards and went out in the water, or up the milk bar to scrounge some leftover stale meat pies kept past their use-by date. One afternoon we ate ten stale meat pies each. Gary knew we were nicking off on the job but at least he got something out of us, more than anyone else did.

Kid gremlins running odd jobs for Gary Trounson: last time we ever worked for another man.

There was special zones on the beach. Us kids were at the Greenmount end with the beach hire and the showers; in the middle was where the clubbies hung, the best part of the beach for swimming where the kiosk was; and then up the Snapper Rocks end was where the surfers hung, in round the park where there was sometimes magic acts and circuses and music bands and these guys knee-paddle out on their huge boards when the swells come. They were miles out of our league. Frank Garsky, who everyone called 'Little Big Shit' cos he had a big brother Dick who was called 'Big Shit', was the only one ever talk to us.

In behind the beach was a line of stick parlours and milk bars and we could hang there long as we didn't go on the machines or tables the surfers or clubbies were playing on. We were just ants to them, little roaches they stomp under their feet if we weren't quick.

There were zones up on the main road too and you had to know where to go and where to avoid. There were surfies joints, there were grommets joints, there were bikies joints and there were rockers joints. During the day everyone keep their distance. But at night, different story. Me and Rod wander down there and eat Sherbies and Choo-Choo Bars and musk sticks and sit in the rocks while all the older guys went in the places where they got plastered.

Problem was, they all had their separate drinking places but there was only one place to dance, called Danceland. About ten pm they'd had enough to drink and all roads led to Danceland. About ten thirty the fights start. Me and Rod watched these battles rage up and down Marine Parade: surfies v clubbies, clubbies v rockers, rockers v bikies, bikies v blackfellas, blackfellas v Brisos, you name it there was a brawl for every taste. Me and Rod lapped it all up from the safety of the lifeguard tower. More they fought, the less blokes there be in the waves the next morning.

At patrol, Keith boys as useful as ashtrays on a longboard. We go walkabout at any excuse, take out a Surfoplane and mow down the swimmers.

Surfoplanes could only go straight but and I wanted to cut across like them boardriders out on the point. I figure out if I wore flippers I could get some steerage. One day in a cyclone swell Rod sees me cutting across, side-slipping and then cutting back up the wave face. He couldn't believe it. But there's no mileage in being a pioneer. Before I knew it Rod and other kids were strapping on flippers too and cutting across and getting deeper than me and stealing my waves, even getting up on their knees.

No mileage in being too far ahead of your time.

. . . yeah . . .

WHILE YOU WERE OUT

. . . the dark, the light, does it in the dark, nobody watching, nobody listening—

Washed up by words in waves, three am, legs over bed, plant the feet, past Mo's room, through the diagonal security grille, down the steps (don't grab them rails), in the garage, past the old people's cars, on the chopper, out the toy roundabouts, over the causeway, out The Other Side, stick in the bush, on the black water . . .

He has mastered it.

He can sit up on his stick.

Without falling off.

Bit of a wobble but he can paddle in a circle and sit up and wait.

In his head he sees a wall of green . . .

Has to think about the sea.

Can't go on the sea in the dark:

Can't see the waves, can't see the sharks.

No point.

What now?

Hungry.

Stick back in the bush, on the chopper, through the stink of frogs and mangroves, back over the causeway, back in town, back through the toy roundabouts, camellias and azaleas, back in the garage, up the steps, don't grab the rails, in the diagonal security grille, past Mo's room, back in bed.

It's still dark.

The radio off.

She's turned the radio off.

MADE IN QLD

Here, do it again:
Like all the truths it started with a big fat lie:

Way before death and rumour, bad times way before the bad name:

She never kept it a secret.
It come out her mouth.
Autumn Saturday, 1961.
Dennis, she said, tremble on her lips turning my name into a whole sentence. *Something you need to know. Yer mother, father, all that.*
There was a Joseph and his name was Joe, and I had a brother, and Joe was the one Rod knew as Dad, but he wasn't Dad. Got it?
Dennis, she said.
I was eleven. Saturday, 1961. Late cyclone season. She held both me hands so I wouldn't float away on the offshore. We're in Point Danger coffee shop. Wooden tables. Birdshit on the wooden seats. The dog, Sam the beagle, asleep at Mo's feet. You were crazy for that beagle. Loyal, up for anything. No questions asked. Lived in the moment just like you. Sam was loose and old and covered in moles. While he slept he yelped and twitched and carried on like he was out hunting.
In the graveyard for sea urchins to save.
I'm looking over Mo's shoulder: offshore, small, standing up nice on the outside bank. Funny how that outside bank only works when the swell's got some east in it.
. . . yeah . . .
Dennis . . .
Tears in her eyes. Mine on the waves. Only a few out. I should of been there on a swiped Surfoplane, only I been out already and come in less than an hour before. Was hosing down my brand new royal blue with yellow competition stripes nylon boardshorts, birthday present from

Mo, when she drug me off to Point Danger, neutral territory. Nobody ever heard of nylon boardshorts before and mine were the ducks nuts, the pride of the coast. Never knew where she got them and there was only one pair, nothing for Rod, sorry, but it wasn't his birthday anyway so why was he so cheesed off.

Must of been a special occasion cos we never went to the coffee shop. She got me three chocky milks. I had the cartons all lined up edge to edge, paper straw in each. She had an instant coffee. Stirring in sugar.

She didn't know where to look.

I did. Was thinking who are them bastards on the outside bank and why was it still offshore, it was meant to be onshore by now and mushing up the little ones. One them bastards trim along a nice right on his Mal, what a waste of a perfect little wave, what a waste to be trimmed off by some kook Mal rider instead of smashed to pieces by a real surfer, smash them lips, carve it to pieces, The Butcher they'll be calling me soon I slice them up, slice and dice . . .

Wasn't all-time or nothing but me teeth were grinding to watch them Mal riders

yeah nah even back then it was the waste I couldn't stand it, the waste. One wasted wave was a crime against nature.

I knew where to look.

But . . . yeah . . .

How she started the conversation. Like that. Over the instant coffee. Over the three chocky milks. Me legs still wet from the hose-down. The coconut smell of Gary Trounson's board wax in me nostrils. They say surfers are always either wet or about to be wet. DK was both.

I nodded sort of shrugging like I knew it all and she didn't have to treat me like a baby, a know-nothing. I was genius. I knew it all.

Her instant coffee going cold.

Me chocky milks going warm.

I heard her breath as she sucked it in like she's about to duck dive a big frothing monster. Deep breath Mo, that's right, and down you go, dive, dive, dive, then kick down on your tail and up, up, up to the light.

That's how you duck dive a big one, Mo. Go on love, commit . . .

I held her breath for her.

She chose that day to tell me.

Okay sure good, I said. Eyes over her shoulder. Them kooks. Them legions of the unjazzed they call them . . .

The ruddy waste . . .

She brought me there to get my attention but she should of known the coffee shop overlooked the D-Bah beachie.

Bastards: two of them take off together, same wave, spoiling it. Someone should nut them both. Has to be some law and order in this world.

Even at eleven that's how I thought and I couldn't even surf yet.

Den love? Yunderstand what I'm saying?

Her instant coffee, even the milk was from powder, never got as cold as my chocky milks at their warmest. Funny how that goes.

I sucked them up, make a big gurgle brought looks from the other ones in the coffee shop who must of thought I was embarrassing my poor old lady so bad I brought her to tears.

Den?

Mo's eyes wet. I could see what the other ones were thinking: *He's only gurgled his milk love, it's not the end of the world love . . .*

Sam give a full-on bark like he seen a cat. Mo looked down at him, me too. This was how we looked at each other: both look at the dog. But he was still asleep.

Den love?

She thought I couldn't hear her but I could, it was just I had to get out there again while it was still offshore, combing nice grooves of corduroy. Sweet! Even if it was small there was rides to be had.

I left her at the milk bar, *Sorry Mo they're going begging.*

Went home for some dry boardies. Ran.

I get out there again that day, had a blinder on the Surfoplane. It was still offshore, but the tide had dropped. Shapely.

DAD 1

There's four of them and they look like Zorro: black hats, black capes, black pencil moustaches, black masks over the eyes.

She's asleep in her room, white nightie, curled up on her bed.

The four masked men whisper to each other, wave their swords, nod in her direction.

They got wicked snarls.

They close in round her. The end.

One of them, him.

KID

Once you had the salt on your skin you liked to let it dry by itself in a crust. You don't shower for days. The sea felt cleaner than fresh water. Most nights you went to bed salted like a hot chip. Your face crackled when it moved.

> You controlled it so it wouldn't break. Didn't smile, didn't react:
> Dennis Keith as a kid.
> Yeah . . .

Kept watching from the beach, from the classroom:

> How waves had a peak and a shoulder.

> How the peak was the sharpest take-off, the hardest place to stand up, but also gave the most speed across the next section and everyone had to get out of your way, off the wave.

> How the shoulder was fatter and easier but someone else might get the wave first.

> How the rips were good for paddling out.

> How there were little ones that drew a bit of water give a better longer ride.

Can't remember being a kook the first time round. Nobody can just pick it up and get on it and ride waves, it's like anything, swimming say, someone throws you in a pool and watch you sink. You must of been a kook but it's like you can't remember how you learnt to walk.

> Late fifties, early sixties. Gold Coast.
> Someone would of laughed. At you.
> Someone would of shouted. At you.
> Someone would of waved a fist.
> At you.
> At him.

At me.

But I learnt and I forgot, I forgot and I learnt.

What you didn't forget was how you want to keep the learners out of the water. They're pollution. They create waste. You don't want them. I didn't want them. They waste Gawd's gift, perfect waves. You can't stand to see waste.

But you must of started as one of them.

Rod was braver than me, not keener but definitely braver. Was dying for a go on a real surfboard. He just needed to do stuff so bad, Rod. He follows Frank Garsky round.

Don't know why Rod picked Little Big Shit, and when Frank come in, drug his whopping great redwood longboard behind in the sand, Rod tag along after him and go, 'Ya gunna gimme a go today?'

And Frank walk along like he's thinking about it and then after a long while goes:

'Nup.'

And that was it, day after day after day. We nick off to the pinball parlour, Funland, where Mo hands out change, or we wanted to steer clear of her we go to the Lazy Jay and play the slot cars. We spent hours in them joints and was unbeatable. Then Rod get a whiff that Little Big Shit was coming in again and so it's down to the beach and Rod:

'Eh Frank, gunna gimme a go now?'

And Frank walking along again like he's thinking about it and then after a long while:

'Nup.'

And it was a bit of a joke on Rod but he get shirty if I bag him.

'Least I'm having a crack, Den.' He'd say it with a sneer. Like I expected everything to be served up on a platter.

Rod pinched hire foam boards from next to the surf club, big floaty Coolites, and thrashed his way out there. He was always bigger than me, whoever my dad was must of been a total weed cos I was narrow-chested and spindle-legged and slow-growing while Rod was big and robust like our Mo.

Also Rod was more trial and error. I had to understand something inside out before I had a go. I had to live and breathe it, think about it day and night, work it all out, head-surf a billion waves before I touch a board. Rod just went and had a go.

Maybe I never was a kook.

Rod was. He get caught in rips and washed out till the other surfers had to paddle him over to a safe little whitewater one and push him in on his chest. Or if it was bigger he get smashed by the shore break, have to come back in to fetch his board. He thrash about for a frothball wave, lurch halfway to his feet and fall off, lose his board again. Thrash, fall off, lose his board, fetch it, paddle back out. Thrash, fall off, lose his board, fetch it, paddle back out. I get knackered watching him.

All I was doing:

Watching.

Then one day completely out of the blue, Little Big Shit thought about it for a bit and went:

'Yep.'

He told Rod he has to swim out on his own. Frank'll paddle the board out the back then give it to him. So that's what they did. I stood on the beach and watched Frank paddle out, Rod swim out, then Frank give Rod the big wooden board and stayed there talking to him in the water, and then Frank left him alone and bodysurfed in, and I was standing there watching when a good wave come and Rod just sitting there rooted to his board, didn't know how to turn it round and start paddling. Besides there was another bloke already riding the wave. This bloke come down the face doing this big soul arch and Rod just squatting there in the impact zone and there was mayhem, Frank's board popping up in the air like a penny bunger and the other surfer falling off and screaming blue murder at Rod, and the next thing I know Rod's dumped Frank's board, bodysurfing in on the next wave, the board's washed in on another, the other surfer's paddling back out, and Rod gets to the sand and doesn't even stop to talk to me he's just bolted in his trunks dripping wet up the hill and up the street to Shangrila, and Frank's picked up his stick and he's not cut up, he's having a chuckle while he checks his wooden board for dings. And I'm standing there like a wombat and Little Big Shit looks at me like I'm gunna ask him for a go, that's what Keith kids do, isn't it, but no way, if Rod can't do it I can't either so I turn round and run up the hill back home after me brother.

•

But then one day, can't have been too long after, Rod got hold of Frank's board again and stood up on a whitewater wave and I mean, we had a lot of fun them days but the look in Rod's eyes was different from anything I ever seen, he was a long way away, he had this look of breakfast with the angels, and I'll never forget it that quiet stare of his and the half smile on his lips, he wasn't even turning it on for me, he was someplace else, far far away . . .

. . . yeah . . .

And told me something I never forget.

Den, he goes, *that is much more fun than it looks.*

Yeah?

Yeah. And it looks like heaps *of fun.*

So I made up me mind. Buggered if I was gunna let him get away from me.

One thing I learnt, from watching:

It was all about how fast you paddled. Riding along the wave was the easy bit. Everything swung on how fast you were going when you stood up. The faster you were moving the easier it was to stand, the better position you were in to slide across the face. So it was all down to the one thing:

Paddle like there's a shark at your feet.

Get fit so you can always paddle like there's a shark at your feet.

Then the next wave, paddle again like there's a shark at your feet.

When you can't paddle no more like there's a shark at your feet, come in, take a rest, you won't catch good waves.

You just gotta be the fastest paddler in the water and the maddest:

What I learnt from watching.

FORK

. . . the dark, the light, does it in the dark, nobody watching, nobody listening.

The hour when the young die

nah when the young are found glassed in.

Washed up by words come in waves, three am, legs over bed, plant the feet, past Mo's room, through the diagonal security grille, down the steps (don't grab them rails), in the garage, past the old people's cars, on the chopper, out the toy roundabouts, over the causeway, out The Other Side, stick in the bush, on the black water . . .

He has mastered it.

He can sit up on his stick.

Without falling off.

Bit of a wobble but he can paddle in a circle and sit up and wait.

In his head he sees a wall of green . . .

Has to think about the sea.

Stick back in the bush, on the chopper, through the stink of frogs and mangroves, back over the causeway, back in—

And snap.

The bike. The chopper. Fork went, wheel bent. Only so many times it could take an eighteen-stoner.

Gone, done.

Kick it off the side of the road in the sandy scrub.

Kick sand over it.

Got it up, check it again: the fork, the wheel.

Sit on the seat.

Fork spread like legs doing the splits. Wheel like spag bol.

Pick it up, hurl it in the sandy scrub.

Get it up, check it again: the fork, the wheel.

Sat on the seat.

Over shoulder, spear throw, in the sandy scrub.

Walk home. Over causeway, in town, sky starting to bruise up purple, quick step in the village, in the unit, past her room, wash hands, in bed sticky and panting from the walk.

It's still dark.

The radio turned off.

Swallowing hard.

On dry pride.

The chopper, my chopper.

Mo bought it for me.

We're in for it now.

WISED UP

You remember the wave.

Rainbow, clean one-foot day, Sam on the beach, squat there arse thrown out to one side, tongue out, give himself a bad back.

You pinched a longboard from Trounson's and gone out with Rod and caught that wave that day.

Little fat ones, offshore, high tide, you must of paddled but you can't remember that, can't remember getting up, what you remember is *being* up, up and away, look down all that green glass in front of you and can't believe you were going, going, hang on! keep on going, yer flying, high in the sky and the wave rolled out in front like a magic carpet, this crease of darker green wrinkle up ahead, the nose of your swiped board glide and slide, glide and slide, your knees bending to stay with it, you going too fast getting ahead of the wave so you stand up tall again and slow down, and the wave catch up with you and the darker green creases out ahead again, on and on and on and on, and when it was done with you you threw a somersault off the board and cracked your head on the sandbank and stood up laughing like a loon arms in the air like you was Nat Young at Sunset, laughing so hard it broke your mouth, wooing and yooping and yeahing and Roddy's out there smiling back at you and he's so far *across*, not so far *out*, but *across*, which means you come that far across to get from there to here, which means you really caught that wave, you didn't just skid down the front straight-handed, you come across, across, across . . .

You took flight. Bird on liquid air.

The way it just kept forming up ahead of you, giving itself to you, giving and giving and giving and you took what it give, and these ten seconds where what—

Everything, everything after that, every littlest thing, was up against . . .

•

Yeah! End of story.

And that was it, you wanted to go straight in and curl up round the glow and cuddle that wave in your hands till the end of time.

But soon as it was over you couldn't remember nothing about it, it was gone.

So you had to go back.

You paddle to Rod, and by the time you got to him you were up to playing it cool and not saying too much and act like it wasn't the first time or the last time or anything special, and so yeah, don't say nothing . . .

Rod just grin out of the side of his head and:

. . . *yeah* . . .

And you:

. . . *yeah* . . .

It was Rod wised you up.

That same first day you stood up and flew on that wave.

It just come back.

It was that day.

We caught our last waves in on the boards we'd nicked and we're sitting on the beach and I was giving Sam a pat. He belonged to me and Rod both. We had to share. I was thinking about that wave, that wave, that wave, that wave, try to bring it back and the more I tried the more it slid away.

Something'd happened to Rod. Bob the owner of the milk bar had short-changed him on a Sunnyboy, and Rod let Bob's tyres down.

I'd gone round telling kids about it. Now when we was on the sand, after our waves, just mellowing, Rod was not mellowing, Roddy was mad at me.

What you been saying about me and Bob?

I shrugged me shoulders. I loved spreading Rod's stories. He was much more of a daredevil than me. Made me feel more of a daredevil to tell his stories.

Just what happened.

Whatcha mean, what happened?

Rod was like a big buried chin pimple in that part when they're turning from red to white. Bubbling up.

I told them ya let his tyres down, that's all.

For short-changing me, Rod said, all aggressive.

I said, tough as nuts, *Yeah that's what ya got to do when they rape ya.*

Rod give me a funny look and said, quiet:

Nobody raped me, Dennis.

He never called me Dennis. I got scared of him when he said Dennis.

But you said he short-changed ya.

He did. So why ya telling people he raped me?

I thought rape meant rip someone off.

Rod explained what rape meant.

He seen me on that wave. Why he was doing this.

Rod wanted to make sure I knew Bob hadn't raped him. That was important to Rod. He had to explain what it meant so I'd know it hadn't happened to him. So I would stop spreading it about that Bob had raped Rod. That meant a lot to Rod.

Once he explained I could see why it mattered to him.

. . . so yeah . . .

He didn't take the piss out of me. It was too serious to take the piss. I was blushing so bad, even worse than getting kooked out in the waves, it was the worst feeling ever, I realised what a dope and a clot I made of meself.

And Den, he goes.

I watched me black stubbed big toe trace waves in the sand.

Mo aint yours, she's mine.

I watched me black stubbed big toe trace waves in the sand.

Yours was some other bird. Had you and took off, you got dumped at Snapper.

I watched me black stubbed big toe tracing figure eights in the sand.

Just saying what happened, Den. Why ya ended up with me and Mo. Ya didn't come from nowhere.

I watched me black stubbed big toe digging right through the sand.

Yeah nah I know I know, Roddy, I'm not some nong.

Yeah well don't say I got raped, right? Okay? Just saying what happened eh.

Wiped out all the good feelings from catching that wave

yeah why he done it

I picked up the log and headed straight back out. Had to catch more, every wave a new swipe with a big wet cloth on the blackboard.

But you can swipe that many times and the mark hasn't went away.

No matter how many waves.

DAD II

She's walking home on her own from a friend's house.

It's late at night.

Little red riding hood.

Strange old lady stops her by the side of the road, ask the way. This old lady's a bit of a witch, wild crazy white hair and a big collie dog she's always taking for walks.

She doesn't have the collie dog with her this night and little red riding hood feels sorry for her

weird old lady leads her off in the bushes up this dirt track to where she lives in a caravan. So rickety this van, if the dog peed on it it fall down.

The collie dog's barking round the caravan, it's the middle of the night.

The weird old lady invites her in for a cup of hot chocolate.

Bird feels sorry for her.

Inside is that young bloke lives with the old lady. Even weirder than she is. Bird knows him. He's big and fat and slow as a wet week.

The door of the caravan shuts hard behind the bird. She hears the little old lady lock it.

Heart like a drum roll.

That big fat slow kid brings out some mates of his, over for a visit. Bird knows them.

They're all in cahoots: the bad boys, the big fat slow weirdo, the crazy little old lady. One of the boys, *him*. Just not the fat one.

PURE NATURAL GENIUS

Never a kook. Been watching them waves so long I knew what to do first up. Had it sorted. Paddled like there was a school of great whites snapping at me toes. Paddle and commit.

Throw everything down that wave. You crash, you wipe out, it's only water.

They mastered one wave, they went after another. First they got the little ones in Rainbow Bay, then the shoulder waves out at Greenmount. Then they went for Little Mali, suck-up inside Snapper. Then there was something else always something else.

Satisfaction of getting the better of one wave only lasted long as you didn't think about the next one. You pat yourself on the back. Then paddle off for what the older blokes was catching.

New Year's Eve, went out for a late night wave. Dead of night. On his own. Thirteen, must of been.

Sat out while the firecrackers went off on Greenmount and all the dumb surfers drink themselves stupid.

Him on his own.

Silent.

Caught the last wave of the old year then the first wave of the new, then went back in and got dry and went to bed.

That's what he did every New Year from now:

Last wave of the old, first of the new.

Genius.

Mo come and watched. Sit herself on the wooden bench on Greenmount Hill. Me and Rod caught waves for her. First time she seen us. We were like performers in a surf comp and she's the crowd.

Between waves me and Rod are chatting out the back, happy as clams, trying not to talk about Mo or look at her. But we was so happy. Swelling like sea monkeys.

Then we come back in, acting like we don't care was she watching or not. We get set to go home and she stops and she's shaking her head.

Watching you ride, she said, *was like watching a beam of light shine across the wave.*

Me and Rod, our necks both snapped. Scope who she was talking to. Him? Me? Us both?

Like a beam of light, she said again and I thought she'd cry.

To Roddy she didn't say nothing.

SWALLOWING IT

Breakfast, the melamine table. Wash hands at the kitchen sink, nice big bowl of muesli and milk, sit down.

Mo.

Her big veiny hands flat on the red melamine.

No rings.

I sit and munch on my muesli. Make me big and strong.

'Might go out for a Splice and a Tarax today.'

Making conversation.

She has no rings on her fingers.

Her hands older than the rest of her.

Her eyes damper than the rest of her.

I push up the aviators. She still knows.

I finish my muesli.

'Think it's time to tell, Den?'

Get up, wash out bowl, hands in the kitchen sink. Dry them on the kitchen towel. Push up the aviators. They're still there.

'Dennis?'

Hate it when she calls me Dennis.

I'm in for it now.

Deep, deep in it.

Me chopper. Me poor poor chopper.

In the sandy scrub on The Other Side.

Deep, deep in it boys.

'Don't tell me then. Where ya been. Sneaky little bugger. Ya been with yer little chickie? Out at night with her? Betcha have.'

Her wobbly old voice close at my shoulder now. Time to swallow my pride, my poor poor chopper, the radio turned off, the kook of the lagoon, my pride, my dry dry pride a hunk of seaweed stuck in my throat . . .

'Ar Den, don't cry, doesn't matter love I don't care just tell me the . . . Here love . . .'

Me dry dry pride. Swallowing it.

Me poor poor chopper.

Wash me hands.

Wipe me eyes. Bow me head in the sink. The kitchen sink.

Mo's old arms flaking off skin and bone, round me round shoulders.

'Here love . . . Here love.'

Mo starts singing. *Baby Face.*

. . . yeah . . .

A long time at the kitchen sink, this and that—

And then:

'I tell you, only you promise me one thing.'

'. . . You've got the cutest little . . . What's that, Den love?'

Push the aviators up the nose. They slip in the wetness. Nose wetter than the rest of me. Redder than the rest of me.

I have conquered the lagoon.

'Take a deep breath love. Deep breath . . .'

I have conquered the lagoon. I will move to the ocean. I will start again. I need to be far away.

Me poor poor chopper.

I need to be far away, where Mo can turn the day into a night.

Me poor poor chopper.

Deep in it now.

'Haven't been with her. If I tell ya have to promise ya won't tell *her.*'

'Den love? When did I ever tell?'

Far away where Mo can turn the day into a night.

EDUCATIONAL

Pure natural genius, ripped everything at school: mainly maths. Top dog in maths. Okay at spelling when it was like maths. Okay at writing when it was like maths. If it was all maths, he'd've been the top doggie hot dog.

Pure genius.

Pretty sweet at art too: cept the only thing he could draw was waves. He drew left-handers, right-handers, A-frames, close-outs, low-tide suckers, fat onshore foamballs, reef breaks, beach breaks, even invented a few upside-down inside-out breaks. Was all he could draw. Nothing else.

But what good was all that schooling anyway. What good could it do ya. Mo been to school and what good had it done. Made her educated at peeling prawns at the fisho and handing out change at Funland. Seven days a week. What good could it do ya? For your week of school work experience, you went to help Mo peel prawns and ate so many you got sick and had to go home. That was work for ya.

Mo left him and Rod down at the beach to look after themself. It wasn't she was neglectful. It was she had nowhere else for them, and if they were at the beach she knew where they were, better than off Lord knows where doing Lord knows what. They might of been wasting their time but at least they were wasting it where she knew where they were.

Like at night times, ever since the night DK had his nightmare, he wakes up he gets to go in with his Mo. Better she knows where he is than

off yeah

They ran in a pack. Sometimes a pack of two. Sometimes other kids with them. Waggers, urchins, wolf cubs. Always running. Making their own rules.

•

Then when they got hungry Mo was there at the end of her day, or between her shifts, on the hill in front of Shangrila. Cept it was called Shagrila now, someone picked off the n probly Rod no doubt.

They come running when they saw their Mo. She didn't need to call, didn't need to drag them off. People said they grovelled to her. Street urchins and mummy's boys. Odd mix.

But she put the meat on their plates.

Other kids pinched food from shops: fruit, lollies, ice creams. Never the Keith boys. Mo drummed it into them:

I feed yous, yous won't need to steal. Yous steal or swear, I'll stop feeding yous.

They knew she meant it and knew she'd find out.

So Dennis never stole nothing cept maybe boards, and never swore.

And Rod never stole nothing cept maybe boards and he also had a name for going through wallets rolled up in towels left on the beach, but they was only kooks' wallets, not anyone anybody knew. He never swore. Sometime he swiped food but only when he was hungry.

Teachers arranged the classroom so the best got to sit in the back row. Worst in the front.

From the back you could see through a broken section of the school fence down, down, all down the headland to Greenmount and Rainbow, and if it was going off down there if it was offshore and peeling you can see it from the back row. Only the back row.

He got top marks.

He looked into the Pacific and the Pacific looked back into him.

Then it all got too much. He was sitting in the back row, earnt his position where he could see the waves, and dying the death of a thousand cutbacks. Hell on earth, watching Greenmount going off from the classroom.

He stopped trying, made his marks drop. So he could sit up front else and not see.

But he knew. He shut his eyes and saw easterly lines. Staircase outside the room was a six-foot drop. Grass bank in the lunch area was a fat shoulder ripe for a roundhouse cutback. His eyes shut, he could see corduroy to the horizon. All-time. Offshore, south swell, breaking mechanical off the rocks. Legs twitching, back tight, pelvis pivoting, making turns, new turns, hook the board to his right, up the lip, reo down off the lip again, cut back, pull in the tube yeah but

but still in his hard wooden school seat.

Hadn't done any them moves yet.

Hell on earth.

Got too much. If it was on, cyclone swell or tradewind, didn't matter, they look round the classroom and Dennis Keith wasn't there no more.

Dennis was that stick figure tracing lines on them corduroy beauties, dancing on water.

Kids in the back row could see him. Top dogs.

Nobody dobbed.

But soon the teachers twigged: when the swell was up and the points were working, Dennis Keith wasn't at school. Cause and effect. Logic. Scientific method.

And Rodney Keith, also gone.

They had boards stashed under Gary Trounson's stall. They hid from the school bus and run out to the waves when it was gone.

Gone, gone.

They only wagged school on days when swell was up and the points were working.

Only them days.

The swell was up and the points were working a lot of days. This was the Goldie. This was the sixties.

Units popping up like shrooms. Him and Rod got to know the developers—not personally just knew their cars. Big yank tanks. Cadillacs, Buicks. Him and Rod watched their cars and the men get out in their suits, fan themselves with their brochures and their folders.

Rod: *If they have to fan themselves so much, why'd they wear suits?*

Didn't teach you the answer to that in school.

What Rod did to the developers once:

Three of them got out of a yank tank, Left Hand Drive and that, to scope out a block on Rainbow Bay.

Rod: *Alien attack!*

Rod worked out that yank tanks had air-conditioning ducts open to the outside.

Rod followed Sam the beagle and scooped up his Sam-poo. In a Glad sandwich bag.

When the aliens walk off round the point trying not to look like aliens Rod snuck up with the bags of Sam-poo and pour them in the air-con ducts.

You watched when the aliens come back to their car and drive off.

Then stopped a few blocks down the road. Stumbling out in their suits, one of them spewing, another one shouting at no-one.

Never would of happened if they hadn't of been wearing suits, Rod said sadly shaking his head.

Eh?

They been wearing T-shirts and boardies like normal ones, Rod said, *they wouldn't of needed air-con. Makes you sick it does.*

Headmaster, Mr Paterson, cut you both a deal.

Yers come to school, I'll take yers surfing. Teach yers proper.

You looked at each other. You looked at him.

He looked at you.

Seen yers trying to cut back on yer front side, he said. *Yer too tight, too stiff.*

Headmaster was a goofy-footer. Out there with the plumbers, the butchers, the newsagents, the police, the house painters. Once, they said, Mr Paterson had skipped a school day when it was all-time at Kirra. He come in afterwards, still the middle of the day, and as he's putting his board in his car he come face to face with his school area inspector. It didn't look good Mr Paterson wagging his own school, not good at all, cept that his inspector, his boss, is walking down the street with a lady who was not his wife. Story went, they took one look at each other, their eyes met, it all went down between them, all understood, and the inspector kept walking and Mr Paterson kept packing his board in the car and not a single nother word was ever said.

Dennis and Rod come to school with their boards and put them on the roof racks of Mr Paterson's station wagon.

Waited till three o'clock and knocked at the headmaster's office.

Time for surf lesson Mr P.

Mr Paterson taught Dennis the basics: how to position his feet, how to press up, never to snatch the rails, taught him front-foot surfing, back-foot surfing.

Taught him etiquette. When not to snake, when not to drop in, when to duck dive, when to get out of the way, when you were in the wrong, when you were in the right.

Dennis didn't know any of that stuff.

Mr Paterson taught him.

Rod sort of hung round the back and pretended not to try to listen. Mr Paterson didn't pay much attention to Rod. Clearly didn't rate Rod's surfing. Figured letting Rod tag along was enough kindness. These lessons was all about you, DK, *the beam of light*, not the wise-guy brother. Even though Rod been surfing before you. Just the way things were.

But a problem:

Three o'clock, sea breezes perking up, turning onshore, waves crumbling, afternoon mush. Better in the morning. In school hours.

Rod come to you and had a quiet word.

Den, we can't let these ones go to waste.

They stop turning up to school again.

When it was on.

Then when the swell dropped you'd get called to the headmaster's office.

Waves are better in the morning Mr P.

As he was caning yous.

End of lesson.

Mo made them go to church but Sunday was a bad deal. Bad, bad deal:

Mass during the morning glass-off.

Mass during the evening glass-off.

Not negotiable.

The death of God.

Mo shook her head: *Not negotiable, yous lot. No church, no baked dinners, no meat on the table. Yous lot.*

That was that. The resurrection. Jesus lives.

No point having a face-off with Mo: only be one winner: Gawd, the Good Lawd.

But . . .

But . . .

. . . Father Aplin, the priest, was this top-ranked oldster surfer.

He been in the Pacific War, Father A, not as a chaplain, back before he found Gawd and that, when he was just a kid aircraft engineer, a whatsit, a *machinist*. Accident-prone, Father A. Always stubbing his toes like you, yous had that in common. *No good on land*, he said. He caught his arm in a propeller once and been told to take up paddling as therapy. Then he got into noseriding big redwood Malibu logs, shipped them from California to the Gold Coast so he could hang ten and do the cheater five, the full fricken repertoire of the old-time log rider. He was one of the pioneers. Then he had a bad wipe-out and speared his redwood board through his thigh. A big football of meat ballooned up out of his leg as he drove himself to the hospital. Turned out he was one fluke away from dying: he punctured his femoral artery and it was bleeding under the muscle, blowing it up, and only the pressure of the blown-up muscle was stopping all his blood gushing out of him. He still had the scar, loved telling the story even more than the one about Jesus walking on water or raising Lazarus.

Story of how he become a priest was, in the forties he used to quit his machinist jobs whenever the surf was up, then go back to work when it was flat. But that was when jobs were everywhere. After the war when all the servicemen come home and there was more competition, he couldn't just duck in and out of work willy-nilly so he had to knuckle down at something. It was either stick at his machinism or quit surfing. So he used his imagination. His initiative. Find a job that didn't matter whether he's in the office or in the waves: and so he become the priest of St Barnabas Cattle-Tick Church at Rainbow Bay. If he missed a service due to a swell, and that happened a fair bit, he tell his bishop he was 'doing some outreach, where it really counts'.

Big-time into shaping, Father A. From his time with the air force he got ideas in his head about 'hydrodynamic planing' and whatnot, started making boards out of sandwiches of plywood, foam and fibreglass in the early sixties. He get you in his vestry behind the church which he converted into a shaping bay, all full of fibreglass dust and holy water, and gibber all this gobbledygook about hydrodynamics and foils and flexible fins and sometimes you wish he shut up and talk about something easier to understand, like the Old Testy say.

•

And the holy wine always had this like film of sawdust floating on the top.

And the communion wafers always tasted a bit like resin.

Father A was always out at Snapper with Mr Paterson, with the butchers, with the plumbers, with the newsagents, with the house painters. There was this deaf one, a deaf chippie, you never knew his name and he never talked much obviously, but Father A told you a story about him, how this deaf chippie been out at ten-foot Kirra one day and come through a massive barrel and when it smashed down behind him, *he heard it*, first time he ever heard a wave break, and as the tube spat him out the exit ramp he had his arms in the air and he was screaming in his mushy deaf-bloke voice, *I heard the tube, I heard the tube!*

Father Aplin got off on repeating that, putting on the mushy voice and all. *I heard the tube! I heard the tube!* It was bigger news than Moses hearing God in the burning bush, Father A said.

Thing was, the waves *mattered*. That's what you took from them old guys. They couldn't say why or how but there was no doubt about it: waves mattered more than anything. So when you grew up down there on that beach, living in the sand and the water days stacking up, before the units, before the developers, before the surfwear companies and the billboards and the like *Gold Coast*, when you grew up in this place same as a barnacle grew on the lava rocks, you knew you were more a part of this coast than any other people were part of any place anywhere, cos you were doing the thing that mattered.

Father A spent his life in the sun but never got burnt. Some weird Jesus-protection in his skin, Factor 15 from God, made it like he been dipped in grey-pink paint head to toe, and he never burnt, never got freckles, never flaked. And he had this comb-over to make himself look less bald only it made him look more. When he was in the surf his comb-over all fell down one side of his head so he was half a hippie. Between waves he tried to paste it back over the top, but no point. You knew he'd got a real good wave if he paddled back out, all his comb-over down one side of his head, and he's forgot to paste it back. On land he took better care of it. Ladies in church probably thought he had a full head.

Father A could get through Mass in world record speed. Nor'-east swell already showing up at Currumbin? Ten-minute Mass. Glassy and building? Five-minute Mass.

Father Aplin had his boards on a rack in the vestry, all built on same lines: nine-footer, three stringer, big raked glassed-in white pine fin. Hawaiian.

Me and Rod wore boardies to Mass. Father A tied up the drawstring of his boardies under his cassock. He knew it was a nine o'clock low tide better than a nine o'clock Mass. Priorities. You go, *When's the evening service, Father?* And he'd go, *Dennis, I can't say exactly, but I do know that it'll be a pretty low low tide and offshore at six thirty-five.* Nothing odd about that at all. Mass could be moved to any time, didn't matter. But you couldn't shift the tide round to suit your routine. God had his schedule and he set it with tides and winds and swells, not with the fricken clock on the wall.

But if it was onshore and small, mushburgers, Father A give Mass the full treatment, all the bells and whistles and incense and holy water sprinkles and calls and responses and Peace Be With Yous, took it serious as the Pope himself, like he was catching up, making up to the Big Fella . . .

. . . yeah religion . . .

WHERE MO CAN TURN THE DAY INTO A NIGHT

The first morning I sleep in till dawn yeah Mo's wake-up time. Breakfast together. I wash hands at kitchen sink, make big bowl of muesli and milk.

In the Sandman panel van sprayed purple and orange, Mo in a pale yellow house dress.

Push up my aviators. They're there.

We drive out through the toy roundabouts, away from the camellias and the azaleas out through the town over the causeway to The Other Side . . .

I don't tell her where my poor poor chopper is.

R—

I—

Fricken—

P.

We go to the bush where my stick is. I get it out the bush and throw it in back of the Sandman panel van sprayed purple and orange.

We drive a long way down The Other Side.

—Hours—

Can't talk. Have to have my mouth open when we drive past a cross street—

Any opening in the curb have to have my mouth open.

Have to have it closed in between.

Lips working away like a guppy

way it's always been.

'How much further, Den love?'

We go hours. There's this break I know. Today it's perfect, tiny, no wind, mid-tide.

Beginner wave.

Hours down The Other Side.

Silence.

Finally we get there.

Someone's out on a Mal.

We sit ten minutes. Him catching a few.

'Well?'

Push up the aviators. They're there.

Shake me head.

'That guy on that Mal he's gunna be there a while.'

We go home.

Me, Mo and the stick in the Sandman panel van sprayed purple and orange.

Open lips when we go past the sandy scrub where I left the poor poor chopper.

Out of respect.

COOLIE AND THE GANG

There was other kids from school from the area, doing what we were. In my class this blond rich kid, Frank Johnson. FJ. There was Glenn Tinkler. Tink. Kinky Tinky, stumpy redheaded bastard. In Rod's class bunch of others. The Peterson brothers, Peter Townend, Wayne Bartholomew—handy surfers, keen as, but never destined for the top. Happy to run round in a mob after me and Rod. Skiving off from club patrol, tooling about on the Surfoplanes, the Coolites, having a crack on the loggers

yeah but not

not just me and Rod. Me and Rod was top of the pecking order. Just you wait.

None of them as poor as us. We were called the zombies on account of living by a graveyard. Rod even earnt coin digging graves when the regular gravies skived off. Five for digging a new hole, two for digging someone out of an old one. Quid. Sometimes he had to dig a new grave for a dead 'un. Sometimes he dig up some Chinese bones. Part of the graveyard was Chinese and the Chinese dig up their dead uncles after a while and stash their bones in a big dish in their bone house. Their relatives come visit play with the bones or whatever. It all smelt sweet of the incense they burnt there. I reckoned if I ever had to die I'd convert to Chinese before I went.

Rod had friends, mates and whatnot, he'd invite them for sleepovers to spin them out at night. Rod knew how to break into the bone house and he grab a skull or a couple of shoulder blades, come up behind his mate and tap him on the shoulder. Or let his mate fall asleep in one of the bedrooms and when they were out cold Rod and me hoist the bed, lug it through the back gate and put it in the Chinese bone house. Then they wake up and see all these bones on shelves round them and well, it was Rod's job to clean the bedsheets afterwards, that's all I'm gunna say.

It might of been fun living by a graveyard but you wouldn't live there if you had any coin and we were the poorest kids on the whole Goldie. There'd be nights

ar there'd be nights yeah

be nights Mo bung a pile of chokoes on the table, fry them in lard and enjoy herself, saying she had that stuff as a kid and good enough for her then it was good enough for us now. Chokoes made us spew and we only keep them down cos we knew if we were having chokoes there wasn't gunna be nothing else that night.

Once Rod had a mate over without warning for dinner and Mo had toast and this one tin of sardines for us. Turned out she only had enough for three people and so she snuck away from the table. Rod and his mate didn't notice, they're wolfing down their sardines in tomato sauce. I looked out the back and saw Mo go in the graveyard and pick some bananas and passionfruit. She sat on a gravestone eating them for dinner. I felt so bad I could of killed Rod's mate. I promised I never let my Mo go hungry again, I'll swipe people's wallets from the beach like Roddy so she won't have to eat fruit from the graveyard ever again.

Gary Trounson's monster loggers, best boards to ride, cost thirty quid new so there was no way we could ever buy one. But one summer this huge cyclone washed away most of the beach, me and Rod beachcombed all the sand on the road and people's yards and scored a good bag of bread been lost over the years. Rod said we picked up twenty years worth of loose change and they should do cyclones more often.

Mo scored me a Coolite for my twelfth birthday. It cost two quid. I lived on it for a summer. I looked like a skinned fricken rabbit all year, polystyrene ripped my chest to mincemeat. Rod called me the pizza man, cos I looked like an uncooked Supreme.

I was so hot on that Coolite, sometimes at the turn of the tide I ride a wave in till it hit the backwash coming back out, fly up on the bump of the collision, twist in the air, land it, and then *ride the backwash back out.* Nobody ever seen nothing like it.

But we couldn't afford a logger. Tink could. FJ could. These kids had two parents each. More than they knew what to do with. More than enough to go round. You'd think. They lived in bigger houses closer to the beach. They hung out in this Hawaiian theme beach hut called the Jungle Hut where they had the best milkshakes. Me and Rod was banned, don't ask me why.

Coppertop Kinky Tinky learnt to surf on a plank swing he had in his backyard, one of them long ones go like a pendulum. He ride it up real high and took zero-gravity drops from the top of the arc. Taught himself to walk up and down the plank and nose ride and everything without even going in the water.

As for FJ his family had a swimming pool. He get dressed for school in the morning and while he was waiting to leave he lay a Coolite in the pool and run at it and jump on it and surf it across to the far edge. He done that back and forward for half an hour till his mum's ready to drive him to school. He said he'd of got a pasting from her if he ever got wet in his uniform but he never did, never fell off once.

I never believed FJ's old lady would paste him. The ones like him and Tink, their folks was always looking after them. But it wasn't the done thing to be well-off so FJ and Tink played poor, getting money from their olds and then blow it all on hamburgers and steak sandwiches and ice creams for their mates so they end up dirt poor like like like say me and Rod. I took a lot of cacks in giving FJ and Tink orders to go buy me a sundae from the Jungle Hut and help their get poor quick scheme. Win–win.

And no harm pinching their boards so me and Rod creep in their garages during me paper round and nick their loggers so we could be first out for the early

early bird catches the wave

FJ got this pretty ten-foot logger in solid balsa, the grain of the wood magnified by the fibreglass, I got lost looking into the wood before Rod give me a clout over the ear and reminds me what we're there for.

Down the beach. We were still too little to get our arms fully round them things so we held on the nose and drug them along behind us.

We were out before the sun. Only blokes on the beach before us was the garbos.

We never beat the garbos.

But we beat all the other surfers. Come sunrise Tink and FJ was down on the rocks screaming at us riding waves on their balsa sticks. We give them the big finger.

When they got them back, they hid their boards inside their houses.

So if they hid their boards we get them in the surf: paddle over on Gary Trounson's waterlogged planks, push FJ off, thank you very much, nice knowing you. Have to be polite in this world eh.

They had more than enough to go round.

Rod suggested an arrangement:

We pinch your boards, you tell your olds they been pinched, they get you new ones.

Tink and FJ spewing. But we was bigger than them and way better surfers and hassled them in the waves so after a few weeks they give in, and their folks scored them new boards and we had the old ones, and then hey presto they tell their folks how they found their old nicked boards again but lost the new ones . . .

More than enough to go round.

Except for waves. Never enough.

Me, them years:

Walking along the street seeing a low wall in front of a house and thinking how if it pitched up this high I could drive up vertical on my forehand side, right up onto the lip, then turn on a brick and fly down again . . .

Riding up hedges and trees . . .

Figure-eight turns off chainlink fences . . .

Smashing the lip of a billboard . . .

Opening and closing me mouth when I crossed a driveway or a street.

Sam was on the way out by then and Mo got us a new mutt. We were hooked on beagles now, infectious, and she got another: mad little bugger, lighter tan colour than Sam, name of Basil. Basil the beagle. Totally mad energy that bloke. Poor old Sam, pretty old and grey by then, didn't know what hit him. Basil always mounting him and shooting all over his back. First thing we knew about all that business: not birds and bees, but beagles and beagles. Basil was a sex maniac. It's no way for a family beagle to grow old, being molested by another dog. But

Basil wasn't just mad he was cunning. He didn't do it in front of Mo, like he knew it'd offend her. So Mo never knew about it. When she was going on about how Basil 'kept Sam young', she didn't have a clue what we were thinking.

The other thing you learnt: It was a war out there.

Every week a few more, a few more out, and now there was guys out full time, living on the dole, not going off to jobs at eight thirty and coming back at five, nah these new guys all day paddling round getting deeper, getting inside everyone else, making the take-offs.

Nobody going behind the granite yet where it sucked up vertical, pure madness, you'll get smashed if you paddle into waves behind the lava rock.

Nobody yet.

But a matter of time. And when someone did others will follow. It was competitive. There was hassling. There was racing. There was snaking. There was dropping in. There was kicking boards. Rod sanded down the rails of his boards so they could draw blood when he kicked them at someone's ankles. Rod got so good at it he could walk down the nose of his board and kick the tail, fins and all, *backwards* at someone *behind* him on the wave. If there was competition points for using boards as weapons Rodney Keith Keith would of been world champ.

Rod was so good at it he could kick his board at someone and intentionally *miss* their face by a couple of inches.

Usually that was enough.

We weren't the only ones doing it. We were just the maddest. It wasn't beautiful or tranquil or bloody oneness with nature.

It was a war.

And you had to be in a *fury*, every fricken wave, to be good enough to get onto them.

And you had to be the most psycho crackpot out there, or at least make everyone else think you are.

Then half the battle's won.

So sayeth Father A.

DAD III

There was blackfellas at school and cos you were long and lean with a heavy brow and a tan deeper than the sun this rumour started that your old man had been a boong. You didn't mind it too much: you were like a flash of Black Lightning on the water. No Abos surfed and you didn't mind them thinking you were the only one in the whole wide world. The Surfing Aboriginal. Black Lightning on the wave. Freak them all out they think you have *black magic* yeah

nah but you could see it, way back in the fifties, them mad post-war years: pack of them, young blokes, laughing and joking the way they always was, passing round a bottle in a brown paper bag. Sitting outside the pub bastard publican wouldn't let them in to drink with whities. Teach him a lesson they sit right there on the street outside his pub and make an exhibition of themself.

Laughing, arguing, laughing again.

Then this tough young bird walks out the pub. Been inside with her girlfriends. Sipping her lemonade. She and drink agree to disagree. But yeah there's one of the Abos she was eyeing off through the window and he saw her too and a lot of eye contact going on while he's pretending to drink and laugh and joke with his mates.

And then the young bird's looked right at him as she come out of the pub, the challenging half of a smile, and she swings off round the corner.

And the bloke, the good-looking one, the funniest one, the one that's less pissed than the others, he wants to follow. Thinks she's shot him an invitation with that look.

But he don't have the hair to get up and leave his mates.

They ask questions.

They won't let him leave on his own.

So he's got this problem: damn sure he wants to follow her but no chance of going up on his own and saying hello and walking her home. On his own. Which is what he wants. So what's he to do, leave her be and let the chance slip?

He gets up. His mates get up too. They leave their spot in front of the pub and swing off round the corner. Joking, laughing. No arguing.

One of them, maybe the good-looking one, maybe one of them others.

Him.

SCREAM IN BLUE

Malvern Star, big dippy handlebars, big spangly sparkly seat. Rod called it a girl's bike but Dennis was in love with it.

Just the right size for him at twelve, thirteen, fourteen.

Then he grew.

Been storing all that food he been eating, all them meat and chips and ice cream and soup and spag bol and meat and meat and meat and even the chokoes in lard, for donkeys it been going nowhere but down in his hollow legs, and then kaboom, one day Dennis grew . . .

But not in order.

First his feet: into flippers.

Then his hands: into buckets.

Then his shoulders: into pistons.

He was a weed with perfect surfing parts, the surfing machine, feet for kicking and controlling the board, hands for paddling and pressing up, shoulders for paddle and twist in turns. Nothing much else grew, only the parts he needed.

Then, one at a time, the rest of him:

Nose.

Mouth.

Backbone.

Legs.

Ears.

Cept the chest, which never grew, just stayed a bony ridge, no pecs, no chest, flat as a tack. His legs and arms stayed short and his centre of gravity low, good for whipping his turns. Surfers built like tortoises, low to the ground and laughable when they weren't on a wave, like bandy-leg race jockeys.

He was the strongest grom and intimidating. Had good ears in the water:

Is that Dennis Keith?

Is that him over there?
Is that the guy?
That DK?
They didn't need to ask.

He was the stringy intimidator, hands like buckets and feet like flippers and always on the move, always paddling, always hassling, imposing order and etiquette as taught by Mr Paterson and Father Aplin, going round them, under them, over them, pushing them off waves, *his* waves, kicking his board at them, the sheriff of the waves yeah

nothing go to waste.

You rode whatever you could: loggers, eggs, Coolites, Surfoplanes, Hawaiian three-stringers, antique boards, orphan boards, cut-downs.

Whatever you could get your hands on.

Whatever you could get your hands on.

In wartime—

Wartime measures.

You paddled round Snapper and Rainbow and Greenmount and Kirra and learnt the waves, learnt where to sit and where not to, learnt how to line yourself up against which agave tree, which rock, which of the blocks of units popping up on the waterfront, which crane, which streetlight. Had names in your head for all of them landmarks: Golden Towers, Blocky-Block, Mary Greenhouse, Nuthead Rock, The Garage, The Boobs, Hair Tree. So on. You lined yourself up and paddled like hell, only needed to think one thing: *Paddle like hell.* Work yourself up into the state, the state, to keep up your energy, your aggro, to paddle like hell and commit yourself you needed to be in a certain state to throw yourself face first down an open wall:

A *fury*, every wave.

. . . yeah . . .

. . . and let nothing go to waste . . .

Let nothing go to some kook gunna waste the wave, pull out of it, fall off his board, or trim it.

Wartime measures.

You had to enforce discipline in wartime. Or else there was no civilisation, right?

Rod was the real sheriff. Once yous both chased this kook all three of yous in your wetsuits on foot across the state border into New South. That kook couldn't surf but could run all right that's for sure. All three of yous in wetsuits. Basil on your heels barking his head off showing his teeth. Basil wouldn't bite a flea, but Rod goes:

Dennis, put the muzzle back on Fang!

Through the town, across the causeway, over The Other Side.

Last you saw of the kook he was still running in his wetsuit into New South Wales.

He'd dropped in on Rod.

Rod was the first kid you knew who was able to whistle properly, tongue between the teeth, loud and no-nonsense, when he was on a wave, *Oi, get out of the way.* Like a man.

You couldn't whistle.

Tried but couldn't manage the sound, not loud enough, not commanding enough.

So you had this scream. This yelp. Like Sam if you trod on his tail by mistake.

Used the scream on waves, the sound from deep inside that someone was in there, someone coming, so get out of the fricken way—

Your calling card: the scream.

Rod and the boys from The Pit give it a name: *The Scream in Blue.*

Tink and FJ were getting good. Had to be good to paddle away from you when they saw you coming. Had to be good to make a wave if you were in the water. Unless they just wanted to sit back off the shoulder and wait for you to pick off the best in each set. Unless they wanted the dregs and the mush.

They didn't. Tink and FJ were good, real fast in the water, they saw sets coming, they knew the line-ups, where to sit, where not to, where to feint and bait and switch, where to look like they were going to be while going somewhere else, yeah, they were good but

but you were better . . .

One day Tink dropped in on you. You were deep, not quite behind the granite but deep in against the point. He didn't mean it. He didn't see you.

He didn't hear the Scream in Blue.

You come across the wave so fast he never heard, never saw you. He thought he was on this perfect little peeler all to himself, deep enough, steep take-off, nor'-east swell, and out of nowhere comes DK, long wet hair flying and flicking, the nose of your board like a torpedo . . .

Too late to pull out, Tink dropped in.

Took your legs out.

Both of yous caught inside smashed by next three waves.

Tink got his board back and paddled out.

Yours got hammered to pieces on the granite.

No more boards.

You swum out.

Best swimmer at Rainbow. Won all the medals. Could of.

You swum out and found Tink.

You got hold of his board.

You took his fin in your right hand and his rail in your left.

Never snatch the rails, except this once.

Wartime measures.

You snapped off his fin.

You sunk your teeth into the rail and put a big chomp in the glass and spit it out.

You flicked what was left of the board back at Tink.

Your best mate sort of but he dropped in on you.

You hated to see waste.

Wartime measures.

Everyone was freaked out. You were meant to be the quiet Keith. Rod was the psycho, Rod policed the waves, Dennis was the one who quietly went about tearing up the surf. The beam of light. But now word spread: DK might be just as psycho as RK. Still waters run deep and all that.

You saw it more simple. Busting off fins was policing the waves. Without fins, they had to go in. That was all you wanted: make them go away.

At school Tink and FJ were friendly as all get out now. Thought you were a mad bastard now. Whole school, talking about you. Loving you. Admiring you. That mad bastard.

They meant it.

The first of the awe.

The first you heard yourself spoken of in that hushed way . . .

Respect.

Legend.

Them days when you got everything that moved and they got nothing. It meant as much to you that they got nothing.

Once they had that awed hush in their voice you had to keep it there. Couldn't let it slip couldn't give an inch.

You said nothing.

You knew who you were, didn't need to prick your finger to know your blood ran red.

But surf:

A war out there.

Loved surfing:

It give you someone to hate.

It wasn't he didn't like people; he just didn't want them in his way.

But you weren't as plain mean as Rod. Better to keep them guessing, be nice once in a while. Also bring Rod into line.

Once he picked on some kid for no reason at all, kid just sitting out on the shoulder like a gummy bear, too scared to get in anyone's way. Rod caught a wave and ploughed over the kid's head then chewed him out for being in the way. When Rod come back out the back Dennis give him a rabbit-punch between the eyes.

Ya do that for?

Show you what it feels when you get sconed by a drongo.

The hell, Den?

Takes one to know one.

Rod looking at you like he didn't know you anymore, like *What's Den doing?*

You got to keep him on his toes.

Made your point.

Another time in front of the whole of Coolie you went out and rescued this bloke and his bird in a canoe. They launched from Greenmount and got took up the sweep past Snapper and were on the way to the Solomons. You seen the bloke's face as he floats past you. Rod and all the boys were cacking themselves. The swell was ten foot and lifeguards couldn't get out.

Then the bloke in the canoe panicked. He jumped out and tried to swim back in. He was on his way to bodysurf a sucky ten-foot mongrel straight into the granite jump-off rock.

You forgot about the waves and paddled, your bucket hands motoring. You risk getting smashed on the rocks yourself. Crowds on the point to watch you get smeared.

You got him on your board and tandemed him halfway into the sand then pushed him in on a wave.

Crowds were shouting, pointing. The bird drifting away into the distance in the canoe. All alone.

You swum out to the line-up, through six monster waves, push Rod off his board, then paddle it out to the canoe. About a k. Then you got to her, the bird's bawling her eyes out and so you get in the canoe with her. Dumped Rod's board. Good riddance. Easy come easy go eh.

You paddled the canoe like you been doing it all your life. You went past Rod who's bobbing about trying to bodysurf in, waiting for a wave that wouldn't chuck him up against the rocks like them sticky jelly figures you chuck at walls and come down in cartwheels.

Need any help bro?

You didn't hear if he had anything to say.

You paddled the bird in, brought her down the face of this solid eight-foot right-hander into Greenmount, biggest wave anyone ever seen a canoe ride on the Gold Coast. Crowds cheering on the point. Bird screaming in terror in your ear.

Nearly deafened you she did. Hope she never set foot in that water again.

You got in shore, dumped her with her bloke then ran to the Rainbow clubhouse to nick a board and get back out there.

You crossed paths with Rod on your way out.

You stopped and clapped your forehead.

Bugger, Rodney, you said.

What? He was shirty about his board.

Forgot to pinch their wallets.

Good Dennis Keith story that one. Have to tell the BFO.

RETURN OF THE BFO

And so now here she is, back, refinanced. Bang another five hundred for Mo's sandwiches, and she's going for walks with you asking about the early days. An investigator, reckons she can crack the cold case.

The cold case still hot in your house.

Dead bird dug up out of Gold Coast sand and fibreglass.

She don't say nothing about running away when you invited her for a sleepover.

How you know *she knows*.

This time round she done some research: interviewed old-timers, some of the ones who were there at the start, talked to them about you:

Chook Draper.

Gary Trounson.

Mr Paterson.

Peter Drouyn.

Kinky Tinky.

FJ.

A bunch of the other retired grommets: the Petersons, Townend, Rabbit.

'Bet your ears have been burning eh!' she goes, all too proud of herself.

Now she reckons she knows what she's asking me. All the school stories, the shaping, the schooling, the churching, the parties, this and that, the other, and reckons just cos she's talked about you with them jokers she knows more than she started out with.

Fat chance.

She's talked to family members and schoolmates and elderly grommets and even tracked down the original Bob, the milk bar owner who gave me my first pine-lime Splice.

Reckons she's a real hotshot bi fricken ographer now.

And everything she asks I push up my aviators (they're still there) and I go,

'Well yeah . . . but no!'

And she laughs at that. She laughs like we're

yeah like we're in on the joke together.

She's moved into a motel reckons she's got me nailed.

'How much they pay ya for this feature, then?'

She shrugs her round meaty shoulders. She's got a face like a plate: flat, round, featureless. Honest face.

'Just expenses,' she says.

Lying face.

'We're a bit strapped,' I say. 'At home.' I push up my aviators. Still there.

She changes the subject.

'Tell me about Keith Surfboards.'

Keith Surfboards/fibreglass dust/hot mix/cold case—

Lying face. I know her.

'Girl,' I go after a long long wait while I'm pulling meself together. '*Suitcase! Shitface!*'

'Eh?' She's looking at me like I've finally cracked up. But she's wrong. I've finally come together. 'Are you all right, Dennis?'

'Girl,' I go with a sly groover's grin and me eyes on the horizon, push up the aviators, 'you're trafficking in shadows now.'

KEITHS SURF BOARDS!

Too many surfers *worshipped* their boards. To you they were tools not the crown jewels. You saw surfers cry when they got a ding. Deadset cry.

Nat Young had this board he called 'Sam' and after he won loads of comps on it he spoke about 'Sam' like his best friend.

You drug yours in the sand, pinged them round the place, used them up till they were busted, then next please. No looking back. No love affairs with hunks of wood and foam and glass.

Nat's Sam got swiped anyway, shot through on him. That's friends for ya.

This was the sixties, pre leashes. Him and Rod lost Tink's board, they lost FJ's board, then they ripped off Tink's and FJ's new boards and lost them too, and suddenly there weren't enough to go round, Mr and Mrs Tinkler and Mrs and Mr Johnson turned off the taps.

When the kids run out of boards they hid in The Pit and scoot out to grab a stick washed in on a foamball. Then scoot back into the agave trees and hide it in the surf club and when the blow-in wanders about looking for his board the kids go, *Mate, saw your wipe-out,* and innocent as the day is long, and the blow-in never guess where his stick gone.

Never got caught. Never get caught. Tink and FJ join in, good boys turned bad by the need for fresh sticks.

There was other ways. Brisos come down to surf weekends then leave their sticks in the lockers, and we knew the locker combos so Monday to Friday it was like a free lending library, dozens of sticks, the catalogue all in your head. You ding one you put it back in its locker. The Briso come back and ask questions, you blame Rod, or Rod blame FJ, or FJ blame Tink, or Tink blame you. Chinese fricken whispers nobody ever get to the bottom of it.

Yeah, you go, *I told Tink not to ride it, bugger didn't listen . . .*

Briso looked at you funny: strips of malice wrapped round wishbones, stinky look in your eye, manky hair to your bare shoulders. Standing there hands on hips. Something told the Briso he had to shrug off his bad luck and get on with his life somewhere else.

Still other ways . . .

The granite points were a wrecking yard for sticks, owners would give up on them. What was he gunna do? We scavenged and scrounged and picked up the pieces, little eddy inside the rocks where the smashed boards floated into, and you could swim in there and take them to Gary Trounson or Dave Chock or Ted Gills or Chook Draper any them ding-fixers, and you even borrow the glassing gear and the sanding gear and the shaping gear and fix them up yourself.

Salvage op.

Rod started to bring them home. He built a board trolley with two wheels he ripped off an old pram and a fruit crate two sides cut off, tied together with a bike inner tube and lined with carpet. He strapped it on the back seat of his pushie and heaved it behind, stuffed with pieces of boards he scrounged from the rocks. Had to get off his bike and walk it up the hill the last bit but he was determined, Rod, and he get them home and start jigsawing together a brand new stick. This was sort of how Keith Surfboards might of been born.

You rebirth them like stolen cars: strip the glass, sand them back, redesign them as a Keith surfboard.

Rod made up a logo:

Modelled on Basil's amazing ball sack.

Rod thought it was a cack. You thought it was a bit off but let him get away with it. Had to keep the operation happy.

Before long yous were selling rebirthed Keith surfboards to groms round Coolie. With the proceeds yous bought more resin, more hardener, more promoter.

Father A might of heard about what you were doing, the legality side of it, and thought he ought to help you do it legit. He line you up some work with Chook Draper from Drape's Shapes.

Chook was the biggest shaper in the Coolie area, brought in his big balsa blanks from down Sydney crafted nice glass loggers for the butchers, the plumbers, the newsagents, the teachers, the cops, the priests.

Chook ankle-deep in balsa shavings smacked a face mask on you and went, *Move an inch and I'll sand yer dick off.*

You stood like a statue while he talks you through what he's doing:

Drawing the pattern.

Sanding the blank.

Letting you rub your hand down the deck. Balsa felt like fur.

Cutting and gluing the stringer.

Mixing the resin and hardener.

Sanding and shaping.

Sanding and shaping.

Feel the wave in yer hands.

Chook's voice muffled under his mask, glass splinters flew everywhere, Chook talking you through it, everything he knew, and he only did it cos he wanted someone to talk to and he knew Father A and your Mo and he felt sorry for you and thought you was a bit of a drongo and not really listening . . .

But Chook was wrong.

Pure natural genius.

You went home and grab Rod and the pair of you gone on a logger hunt. Now you really knew what to do with them.

Nicked two old planks from Gary Trounson's shop. Found some more abandoned in the surf club. Dinged up loggers round the rocks. Loggers abandoned in garages.

Under their houses.

In their rat cellars.

Soil infiltrated with fibreglass.

Didn't matter. Yous couldn't afford to buy blanks yourself.

Chook had more sanders, more knives, more resin and promoter and hardener than he needed. You swiped some of that and Rod nicked some hydrogen peroxide from the hardware to bleach the blanks.

Rod dug the challenge, rebirthing stolen ones. You were uncomfortable with all that, preferred to be legit if you could of.

Rod found a couple of sawhorses from a building site and you set them up under Shagrila, in your rat cellar.

Cellar swimming with glass dust.

Two dangerous kids, no more dancing for you, DK.

Then one night you come home and find this stick Roddy's redecorated. He's rewrote the writing on it.

You storm upstairs with it, stand it in front of him. He's on a beanbag, picking his latest knee scab.

'What's this then?'

'What's what Den?'

You nod at what he done. Not that you're a stickler, but this is—

'Didn't you get no education?' you go.

Rod's cacking himself silly.

'Read it again Den. Read it closer.'

I read it again and I read it closer.

'Yeah,' I went. 'Right.'

'We're the *only* ones with education,' Rod goes.

And so yeah, this is how Keith Surfboards got turned into Keiths Surf Boards.

And everyone who ever saw our boards, every last one, in the whole wide world, Perth to Hawaii, everyone always thought we'd spelt it wrong.

You done your reading, your late-night study. *Surfer. Surfing.*

Your Nat posters, your Midget posters. They didn't even need second names, Nat and Midget. Miki, David, Da Bull. You had no idea who they were but you knew them by their first names. All you needed to power you on. The words: *Nat. Midget. Bull. Miki.*

Yeah!

You had a bear trap outside your window and posters of Hawaii on your bedroom wall: Pipeline, Sunset, Haleiwa. The famous right-hander at Laniakea called The Boat, where they lined up in the water off a big wreck and paddled into perfect eight-footers. Sunset, field of dreams, hardest wave in the world cos it comes from all different directions and peaks from flat to eight foot in half a second. The Pipe, 'the meanest slab of water on earth' your poster said, which no-one rode till the year you turned twelve, the hollow tunnel steaming over Banzai reef, a picture of Butch crouching in that tunnel hoping like hell he's gunna make it out alive. Cos so many didn't. That Pipe ate men.

You lay in bed looking at them posters, hours pumping into hours. Hawaii. The waves more than the surfers. The waves that started up in some country-sized storm in the north Pacific, gallop across the world nothing to stop them, get bigger and bigger and piling on water, till they hit The Rock, the north shore of Oahu, jack straight up on them reefs into thirty-foot blue-green monsters . . .

Them Hawaiian surfers were the old gods, the calm cruisers, the water poets. Everything about Hawaiian surfing was relaxed, let the wave steal the show. When you looked at them posters you get in a fight with yourself. The Hawaiians were gods. But they *wasted* them waves. Didn't leave a mark on them. Didn't subdue them or demolish them or rip them or carve them. Not that you could ever say this but you hated the Hawaiians. Any kook could understand a big wave. These Hawaiians, all pose, all grace, surfing sculptures, glorified kooks on longboards too busy looking pretty to take any risks and get involved with the wave. They danced with the wave like the handbags who danced with the birds at Danceland

yeah didn't do that much.

You hated that you really did. What a waste. They were only one step up from Californians who pretty much stood on surfboards and modelled clothing. You saw them in the surf movies they showed down the civic centre on Friday nights, Californians and Hawaiians, none of them was surfing like you, doing stuff with the wave every second, ripping it up, squeezing it dry, big part of you wanted to step in them posters and movies and tear the whole joint to shreds.

Didn't matter that you were a teenager who hadn't been out of Coolangatta yet . . .

You were already better than all of them. Hawaiians, Americans, even Midget and Nat.

With your mind you surfed past them, you done what they couldn't do.

MALCOLM KNOX

And then in the water:

Rod, did I look like Nat on that one? Was that wave like ten-foot Sunset or what?

Yeah nah in yer dreams Den.

Didn't matter what you really looked like. Rod had a job to do. Keep your feet on the ground. In your wax.

THE OTHER SIDE

Done a lot of talking with this girl. A lot for me anyway.

But now the hotshot BFO wants to go away again couple of days. She's in, she's out, she's in, she's out. Just when I'm getting warmed up.

'Where you goin?'

'Score some waves.'

'You're kidding,' says The Great Man.

Her: nothing.

'Birds don't surf eh? What ya really doin?'

Her: nothing.

'Suit yourself. Yeah nah don't tell me then.'

She rolls her eyes but not for show, not that kind of rolling, the other kind she can't hold down. Doesn't know if I was taking the mickey or not. Getting sick of me already.

I watch her get in her ute. She drives a ute. It says 'Rip Curl', like it must be half car, half wetsuit.

Next morning me and Mo tootle off again down The Other Side. Onshore, cloudy, rainy, miserable. Figure I got to find somewhere.

There we are: Mo behind the wheel of the Sandman panel van sprayed purple and orange. DK squashed in the passenger seat. Mo's white hair bouncing round.

Big-game hunter signature DK stick up against the back window, down the middle, jammed between us into the front.

Aviators on me nose.

Mouth opening closing.

Poor poor chopper somewhere in the bush.

Mo can't use second or fourth gears: no room for the gearstick with my gun in there.

Off we go over the causeway down The Other Side, all me secret spots. Not saying nothing. Butterflies in my stomach. Need to do a poo.

That nervous.

We stop at all the secret spots.

Wearing my boardies. Me sleeping boardies.

All set and ready.

But always someone out.

Every secret spot:

Someone out.

Or someone in the car park.

Or someone going for a walk.

Or someone with a camera taking holiday snaps.

Always someone.

'I want to go home Mo.'

Mo says nothing. Cranks the Sandman panel van sprayed purple and orange in reverse and we're home in time for morning tea. I go down Bob's.

Sign autographs.

No rumours here: no parents to spread them or give you the stink-eye.

No BFOs on the case.

Yesterday, the last day I was with that BFO, we had a blue.

She had her notebook out. Here's how this blue went: Her voice tight like a rubber band about to break:

'So Dennis, when you gunna start telling me about Rodney?'

Rodney/Sydney/Hate me/Rob me cut it out man—

'Rob me,' I said.

'What?'

That face of hers, like I'm just another bloke come to lead her up the garden path and drop her stone cold.

I went in my room and shut the door.

Then this morning she decides to go on a surfing trip.

Yeah that was the blue but that's always

Yeah, forget it.

LEAST OF ALL

Lot of things been said about you and Rod.

Only Mo knew the truth.

And Mo didn't know the half of it.

But she was the only one knew that much.

Except for you.

Rod didn't.

Rod was a pretty good surfer you had to give him that. Better than Tink, better than FJ, the 'world champions'. They were kooks next to Rod eh.

But Rod was not good enough to wax your board.

That's how good Rod was. That's how good you were.

Rod was the only one ever, out of all of them really, the only one who liked you.

Even when you was in the water Rod got plenty of waves. You didn't hate Rod the way you hated FJ and Tink and the others. Not to mention kooks and blow-ins and wave-wasters.

There's no word for what you thought about surfers from other clubs. Other beaches. Anyone you didn't know.

You knew no limits.

Rod was better with money than you he always had this magic way of coming up with coin.

This night on the beach at Rainbow. You and Rod often slept on the beach, or The Pit, or Greenmount Hill. On a warm night you collapse in your Levis and T-shirts so you'll be there at sparrow fart. Local cops and business owners didn't go much on it. You were all meant to be part of the Youth Rebellion and whatnot. Queensland brought in these laws where if you didn't have any coin in your pocket, didn't matter who you were, you get took in as a vagrant. When Wayne Lynch come up from Victoria to Coolie, best surfer in the world, he had nowhere to stay so he crashed on the beach. Pigs drug him in a Black Maria and cos he looked like Jesus and didn't have no coin they dump him over the border in New South.

Queensland! Best surfer in the world turns up, they chuck him out for being a vagrant! Barbarians them police.

Yeah and

and but so this one night you woke up in The Pit with a size-14 in your ribs and a copper saying empty your pockets. Rod been asleep beside you last you looked, now nowhere to be seen.

You emptied your pockets. Triumph!

There yers go, I got nothing. Can't rob me, ya maggots.

All right son, you're coming in.

I'm shaking them off me elbows.

What yers doing?

Vagrancy Act, you're under arrest son, no money.

They're dragging you off to their van, the Black Maria everyone called it on account of it was black. You were about to do your block when out of nowhere Rod appears. Hands full of silver change.

Here, he cacks, *here we're not vagrants, we're millionaires sleeping rough!*

Pigs couldn't take us in for vagrancy now. Instead they swipe the coin and give us a boot up the arse and bark at us to go home or they tell our mum.

Can't tell my *mum eh!* I shout at them.

Rod looking at me and shaking his head like I'm a drongo.

Well they can't can they, I go.

Got to come in useful sometimes, the no mum thing.

Rod never did tell me where he got them funds from. Someone's wallet eh, I reckon.

But even though Rod was the only one who liked you he was the one who copped the worst of it. From you. For you. One day at Kirra he had the squirts for some reason and kept fading you. It was a sunny day and he stayed out longer than usual and got sunburnt.

When you caught up with him in the rat cellar under the house you bound his face in duct tape. Like a mummy. All except his eyes. But then you saw the way he was looking at you, like he finally twigged you were some kind of psycho, like for real, and he's thinking you're really truly gunna kill him.

Accidentally?

On purpose?

Didn't matter:

Accidentally on purpose.

But he was your brother, good as, and so you ripped the duct tape off him.

Second-best part of it was seeing his relief: you might of been a psycho but you weren't a total fruitcake.

Best part of it was seeing his skin: you ripped off all his peeling sheets of face with his sunburn and him now pink and wet and slimy as a newborn dog.

He went round with ointment on him for days. Couldn't go out in the sun. Couldn't go out in the water.

Couldn't fade you.

But you needed him:

Rod, did I look like Nat on that one?

Yeah nah in yer dreams Den.

Once you got Rod good. You were sitting out the back at Snapper and felt something on your leg. You shook it round then looked down and saw something make your heart stop:

A squid, wrapped round your leg.

Size of a doormat. You pulled off one tentacle and it starts wrapping itself round your hand. All them little suckers, you felt every one of them. Sucky feeling, totally freaked you. You start gasping, panic attack, wrestled with the big slimy purple thing.

Few yards away, Rod laughing so hard he fell off his board. He broke his mouth. Making sure everyone else was looking at you in your life-and-death combat with this fricken squid.

You were bugging out now, off your board, but still got your head on your shoulders. Squiddy hadn't sucked everything out of you.

Rod . . . ROD YA BLOODY—!

He got on his board and paddled over to you, still cacking himself. You were wrestling with squiddy underwater. Rod's face a little concerned by now, you might be in proper trouble, which was your cue . . .

Faaaark!

Suddenly Rod's gripping his face and falling off his board. Squiddy's shot up out the water and wrapped himself round Rod's ugly mug. Rod's screaming. Now everyone's pissing themself. They're all distracted from the new set rolling in. You turn and paddle and catch a ripping barrel while everyone's watching Rod get eaten by squiddy.

But nah it wasn't all one-way traffic.

Dennis loved making jigsaw puzzles. Was good at following instructions. Lego, Meccano, Airfix, anything with numbered steps and exact pieces: he never made a thing that wasn't from the plan. Genius at jigsaw puzzles.

Had to have them just like they were on the picture on the front of the box, and then he tape them up flat and stick them on his wall. Regular art gallery in there. Only ever done each puzzle once. Art yeah

and he's this is the thing I'm telling and she's not listening

for revenge Rod grabbed a piece from this 5000-piece jigsaw you were doing and hid it. You never suspect him. You never suspect your worst enemy of hiding a piece of a jigsaw puzzle. Naïve that way yeah

but nah and you opened the box and shut it.

Looked underneath.

Round the sides.

Lifted up all the furniture.

Searched every drawer.

Every corner.

Through your clothes.

Done it all again.

Through the box a hundred times.

Ready to explode.

Shouting at Basil: *Yav eaten it haven't ya ya greedy mongrel!*

Rod watched it all till he felt sorry for you. But brothers don't feel sorry for big little brothers. Brothers let it ride long as they can before the roof is hit and the top is blown and the block is done.

Yeah like we really was brothers now, this is how I knew we was.

Rod watched your torment for two days. Three days. Couldn't hold himself in no longer nor could you.

Sadistic your brother.

His revenge.

He put the piece back in the box and the hundred and first time you searched for it, you found it.

Looked at it and went, *I thought I looked there*. Then you got on with your business.

You never suspected a thing.

Naïve that way, yeah always assumed the best of people.

When he was seventeen Rod got his driver's licence. Keiths couldn't afford a car, but this is Coolie in the sixties and everything was everyone's and Rod just rock up on the doorstep with this car from some neighbour and the back of it full of sticks and some of the boys, and if it was blown out at Snapper or Kirra you hop in and Rod hook the nose of the station wagon or panel van or family sedan south or north and yous're off, the mob of yous, Rod, you, FJ, Tink, couple of others if they showed, jabbering away, typical hens night.

You claustrophobic in the back seat with too many people.

Could of murdered a wave.

Needed to get out that bad.

In a barrel, where nobody could see you.

Rod drove like a wingnut. From day one. You didn't want to drive, didn't want the complication in your life. Cars no, too many instruments, too many things to go wrong. No cars no go.

But even though you were scared of driving you go with Rod who was a whole lot worse. He should of been scared of driving yeah but he wasn't. That was the problem. He wasn't scared enough. You never knew what he's gunna do. You watched him. Seemed to only make his mind up at the last second. He was off with the fairies or looking at the waves or the bikini girls or talking his head off and then he suddenly pull a stop at a traffic light or a right turn or a U-turn. Hair-raising. But not enough to make you go get a licence yourself. No cars, no go.

Yeah but having a driver broadened your horizons. Nobody gets good surfing the same wave all their life, especially mechanical right-hander like Snapper or Kirra. You lay awake worrying you couldn't surf back-handers. You had this one bad day on left-handers at the beachie at D-Bah and drive Mo crazy with your all-night fretting and talking, sit on the end of her bed going through every wave you wiped out on. You were like a caged bull. You could surf right-handers in your sleep but your back to the wave you were kookarama. An embarrassment to yourself and your family.

Mo said, *You learn back-handers there won't be nobody in the world'll stop you winning.*

So you made Rod drive to all the left-hand breaks up and down the coast. FJ and Tink whinged and moaned but knew not to argue. You had to master your back-handers. You wanted barrels on your back hand. Back to the wave. Tuck in behind the silver curtain. Where they couldn't see you.

A BIG SHOW

We're a big show me and me Mo, cruising down the coast highway to all the secret spots first thing in the morning or last at night, the seventy-five-year-old lady in her pale yellow house dress in her Sandman panel van sprayed purple and orange with her fifty-eight-year-old Den squashed in the passenger seat and the car can't do second or fourth cos the big DK gun is jammed down between the seats . . .

'Gunna go out today,' I go.

'Gunna go in, right?'

Mo's never been able to figure the right words, with surfing. I tried explaining it to her years ago.

In means in, on land.

Out means out, in the water.

Deep means inside the peakiest part of the wave.

Wide means out on the shoulder.

Inside means closer to the shore.

Outside means further from the shore.

Don't matter how many times I explain it she always gets it wrong-end up.

Don't matter how many times.

This is your conversation, in the car. Most you've ever talked at once. Mo's in your corner, she is. Gets you copies of *Surfing* and *Surfer* and *Tracks* and whatnot, and just now and then she looks at them pictures and lets drop a little stinger, like:

'They're still not as good as you Den.'

Or:

'Thirty years and they're still trying to match you.'

Or:

'You go in the world tour now Den, they won't know what hit them.'

•

But someone's always out there. Twelve days, twelve drives and you still haven't been out.

Someone always out there.

CATHEDRAL

Sam died that year. Nineteen sixty-five or six. Basil'd used him up and wore him out. Now our only dog was Basil and Basil was a different kettle of fish. Unpredictable. Only cared about number one. Basil ate pretty much anything. All food, for a start. But also other stuff. Once he ate batteries. Once a packet of ciggies. Once a wooden box that used to have chocolates in it. He wasn't fussy. One thing he had in common with Sam was when you took him down the beach you didn't have to tie him up. He loved sitting there watching waves.

But Basil was getting out of hand so Mo made you try to train him. You took Basil to classes where all the dogs and the dog owners stood in a circle round the trainer. First day, trainer's explaining how to reward dogs for following instructions. He give them a bikkie out of this bag he held up. All about rewards and bikkies.

And but so while he was saying this, Basil tore out and charged the trainer, knocked him down, ripped the bikkies out of his hand and hoed in. Too much like his master. Except everyone said you weren't Basil's master, they said you were his father. He took after you that much.

You finished your confirmation classes. Father Aplin said Dennis knew the New Testament off by heart, just about.

Dennis said he liked the Old Testy more. But hard to remember all them names.

Mo didn't often kiss him. But when he got confirmed in St Barnabas—stubbed his toe and howled as he walked up the steps to the altar, Father A smiling away in sympathy, *Lost count of how many times I've done that meself*, he went—when it was over Mo cried and covered Den with sloppy wet ones.

He was confirmed now: Mo thought he was going to heaven.

•

Wrong. Dennis was already there.

At Snapper, at D-Bah, at Rainbow, at Greenmount.

At Kirra.

That was the summer you rode your first barrel. You had photos of Nat Young in barrels on your walls. Rod said you couldn't do it, said no-one could on the boards you were using. Meaning, you couldn't do it, nor could he, nor could Tink or FJ or any other of the kids around.

But you found the other cathedral, the green one, this day at Kirra.

Paddled into the wave, stood up, hooked right towards the shoulder, and somehow you were too far back on your board, the tail stalled in the water. You looked up at the lip about to smash down on your head and ducked. As you ducked you bent your knees and the board rode higher up into the wall, which was pitching and straightening ready to chuck you down on the sandbank.

But it didn't.

You weren't even there, you were just waiting for the lip to come down and smash you.

But it didn't.

The lip stretched out like bubble gum and went over your head, like someone was tying a knot round you. It wrapped round you. The lip was now over your head and washing the side of your face. Meanwhile your board was scooting along, sticking like a fly to the wall.

Waves made this tunnel.

Just people didn't often happen to be there.

But this time, you were.

It shot you through, spat you out, and you were in the open air again. You stood upright and cruised off the wave's shoulder.

Your arms hanging by your sides. Inside you they were raised to the sky, in praise. This was what Father A and Mo meant by: *Praise. Ecstasy.*

You didn't know what had happened.

Yes you did.

You seen it.

Dreamt it.

Now you done it.

You'd rode a barrel.

•

You wanted to go straight in and sit on the beach and think about it, without moving, without eating, without surfing, for like a week. Wanted to live the rest of your life thinking about that place you just been. Think about it and cradle it and not let it be spoilt. You just wanted to *finish*.

You didn't go in.

You paddled back out to do it again.

And Roddy, sitting out there in the line-up. At first he said nothing, like he hadn't seen you.

You began to wonder had it happened. If Rod hadn't seen it, was it real?

He paddled for a few waves and got wiped out going too deep, aiming for the barrel.

That was how you knew he'd seen.

You tried it again that afternoon, made a couple more, wiped out a heap. You were a barrel rider. That was what you were going to be now.

But Roddy still acted like he never saw you.

Getting dark, he finally goes:

Fuck it, Den, been trying all day and I can't do it.

Do what?

You bloody bastard. You done it, eh.

You saw me right?

The way he was looking at me I didn't know if he was gunna kill me there and then, sitting in the water, just dunk my head and hold me under and drown me—or burst into tears and tell me he loved me.

I saw ya Den.

Just shaking his head.

We gotta start entering you in a conness, he went. *Otherwise you and me's gunna end up doing each other in.*

And yeah, that was it:

Your next love:

Competition.

BE PREPARED TO FIGHT

Dennis won his first conness: Kirra Juniors. December 11, 1966. Should of won a trophy but the guy at the preso, the club president, had lost it somewhere or it been pinched.

Dunno how to say sorry, the president said. *Dunno what else I can give you. How bout these?*

Dennis liked the sunglasses the president was wearing: aviator style, gold rims, blue-tinted mirror lenses. He was too quick for the president, who threw out a hand to get them back but they was already on Dennis's face.

First trophy.

But after that, it got good with the trophies. He win an age conness and they take him to The Shop—surf shop that sponsored the event—and he get a voucher to buy shorts or a shirt or whatnot. He thought all his xmases come at once. Brand new money: $$ and c. No more pounds shillings and pennies. Dollars and sense now. Couldn't believe they were paying him to shoplift.

Competition was mostly on the right-handed points. Your bread and butter. You won the Kirra Boardriders. Before the zone juniors at Greenmount you broke the nose off your board, a whole ten inches snapped on a sandbank. You couldn't swipe another and that was your favourite so you just rode it with no nose. You won. Then on the same busted stick you won state juniors at Snapper. All right-handers. You would of won the state open title against the men at Burleigh except your board snapped clean in half as you come out of a barrel and that was it, not even you could surf half a board.

You figured your back-hands out. You experimented with new boards you made in the rat cellar, and new moves. There was other ripping surfers but DK was ahead of them all. You were the Legend and the Messiah. They all knew if you was out the back. Nobody faded you. Nobody dropped in on you. If they was inside you and paddling out while DK was on a wave they got the hell out of the way. Like you had a force field.

Even free surfing you had to be the best in the water. If FJ got some kind of smoking barrel you would stay until you got a smokinger one.

Rod baited you: *Nah, Tink got the best waves today.*

You wouldn't sleep till you got out there again and outsurfed Tink.

Rod was usually joking.

You didn't get jokes.

Jokes weren't your thing.

You got edgy about the number three and the number nine. You saw a car numberplate with a three or a nine on it on your way to a comp, you knew it was your day. You heard someone mention three or nine on the radio news, you knew you'd win that day. If there was no threes or nines in your life, you got a bad feeling. The day before the state junior titles at Snapper, you were frantic looking for threes or nines on letterboxes, grocery shop hoardings, car numberplates, everywhere, but there was none, not one, and sure enough your board got nicked. You ducked into Bob's milk bar for a minute and when you come out your stick was gone.

Gone.

Your best Keiths Surf Boards rebirthed stick.

Day before the state juniors in your own backyard.

Never mind.

Rod had a brand new Draper board. Rod always rode someone else's board, never a Keiths Surf Boards board. Rod was funny like that. He didn't want your boards no more. He thought you shaped them weird on purpose so he couldn't ride them. He said the only one who could ride them was you. Said the name should of been Keith Surfs Boards, not that he was getting you to change it, he still wanted to be advertised but he didn't want what you shaped. So he swipe a board from someone else and ride that.

When you got home, Rod's new Draper stick was in the rat cellar. You worked the glass off it then set about reshaping it. Planing the rails and the tail so it was an exact replica of your best stick, the stolen one.

•

Then you reglassed it. All afternoon and all night. Missed your late surf but you be ready for the state juniors next day.

Rod wasn't happy when he come home.

What ya done with me stick?

He saw his Draper glass, just the glass sheath but no board in it, standing up against a pylon like a snake's skin.

Bugger ya, he said.

State juniors tomorrow, you said. *Me stick got nicked outside Bob's.*

Rod looking at you like you'd finally flipped, you'd lost it, you'd went barking mad.

We can both use this one, you said encouragingly, gave the new re-birthed board a tap on the tail. *You'll love it, it's better than it was before.*

Dennis, Rod said. *Come outside.*

You were a bit sheepish, so you followed him. You knew how it looked to Rod. But state juniors was next day. He'd understand.

You followed him to the front yard.

There on the grass was your stick. Your best DK.

It was nicked, you said.

It wasn't nicked, Rod said. *Mrs Dolethorpe was walking past with Father A, they saw it lying on the path, they knew the state juniors was tomorrow, they figured some punk must of pinched it off you. So they took it for safekeeping. When I saw Father A this arvo he said tell you your stick was at Mrs Dolethorpe's. Right next door. It wasn't nicked, Dennis. Nobody's got the hair to nick your board. They wouldn't make it out of Coolie alive.*

Far out, I went. Looking at my beautiful Keith stick. My fave at the time. It was better than the Draper one I'd just reshaped. I could see it now. I hadn't got the Draper's rails tucked under right. Wasn't enough wood left on it.

You can have your one back, I went.

Yeah but it's not really the same stick, is it?

Nah, I went. *It's better.*

Rod didn't believe me but what could he do. He was in the state juniors as well. He just walked away shaking his head.

But he made top ten, on that custom reshaped Draper.

I won. I told Rod he should always surf Keiths Surf Boards boards now.

He went quiet. Shaking his head a lot. Like I'd entered a new realm of craziness.

Rod was the one who couldn't take a joke.

That type of thing.

I never knew how bad he wanted to win something.

Tink was with you and Rod pretty tight, and FJ, and a crew of others, but Dennis Keith discovered something early on:

He breathed surfing, he lived surfing, he dreamt surfing, he lived surfing, he breathed surfing—but he didn't like surfers.

Everyone talked, like a mothers' group, in and out the water, gabbing away, about this, about that, bugged hell out of him, like surfing was some kind of social occasion, and half of them talking so much they miss a set, talking so much they let waves go to waste, unforgivable waste . . .

. . . babble babble babble . . .

The Pit was in a gap between the Snapper car park and the jump-off rock where you had to go through if you wanted an easy paddle-out. The Pit was a natural semicircle theatre, with rocks you could sit on and rocks you could lay your board on, and the boys chose The Pit as their hangout.

Someone'd spraypainted a big sentence on a boulder at the mouth of The Pit . . .

They had bonfires and scoped the waves and claimed it as their cave, their clubhouse, that kind of thing. And if you was a drive-in surfer from Briso or blown in on a hot offshore from out west or even coming from close by like Burleigh, and you parked in the car park, then you had to walk through The Pit if you wanted to get to the jump-off rock, and if you had to walk through The Pit you had to run the gauntlet of what the boys say to you. And they'd say what they'd say.

Welcome to Coolangatta . . . not!

Didn't matter what they said, it was all dribble most of it, what mattered was they laughed, cacked themselves like crazy, send people mad with paranoia.

Someone'd spraypainted a boulder at the mouth of The Pit . . .

They got a rep, boys in The Pit. Rod was in there with the worst of it. They weren't bad boys, their bark was worse than their bite, but this was the whole point, they had to act more psycho than they were so they wouldn't *have* to bite.

The Pit was nasty to walk through . . .

But not DK not personally. He didn't open his mouth. He never said a word. He didn't like it. Abusing strangers just cos they were walking in from the car park. Wouldn't have a bar of it.

He just sat leaning against a rock that curved in the shape of an armchair cradling his back, a rock in The Pit that gave him support at every point where he needed it, sat there and let it all wash over him.

He never abused a soul in The Pit.

Didn't mean he didn't get a reputation for it.

Whenever anyone grizzled about the nasty boys in The Pit, they'd say, *It was that Dennis Keith and his mates.*

And Dennis never said a word to deserve it.

Didn't even approve of it.

So there you go. Reputation.

Like The Pit was your voice, the rocks spoke for you, them rocks you grow out of . . .

The words in the spraypaint:

BE PREPARED TO FIGHT

When he surfed, he didn't like to talk. He was on the move, on the move, getting more waves, paddling and paddling, more waves.

No talking.

Half the time they were talking about him anyway.

Why they always have to talk?

Plenty of time for talking on land. Why waste surfing time with talk? Why?

It bugged him, bugged him, bugged him.

Riding the wave was between you and it, personal, one on one. You start bringing other people into it, gasbagging, you break the dream. You slit it open. You kill it.

He heard someone talking he'd have no hesitation dropping in on them. Teach them silence.

They made too much noise. Like dogs pissing on their territory. But the only way to assert your territorial rights was to catch waves. Pretty simple. Just shut up. Shut *up*.

The only talking you did was to yourself, out the back. You get onto a gibber with yourself, both ends of the conversation about this or that, mad about a wave you missed, that kind of thing.

Also let yourself have the odd temper tantrum too, out there:

But only under the water. A good growling yell at yourself, when you were under the water.

Unheard.

He had these tricks to psyche the others out. During a lull, he sit further out the back. Sometimes he take his lunch out with him, a spring roll in a paper bag, and eat it sitting on his board. It freaked them out that he was so sure of himself on his board he knew he could paddle out without getting his lunch wet.

If the lull went on, he stand up on his board—in the still water. Kids always trying this, standing up on a still board. They wobble, stay up for a second or two, then fall.

He could stand up—five, ten seconds, as long as a wave. On a stationary board.

They couldn't believe that. Another DK story.

Silence, his habit.

Even on land, no need to overdo the talking bit.

On land, he was still surfing. In his head. Still surfing. Shut up. Talk and you'll miss something.

In his head he was paddling into another wave.

In his head he was gliding on glass.

The way it felt like you were going downhill.

The way it kept walling up in front of you.

The colour of that glass.

The silence of it.

This was in his head, on land, or in his head, in the water, or in his head, on the wave:

Shut *up*.

Mr Paterson and Father A liked Dennis: he was quiet. Liked him more than Rod, gasbagger. When they took Dennis to the beach he didn't say boo. He listened. Watched. Learnt. Adults liked that in him. He didn't need supervision: they only had to give him a board and let him go, he wouldn't give them a moment's worry. Self-sufficient Dennis.

Adults thought that meant he was grown up. Unlike Roddy.

Because you wouldn't speak much, wouldn't trust, wouldn't make friends, Rod become your interpreter. Rod turned up at school and told the latest story about what Dennis done. Rod sat in the line-up and described Dennis's last wave: some incredible manoeuvre no-one ever tried.

Dennis paddled away from Rod's little show, looking to get deeper, deeper. Looking to get into that take-off spot right in behind the black granite.

If he got to that take-off, that vertical slot, nobody could follow.

He went in there and wiped out.

Nobody caught more waves than Dennis, not even the plumbers and the butchers and the newsagents and the house painters and the headmaster and the priest, none of the grommets, none of the blow-ins.

But also, nobody wiped out more than Dennis.

And the old heads saw him wipe out behind the black granite and said:

Kid's mad.

Cracked in the head.

Nobody can take off behind there.

Sweep's too strong.

Take-off's too vertical.

Too sucky.

He always wipes out in there.

Gunna kill himself.

How they justified themselves.

Dennis kept going in, paddled against the sweep to hold his position, the only one strong enough to turn and paddle into the waves against the sweep, but when it sucked up and went big and vertical he couldn't get the old board shape, the seven-eleven with the big raked fin, couldn't get it to hook hard enough, so he come down too face-on and wipe out where it sucked up behind the black granite.

And they all thought he was mad.

And they all thought they were right sitting where they were.

But you didn't mind wiping out: the fingers of white pulling you down and roughing you up. Only water. Didn't hurt. Gave you a tickle in fact, made you giggle. Your body's ninety percent sea anyway. You and the sea, you were just finding each other.

Water, meet water.

Wiping out you also learnt your learning:

The secret to surfing:

You hesitate for a micro-micro-second, you're gone.

You got to commit. Throw the kitchen sink at it. You got to be in a frenzy. Kill that wave. You got to surf angry, like your life depends on it.

A frenzy of anger.

Got to be in that state:

Fury.

Every wave:

Fury.

COS

The BFO come back from her 'surfing' trip. She looks pumped in the shoulders. I ask her has she been in the ladies' gym. She blanks me and sits down with her notebook and asks me about my mates from old days. She's Miss Nancy Drew again, on her cold case. Reckons she's the one kid in this whole golden coast who knows the truth about what I'm meant to have done.

'Didn't really have mates.'

'You musta had mates. Glenn Tinkler, Frank Johnson, Michael Peterson?'

'They weren't mates. They were surfers.'

'A surfer couldn't be a mate?'

'Not if he was in the water.'

'Not even if he was your brother?'

Give her a long look, chill her to the bone. Check if your aviators are still there.

'Least of all if he was my brother.'

'You don't believe you had any friends among the surfing community?'

'Contradiction, girl. Surfing community. If they were surfing, they were trying to steal my waves. Waste them.'

'*Your* waves.' The BFO can't hold down that smirk. It gets out and runs round her face like a puppy being took for a walk.

'They were all my waves. That's where I lived.'

She writes in her notepad. You won't try to sneak a look. Wouldn't want to give her the pleasure.

'So . . . outside surfing? You had your mates from outside the surfing community?'

'What's "outside the surfing community"?'

'Non-surfers?'

'Can't say I ever had time for anyone who didn't surf. Cept birds.'

'You liked . . . *girls* if they didn't surf?'

'Nope.'

I shoot her a look. She must see herself reflected in my aviators. I give them a push back up my nose. Still there.

'I liked birds *because* they didn't surf.'

FLAT

Flat flat flaaaaaat.

He hadn't been into surfing long enough to know what a flat spell meant.
    The depression.
    The pain.
    The boredom.

The Gold Coast was a village of bored teenage boys at the best of times.
    When it was flat it was murder.

Spring of his eighteenth year, 1968, the warmest, balmiest, summeriest
on record.
    Flattest.

The depression.
    The pain.
    The boredom.

He got up every day and his heart sank: big sheet of plastic stretched
to the horizon. Mums and bubs splashing in Rainbow Bay.
    Had to go to school. Eyes met Mr Paterson's: a shake of the head.
The headmaster's eyes as dead flat as the Pacific. Depressed, bored.
Mr Paterson had taught him how to read the weather charts he got

faxed in from the bureau. And for what? For what? All they showed was big monster highs plonked like dead dinosaurs on the sea, squashing it.

Had to go to church. Stubbed his toe. Father A's Masses went the full duration, Latin and all. Prayers for some action: *Dear Gawd, just some two-foot wind swell would do. Not asking for much, not even ground swell, just something rideable.*

Dennis turned to religion. The flat spell went on. So he lost his faith.

Worst part of the Big Flat was when you were on land you had to socialise. Rod held parties at the QUEENSLANDER. The downstairs rat cellar become the disco for all the bored kids from the neighbourhood. All the groms was there every night, drinking and playing crud music. They played it real loud and you tell Rod to shut them up.

Who's gunna complain? Rod said, all cheek. *We've only got dead 'uns for neighbours and I don't think they're gunna be calling the Black Maria.*

Before long there be kids, boys and girls, sneak off at night to do their bits and pieces among the tombstones. They got off on it, everyone knew that. They come back with a zombied-out look. Or just pass out on the graves.

Who's gunna complain?

Unlike you Rod loved a drink and when he was with his mates and he run out of money he'd do dares for a drink, like eat a raw snail, shell and all, or run starkers through the shopping centre, and wasn't really about how thirsty he was but what a mug lair and a show pony he was for his mates.

Meanwhile: you run your own race.

Rod wanted you to have more mates, like he had, but you didn't need friends, friends wasted waves, friends dropped in on you.

And friends couldn't bring some waves in, couldn't break the Big Flat, could they.

Let them think you're weird.

Doesn't matter eh.

The depression.
The pain.
The toes stubbed purple.
The boredom.

Big Flat during school hols that spring. Dennis grinding his teeth all night. Took it all out on his bro, had him washing up, scrubbing the toilets, sweeping the floors, bringing the clothes off the line, hanging them up, mowing the lawn . . .

Mo close the door behind her going out to work and Roddy's eyes go to Dennis, who's up with a snarl on his face and a list of chores.

Here we go, Rod went.

Rod's problem was, Rod was disobedient. When Mo went out and you took over, Rod wouldn't listen to orders. Must of been Vietnam, the protest movement putting ideas in his head. The Prime Minister going missing in the surf down in Vicco. Roddy getting ideas about himself.

You told Rod do the washing-up.

Rod said no.

You told him how many times.

Rod said no.

You said, *How many times am I gunna have to tell you?*

Rod said, *Nick off.* Walked off down the hallway.

You picked something up and chucked it.

Wooden coathanger.

Clocked him back of the head. He saw it on the floor and thought you'd chucked a boomerang.

Didn't come back ta ya, he said.

So you went him. Chasing him round the house and collared him and crow-pecked the top of his head.

You give him Chinese burns.

You give him nipple cripples.

You give him Russian braces.

You give him the sleeper hold.

I still ain't doing the washing up ya dickhead!

You grabbed him and poleaxed him through the kitchen wall.

Mrs Dolethorpe, the next-door neighbour, was hanging out her washing when she looked up from her yard through the rubber trees and went: *G'day Rodney.*

Rod was half out the wall of your house like the figurehead on a boat.

G'day Mrs Dolethorpe.

When's your mum get home?

Couple of hours I reckon?

Yous've got a bit of work to do then, don't yous?

Spot on, Mrs D.

If Mo come home on time she'd impale you on a fricken gravestone. You pulled Roddy out the wall. You taped a Nat Young poster over the hole on the inside and hoped like hell Mo wouldn't see the outside.

At the end of it, brothers again, job done.

Rod: *Still ain't doing the washing-up. I cooked, you can wash up.*

It was true, Rod had cooked. He'd cooked with the big saucepan. Fried eggs and potatoes. You picked up the saucepan to acknowledge his effort.

You smacked him with it on the head. Blood dripping in the sink. On the dishes.

You better wash up that blood too, Rodney.

When you called him Rodney he knew you were serious. Just like if him or Mo called you Dennis. He was in a daze, spinning round like he been nailed by a six-foot close-out set. His hand on his forehead where you touched him. He lifted it and had a big grey mouse above his eye.

Must of knocked some sense into him. No more fighting. He washed up.

After Mo get home and went to bed, you and Rod patched up the outside wall with bits of old board offcuts. She knew but she didn't say nothing. Her sharp blind eye. You and Rod done that together. Next day yous had a good surf.

Rod escaped to The Pit, where you wouldn't go when it was crowded. The Pit got renovated during the Big Flat. Bored groms drug down old couches and foot stools, standing lamps, even a TV and a phone, so it was just like a living room. Not that there was any electricity for the TV and phone and lamps, but that wasn't the point. The Pit was the clubhouse. Rod was right into the building program. Rod helped bring in a 'borrowed' nest of tables and some 'lent' vases. He even got this Persian rug from somewhere definitely not Persia.

Eventually Rod and some others got the shell of a car from somewhere and it turned up half buried in the sand in The Pit so there was a real roof over their heads. They whacked in an armchair and a sofa and a coffee table and lived in that car. It even had a loose steering wheel so they could 'drive' it when they were wasted. Couple of Rod's mates even lived in that car for a while, coming up to Shagrila to use the shower and give a surf report. Cept now it was called Shaga due to some more letters gone missing eh.

Flat.

Loads of talk in The Pit. Too much for you. Mostly rubbish, their dreams of The Life. The Life was this mythic world where you could surf as much as you want, every day, any day, go anywhere it was good. Big swells coming into Hawaii? You hopped in a jet plane. Not that anyone wanted to go to Hawaii, or even New South Wales. They just wanted to be able to surf Snapper and Greenmount and Kirra every day till the day they died and not be tied down when the waves was good. Apparently there was some guys somewhere, America or Hawaii or something, who had The Life—made a living from surfing in comps and selling and shaping boards and maybe giving surf lessons and still surfed whenever they wanted. You never seen them and thought The Life was a bit of a hoax. Surfers took themself too serious, you knew that for sure, surfers took themself so serious they ended up not talking to each other for years cos of *one wave*, surfers could freeze a bloke out cos he was wearing a panel of colour on his wetsuit or if his board was three inches too long or too wide, surfers could stand on a beach and burst into tears cos they arrived an hour too late and now the wind and tide had went screwy on them, surfers regretted too much, they always should of been here an hour ago.

You knew all this cos it was all you.

But yeah, still flat.

Out of desperation, Rod made a skateboard. Keith kids couldn't afford one so he cut a piece of wood from the rat cellar into the shape of a mini-board, then swiped a single rollerskate from the school gym. Hacksawed the rollerskate in half, screwed one wheel under the front of the board, other under the back.

Hey presto, skateboarding.

Rod was pretty good at it, haring off down big hill streets off Point Danger into Rainbow Bay, wiped out, got up smiling. Rod never saw no danger in nothing. That was his big problem. You saw danger in everything that wasn't water. That was yours.

•

He found an empty swimming pool in some under-construction house at Tweed, and experimented with drops off the edge into the bowl.

Dennis, never no good at it. Only time he stayed on the board was when him and Rod did some crabbing, sitting both ends legs locked together. Rod controlled that, and Dennis dug it. But once he got on the skateboard on his own, Dennis kept trying miracle moves and getting horrendously skin-sheeted by pebblecrete.

No good out of the water, Rod laughed.

You just needed waves.

You didn't notice the birds or the dope till they were already there. They arrived with the Big Flat. The late nights when Rod and his mates had finished gasbagging in The Pit or working on the boards in the rat cellar and went upstairs to party, when you scuttled downstairs to do your all-nighters on new shapes, there was something going on upstairs, you knew that from the OP Frigate Rum and the music, the Hendrix and the Cream and the The Doors, but you shut it all out, you was thinking shapes and waves, shapes and waves.

It been going on for a while when you noticed.

It was dug in.

Rod had a new world going on up there.

This one night, you only had one board to work on and you sanded it down so thin it had wore through and broke on the sawhorse. Must of been round midnight you went upstairs. You checked on Basil. Asleep, snoring, big lipstick out, dreaming about rooting grey old beagles. Rod in the sleepout making a din with his mates.

You went out there and could hardly see them for the clouds. Your nose was numbed-out with resin and glass but you could smell this smell, clouds of smell like earth, sweet planet earth.

You didn't say nothing. Rod had four or five of his mates, four or five birds too. Lying round the floor on blankets, scattered like a strong wind come in and blew them off the furniture. Like rubbish.

Rod croaking: *What's up, bro?*

His eyes them red beads.

You didn't like that word. *Bro.*

You were peed off about the board you'd sanded through. You didn't know what to do with all this crew lying round with red eyes and lazy smiles smiling up at you.

There was this bird and she passed you a ciggie.

You knew what birds were: ones that come up to you and said they liked you and ran off giggling, like they done it for a dare to set you up and laugh at you. That was birds.

You knew what the ciggie was.

The smell.

You grunted something and sat down on the floor. You took a drag.

Oh far out, you heard Rod say. There was this bird with her arm round your shoulder.

The despair and disappointment in Rod's voice, first you thought you'd taken some of his smoke or moved in on one of his birds, but it was different this look in his eye, like he'd had a flash and seen the whole future rolled out in front of him, and realised it was too late to stop, the point of no return just been passed.

The point of no return.

The despair and disappointment.

His despair: he'd of kept you hidden under the house shaping your board till the end of time. His disappointment: with himself, for letting it into the house.

They tried to get you to talk, but you wouldn't. Couldn't.

Birds, all over you by then. Distracting you from the waves. You figured out they weren't taking the mickey out of you anymore. They were serious about you. Running their hands through your hair.

That Big Flat summer you shaved all your hair off, they seemed to dig it so much. You figured if you had no hair then birds wouldn't come after you.

Didn't make no difference.

They were there, they were everywhere, they wouldn't leave you alone. Rod would interpret them for you. He'd say, *Birds they're just like blokes, just like you want to surf the most challenging and enjoyable wave they want to go off with the most challenging and enjoyable bloke. Which is you, ya dipstick,* he added, not holding down his despair and disappointment.

But I'm not challenging. I never say no.

Yeah, Rod said. *But ya never say yes either. Ya never say nothin eh.*

And I'm not enjoyable, you said. You didn't want to add anything to that, any explanation.

Yeah, Rod said again. *But birds don't know that do they.*

His despair and disappointment. You didn't get that. Plenty of girls dug Rod and he always had a few on the go. But he seemed to think you were always getting a better end of the deal. Like you didn't have to try hard enough. Like you were too much of a legend and a Messiah and too good-looking and it didn't matter how many chicks Rod had on the go, it still wouldn't be enough to throw in and bury over the top of you.

Yourself, you couldn't see what the girls saw in you. Not that you were rude or mean or slapped them or nothing. You just didn't offer a lot. You never went up to a girl and made nice conversation and asked her out. Wouldn't of known how to. Couldn't see the point. Probably would of made a goose of yourself. So why do it? There was plenty of birds rock up at the Queenslander all night, smoking pot, willing and able, slim girls in bikinis and wraparound sarongs, girls with long straight hair and sunburnt noses and tan shoulders, just nice kids looking for fun.

They dug Basil so that gave you something to talk about. You kept saying rubbish like, *If you really knew this dog you wouldn't dig him so much.* Like you were talking about yourself.

You go off with them and kiss them a bit and sometimes when you got real close and eye to eye with them and they broke through into some hidden soft space, you saw them changed from the fun laughing long-haired girl into a gentle baby who cuddled you like they cuddled their teddy bear and you were right inside their space and their heads and their dreams . . .

. . . totally freaked you out so

so you steered clear of that. Keep them at arms length. Keep the aviators on.

Cos if you saw that deep into them, they were seeing that deep into you.

Freaked you out. Till Lisa Exmire.

SURFER GIRL

Always liked walking. It slows your thoughts. I walk every day from this retirement village to the shops. I go to Bob's milk bar for a pine-lime Splice and an orange Tarax. I walk over Greenmount Hill where me and Rod used to camp in a two-man hootchie and sit round the fire. Once we burnt the headland down. You'd never know it now. Now it's all landscaped and beautiful eh, every square inch accounted for, paving and edging, edging and paving. Not careful, you get run over by old people power-walking. DK always been freaked by old people. Still is, even when the old people are younger than him.

The surfboard-shaped benches are out of control here, rampant like lantana. Place been turned into some theme park of surf. *Surfworld/ Jerkwild/Porkwheel/Far out stop it man eh.*

Now the BFO likes to do the walk with me.

I don't mind. I just want to keep her away from Mo. If the price I have to pay is her and her questions on my walks, then okay.

She's all right.

We sit on Greenmount and watch waves.

Only when she's crook at me she ask me if I miss it. Otherwise she knows better.

Mostly we walk and sit in silence. Always liked silence. Me element. That's the price she has to pay.

She nods down to The Pit, the big spraypainted boulder at Snapper.

'It's always said that?'

I shake my head.

'Used to say something else.'

She doesn't know what it used to say.

But she been doing her research. She says:

'It used to say, DK RULES, or DK WAS HERE, or DK FOREVER. Every time council had it cleaned up, it got repainted. Always for you.'

'Not always for me.'

She doesn't know what it used to say.

She says: 'Ironic though, isn't it?'

I sneak a look down at the sign. It says what it says.

Be Prepared To Fight/Be Prepared For Night/Beware of the Bite/Maximum Height/Last One Out Turn Off The Light.

Open and close me lips like I'm crossing a driveway.

She's asked me a few times about the girls, the dope. She's shy about it. She drops it in conversation, like, if we're talking about the '69 nationals at Bells she'll say, *So was that the period when you were with Lisa Exmire?* and I'll say nothing and just keep on about the rogue right-hander I jagged in the quarter-finals. Or we'll be talking about the '68 state titles at D-Bah and she'll say, *So was that the period when you were first into the grass and stuff?* and I'll say nothing and just keep on about the best back-handed barrel I ever got when I was in a heat with Tink and FJ and they just sat back and clapped and paddled in, they knew how much it meant to me, how much practice I put in up and down the coast working on left-handers cos they were the ones I drug along with me in Rod's borrowed cars, and they knew they couldn't beat me . . .

I feel the BFO probing, how hungry she wants it, do anything for it, but I push my aviators up the bridge of my nose (they're still there) and keep on.

She gets her best surfing material out of me when she's asking me to talk about the birds or the dope. Maybe if she asks me about surfing I'll tell her about the birds.

Material. That's what she calls it. Even though she's not always carrying her notepad or her tape recorder. I've noticed that.

Another ruse. She pretends she's not interviewing me. Pretends she's my Psy Fricken Chologist or something. My PFC not my BFO.

That type of thing.

But I'm not giving her what she wants, her soap opera, she can go to Mark Occhilupo or Mick Fanning if that's what she wants. She wants to write a serious story about surfing, she can come to The Great One.

Yeah.

Serious material, that's what I'm giving her.

•

Then we come home to Mo and I wash my hands and we have a big pie or a salad or sandwiches the BFO has bought. Sometimes she hands over 'the change' to Mo. Another hundred, two hundred.

Quite the little cash cow, our BFO is turning out to be.

Longer I can string her out the better.

She wants it so bad she's aching.

But she knows better than to raise the subjects, the birds and the dope, with Mo. These were never subjects to raise with Mrs Keith.

BFO's smart enough to know that.

Our little cash cow.

I take her out for a walk. Or she takes me, she's probably thinking. I dump her at her motel. Before dawn next morning me and Mo drive to The Other Side. But it's summer now, tourist season, school holidays. No hope of finding anywhere. A five-thousand-mile coast and not one secret spot left: what the world's come to.

I'm getting jack of trying to find somewhere no-one can see.

Can feel Mo getting jack too. Or jill. Whatever it is, she's getting it.

But she doesn't say nothing. She just goes, *You take your green and your white and your blue today?*

That type of thing.

SAD LISA

Lisa Exmire wasn't sad, the least sad person he knew, but in them first days he called her 'Sad Lisa' cos she played that Cat Stevens song on her guitar for him at night with a grand smile on her face and tongue pushing through her cheek and he loved that song, loved it, hummed it to himself in the waves.

He didn't mind Cat Stevens but he dig heavier stuff more: the new sounds: Santana, Floyd, Hendrix, songs without so many words. You couldn't avoid music in them days and he didn't want to. Once he got into the green he saw new dimensions of music. Music gained depth and life, like waves. He could listen to whole tracks but only hear one instrument: the drum, or the bass. He preferred the long instrumentals. Words got in the way. Didn't have time for words.

Rod was into his music too and always going out to bands with his mates and birds. Dennis tag along but couldn't cop the crowds. He wore a snazzy suede suit with lapels big as longboards and Florsheim shoes, he loved them clothes and Mo always told him he had to look nice when he went out 'socially'.

You couldn't work yourself out. Sometimes you wanted to be seen. You show up at The Pit in a big open-necked aloha shirt. Sometimes a cricket sweater. Had a collection of trench coats and bathrobes. Capes, Panama hats. Stand there at The Pit till everyone seen you. Then turn round and run off back home to the shaping cellar.

You dug clothes. Problem was, people noticed them. You couldn't work out how to enjoy clothes *and* not be seen in them.

This night Dennis Keith stuck to the dark corners. Already kids coming up wanting an autograph. Already whispering behind their hands: *There—that's him.* He didn't want to be *him.* He wanted to be *me.* Or at least *you.* But he couldn't. The moment he stepped out he was him,

DK, The Man, the state junior champion, the freakazoid, the blitzer, the mysto mad genius. That kind of thing.

Only go to The Patch if people promised to pretend he wasn't there. This night it got ridiculous, three hundred locals all talking about Dennis Keith but having to make like he wasn't that bloke sucking lemonade in the shadows, like he wasn't even there, like if they even looked at him for a second, pouf, he'd disappear.

So Dennis, him, you, skulks in the corner with a glass of lemonade he pretended was vodka. He didn't much like lemonade neither so he made it last all night.

Birds come up. He said nothing. Birds hung round.

Lemonade birds: he could pretend they were the real thing.

Birds were like waves but not like waves.

Like waves: there was always another one.

Not like waves: it didn't matter if you wasted one.

Like waves: they give you a sweet feeling on the edge between dreaming and awake, like all your happiness was in those moments alone with them, and then when it was over you couldn't remember it.

Not like waves: you didn't have to go back and back and back again to imprint the memory till you could hold it in your head while you were lying awake at night. You were happy with what come your way but you didn't go out looking for them.

Like waves: they loved you, you were a natural for them, you were part of their element and they were part of yours.

Not like waves: you didn't feel a natural for them.

So stoned now, at this club, he was feeling normal. He was there for the music.

He looked at the bistro menu blackboard: Steaks $3.33. Lobsters $9.99. Beers $0.99.

Got a *good* feeling and—

And so this bird comes on with her band. Sang like Janis, more on the heavy 'Take a Little Piece of My Heart' side than the folk or romantic. Her songs went fast. She wore denim all the way up and down. She was kind of country but kind of surfer. She had skin like a morning glass-off.

Dennis closed his eyes and listened to her wild singing. He was invisible in her music.

Then she played this instrumental.

After she finished her set she seemed to know who you were. She was at this table with her band and a couple of Rod's mates. That give Rod the opening. He drug you in. The table all got along real well except you.

Freakazoid.

You behind your aviators and stared at her all night. In your midnight-blue velour suit.

Never a word.

You get Rod to leave early with you.

Rod said as you walked home: *She'll either root you or have you arrested.*

You didn't say nothing. You couldn't.

You got home and still before midnight. You washed your hands. You worked in the shaping bay. You buggered up a good blank.

You washed your hands. You went and picked up a stick and got on your chopper and rode back down to Coolie.

Only five hours till dawn. Still flat. And dark.

You smoked a doob pinched from Rod's stash.

You straddled your poor old chopper with your stick under your arm and stood outside the club where she sung.

Closing time, she come out. Her arms round two of her band members. You didn't clock the bloke.

You clock her scoping you out the corner of her eye.

You just stood there.

It's one o'clock in the morning. She come up grinning. *Surfer boy.*

Laughing at you.

You DK Surfer Boy was wearing your aviators. With your free hand you pushed them up your nose. They were still there.

But without any hands and your legs too far apart, your chopper slid out from under you and knobbed her leg.

Nice move, she grinned.

You lift your chin at her band mates.

They ya boyfriends?

She clapped her hand to her mouth. *My God, it speaks!*

You didn't say no more till she said:

So what if they are?

You shrugged. You pushed up your aviators (still there).

She looked round at her band, made some kind of signal you didn't see, they started drifting off towards Danceland.

The buzzing ball in your stomach catch fire again. You were hurting. You needed a joint. Or a surf.

You needed a joint then a surf.

But it was still Flat.

The night is young, she said, like she was quoting someone else, some song maybe.

Then she fixed you with a real, real serious face and said:

Got any weed?

Yeah why?

Cos you probably won't have the hair to kiss me till you're more stoned.

Who says I'm gunna kiss you? I haven't yet.

That's cos if you start you're gunna need a crowbar to get off me.

I couldn't say nothing to that.

Doesn't seem any reason not to try, she went all grins.

Lisa Exmire pashed you on Greenmount Hill. February 8, 1969. She got on top of you and went after every piece of you, indirect, like she was taking the full scenic tour before she got down to the thing that was busting open. You were in agony as she wandered round parts of your body you didn't even know existed and for sure didn't want them to exist now. She kept finding new places. Took hours. Made little gasps and comments to herself, like she was marking your exam paper or whatnot. You just dying there while she took her sweet time. Then you couldn't wait no longer, and it turned out this was what she'd been waiting for, she was ready the whole time, she just been waiting for you to *fricken do something*. So you done it and she took you. You never done that before. You been with tens of birds, every last one of them forward enough to make the first move and ask you to go off with them, but not a single one of them forward enough to make the last.

You had no initiative. You just did what you were asked.

So you never done it. And now Lisa Exmire was getting you to do it. So you done it.

The moon a fingernail.

She took your aviators off and got inside you.

You inside her, she inside you. Too close but comfortable.

In the open air, under the open sky, your chopper and your board lying beside yous.

You and Lisa side by side on your backs, smoke another doob looking at the stars.

You said nothing.

She sang quiet tunes, not the ones she did for the crowd, more like little nursery tunes.

Baby Face.

You couldn't speak.

She didn't mind.

Mo's song.

You both drifted off to sleep a while.

You heard the waves first and sat up.

Nor'-east swell come up, out of nowhere. You couldn't see it but could smell it. First rosy glow on the horizon.

Lisa sat up beside you, stretched her arms.

You smoked Roddy's last doob with her and got up and picked up your stick.

You're not going surfing, are you?

She rubbed her eyes. You saw how rumpled-up her face was with sleeping creases and you wanted to die right there and then.

You shrugged one shoulder and pushed your aviators up your nose (still there. there again.).

My God, you're just like me, she said.

You threw a leg over your chopper.

She said: *Anyone else I know, a doob like that would wipe them out. It picks you up, doesn't it?*

You were having the most feelings of your life. You were coming apart with feelings.

And now, she said, *yer gunna surf. In the dark.*

First waves, you said. *Light soon, it'll be like Cavill Mall.*

It speaks! she cried again, delighted.

You were both delighted. You cycled down the hill to Rainbow. You kept looking up to Greenmount see if she was watching.

When you got there, the granite's lit up with huge smashing sucking six-footers. You dropped to your knees.

It was all-time.

She ended the Big Flat.

You cried to yourself as you paddled out.

Rod was out there. He believed in God.

Mr Paterson was out there. He believed in his bureau faxes.

The plumbers, the butchers, the chippies, the newsagents. Everyone was out there.

FJ and Tink were out there.

They'd all got up before first light.

They'd beaten you.

You: filthy.

You looked up to the hill to see was she watching.

With the big swell, the sweep was dragging hard and everyone had to paddle non-stop to stay in position, just to stay on the point.

As the sun rose the bay lit up with cries:

Woohoo!

Yeeuuu!

Wooooooo!

The drought broke by prayer.

And you were filthy, cos there was so many out there, Cavill Fricken Mall.

You'd lost condition. Your arms weak after the Big Flat. All the paddling to stay in position.

By the time the sun was well up and the water was blue, it was turning into the worst surf of your life. You were missing waves from behind, you were getting outpaddled, you were going too deep and wiping out, you were having to drop in on people but they were shouting you off, you just weren't getting no waves.

Filthy.

You didn't look up to the hill to see was she watching.

You let the sweep take you off, then when it dumped you you paddled round the back of the black granite lava rock:

In behind Snapper.

Where it was jacking up vertical and nobody ever took off.

In a nor'-east swell.

You didn't even sit on your board, you just kept paddling, didn't look behind you, just kept paddling—

And without meaning it, without thinking about what you were doing, you were being lifted high high on the brow of a set wave, up above the black lava rock so you could see the agave trees, you could see the Rainbow Bay surf club, you could see the Point Danger nav station, you could see up the Tweedmouth to The Other Side.

You didn't look up Greenmount.

You were on your feet.

You hooked it right and tucked in.

All you remember coming out from behind the black granite is their faces as they were scratching to get over this set wave, paddling in the opposite direction to you, panic on their faces, monster wave, not wanting to get cleaned up, they were paddling and paddling and you remember the faces as they turned from panic to wonder:

Rod.

Mr Paterson.

Tink.

FJ.

Everyone else.

The butchers.

The plumbers.

The chippies.

The newsagent.

Chook Draper of Drape's Shapes.

Michael Peterson, the local choir boy.

Everyone was out there, except Father A.

And her.

You sliced through them like Alexander the Fricken Great through a guard of honour.

They didn't know where you come from.

The wonder.

Paddling over the shoulder, their faces on you.

Rod was the only one who stopped paddling.

Rod stopped paddling and sit up on his board and raised his arms in two fists above his head and screamed:

Yeeeuuuuuuuuuuwwwwwwwwwwwwwwwwwwwwwww!!!!!!!!!

You drop in the pocket and bottom turn up to the lip.

The last you saw of Rod is him getting sucked over the falls and nailed by that lip—

—cos he stopped paddling to watch you go through.

The wave went on and on.

As it entered the bay it turned into a normal wave, like others you caught, like something out of a machine. You must of ridden it, turning up, turning down, turning up, turning down, your knees and thighs turning to fire, but you don't remember that.

You just remember the beginning when you come out from behind the black granite when you cut through that guard of honour . . .

It could be done.

Yeah . . .

You could take off in deep behind the lava rock.

They said Father A was still on the beach that day, getting ready to come out. He been late cos he given up on praying for waves and was running a normal Mass. Then he drops the chasuble when he heard the sets come in and now he was on the sand getting rubbered up.

When he saw you come out from behind the black granite, they said he rolled around on the sand half mad, half laughing his head off and gibbering, *Miracle! Miracle! Nobody does that! It's a miracle!*

They said.

Your first thought, once you flicked off the wave, was the same first thought whenever you got a real real real good one:

You wanted to finish.

You wanted to take that wave up onto the hill and show it to her cupped in your hands, just look at it, look at it with love and stop it melting away.

It was so good, all you wanted to do was finish.

Prolong that.

With her.

Your second thought was the opposite. Took over the first:

    Only way to prolong the feeling was to do it again.

    You paddled back out behind the granite.

You wrote words for her on the waves. Poems. Songs.

    You wouldn't look up see was she watching.

    You surfed two hours, only caught eight or nine waves, every one a song you wrote for her.

    You run back up Greenmount Hill.

    See if she'd read your music.

    She wasn't there.

She wasn't there.

    She wasn't there.

SUMMER'S ALMOST WENT

Summer's almost went. The BFO's went, with her sly deposits. The tourists went.

Only dragging Mo out on our morning drives if the conditions are promising:

Rain, wind, chop, onshore, run-off pollution.

They're the only days we'll try the secret spots now.

Then it happens. Driving rain against the windows, against the diagonals in the steel door grille, rain that springs a leak in the bathroom. Devil wind is onshore, due east. Been raining all night so the stormwater drains are gushers.

Yeah . . .

Stand in my sleeping boardies and my sleeping T-shirt with my aviators on and I push them up my nose (they're still there) and I've washed my hands and mixed a bowl of muesli and milk and ready now to sit at the head of the melamine table and Mo walks into the kitchen and:

'You got a big smile on your mug this morning my boy.'

You nod. You sit down and start in on your muesli. You feel the short-period wind chop in your thighs, in your waters . . .

'Today the day?'

You nod. Your mouth is full.

'Taken your green and your white? Your blue?'

You nod. Your mouth runneth over.

'You're the champion of the world, Den. Just remember that.'

Into the Sandman panel van sprayed purple and orange, the DK gun between you, no second or fourth, out through the toy roundabouts but no smell of planted flowers today, the rain and the wind drive too hard.

Mouth opens and closes round the driveways. Out of town, over the causeway to The Other Side. Down past the bush where your poor poor chopper lives, Rest in Peace. Turn off the highway onto a bush track turned to glue. Your Mo handling the Sandman panel van sprayed purple and orange like a pro rally ace. So proud of her you could cry. The buzzing ball in your stomach is raging. You need to do a poo. You will do a poo in the bushes.

You get there. Mo pulls up in the sandy parking area. It's a bog with all the rain.

The secret spot where someone is always out.

The wind belts in from the east. The waves are choppy, disorganised, all over the shop. There's brown water running off into a big stinking slick wrapping round the point. The rip is sweeping out along the rocks. The tide is all wrong. There is so much rain you can't see far beyond the point but you can see far enough.

You turn your head hard away from Mo. You love her too much. 'Nobody out today, Mo.'

COOKING

Summer '68–69, you was cooking. After the Big Flat was the Big Summer —cyclones queuing up in the Coral Sea churning out swell event after swell event. It was all-time out there.

This was the sixties and you pretty much declared yourself a self-governing nation. You could do that in them days. You was good at maths, pure natural genius at business. You done ding repairs for fifty cents. You sold your rebirthed boards to groms on hire purchase, a dollar a week for fifty weeks. You repo them when they missed a payment. Quick smart. Keiths Surf Boards was ruthless. Businesslike.

You didn't need to enforce payments. Everyone knew who you were. Seen you out in the water. Everyone talk about DK.

When groms couldn't pay—and we know this for sure, cos we know their families, we'd eaten steak and chops at their houses, we know who they were—when they deadset couldn't pay, we put them to work in the rat cellar: the dirty work, the sanding and planing and glassing. They was getting their education. You never showed them no designs or shared your *ideas*. That was old Chook Draper's mistake. You kept tight-lipped. Instead you broke up the production line so one kid did one part of the job: some sanding, some planing, some glassing. And you kept control of the big picture. Most of all the designs.

You never done no drawings.

Kept the drawings in your head.

Ran the tests, experiments, stored the results and the learnings, all in your head.

Pure natural genius.

So businesslike, you figured out you could avoid paying tax if you sponsored a surfer with your profits—so you come upon the idea of sponsoring yourself! Keiths Surf Boards paid DK twenty bucks a month to surf their boards. You couldn't believe someone pay you to surf! You couldn't believe *you* could pay you to surf! Right on! Then you upped your retainer to twenty bucks a week, cos that was what Wayne Lynch was getting. You were up there!

There was this conness going on down at Newcastle, New South Wales juniors or something, and you was already going as the Queensland junior champion and marquee surfer for Keiths Surf Boards, but Rod wasn't. Meanwhile Tink at school was organising these Casual Clothes Days, where everyone bring in 20c to fund him going to Newcastle on the bus and stay the night in a motel. You couldn't believe it, how low the guy would go when his parents could of afforded to probably buy the motel if they wanted. You saw the whole racket as organised theft.

One day Kinky Tinky come cycling down the hill at Greenmount his red hair shining and a great big jingle, like he had fifty bucks worth of 20c pieces in his schoolbag. He just ripped off the entire school. You couldn't stand for it. Rod set up an ambush, cast a fishing line across the road and took Tink out. It was like you were the Kelly Gang, Robin Hood and his merry men, bailing him up.

Hand over yer cash ya thief!

Tinky's mouth flapping away.

We're robbing the rich and giving to the poor! Rod bellowed.

Tink handed over the money, grizzling.

Turned out Rod was able to go to the Newcastle conness with you, late entry. Mo was gunna come down with you when it was only you, but now Rod was in it she said she wouldn't be bothered. Rod was spewing but got a big bag of mull for the trip, helped him over his disappointment. He didn't do no good in the event but you won it and these things are always best when you can share your victory with your fam.

Ooh yeah, you were cooking in the business world.

You put in new electrical wiring, laid down tarps on the earth floor of the rat cellar so it wouldn't pile too high with glass dust. Basil sit and watch while you relaid the lino upstairs, above your shaping bay, so glass dust won't blow up through the floorboards. You accept payment in resin, in blanks, in old loggers fallen off the back of a truck . . . You reinvest all your earnings in the business. Keiths Surf Boards. You liked that name now, it'd grew on you. Three words better than two.

You changed the scroty logo into something more elegant, classical. There was this shape you seen somewhere—cool shape, bit like a spinning firecracker inside a circle. You got Rod to put it on your board and you took it out a few times till Father Aplin saw you out the back pulling a big sweeping cutback and he absolutely did his nana.

Mate, you've got to get that off your board.

Too cool for school eh! You and your big mouth.

Father Aplin shook his head, looking real sad and old.

You couldn't work it out. You hadn't ripped off someone else's logo had you?

Finally Father A got his head standing still long enough to say:

What on earth possessed you to put a swastika on your board?

A what sticker? you said.

You had no idea. You just seen it somewhere. You didn't want to cause offence. Once Father Aplin explained, you were happy to change it again, though Rod was a bit whingey. The painting and glassing had took him all day.

You didn't want to cause offence.

You were smart as Einstein. But you didn't pay attention in history.

You then did 'DK' in a Superman shield.

More like it.

Other ones followed you out behind the black lava rock, watched you taking off there. Many tried. Not many succeeded. The ones succeeded, you targeted them, shadowed them, snaked them . . .

You wouldn't drop in on them, not there, be as good as killing them, they come off a deep wave in behind and end up mincemeat on the granite. Though it might net you a new board to take back to Keiths Surf Boards. Tempting, but no, no dropping in there.

There was rules.

But you paddle about and make them think you was going to. You surfed full-on, hassling and snaking, like every session was the final of a conness and you needed the next wave to win and'd take it at any cost.

If they saw you, they be so scared you was gunna drop in on them they pull back and leave the wave for you.

All working nicely now.

•

You done your own design testing. You take a new board out for an hour and ride a few waves and bring it back home and narrow down the rail or carve up the tail or change the fin position or glass in a new fin . . . Then you cycle back to the beach and paddle out on it again, test it again.

No-one in the whole world was testing surfboards the way you were. You were ahead of the whole wide world.

Yeah . . .

At age eighteen.

Not that you knew that.

Not that you cared.

And you made sure you never looked for *her*, never asked about *her*—

You made sure nobody saw you looking for *her*, thinking about *her*—

You kept riding and making and designing and making and riding and refining. Loggers was designed for grown men. Groms surfed cut-downs, butchered versions of their dads' boards. But you developed whole new designs that could come down shorter. So how short could you make it? Six ten? Six six?

Right down to six three or six four?

How short?

You went below six foot. Rode all right.

You went down to five eight.

Five seven.

Five six.

You and Rod cut a couple of boards at four eleven, with massive plywood raked fins.

You took your tiny cut-downs out to Big Kirra one day and got smashed, totalled, Rod come in and cried, he thought he was gunna drown.

Maybe under five foot was too short.

It wasn't just length. You made them fat, you made them sleek, you made them thick, you made them toothpick-thin. You made the rails boxy and round and razor-sharp. You cut pin tails and round tails and swallow tails and square tails, and every tail in between. You used a long fin, a short fin, a hard fin, a whippy fin, you moved the fin position up and down the tail. You even tried a central fin. You tried flexible fins copied from a tuna's tail, thought about Father Aplin and his gibberish about hydrodynamics and the energy stored by fish. Suddenly it was making sense.

You tried two fins then three, but they didn't give the same as a single fin so you dumped that idea. More than one fin, it'd never catch on.

Your boards were mostly shit but. For the clients. You tested them for yourself, with your skills, and yeah they worked good for you. But then you hand it to its owner, and he'd look at it like it had come from Mars, and he take it out and not be able to paddle it, not be able to stand up on it, not be able to do anything with it but bring it back to you and ask for a trade-in.

Turned out to be a good business decision, earnt you a bulk on trade-ins. Then you get your hands on the unsurfable surfboard, ride it a bit yourself, then turn it into something else you can sell.

Sweet.

Frank Johnson didn't need to buy his boards from you. FJ's family had money, heaps of coin for pies, drinks and lollies at Bob's. FJ was a golden boy. Golden hair, golden nuts, rainbow up his arse. When he been in the surf lifesaving club, FJ saved someone and told the local paper, which was totally bad form. He'd went in after an American tourist's kid who sunk to the bottom of Rainbow Bay, helped drag the kid out, then pumped the whole heart-massage mouth-to-mouth jag even though the kid's face was blue and purple, and FJ they said was going bananas screaming at everyone, screaming at the kid to *Come back! Come back!* And everyone given up the ghost but FJ the hero still pumping away, the kid was the same age as us and Frank must of seen something scary in him lying dead there, and finally the kid threw up *into* FJ's mouth. He was alive eh. But totally gross, disgusting. Imagine someone vomiting in your mouth, someone you didn't even know. Sure, everyone said how brave and super-duper FJ was but you never got over it. They gave FJ a bravery award but you could smell American ralph on his breath.

FJ, bona fide golden boy of the Gold Coast. He was a publicity machine before they invented publicity. After he won the local juniors (you were a month over-age, but free surfed that day and would

of smashed him), FJ's mum and dad bought him a board from Joe
Larkin up the coast. Keiths Surf Boards boards sold for fifty bucks. A
Joe Larkin sell for three hundred. Top of the line. FJ's had 'FJ' painted
into the glass.

Wow, Rod said as you sat out the back. *Must be hot shit that FJ, he's
got his own name on his Joe Larkin board!*

You wanted a Joe Larkin with 'DK' on it. To go with all your DKs
with 'DK' on them. Suddenly they didn't count for much.

Even though all the kids had 'DK' on their Keith boards, you
wanted a Joe Larkin with 'DK' on it.

Or better, you wanted FJ to surf a DK.

So you paddled round behind the black granite on a day when it
wasn't breaking right, it was sucky up too close behind the rocks. FJ
newly crowned local junior champ on his brand new Joe Larkin stick
paddled round with you.

A set come. You steamed in, your big bucket hands.

It reared up close to the rocks. You pulled off it.

FJ looked at you. His golden skin, his golden hair, his pearly teeth.
You looked at him, shrugged.

Better paddle back in the bay where it's safe, champ, you said.

FJ noticed:

Champ.

Touch of glimmer come off him.

Bit of a wait for the next set, but when it come FJ paddled like mad
to get inside you. You pretended to race him, but let him get in there.

He was right in behind the granite lava rock, turning and paddling
into the wave.

You got out on the shoulder and started paddling like a maniac.

Just as FJ was on his feet, he saw you on the shoulder outside him,
cutting him off.

He thought you were about to drop in on him.

You didn't. But you paddled hard enough, before pulling off, that
you distracted him.

Wasn't a wave to mess with.

FJ got out of it sweet. Kept his life at least.

Not his Larkin board, his 'FJ'.

Shame, you said when he swum out after a nasty little spell in the
impact zone on the black granite. He was heaving breaths, dry-spewing,

doing his best to not cry from the stress of it. He freestyled over and hung on the nose of your board.

Thought you were dropping in on me, he panted.

Wouldn't do that eh, you went. *What ya think I am? Uncivilised?*

FJ panted and burped and lay his head on the nose of your board.

You nodded towards the rocks. A piece of his Joe Larkin was trying to climb up the granite.

Don't really hold together, them Larkins, you said. *I'll make you a nice new Keiths stick.*

You made FJ a nice new DK. You give it to him for sixty bucks. It was bright purple and it had three cockroaches from your rat cellar glassed into the deck. It was a total shocker and he was ashamed to be seen with it, but even more afraid of paddling out there and some heavy type like Rod seeing him without it. So he had to use it.

You made him a board only you could surf.

But FJ figured it out. In time. Worked his arse off. Learnt to surf all over again from scratch. Had to, with that heap of unrideable crap you made for him.

Called it his 'Magic Board'. Said it was the board that turned him into a bona fide shortboard surfer. He loved that board. It made him into a world champion.

Still talks about it.

See, you weren't such a bad bloke.

You didn't see *her* the rest of that summer. You scoped the bill posters for bands. All them names but no Lisa Exmire.

You tried to forget and surf. Your surfing grew a new edge. You didn't think about what you done with her. It hurt. You didn't tell nobody, not even Mo.

You just surfed.

They said, *Dennis Keith lets his surfing do his talking for him.*

Lost count of the number of ones wrote that.

Only truly accurate thing you ever saw in the surfing press.

Most of all didn't tell Mo.

•

You done a deal with the world:

You had nothing else to say till she come back. No words. Just your writing on water.

Like it could bring her.

TO KOOKDOM COME

Stand in the shore break with stick in hand and wait for a gap, Mo up behind me in the Sandman panel van sprayed purple and orange in the bog car park. My poo hot in the scrub.

Mo: reading a *Tracks*. Keep up with the world tour news. Brought it for my benefit. Not wanting me to think she's watching.

Maybe she's not. Maybe she don't care.

A gap come. I lunge forward on me belly. Thrash out in the brown froth. Arms seem to be working. Legs move. Chop's throwing the nose of me board all over the shop but I haven't fallen off yet, haven't embarrassed myself in the first ten seconds.

A chop rises up and throws the nose. I fall off.

I climb back on like a shipwrecked sailor. Who can't swim.

Keep on paddling. No lulls: onshore chop just keeps on punching, light combinations. I keep paddling. Can't see any calm out the back.

Chop rises, smashes down unpredictable, you never know where it's coming from, left, right, cross-waves, backwash.

A bigger one: duck dive.

Lose me board behind me. Leash keeps it on.

Climb back on in about six movements.

Keep paddling.

This is shit. This is total shit.

Keep paddling, chop after chop after chop, awful, not remotely surfable waves, what are you doing.

Keep paddling.

After an hour or ten minutes I get out to where it's more grey-brown than brown-white. Beyond the break, if you can call it a break.

This is shit. This is total shit.

I sit up on the board to take a breather.

I fall off.

Shit. Total shit.

I lie on the board. Wind swell throws us. I sit up again. Wobble about. Throw an arm to one side to stop falling over.

Kind of a wave?

I turn, fall on me belly, paddle.

Not strong enough. Wave doesn't break anyway.

Now I turn. Caught inside. Duck dive. Lose the board again.

This is shit. This is total shit.

Keep paddling.

Been out here fifteen minutes and totally rooted. Can hardly breathe. Don't dare look up to the Sandman panel van sprayed purple and orange.

Paddle for a wave in. It picks me up!

The old stick is surfing but me on me belly still.

I push up . . .

Nothing.

No strength.

Noodle arms.

Wave washes me in on me belly.

I've bellied a wave in to shore.

I'm rooted. Rain pinging against me fat old face.

This is shit. This was total shit.

I get up to the car. Put the aviators on. Towel down.

Mo makes like she hasn't stopped reading her *Tracks*.

Ready to go home then love? she says.

I don't say a word. Wrap the towel round me and shove the stick between the seats.

When we are passing the bush where my poor poor chopper rests in peace, I go:

Have to do that again soon.

Mo changes gear from third down to first and pulls up at the causeway. Her face so old it has red spiders in her cheeks.

Bells at Easter, she goes. *Big comeback, they won't know what hit them.*

I don't say nothing.

Or, she goes, not looking at me, letting her mouth do the talking, *wait till December. Hawaii. Triple Crown.*

My Mo. Man, if that woman had surfed she'd of cleared the water.

I go:

Can we go to church now?

Mo says, like it's the most natural thing in the world, *Have to get you showered and changed first.*

She drives us back through the toy roundabouts into the garage. We go up the stairs. I don't grab the rail. Security grille makes me nervous. I blurt out:

I was the best in the world Mo.

Me and Mo standing in the little hallway area where the diagonals are all wrong for me, all wrong, I can't stand still. Push the aviators up my nose (still there).

Mo doesn't let her face break.

Go and have yer shower, get changed and we'll go to church. We'll get a Splice afterwards. It's cold, I don't want ya getting sick.

She goes off with her *Tracks* rolled up in her hand like a torch.

I wonder if I said it, or thought it.

Mo don't give me no clues neither way.

Until we're about to head inside St Barnabas and she whispers:

Den?

Yeah?

Look.

I follow her eyes and we're scoping the old J-man, the old surf dog overlooking the waves from his high possie, arms outstretched, feet pinned together, crown of thorns, and a look on his face like it's onshore slop third day in a row.

Thirty years, Mo goes, looking at the J-man but talking to you, *and still to this day none of them surfing within a bull's roar of you.*

Now she looks at you direct. You look away. Aviators still there.

Den, and they thought three days was a miracle! What're they gunna say when the resurrection comes after thirty years?

And leads me elbow down the aisle to the front pews, and I get a flash: I'm the invalid old man and she's the daughter gone crazy looking after me.

FULLY PRO

End of the sixties, the Goldie becoming an interesting place and not in a good way. More tower blocks mushrooming at Surfers. Developers cruising Coolie, licking their chops at all that fibro. They ate fibro and shat out bricks and concrete. Turned one storey into ten, must of thought they were Gawd. Queensland politicians squiring them in govt cars. Deals done, cut taxes, encourage investment. One winter, a row of QUEENSLANDERS was knocked down at Rainbow Bay and a block of brand new brick holiday units got bunged up in a month. American-style, hotel motel. Parking lot behind it. Interesting times.

You sit out in the waves and scope the building site. Half the surfers round that time working as brickies' labourers.

Something coming.

But you DK was coming. Father Aplin called you the Messiah after you won the state opens in '68. You would live forever.

The awe in their faces.

Your hands like buckets like a waterwheel scooping gallons, paddling away from the pack to where the next set was going to break.

Inside a barrel.

Where they couldn't see you.

Your best year then. Dennis Keith, eighteen, self-made businessman, self-governing nation. Full-time surfer and shaper, part-time school student. Keiths Surf Boards—now known as KSB—off its head. Costs nil. Revenues growing. This was the Gold Coast, the new California: pineapples, bananas, straw hats. Drive-ins, drive-throughs. Dennis shaping all night while Rod partied upstairs. Mo off at the Rissole Club handing out change. Then in the morning, Dennis took the new board out and everyone else had to wait till he'd had his go, caught the best of the dawn glass-off.

Then some muesli and a lie-down, then maybe school. But not much strain before the afternoon surf.

Mo peeling prawns and working night shifts at the hospital. Lugging buckets of old people's poo.

Mo hardly ever had time to come watch him surf connesses. But one day she's standing there at D-Bah in the rain under her umbrella, big broad-shouldered lady the only one on the sand watching. Crowd of one. The wind turned, the sun arrived. He surfed his brain out, won easy in three-footers combed straight as an altar boy's hair.

When he come in but, Mo wasn't smiling.

She goes:

Ya should be surfing in rubbish waves like it was earlier, these nice ones ain't no good for ya. Nobody ever gets good in perfect waves.

Took the wind out of his sails. But while they walked home together, Mo first, DK trailing behind her his board under his arm, he thought about it. Not another word spoken between them but he knew she was right. Without knowing a thing about it, Mo knew everything.

But she didn't know how good Keiths Surf Boards was doing.

That Christmas, she said she buy him a brand new Joe Larkin. She thought he'd dig a new board, instead of the cut-downs and crack-ups and waterlogged loggers he drug in and rebirthed downstairs.

She cut a deal. She gave him a choice. She give him a new Larkin surfboard if he:

Passed his leaving exams.

Got a job. Any job.

Went to church with her now and then.

Mo, she was good to him. Held out her hand to shake on the deal.

Dennis wouldn't come at it.

Not even for your old Mo? Mo said. Eyes wetter than the rest of her.

Dennis said nothing.

Instead went down the rat cellar and took some cash out of the old resin tin where he kept the new $$$ all rolled up and neat. Cycled to the bank. Left his chopper and fresh experiment, a Coolite with glassed-in fins, on the footpath. Six foot that day, cranking at Kirra but wild and woolly with onshores. Went into the bank, asked the manager could he pay the mortgage on Shaga. The bank manager looked at this kid with dark blond hair down past his shoulders, two-surf-a-day tan, hands like buckets, holey T-shirt, reek of chemicals. Would of thought twice about his sea-green eyes except for the aviators.

Dennis pushed them up his nose. Still there.

Bank manager took his cash. It come to two weeks of the mortgage.

Then Dennis cycled to church and told Father Aplin he wanted to enrol in youth leadership group.

Father Aplin scratched his nose and patted down his comb-over and winced: *Swell's gunna have more south in it on Sunday, offshores, clean it right up.*

Dennis: *I'll start the Sunday after then.*

Father Aplin: *Deal.*

Dennis went back outside, good works done, ready to take on wild Kirra. But the glass has melted and eaten away the foam of the Coolite. Some reaction between resin and Coolite foam. All that's there next to his chopper is half a board and a pile of evil chemicals bubbling on the footpath.

Father A standing next to him. *No good deed goes unpunished, Den.*

You just shook your head, staring at what was left of your board.

I thought God'd look after me after all I done.

You tried to glass fins into a Coolite for six-foot Kirra? Father A give you a look like you got shit for brains and there isn't much any God can do about that.

You shrug one shoulder. *We're just battlers, Father A. Make do with what we can. I thought God was meant to respect that. He's meant to be on my side eh?*

Father A looked at the melted board and give a sniff. *You thought you could go out on that? In six-foot Kirra? What makes you think God's sending you a bad sign?*

Once he walked off you kind of got what he was saying.

So Mo had her Christmas present for that year. Dennis wouldn't let her get him the Larkin surfboard.

Said his KSBs were better anyway.

•

Joe Larkin offered him his boards to ride for free, as advertising. Joe wanted the famous DK to be seen on his sticks.

DK took them out and sold them instead.

Had them all spooked in the comps. Whenever he needed a wave he seemed to get one, no matter where he was sitting he was right spot right time.

They said he had a magical connection with the sea . . .

Yeah . . .

The Big Secret . . .

It happened so often, when he looked like he was out of the conness, this wave come right at the end, the perfect peeler peaking just where he was sitting, they were all spooked said he could murmur what he needed into the ocean's ear . . .

When the truth was, he was *always ready*. Every moment, every second. Ready for the wave to come. Always. Not an instant excepted. Ready.

Nobody did ask.

They preferred to believe he had The Secret.

Even the ones he beat.

They preferred to believe in The Great DK.

Even them. Most of all them. Made them feel better about losing.

There was weekend comps at the different points: Snapper, Greenmount, Kirra, Burleigh. You were only allowed to join one boardriders' club, cos they competed against each other. He joined Snapper. Then he joined Greenmount. Then he joined Kirra. Kirra was the best: had the most connesses. He went up and down the coast surfing for Kirra.

Zone championships, he come second to Peter Drouyn, grown man, national open champ. DK brought the trophy home: gold-painted plastic man on a board, on a wave. Couldn't wait to tell Mo.

Mo, Mo, look what I won!

Mo looked at the trophy which already had bits of gold paint coming off it.

Second, eh?

Yeah Mo, second in the zone! Second to the Australian open champion!

She walked up and took his face in her hands.

Nobody remembers who come second, love. Nobody. Not a sausage.

You stared at her till you fell in her bloodshot green eyes and drowned.

Then Mo smiled and ruffled your hair. Since you stopped having nightmares, stayed in your own room, you didn't know as good as before where you stood with her. Like where she was coming from eh.

Just make sure ya come first next time, eh?

Mo?

Yeah, love?

I got enough money downstairs so ya don't have to peel no more prawns.

When he wasn't surfing he was shaping: for himself, for Chook Draper at Drape's Shapes. They never seen anyone could take a blank and knock it into a finished stick so fast. He was a blur. Give him a hunk of wood, he saw the board move in the wave. Something programmed inside of him.

His hand was the wave. His brain the God.

Sometimes overdone it: shaved blanks so thin they had to be thrown out. Glassed boards so thick they wouldn't flex.

His designs were so special, when anyone come in his bay he'd stop working and hide his things.

It got so he rigged a shower curtain round his bay.

Then hid his stuff when he left.

No-one could see.

No-one.

Paid half of Mo's mortgage. Said he'd do her a deal:

Ya stop working peeling prawns, I'll win a state championship for ya.

I dunno love, it's a nice thought but them conness judges, they got it in for you and it won't be your fault if you don't . . .

He pushed his aviators up his nose. Still there.

Don't argue Mo. It's done.

Mo was able to quit her job peeling prawns. But she didn't come home more. She just worked more hours carting poo at the hospital and handing out change at Funland and the Rissole.

•

No Mo, no *her.* Just winning comps in the day and Rod's crew at night.

You tried alcohol and it made you sick, you vomited and woke up with a headache and worst of all couldn't surf.

But the dope was instant love:

Your fourth love.

It slowed you down, it helped you concentrate and appreciate the music on the stereo or the flower in the palm of your hand. Normally you were racing, too much to do, too little time . . . But when you smoked weed that ball of nerves in your stomach went all caramel.

First time you smoked it, you realised that buzzing ball had been in your stomach your whole life. And now you made it warm and calm.

Mo must of had that buzzing ball too. For some reason that thought come to you.

This was another thing: the thoughts that come to you. The way you'd analyse them and see where they come from and even though you forget what you were saying you could remember all the thoughts in a line-up that led up to that point, so you could go back and fetch it again.

Rod and the others, on the green they laughed to break the mouth and danced and cacked themselves silly. If one of his mates passed out from smoking too much, Rod load him into a wheelbarrow, glue his eyes shut with board resin, and dump him in the bone yard behind Shaga. There was this one kid who when he woke up couldn't see anything and thought he was dead, in the cemetery. Rod and that pissed themself.

For you but, green was more like philosophical. You wanted to use it for your surfing. You didn't giggle. It clarified things for you. It was like it took a snapshot of everything around you, made the world stand still so you could stroll about in it like a waxworks museum. Weed helped you see the patterns underneath. Weed helped you focus on one thing at a time. Made you a real brainiac. You did your school leaving exams stoned. You outdone everyone's expectations.

Rod and them others, they passed out when they had too much.

When you had too much, you felt ready to focus.

Nineteen sixty-nine. Summer of no love.

Rod's despair: when you smoked weed, you knew you could surf better. That's what he saw, that first night he give it to you.

If there wasn't waves for a few days you panicked. Nothing to do with the dope. How it was ever since the first Big Flat. You couldn't function till you got a few waves. It was like your medicine. When the surf was flat or blown-out, you could go into a full-on panic which would turn into a full-on rage at Rod or one of his crew. They were scared witless of you.

You thought the ocean had stopped moving forever.

You were grieving.

But yeah, the waves come again and you're sweet. Your morning routine was set. Up in darkness, down in the rat cellar selecting boards. Wash your hands and fill a mixing bowl with muesli and milk. Scarf handfuls of dried apricots and sunflower seeds and slivered almonds. You were a health freak. Ahead of your time. While all them other boys was wasting their bodies on beer, chips and hamburgers, your body was a machine tuned for one thing.

You could hear the waves break on Snapper and the buzzing ball in your stomach rev up another gear.

Make that stomach caramel: roll yourself one from Rod's gear, calm you down and set you up and focus you.

A board under each arm, down the hill. Light breaking. You scope the waves. Pick one board and put the other under the clubhouse at Rainbow. It stunk of wee in that clubhouse. They never cleaned the troughs. You hated it and never went in that toilet. Surfers are pigs, unclean animals, you wished you didn't have to know them. Salt water rot their brains.

Walk round the rocks and jump off and be first out. This was central: they know that no matter how early they got up, the best they could hope for was second to DK.

Set the tone.

You wait for the small grower, the one didn't look big but drew all the water, that's the first one you paddle into.

The one knocked the froth off.

The one settled you.

You wouldn't do much on it: no cutbacks, no reos, no pulling into barrels, just trim along on a high line like an old-fashioned logger rider, soul surfing, cruising your first wave.

Get your feet in the wax.

And that with the pre-dawn joint and the muesli get you all set up.

Others be out with you now, chirping their good mornings and gdays.

And you, you'd be ready for war.

TRUE COLOURS

Shit, total shit next day too and you beauty I think as I get out of bed hearing the rain hammer the diagonal security grilles and soon I have poor Mo behind the vinyl steering wheel and down it is to the secret spot and . . .

. . . yeah . . .

My pride well swallowed, digested, sit in my intestines, broken down by me gastric juices . . .

Mo in the car with her *Tracks* on the bluff over the secret spot.

Getting a taste for it I paddle into the slush and this is so bad you laugh inside, such shit, mush, total rubbish and I have my sense of humour back. First chuckle in about thirty-five years, first laugh along with myself since Hawaii.

Progress.

Laughing thinking, *So this is why nobody but kooks go out in crap onshore mush crap . . . cos it's crap!* That I find funny. I never surfed rubbish like this my entire life. These waves are like a teenager's bedroom, only messier. And no power, no lift. On one wave I'm going and get up on one knee, but the old gun is wobbling away and losing power in the slush and it slows down and I slow down and over we go, face plant.

The water's brown and seaweedy and rippy and sandy and has the sick freshwater smell of run-off and I love it I love it I love it.

How'd I ever forget it?

After thirty minutes I've had enough. Still not a wave. Still King Kook. But crazy-happy. Dunno what's got into me.

I belly one in and the stick gets spat out on the sandbank. I froth about but the leash acts like a slingshot and fires the gun back at me and I'm not ready as I look up and . . .

. . . yeah no . . .

It comes back how pain has a colour. Getting held down under two waves at Pipeline or Big Kirra, when you think you're about to drown, that colour's bluey grey.

When you go down on razor-sharp reef and dragged on your back and knees, that colour's red.

When you snap your hamstring or Achilles, that's green.

When you went in a hollow Burleigh cement mixer and the compression of the wave caught your foot and broke every bone in it, bits and pieces of foot-bone sticking up through the skin—that's purple.

When you get a fin chop or a board in your face, that's yellow.

The colours of the pain you see behind your shut eyes.

I'm seeing yellow. Hands at my face. Knowing already it's the eye.

Stumble on the sand. Stick dragging on the leash like a dog doesn't want to finish his walk.

Clutching me face. Yellow.

Mo's with me and got a towel to my eye and we're in the driving rain on the beach in the secret spot and she's trying to get a look at me and she's like the risen moon her big white face and halo of white hair, all I can see out me one good eye.

In the Sandman panel van sprayed purple and orange, back down the track, back onto the highway safe into Queensland, Mo pulling over again to have another look.

'Didn't get yer eye anyway,' her voice goes. 'Just above it.'

Mo used to be a nurse. Or worked in hospitals anyway.

My yellow dims down to normal colours, blacks and deep reds.

'Am I all right?'

'Yer all right love.'

We drive on.

I pass out.

On me bed in clean boardies and sleeping T-shirt. Bandage over the cut above me left eye. Sore and swollen but I didn't need to go to hospital, didn't need stitches.

Voices. Ladies, the kitchen.

I go to the door. Mo and the BFO at the melamine table. Biscuits and tea.

I back back in my room and pull the door shut.

Please Mo don't say a word.

The voices, on and on.

Please Mo not a word.

I drink my tea. Hands shaking.

Lie back down.

Please Mo . . .

Mo used to work in hospitals.

I blacked out.

Mo changed me clothes on me when I was blacked out.

She says a word about this to the BFO, DK will not be answerable for his actions.

ANOTHER STATE

Competition had a bad name till you. Nat give up and went native at Angourie. Some went off to India like Beatles with their gurus. Keith Paull had found his inner guru in a gold top mushroom from the Pigabeen Valley and arrived at a preso driving his van into the pub then running out in nothing but ugg boots and rolling round in the shore break and telling a TV reporter he was an oyster. Deadset. Ted Spencer was a Hare Krishna. Midget Farrelly was in 'self-imposed exile', whatever that was. Rolf Aurness won the world title at Bells, said, *Far out*, and walked into the sunset.

Higher plane where they didn't need to win no more. All them hippie-dippies on their trip about *It's not about winning, man* and *You only talk about who won when you're too tired to surf . . .* and *No surfer, no matter how much he rips, can ever look as good as an unridden wave . . .*

And yeah right this was the end of the sixties and nobody wanted to win no more. Winning was old hat. Uncool. Capitalist. Selling out to the man.

And but so you thought:

Yeah!

That summer you won the state seniors against the men, as well as Tink, FJ, all the kids. Rod made quarters.

Not a wave went by when you weren't thinking about *her*.

March 30, 1969. You DK was interviewed in a rust-coloured Anthony Squires blazer and gold-thread Miller shirt and moccasins on the preso stage where they give you the trophy which was another gold-painted plastic man on a surfboard on a wave. You looked at yourself and got paranoid about what you were wearing. Everyone be laughing at you. You screwed up again. In a full-flow sweat you coined your signature speech. Interviewer said,

So DK, what was your inspiration out there today? You were totally stoked!

You said:

Well yeah . . . but no!

End of interview.

You were thinking of her.

Well yeah . . . but no.

A line from one of them little songs she cooed in your ear on Greenmount Hill in the agave trees under the fingernail moon.

They didn't need to know that.

You were one of the first to use the leash, the leggie. The longboard boys called them 'kook cords'. Definitely uncool to have a safety line joining you to your board. Nobody used one, nobody good anyway. Nobody'd even heard of them. Surfers kept hold of their boards.

But you saw something else.

Eyes only for the barrel.

You were the barrel rider.

And hardly any them other guys tried to get inside the tube, not in a comp anyway, cos wiping out meant they waste all their energy swimming in to pick up their board. So they wouldn't try for barrels. For them it was all about an elegant trim and hopping off with their stick in their hands.

For you it was all about the green cathedral.

You got Mo to make you this cord out of an occy strap and some cloth to tie it round your ankle. You drilled a hole in the base of the fin and tied the strap through it.

It wasn't cool, it wasn't what surfers done, but with your leash on you could take the risk and if you got wiped out your board was right there with you, no swimming necessary.

You used it and you won and you were The Great DK, and within a couple of years there was leg ropes getting sold round the world and all the others were on the leash too trying to get in that green room with you. Before long your leash was making a lot of breaks available to kooks, now they could keep their boards no matter how often they got wiped out and so they come out to Kirra, Lennox, even Snapper behind the lava rock, and you prowling the beach with your fishing knife cutting kooks' leashes so they wouldn't come out into your breaks, but it was too late, you weren't careful enough of what you wished for, you been too damn smart and started yourself a trend, the whole world following you.

Always following you.

In '69 you DK was on fire. Winning the state title qualified you for your first national opens, and your first trip to Bells Beach, Victoria.

You knew about Bells. Posters on your walls. The world knew about Bells. You weren't that much of a hick. You knew the whole wide world: Bells, Jeffreys Bay, Margaret River, Pipeline, Haleiwa, Sunset, Huntington. You were gunna surf all them places and you were gunna kill every other surfer out there. Kill kill kill.

You were going to surf all the posters on your bedroom wall.

But you had to do Bells first.
First things first.

Easter '69. Rod drove you down in Gary Trounson's panel van. Yous had bugger-all coin but someone had got hold of a bag of red-headed buds so yous were set. The windscreen was smashed in but Rod fixed it by ripping out the passenger side window and clamping it in front of the steering wheel. So you, in the passenger seat, froze your eyes out with no windscreen and no side window.

Cold didn't bother you. Wind blowing out your lighter or your mull did. You hunched under the glovebox, your hand over the light and the billy.

Basil sat in back. You had your favourite cassette, *Santana* by Santana, and played it all the way except when Rod got the squirts and put on *Disraeli Gears*. For all them days on the road that was all yous listened to, end on end, them two albums. Yous choofed all the way and camped on the side of the road. Two days later yous were at Bells, national titles, and the sight of it at the end of that long road the Southern Ocean, the freeze-dried toenail of the mainland, spun you out so bad that Rod and Basil lost you in the crowd and only found you when they smelt the cloud coming out the deserted dunes east of the beach.

What's up bro? Rod went.

You looked at Rod and hated him. Yous both wandered in the same Disneyland and Rod lapped it all up. Hotshots from your bedroom walls: Peter Drouyn, Wayne Lynch, Terry Fitzgerald. Up-and-coming shortboard superstars: Peterson, FJ, Tink, Rabbit, Mark Warren. Rod walked round his mouth trapping flies.

And the big news: Nat Young making a comeback in the conness. Roddy was wetting himself. Stoked. You was wetting yourself. Definitely un-stoked.

He found you crouched over an emergency billy in the dunes. Settling. Yeah.

For four years you been asking Rod if you looked like Nat Young on a wave. *Rod, did I look like Nat on that one?* And Rod said, every single time, *Yeah nah in yer dreams Den.*

Every time the same.

He settled down in the sand and you packed him a cone. Yous called them C-1s. As in C-Ones.

Know what? Rod said, his voice a croak as he held the smoke. *Ya don't look like Nat when ya surf.*

You wanted to go to the panel van and hit the road home. That was all you wanted since that sick moment when you drove in and seen all the flags and the banners and the people and Nat Nat Nat . . .

Nah, Rod said. *Yer better.*

The buzzing ball went caramel. Inside, you felt nothing. But ready to surf again.

Yer the best here, Rod said. *Only bad luck or cheatin judges can stop ya.*

You thought Rod was crazy. It helped.

The pair yous got up and walked over to the big hullabaloo and found the BBQ and hoed into the sausage sizzle. Basil got in there and nicked a sossie or ten. Everything sweet.

You went and had a free surf, and Rod made money by parking the van across two spaces and selling them when the car park was filling up. Someone come up to him and pull open the van door and go:

Hey man, can you repark so I can fit my wheels into the space?

And Rod:

Sure man. Two bucks and it's yours.

Did it every day.

Did it every year he went to Bells. Made a load of coin.

He always said they had to improve their parking situation there. Reckoned they should put up a three-storey garage with timed meters.

Yeah but . . .

Easter '69 . . .

Next morning you got up and had your first doob and your bowl of muesli and washed your hands and put on your wetsuit and . . .

Rod where's me wetty?

Rod crawled out of Gary's shaggin wagon.

You put it in, he said. Rubbing his eyes.

Nah you *did eh!*

Brothers, brotherly love, brothers at war.

You had no wetty. Bells, sixteen degrees in the air, fifteen in the water, everyone in steamers, and you DK was going in the first round of the conness in boardies and a T-shirt.

Nobody knew who you was, you was just this mad Queensland cunt in shorts. You were tall, your hands was buckets and your feet was flippers, but you were also young. Your first pro conness.

No one-on-one heats them days. Just you in a bunch.

Five blokes in the line-up.

Except the five had Mark Warren, Peter Drouyn, Wayne Lynch and Nat.

Nat's Nat, that's that.

You didn't watch them on their waves. Bells was working well, offshore and five foot. Nat took off, Peter took off, Warren took off.

You paddled and hassled and tried to take charge of the long right-hander like it was Snapper.

You got one and pulled your moves:

Hack, cuttie, roundhouse, hack, cuttie, roundhouse . . .

Motion in poetry.

Bells was easier than your home waves, fatter on the take-off, big fat long rollers, offshore spitting spray in your face.

You cut them to pieces. You smashed them. You killed them.

You come out the water octopus-blue. Coldest in your life. You saw Rod up in the stand and give him a thumbs-up. He give you one back.

You hadn't clocked any of the others in the heat but you knew like you'd always know deep down when you was the best out there . . .

Killed them. Smashed them. Cut them to pieces.

When you come in on your last wave, you done a massive bottom turn with your front to the wave, back to the shore, and your shorts split open down the back seam. People thought you were mooning the judges but you weren't, it was just your boardies split, accidents happen eh.

Didn't matter. Crowd went berserk.

And you—
You DK was judged fifth of five.
Out in round one.

You and Rod standing side by side as they read out the results:
Young, Lynch, Drouyn, Warren, Keith.
Young, Lynch and Drouyn to progress to the next round.
Warren and Keith, see yers next year.
Out in round one.
Rod wanted to blue with someone. He charged into the judges' tent, raging.
You already walking off to the dunes.
Stick under your arm.
Blue.

You were on the back tray of the panel van. Somewhere over the dune crowds were cheering round two.
You had a C-1.
Got any more?
Her voice up behind the van, almost made you jump out of your skin. Your blue skin.

She put her arms round you, not another word. You were froze solid. It was like she been waiting your whole life to come up here and give you what you needed but she had to wait and wait and wait till you needed it most.
The warm of her heart, the warm of her arms.
She thawed you out all by herself.

After she had one, she lay back and blew out and said:
Man, you're still grey. You need more cuddles.
She pushed Basil out the van. Hate at first sight. Like she was jealous of him. Normally when someone didn't like Basil, you catch up to them in the surf and kick your board at them. You didn't tolerate ones who were mean to your beagle. Cept her.
He give a snarl and a yelp and pissed off to look for Rod. Reckon it was then that Bas started seeing you as a fair-weather friend.

Lisa. She altered your state.

First time you seen her since that morning back at Greenmount. Turned out Lisa's band been booked as bar entertainment up at Torquay. She hadn't known you were in the conness, she just wandered down, see what's going on. Her swaggering chunky gym rat's walk and hair feathercut over ears and neck, like a duckling, brown and gold.

Her walk: the thing about her. When she walked she rocked from side to side . . .

I saw your heat, she said. *You were insane, man. And that stunt mooning the judges—so totally rad, man!*

Come last. And I didn't moo—

Ar fuck that, she said. *You were miles ahead. All those other guys, smooth as silk but lazy, you know? They just cruise down those waves like they're doing a ballroom waltz. But you, man, you were like jazz, you were rock and roll, you were, I dunno, you were just doing so many things, so much, you looked like you were fucken epileptic or something, you know?*

Come last.

In whose eyes? Just some bunch of old has-beens? Don't worry, man, you're ahead of your time. You were so far ahead of your time nobody knew what to make of you. You made them all look like they were on Valium, man, and you were on, like, whiz. You were so much better, you had so much more power, like you were, I dunno, taking the mickey out of all of them, they were doing some kind of Hawaiian aloha Elvis thing and you were doing Deep Purple, so rad when you mooned them . . .

You wanted her to hear you—*Come last, didn't moon no-one*—but she was laughing, all arse, like she knew better than the judges and you knew better and yous both knew better and yous were looking back on this day from years ahead, when you was world champion and she's still your bird and yous can look back on when the sport still hadn't caught up with you, and she was that confident, that super-sure you were ahead of your time, and . . .

. . . yeah . . .

Butting in:

You spoiling the moment:

If you don't come back to Coolie with me then we're done.

Lisa stopped laughing at the judges, stopped looking back on this day from twenty years on, and looked at you.

You didn't look back.

Yous were lying side by side in the back of Gary Trounson's shaggin wagon.

You didn't know where you'd left the aviators.

You got up and went through your gear. Stubbed your toe on the wheel well.

There they were, on the dashboard.

You come back and sat with Lisa on the tailgate and pushed the aviators up your nose. There. Rubbed your toe. Black and blue your whole life.

I live in Coolie, she goes.

Soft. With that gentleness she had when you were inside her face and she was inside yours.

You thought she's pulling your leg. Always pulling your leg, this girl. You grunted and packed another billy.

It's true, she said. Still tender. *I didn't want you to know it cos I wasn't sure how deep I wanted to get in this.*

You pass her the bong. Stop her talking.

She put her hand on your knee.

Dry land just doesn't suit you, eh Dennis Keith? You should have a sign on you.

What sign?

She had this dimple, just one, in her right cheek. Like her grin was reaching out for you.

Just add water.

Easter Monday 1969. Rod and Basil let the two of yous drive back to Coolie alone.

Her and you. She took the wheel in both hands and left her band behind.

Rod stayed at Bells. He'd made some new friends. Bas stayed with him, keep an eye on him.

Nat won.

Lisa come and moved in with you at Shaga. Only another letter'd fallen off. Now it was: Saga.

You won.

YELLOW EYE

The BFO scopes me coming out the bathroom. Why's she still here? What's Mo telling her?

'What you done to your eye?'

I'm standing in the hallway of this retirement unit and I've left my aviators in the bedroom.

Clap me hand over the eye.

The BFO isn't surprised I've locked myself away from her for three days. Not annoyed about the time of hers I'm wasting.

I don't trust Mo.

Why's this one still here?

I go: 'Walked into a door.'

Shuffle back to my room to listen to the radio. Turn it up.

Her sniffy laughter behind me, like we're in someone else's joke together.

LADIES THEN

The all-time winter: 1969. You get warmed up on that number. Five big swells end on end, right-handers breaking Snapper to Kirra. Waves so long blokes would jump off cos their legs got tired or they got bored.

You never jumped off. Your legs never got tired or bored. Never let a one go to waste.

Longboarders let the best part of the wave go to waste. Criminal. Take off when it was big and fat, cruise through, but when it hit the sandbank and started to wall up and barrel they kicked off, boards flying into the air on the offshore, and . . .

. . . criminal.

For you the wave didn't really get started till it hit the sand and got real fast and the longboarders bailed out, you tucked yourself into a ball and drilled into the pit down and through till the barrel spat you out the other side. Crowds on the beach and point cheer and whoop.

Surfers sit on the beach till their heart rate come back down and they can feel their arms again. When it was big like this they couldn't get back out.

You were the only one. Your stamina. You sucked up the white pain of that paddle.

This was the summer you made your name: the cult hero DK.

In the barrel.

Where none of them could see you.

That year you became DK, *you* became *he*.

DK stories in *Tracks*, in *Surfer*, in *Surfing*. Pictures, loads of pictures. Couldn't take your eyes off DK. And films they made: DK's trademark hand chops, like whipping a horse. You didn't know that. Best waves of your life, on film. You become a flick buff as long as you were in it. And then they tell stories, in the flicks, the pics, the mags. How everyone knew Basil, like you were partners in crime. Just when Bas had give up on you and signed up with Rod. But when you read about you and Bas in the magazines, you believed it and had a big bust-up with Rod when you couldn't ever find Bas.

You took up reading. How Tink and FJ said they idolised you more than Nat or Midget. You didn't know that. How DK's brain worked so fast that even when he was ripping down the line on an eight-foot right-hander, his arms chopped round like he was *impatient*, waiting for the wave to catch up with his brain, and when it did he pull one of these massive cutbacks to give something back to the wave, let it catch him, then turn away and rip off down the line. Tricks like this on waves nobody else could catch.

The cutback defined: when the surfer's brain works too fast, his body works too fast, he's outrun the wave, outsurfed the wave, defeated the wave, so what does he do? He jams down his back foot, turns his board, and goes back to the wave to let it have him again.

Generous. Give something back to the wave. A big bucket of spray fired out of your tail block, like your board was a spraycan and you were the graffiti artist painting your tag on them shiny green walls—

And that surfer, the original cutback surfer, was DK.

You.

Him.

You never thought of it in so many words.

DK, DK, DK . . .

They never dropped in on DK no more. They hardly even caught waves. They paddle up on the shoulder and look deep in the barrel and listen for the Scream in Blue.

DK, DK, DK . . .

Had them spooked. He drove up to Burleigh with his mates and paddled in his first wave and disappeared in a ten-second barrel. The Burleigh boys' chins hit their chests.

Who was he?

He was DK eh.

Ar so that's DK eh.

They admired him. They wanted to know him. They welcomed him to their break.

But when the Burleigh boys come down to Kirra, in their flash Holden Toranas and Ford Fairlanes and VW Passats, you and Rod sit out the back and hassled them till they left.

Don't yous remember us? the Burleigh boys said.

You and Rod looked at each other and then back at this pack of Burleigh drongos.

Piss off, this is our wave eh.

Had to make sure nothing got wasted.

Had to be some order in the world, some rules, some respect.

Nineteen sixty-nine, Summer of Love, *Pet Sounds*, *Sergeant Pepper's*, Woodstock, Altamont. A man walked on the moon and Hawaii had its all-time biggest swells and Keiths Surf Boards opened up in the mini-mall on Marine Parade. Had to be some connection.

Prime possie. Gary Trounson passed his lease to you, paid out six months. The blokes you done shaping for like Chook Draper and Joe Larkin give you stock on consignment. You were set up. Nineteen years old and a self-made businessman. Bought a rack of Anthony Squires suits. Put some kids on the payroll to glass and sand your boards and stand in the shop and rake in the coin.

Spent a bit of time in the shop yourself: the main attraction. You were doing fashion as well: tie-string canvas boardshorts, Jesus sandals, psychedelic Indian shirts, puka shell necklaces. You were raking it, raking it, raking it in. An article said you were gunna be surfing's first millionaire.

You took up reading:

DK's thousand-yard stare.

When DK enters the water, it's like Moses parting the Red Sea.

DK doesn't need to talk. Fifteen-second barrels speak for themselves.

You'd like to meet this DK. You'd like to see him carve. You'd like to drop in on him, scare him out the water, take him on. He sounded like he was getting big for his ugg boots.

All this and since Bells you hadn't been in a single conness. Bugger them.

Lisa was living in the QUEENSLANDER with you now and behind you all the way. She and Bas snarled at each other. She whispered over the pillow how Mo was jealous of her.

Lisa's dimple never lied.

Rod done his leg that year. Riding cyclone waves wrapping round Point Danger into D-Bah, big sucky one threw him down against the breakwall. Said he felt like he been punched in the leg, nothing worse. Swam to get on his board and felt something hit him on the back of his head.

And I looked round to see what hit me, and it was me own foot!

Then he passed out. Lucky someone—not you—found him floating and drug him in, took him to hospital. Busted femur bone. Busted in two.

The pain changed Rod. Spent the whole season in his room with his leg in a cast. Stewing about all them waves he wasn't catching.

Mo come in every morning, tidy up his room, make casual remarks about how Dennis was carving that day on clean offshore eight-footers behind the lava rock.

He's gunna be world champion Rodney, just you wait.

That was one thing Rod, lying on his bed in his cast, could do: Wait.

Felt a lot of pain and needed to press it down.

If there was a lull and you knew you wouldn't be surfing at dawn, you and Lisa sat up all night. She done most of the talking. When she talked about music, the way songs had a natural fall line, a rhythm of pits and rises, you saw waves. She could play slack-key Hawaiian guitar, which you *really* liked. She bit the guitar neck while she played a song so the music flows straight into her soul. When she played slack key, she took you in the posters on your wall, Sunset and Pipe and Waimea.

Mo pop her face in the door and cop a look and shoot one at you:

Bird knows what she's doing all right. Gotcha ya dill.

Mo and Lisa, at each other guerilla-style, Viet Cong in Saga.

Lisa started to write songs based on 'the similarity between music and waves', music with pits and barrels and shoulders and ramps, and when she played them you could see what she meant, you could see waves with your ears. That might of been the only way she could get through to you but get through she did.

Music's so much like surfing, she said.

Yeah right, you said. *Once you've done it it's gone.*

She looked at you funny and thought for a minute, then said:

But the big trick is to find out how to hold that last note.

And she looked at you a long time, so long that eventually you had to look back at her, and that was the last note, she was saying, that was the last note and you have to hold it or else nothing ever means nothing.

You and Lisa had heaps in common but one thing above all: yous dug competing and yous liked to win. Her and you could turn brushing your teeth, getting dressed, sweeping the house, into a fricken race. Made life interesting. In the evenings yous played chess, checkers, backgammon, Monopoly, Mastermind, cards. Totem Tennis. She was the only person you ever met who liked winning as much as you did. Even more than Roddy. But it never got heated between her and you. Yous had mutual respect. That was another great thing about her: she loved winning but she didn't take losing personal. Grown-up about it. If she lost a game, she just flick her hair out of her eyes and flash that dimple and go, *Best of three?*

Sometimes yous bet money, fifty or a hundred bucks on a game of poker. Sometimes yous bet favours: make dinner, give massage, do shopping, mow lawn. Once yous bet the job of picking the fleas off Basil over a game of Twister, but you had no hope, Lisa had a fire in her eyes that would never be beat on that one.

If she surfed, Lisa would of been pretty much the perfect chick.

Or not—if she surfed, she probably would of snaked waves off you and you'd of had to kick your board at her head or something.

But she knew how to watch surfing. She become knowledgeable about anything real quick.

Lisa said you were light years ahead, you proved it at Bells, you just had to take a holiday till the professional world caught up with you.

Mo said you won Bells really, they cheated you out of it, and you should be surfing every conness.

Lisa and Mo were always nice to each other to their face, except when it come to your surfing.

Mo thought you should be winning all the comps.

Lisa thought you should tell the comps to get stuffed.

Mo saw you as world champion.

Lisa saw you as a cult hero and an artist.

All you saw was DK.

Lisa talked about Rolf Aurness. Everyone knew about Rolf Aurness: won the title at Bells, collected his trophy, said, *Far out!*, then walked out, went bush, never competed again. Total outsider. That was supreme, in Lisa's eyes.

Mo said you were sulking cos you'd lost.

Lisa said you were doing things nobody understood yet, you were avant-garde.

Mo didn't speak French. Mo get up and left the table.

Mo didn't dig you shacked up with this singer in your room smoking dope all night. Mo didn't dig another bird in the house. She was happy with all the rubbish Rod dragged in, but she didn't want another bird in the house. She was happy with the cockroaches everywhere, and when she saw Lisa turning up her nose at the ants in the kitchen between the skirting board and the cereal cupboard, it was like Mo took the ants' side. She rather have them in the house than have Lisa.

That's what Lisa told you anyway. Lisa said how when she tried to throw something out, old food or whatnot, Mo got it back out of the bin and put it in the fridge, right in front of her. No arguing, it just happened. Lisa said Mo wouldn't even let her throw out Glad Wrap—had to be used again till it wore out. And Lisa couldn't figure out why Mo always pulled the appliances' plugs out of the walls when they weren't on. *Save electricity*, you said. Lisa laughed. But you were used to Mo's ways, Lisa wasn't.

Lisa didn't get *hardscrabble*.

Mo hated that Lisa didn't get it.

You loved it.

Ladies eh.

PINE-LIME SPLICE AND ORANGE TARAX

When the BFO has went and I come out me bedroom, the diagonals in the retirement unit are giving me ants in the pants so Mo agrees to drive me down the milk bar. I can't go in: me eye. So I sit in the Sandman panel van sprayed purple and orange while she gets me pine-lime Splice and orange Tarax from Bob.

We drive back. I keep my lips apart while we cross driveways and cross streets which is hard when you're trying to eat an ice block and drink a can of drink.

Out the side of her mouth Mo goes:

'Not a bad bird that one eh.'

'What, ya reckon I should go out with her?'

I push the aviators up my nose (still there).

She never said that about any girlfriend. Never said that about Lisa.

Mo gave a grunt. She battled on well, Mo, everything considered.

'Talked to her about your brother today.'

Brother/Sister/Mother/Daughter/Slaughter, I think. But don't say nothing.

'She wants to know if ya'd talk to her about him.'

'Yeah and what'd ya say?'

A papery creasing round Mo's jaw.

'I said: *He'd say yeah . . . but no.*'

Wipe my mouth. Orange Tarax in the ends of my moustache bristles. Don't want to talk to her about Rod. Not her and not *her* neither.

HORRORS

Lisa can't surf but she done everything else with you. Get up at dawn and drive you round the breaks, surf check. Driving more efficient than walking, she said. Sure was, for Rod anyway, sitting in the back with his gammy leg going through the motions.

Not that it made him like her. Rod was different that year, after the leg: quiet.

Lisa was all about improving your efficiency. She'd have you eating your muesli in the car as you drove round. Lisa rolled the doobs and smoked them with you. Lisa helped you plane yourself down into the machine you became.

Like his mother Rod didn't go much on Lisa. But her driving him round and feeding him and rolling his doobs too, what could he say.

What could he do eh.

Basil just give her the cold shoulder.

You smoked a bit of grass them days and people said you was a dealer. Exaggeration comes natural to some. You didn't really deal, you shared and sometimes give it away as contra. But you weren't like a dealer.

Sometimes you'd need to throw people off the scent. A group of well-known surfers come up from Sydney, scoped you out and invited you over to their bonfire on Point Danger looking down on D-Bah. All excited to be meeting you. One of them pushed a big fat doob in your direction. Like you DK was this legend smoker.

You give him a look so cold it made his balls shrivel.

I don't do drugs, you said. *And I don't have anything to do with ones who do eh.*

Then you walked off.

Good way to get them to quiet down their party.

·

You and Lisa and Rod and Mo and Basil turned up at the screening of this flick when it come to Coolie. On a big outdoor screen. Breeze puffing out the screen like it was a sailing boat. Night-time. Lisa holding your hand. She done some of the music. Apparently.

They were everywhere, the people, in the big football field where the screen been set up. Once they saw you there was a bit of a mob-type effect. *DK, DK, DK* . . . And they hadn't even seen the flick yet.

Which was all about you.

Everyone there, grommets, plumbers, butchers, teachers, priests, coppers, mums, dads, that type of thing.

Milling round.

Closing in.

Gotta go, you said to Mo.

Lisa looked at you with horror movies streaked across her face. Her big round beautiful face a screen for horror and terror.

Come on Den. She took your hand.

You'd given Mo your other.

Two of them, one hand each.

What was Rod gunna grab onto, your bean?

Rod disappeared into the crowd with Bas. Bugger you, he was going to enjoy being DK's brother, celebrity enough for what Rod wanted out of it.

But you, you were on a cross like the J-man: one hand nailed by Mo, the other by Lisa. They better not start pulling.

You'll enjoy it, Lisa said.

Mo said nothing.

Relax, man, Lisa said.

Mo said nothing.

People everywhere, you're pepper in a mill.

Screen bursting like a sailing boat sail.

Gotta go.

Mo drove you home. You went down the shaping bay and lit a doob and got back to work.

Lisa stayed at the flick. Apparently it was a knockout. She took a bow at the end, for her music, apparently.

Next morning she was up with you and giving you maximum efficiency.

●

You heard later, Rod stayed at the movie cos he brought a big petrol tin full of moths.

Yeah—*moths*.

And after this big Bells scene with DK in it, Rod took the lid off his tin and released the moths so they all fly at the projector.

The screen filled up with giant moth shadows.

They had to call the movie off for fifteen minutes. Too many surfing moths dropping in on the waves.

Last scene before the moth storm was the one with DK.

Before she moved in, Lisa lived with her parents, the Mr and Mrs Exmire. DK only met them once. They lived in a brick house other side of Coolie, up closer to Burleigh. Nice spot on a hill with a view and a looked-after garden.

So, Dennis, you like, er, surfing? said the Mr Exmire. He was bald. Some kind of businessman. Or publican, public servant. That sort of thing.

So, Dennis, you have a business selling—surfboards? said the Mrs Exmire. She was bringing you a big pile of food that had no meat. She was vego. That sort of thing.

DK too gone to say nothing.

Lisa gone too, but kept up both ends of the conversation.

At the end of the night, Lisa driving you back to Saga, tears on her cheeks.

DK too sad to say nothing.

That was the night of the ghost.

You and Lisa got home and Lisa didn't want to sleep in your room. You didn't have a fight or nothing. You never did. Her dimple just went soft and shallow.

Want to be on my own tonight.

She went to the sleepout.

DK didn't stand in her way. DK went downstairs and got out the sander. Make some noise for his head.

Some time later, don't know how long, you heard a scream upstairs. It could of been going while you had the sander on.

You raced up the stairs and Lisa was running out of the sleepout. Shivering. Arms crossed against her throat like she was praying. Fingers knit together.

Eyes wide like flying saucers.

She fell in your arms and bawled her head off.

Something was stroking my hair . . . something in there . . .

You stroked her hair, rub it out.

You put your mouth on the crown of her head and the tips of her ears. You held her close.

Mo come out. No Rod. You didn't know if Rod come home that night.

When Mo heard Lisa talking about *something in there*, Mo tut-tutted about frightening everyone and shuffled back off.

To show Lisa there wasn't nothing in there, you led her back in the sleepout. She was still shaking.

Nothing in there, you said.

Lisa said: *There's a ghost . . .*

She believed in ghosts.

Deadset.

Lisa wouldn't sleep in there no more. She went in your room then, moved right back, wouldn't let you go.

BODYBASH KING

Lisa had to go off and do her singing gigs. Her band was doing all right. You didn't go much—didn't dig them creeps played instruments behind her, didn't go much on the way they scoped you. Didn't dig pubs and clubs. Too many people knew DK.

You were busy shaping, surfing, surfing, shaping. Eating. Smoking. Surfing.

Busy busy.

Busy doing surf trips. Easter '70, you went down south to free surf Bells. Left Mo behind to look after the shop. Stopped at Pam's Rivermouth: six foot, offshore, clean, only two out at a break that went off about once every five years. You was with FJ and Tink. Just for fun you smeared butter on their boards before sun-up. So you could get there first. You surfed six hours straight.

Killing them.

They couldn't believe you were hassling, dropping in, surf ratting them, snaking, at this pristine break down middle of nowhere. You chased the two locals out the water.

What ya doin DK? Snot a conness or nothin eh!

You didn't care. If you couldn't surf in comps, it didn't matter. Everything was a conness.

You surfed six hours and went up the campsite to fry a steak. Buggered. But while you fried your steak you saw FJ get one okay barrel.

Be getting ideas about himself.

You pulled the steak off the fire and crawled in your soaking sticky wetsuit. Bones rusted together after the six-hour session but you slogged down the shore and paddled back out.

Dropped in on blondie, scored a better barrel.

Hey DK—you went in eh! What ya doin?

Couldn't let him be getting ideas about himself.

•

You stole their birds too. They knew you had the most beautiful chickie on the whole east coast, the coolest too, this amazing bird so far out of their league they couldn't imagine even talking to her. But on surf trips, or while Lisa was off on one of her tours, you snake in on the boys' birds.

It was expected of The Great DK, that sort of thing.

FJ or Tink would pick up some dolly in a pub, and you had to do your duty. On behalf of DK.

Not that you made the girls do nothing. All you wanted was lure them away from Tink or FJ and spend a few hours with you.

All you do with them was smoke doobs and listen to music.

You never made them do nothing. They tried, but you weren't playing that game.

You DK was playing another game.

All you asked was they made sure Tink or FJ knew who they been with.

You free surfed Bells the same fortnight they had the Australian titles. Easter '70. Bells was everything surfing was not meant to be: jumpers and five-mil steamers, icy rain and mud everywhere, the smoky shut-in Torquay pub, the big cliffs over the break that set the crowds up like the Colosseum looking down on you, clapping your waves. Public had to pay a fee to stand there and clap the surfers. What crap. You hated it all. You hated the promoters, all the Rip Curls and whatnot they had down there flogging their gear and paying surfers to wiggle their bums like clothing models, all the commercialism that sprung up there before it really took hold in the civilised part of the world, Queensland.

The cold went in your bones and never left. But still free surfed eight hours a day. Meanwhile the Bells comp was getting started: Drouyn, Neilsen, FJ, Giblet, Lynch, Cairns, Warren, Peterson. All waiting for you to enter the conness. Expecting you to shrug your shoulders at the last minute and go, fake reluctant, *Well I gotta do it*, and blitz them all. They thought DK was some kind of actor, some kind of prima donna, that sort of thing. You lurked in the sandhills freaking them out. You went up to Winki Pop and free surfed. Everyone expected you to bob up in their heat. Driving themself mad. FJ was progressing through the rounds but telling everyone DK had some kind of wildcard exemption through to the finals . . .

Yeah bugger them. Sidelong you watched the heats, the judging. Registered the point.

Always good on numbers.

You had it worked out sweet.

They were catching up to you but not there yet.

So there it was:

Australian titles, Bells, final rounds, FJ, Peter Townend, Drouyn, Terry Fitzgerald, Neilsen, cream of the crop.

But most of the crowd round the corner watching DK free surfing Winki alone. Smoking barrel after barrel.

You got surfer's ear from the cold water. Surfer's ear is when them bones round your eardrum swell up to protect the eardrum against the cold. Makes as much sense as bricking up a fourth wall round your garage to stop anyone nicking your car. But that's the body eh. You went deaf, left ear only. Got a spare one eh.

Kept on free surfing.

On the last day you entered the *bodysurfing* conness.

Made the semis.

This article:

While the national titles proceeded to their anticlimax, enigmatic Gold Coast surfer Dennis Keith made an appearance in the bodysurfing contest. The organisers failed in their efforts to contact Keith and invite him into the main contest.

That boy. You didn't know what to do with him.

DAD IV

But he must of been a surfer. Stood to reason. That genius had to come from somewhere.

Yeah.

You saw a pack of them: Windansea types, from up north, full of themselves and their money and looking down their noses at Kirra and Snapper boardriders. Windansea was some fancy-pants club in America, branches all round the world. They wouldn't dare set one up at Coolangatta, but they felt safe among the ponces up at Surfers Paradise. You saw them ride down into Coolie in their spruced-up yank tanks, Buicks and Cadillacs, the only ones on the coast, with their Left Hand Drive and hair slicked back and their loggers on their roof. Down to pinch waves and birds from the Coolie kids.

Windansea types, educated, fully year-12, two parents apiece. Rulers of the world.

In the waves one minute, the next run out of the joint like they'd went in the wrong pub. Tails between their legs. Spoilt brats, back on shore, spewing over the way they been treated.

End of war bloodbaths:

Coolangatta full of returned soldiers.

Windansea mob, beaten to a pulp, working up their outrage. Revenge fantasies. They can't take on any of the local blokes, so being cowards they take it out on the birds.

And here she comes: alone, home from work.

'Hey, darling, what brings you out on a night like this?'

'You come here often?'

All charm, these Windansea types. Educated. Athletic. Just got their arses kicked. Heads full of revenge.

Him. Some of them could really surf. Him.

RINGING THE BELL

Them two years, '69 and '70, when yous went down to Bells, Rod and Bas didn't come back with you. Thick as thieves them two. Rod saw himself spending the rest of his life lying in a beanbag eating chocolate. Bas pictured the rest of his life exact same way. Soul mates, same dreams and aspirations.

They come back later and when Rod come back he come back with some new friends.

Some friends called Harry in little baggies.

Better part of Rod never come back.

You been trying the full smorgasbord, not just dope and hash. One afternoon in late summer of '70 you driven with Lisa up the Pigabeen hinterland after a thunderstorm.

There was no surf. Flat tacky. She said you could pick mushies.

You'd never had mushies. You climbed over a fence into a field and tromped round. Lisa said they grew in cow pats. You picked a few out of cow pats but Lisa said they was toadstools. You tromped round some more and smoked a C-1. You tromped round and Lisa found something. She called you over. Mushroom with a brownish cap and white stalk, black gills. When she broke the stem it bruised blue.

That's how ya know, she said with this devil in her dimple.

She slipped it in her pocket.

It took you two hours in a bunch of different cow paddocks but you collected six mushies, what Lisa said would be enough. She had them in her pockets and drove down The Other Side, the big open windswept beach with no buildings.

Safer in New South, she said.

Everyone knew Queensland coppers was the most bent in the nation and the drug laws so strict you could be put away for life for having a tiny little ounce of weed, so if you were gunna do serious trips it might be a good idea to pop across the border.

Also you weren't gunna see no-one on The Other Side.

You ate three, she ate three. You didn't like the cold dirt taste but pushed them down. Then in the car Lisa rolled this big doob, twinkle in her eye, you passed it back and forth and waited.

Nothing.

You looked at the no surf. 'Flat as,' you said to make conversation.

'You're kind of an addict, aren't ya?' Lisa said. 'Surf addict.'

'Yeah well I'm in withdrawal now.'

'Like a caged lion.' She pinched the top of your thigh. Was always pinching you, Lisa. Them strong guitar fingers. 'You get wild when there's no surf. And but you're even wilder when there is surf.' She sang, like it was a line of a song she was making up right there: 'Can't live with it, can't live without it.'

Still no effect from them mushies. 'Can't live with it, can't live without it,' you repeated, speaking but, not singing.

'Same as with me eh,' she said, showing her dimple. 'You can't live with me, can't live without me.'

'Yeah right.' Then you thought a bit. 'Except for the first bit.'

Lisa thought about that, and when the penny dropped she said: 'That right?' And she was so stoked, these tears come to her eyes, stoked that you told her you could live with her, just couldn't live without her. Nearest you come to an admission of like . . .

She could see you struggling.

'Salright Den, I know.' She squeezed your hand. 'I love ya too.'

That was it, that was the moment to go for it, go after her like paddling for the big set wave, commit. That day in the car on The Other Side was when you should of asked her to get hitched or whatnot. Only you couldn't handle the thought. Couldn't handle the idea of being up there in front of a big crowd, centre of attention and that. If you could do it here in the car, nobody else knowing, you'd of done it.

Yeah. Nah. Couldn't say it but.

She's still looking at you and her eyes was full up. Car reeks of dutch oven dope smoke. You wind down the window. Lisa's still gazing at you, stroking your shoulder and dragging her finger all the way down to squeeze your hand. She's so stoked by what you said and what she knew you was thinking. And you were stoked by how much she was stoked. You never knew what she saw in you. When it was clear she did see something, you couldn't believe your luck.

Yeah but driving you crazy and now your hands, where she squeezes them, your hands are numb and pins and needles in the fingertips.

'Let's take a dip,' she goes.

The water was body temperature. Lisa wearing her T-shirt wet, then pulled it off. You took your boardies off and you're both frolicking in the nuddy.

She swim up to you and popped jiggling out the water.

Oh my God, she said. Clapped her hand over her mouth, like something really bad had happened but was too funny to tell.

What?

Den, you're all . . . blue . . .

You don't know what happened or what you looked like but Lisa swore you must of lost all the oxygen out of your bloodstream or something . . .

. . . yeah . . .

But anyway yous got it together and romped round the sandhills finding blue things: berries, flowers, chip packets. The sky. The sea. It was all blue.

Nineteen seventy.

Lisa loved mushies and loved tripping. It was a bit much for you, at least you enjoyed it with her but it didn't help your surfing. It wasn't like dope, which focused you. Acid and mushies sent you into spirals of thoughts and laughter and mazes and puzzles and if you went surfing on it you didn't find the surf all that interesting. You'd read Nat saying surfing on acid, he saw new colours in the water, like wearing polarised sunglasses, or rainbow oil patterns in the waves, surfing on acid was the best thing he done in his whole life, like carving curves on clouds, but you couldn't see it. You gobble some mushies with Lisa and go paddle out the back and sit staring at the patterns of the clouds in the sky or dive off your board and swim round looking at your hand and the way the sunlight reflected off it underwater. Inside your head it was calm and ordinary, everyday. Quiet.

That sort of thing. You was the only person you heard of who said LSD and mushies made you normal.

But you was only interested in gear if it improved your surfing.

You tried whiz which was all round Coolie those years and that didn't agree with you too good. It sped you up too fast and you get paranoid and agitated. You had to agree to disagree with Lisa on whiz. She loved it. Said it was her fave. But no, yeah, for you, speed too zippy and acid too spacey. What you liked was mull.

When Lisa come to bed on whiz, she went funny on you—like she wasn't into cuddling, more like wrestling and then edgier, like real cage fighting. Yous were mucking round this one night and you were laughing along and kidding round and all of a sudden you got this clout on your ear and your head was ringing like you been wiped out bottom of a six-foot wave with a board in your head.

'What's that for?' you go, stopping to rub your ear which is throbbing like a gong.

Then she went you again—smack! Right hook across the jaw.

'Oi!'

She had this look of devil in her, crawling round the bed on all fours. Dimple right down to the bone. Whizzy eyes.

'Carn,' she goes. 'Show us what yer made of, DK.'

Then she come up and cuddle your head against her chest, and while you're taking a deep breath there's this thump again and you're seeing stars, she's crow-pecked you on the top of your head.

'Sthat for?' You felt like crying. It really hurt.

'Carn,' she goes again. She's spoiling for a fight. Not that you got nothing to fight over. She's just whizzy and when she's like that she only wants to root after you've fooled a bit, usually it's tumbling cuddles, this time it's got to go a bit harder, got to see some bruises or blood running. Like she gets off on it. All she wants is for you to belt her, give her a black eye, then she'll go off like a firecracker.

'Nah.' You rubbed all the places your head hurt. 'Not into that.'

Lisa sort of accepted it, pretended not to be too disappointed in you. But you could tell she was. Cos every time she got too whizzy and come to bed, she'd sneak in a bit of a whack or a hard pinch or a bite, like she's goading you into full-bore pain, see if you'll be in it, and but you won't be in it. It's not you. And when she gets that message, some of the air goes out of her.

Only when she was over-whizzed but. Other times she was normal.

•

What Rod liked was smack. It broke Mo's heart when she found him passed out in his room, needle at his bedside baggie on his drawer. He tried to deny it, but Mo worked in hospitals, almost a nurse, she wasn't swallowing his story that he become a diabetic and was injecting insulin.

One night you were up late with Rod and Lisa, and Bas come in the kitchen. Beagle blown up to twice his size and lumpy like he been stuffed with potatoes. His eyes black and the size of dishes, and pissing uncontrollable. Skating round the lino floor like it was ice.

Fark, said Rod who was on his smack that night.

Fark, said DK who was stoned on weed.

Oh my Gawd, racing round the kitchen cleaning up was Lisa who was on the whiz.

Yous couldn't get Bas to drink or calm down and yous didn't know what it was so Lisa ring a vet. Told the bloke yous had a freaking beagle who was freaking out. Yous took him in and left him overnight. When yous got back home, yous all had to have a dose to settle. Lisa needed a doob to take the edge off her speed downer. You were boiling a pot of tea when Rod come in the kitchen and goes:

Eh where'd ya leave yer stash?

Which stash, Lisa said, *the mull, the whiz or your shit?*

The mull, said Rod.

Taped to the tree like always, you said. You always taped your bags of weed to a palm tree out the backyard. In case the cops come with the Black Maria. Your idea.

Well it's not there eh.

When you added two and two it was cacksville. Least Bas wasn't gunna die. Just ripped off his noggin. Serve the little bugger right for not controlling his appetite.

Next day we told the vet what it was.

Yeah right, bloke said. *Thought it might've been something like that.* And looking at us like it wasn't the dog that needed treatment.

Not that Mo was all that wised up. She thought you was doing so well running the business, the shop and that, you wouldn't need to do anything stupid like for instance:

Decided to grow some dope plants in the long grass out in the graveyard. One day you come in from your morning sesh and found six plants lined up on the melamine kitchen table.

Mo with red eyes dripping in the sink.

Nothing much you could say.

You stood there and went to the fridge and found something to eat.

Mo rounded on you, screamed:

But why, Den? Why do you want to smoke heroin?

Poor Mo. Clear on the big picture, knew her boys was doing drugs and she didn't want nothing to do with it, not so accurate on the smaller details. Poor Mo.

Poor Rod. He offered you his baggie mate, but it was the one thing you weren't game for. You'd tried ether and morning glory and datura and angel dust but good old doctor green was the only one you really loved. That really loved you. Mutual respect. Love.

Rod was getting into smack just when you were gearing up to hit comps again. You walked in his room one day, after he come back from Victoria late with Bas, must of been mid-'70, and he's squatting there with these skanky Vicco friends of his, all black jeans and black T-shirts and that Victorian thing of skin greyer than their grey hair, hadn't seen sunshine in about a decade, and they were smoking cigarettes and shooting up.

Rod motioned you to pull up a beanbag.

You sat down and punched a C-1.

He held out his rubber tie for you. You shook your head.

Rod said to his friends:

Fucken women.

They sat there sniggering like schoolkids.

They thought Rod was calling you a woman.

They didn't know who he was talking about.

Mo loved you till the end of time. Do anything for you, lay down her life, that sort of thing. Would Lisa do that? Would Lisa *lay down her life*? Mo blamed Lisa for leading you into drugs. Mo blamed Lisa for leading Rod into smack. Her reasoning being, if Lisa hadn't took me away, Rod would of been surfing more with me and the way she saw it, me and Rod was always gunna be the same two harmless mischief-makers we were as kids, and if it wasn't turning out that way that wasn't Rod's fault or my fault or the fault of us both growing up a tiny bit different from each other, but Lisa's fault.

Lisa might as well of plugged it into Rod's arm herself. Far as Mo was concerned.

Lisa was ropable. One night while we're lying in bed she goes off:

You know, it's good that I'm so convenient for your mother.

How so? I was falling asleep.

I come in handy for lots of things.

Eh?

Like diverting the blame. Like she can blame me, by whatever reasoning she can work out, for Rod being on smack. Which makes it easy for her to forget what she's *done to Rod.*

What she's done?

Oh, Den, you don't see it, do you?

Lisa held my face in her hands and tried to read me like she was looking at this music score sheet for the fiftieth time for some note that wasn't there, and she couldn't believe that no matter how many times she read it it still wasn't there.

Oh my love, you just don't see it eh.

Then Lisa's sister come up to stay a night. Like sent up as a spy by the Mr and the Mrs Exmire. But before she even got through the front door she was having a fainting fit seeing what her sister had landed in: you looking like the Wild Man of Borneo, Lisa wandering round with her guitar round her neck and a head full of mushies, Rod bombed out to Black Sabbath, a bunch of groms covered in fibreglass dust, Basil running round like a feral hunting dog, and somewhere among this Mo storming round in her pale floral house dress looking for someone to tell her why the garden hose wasn't reaching her flowerbeds at the back fence no more.

And then there was the graveyard. You saw how this bird saw all the tombstones and whatnot, ticking over in her head, haunted house and all that, zombies and undead, and she's freaked as a bunch of bananas before she's took two steps into Saga.

Late that night, you was down the rat cellar with your sander full bore when you heard the screaming and that.

Lisa all over again.

Her sister crying and whimpering about ghosts, something in the sleepout stroking her hair, she was sure it was there but when she turned on the lights there was nothing.

Lisa didn't say nothing. She didn't want the cops, they'd drag her home.

Mo tut-tutted about these girls waking her up.

Rod was out of his room in his undies.

He looked at you.

You didn't look at him. You had your aviators on. Pushed them up me nose. Still there.

The sister reported back home. We lived in a haunted house in a graveyard, that was all the Exmires needed to know. We never heard a peep from the Mr and the Mrs.

THE THING PT 1

I don't never sleep in, not since I was fifteen and found out what the dawn had for me. Never even if I was up all night doing who knows what, that type of thing. If I was up till dawn, I'd be up at dawn. If need be, cut out the middleman: sleep.

Mo never sleeps in, not since she was a kid and found out what the night had for her. Never even if she was in bed early and tuckered out after raising her children all on her own, that type of thing. If she was up and down all night, she still couldn't sleep in. If need be, cut out the doctor: sleep.

We was up at the same time now.

My eye: yellow.

My eye from the inside: yellow.

Me and me Mo, surfing buddies.

The old lady with her white hair brushing the droopy vinyl ceiling of the Sandman panel van sprayed purple and orange. Her oversize boy, fifty-eight years and eighteen stone packed into the seat beside her. Not a panel of vinyl in the car without a crack in it. His gun down the middle: no second, no fourth. First and third only.

. . . out the toy roundabouts, over the causeway, out The Other Side, down the dirt track, up the dunes to the secret spot . . .

Watch that mouth there . . .

First and third only.

Surfing buddies.

In her pale floral house dress. Green, pink, yellow, grey, blue. All the pastels of the rainbow.

And now, this one morning: The Thing.

She been up during the night. Over the voices of National Public Radio and BBC World Service I heard her. Through the voices. Under the voices. Round the sides of the voices.

Stood there in sleeping boardies, sleeping T-shirt, scratching me head. Pushed up the aviators (still there).

Looking at it. Looking away from it. Looking back at it. Can't help looking. Squeezed in the living room of this place, crossing six or seven different diagonals, all wrong, wrong and evil, wrong and crossed.

Yellow, white, black. Disgusting, evil, abomination.

What?

What??

Mo beside it, in its shadow, pretending it wasn't her that got it for me.

Mo, she'd do anything for me.

Even insult me.

Even break me heart.

Don't say nothing. Can't say nothing. What can I?

My Mo loves me.

Here's what she's got for me. These things cost a grand. Unless she got a deal. But she could only have got a deal if she . . .

No.

The Thing.

Her red eyes about to drip onto her house dress.

She looks at me with a question, the only question:

Ready to go then love?

I need a bowl of muesli.

WINNING

Nineteen seventy-one. Nineteen seventy-two. You liked them years, the shape of the numbers.

DK: the Gold Coast's newest tourist attraction.

They come to Coolie to buy your boards, your boardshorts, your imported shirts. You used the till as your personal bank. Soon as it come in you took it out. You paid the glassers in hemp seeds: something to invest for the future. Doing them a favour: you'd paid in coin, they spend it.

They come to Coolie to scope you surf. They sit on their boards in the channel and scoped you. They got out your way and sit on the black granite to scope you.

Hawaiians come to Coolangatta airport and the taxi drivers looked at their boards and said:

Surfer are ya?

Sure, brah.

We got a surfer. Dennis Keith. Heard of him? Course ya have eh.

I'm surfing in the pro-am, brah.

Course y'are. He'd smack yer bum, mate. But he couldn't be buggered going in the comp eh!

To the Hawaiian gods . . .

Birds come up to you, fell to pieces. Not taking the mickey no more. If they ever had been.

You hugging the corner sucking a lemonade wishing you wasn't there. In your fancy velour suit and frilled white shirt. Bad dress sense again DK. You had no idea. Didn't want nobody to see you, wanted to run and run, but instead:

Are you really Dennis Keith do you stand up on the wave or inside it are you on the water or under it are you scared of sharks does it hurt if you fall off my brother is in love with you can you sign my tummy what are you doing after is it really that fun do you think I should try it?

Well yeah . . . but no.

Rod'd turned Saga into this all-time surf hostel. During cyclone season there was nights thirty surfers sleeping in the Queenslander, in the rat cellar, in the yard. Sixty boards lying round. Plenty of pickings for the early bird, first up, took your choice. Nobody argued.

Rod set the house rules. House *rule*:

No rent but clean up after yous.

Lisa set the other house rule:

DK is God.

The Keiths Surf Boards shop was going gangbusters though management was a challenge. You leave instructions for the shapers written with your fingertip in the wood dust on the walls. When bills come you thought they was fan letters and threw them out. When the supplier turned up you paid him in cash or dope.

But you wasn't a businessman, no matter how successful. DK was a surfer. Lisa said you DK was ready to have another crack. At comps. Surfing was dying without you, she said. They were aching for you. Begging for you. They were talking about a genuine world surfing tour, Australia, California, Hawaii. You been the outlaw two years, doing your own thing, thumbing your nose at them.

Now they caught up with you. They needed you.

Pure natural genius eh. Lisa's words, not yours. *They can't carry on a world surfing championship without the world's best surfer.*

You'd won. The pair of you, you and Lisa. Before you strapped on your leg rope for your first heat of your first event you'd already won.

You had a letter inviting you to the Queensland Open, then the Aussie Open down in Sydney. Then Huntington Beach for the US Open.

You hadn't done nothing to deserve it except ignore them.

You hadn't done nothing except surfed on another planet, Planet Keith.

You'd won.

You'd lost the lot.

Your first start was '72 Queensland Open titles, up the road at Burleigh.

Their break.

The northerners. All in there, as well as you and the Coolie kids: FJ, Townend, Peterson, the rest.

The prize was a $150 money order for a menswear store.

Northerners, Hawaiians, Californians, all there for a good time. They didn't know how to value winning. They didn't know you done a thousand club comps school comps comps with Rod states under-ages nationals under-ages trials pro-ams comps comps comps in your head . . .

Yeah they didn't know that for DK, even when he was sitting on the sidelines refusing to go up before the judges, every single surf session was a fricken *conness*. They didn't know DK could suck all the energy out of any wave, no matter how small or scrappy or big and hollow, any wave, and turn into a mad cyclone of energy wild as the ocean itself. Destructive and unbeatable yeah but

but you can't

nah

yeah

he could be in the water with a retired carpenter, two groms and a girl, and all he wanted was to smash them into submission.

What they never understood was, the ocean itself was into competition.

Nobody within a bull's roar.

Long right-handers. Your bread and butter, your face to the wave, you dropped into the pit and wrote your signature on good-size Burleigh. Into the pit, up on the lip, roundhouse cutback, down again, chop the hands, build up speed, through the next section, up on the lip, hack a big bucket of spray out of it, drop down again . . .

. . . yeah . . .

They didn't know what hit them. Except the ones that did. Frank Johnson and Michael Peterson in the final heat but in your wake, carry you up the beach on their shoulders. Local newspapers snapping away. You pull a stink-eye. Didn't like them photographers.

At the preso, Nat Young walked out of a poster on your bedroom wall and give you the trophy. Nat was up from New South to scope you. Handed you your money in a white envelope. It had a bulge in it.

Nat hadn't entered the conness. It was beneath him. Like only the plebs, only the scumbags would worry about something as warty and working class as *competing*.

Would of killed him for that too.

A bunch of Coolie boys was there in the crowd. Nat was making some kind of political speech, urging revolution or whatnot, and halfway through the boys started chanting:

DK! DK! DK!

Shouting down the best surfer in Australian history.

Gary Trounson going off his head. Father Aplin, wearing a new style of Mexican wedding shirt you hadn't seen before, and baggy corduroy pants. Always ahead of the curve, Father A. More traditionally turned out in singlets and stubbies: the butchers, the plumbers, the newsagents. Was one of them that yelled out:

Just get out the way and give him his trophy, Young!

One of them that yelled out:

Your day's over, Young! DK's gotcha!

Nat Young, The Animal, handed over the mike.

DK mumbled: *Yeah thanks . . . yeah . . . And, um, yeah.*

Coolie mob went bananas.

Lisa up the back, slow handclapping above her head. Like she was at a concert. Hearing the music you were playing.

Dimple deep as a low C. Bangles tinkling on her wrists.

All the boys went down the pubs, the clubs, to celebrate. Got on the whiz, on the gear.

You went home with Lisa and sat in your room and pulled C-1s. Deep Purple, Hendrix, Santana instrumentals.

You didn't mess round or nothing. You just sat and pulled C-1s and listened to music. Posters of Nat Young and Hawaiian waves on your wall.

Celebration.

Then down to Sydney, the nationals. Rod shown up again from wherever he been. Bas with him, pretty emaciated these days, more the junkie dog. Bas reckoned he'd been onto a good thing hanging with Rod— some buddy who'd feed him and ferry him round and entertain him and do all his chores for him. Bas thought he swung it sweet but then he didn't figure on Rod's other mate, the one in the bag, moving in as well.

Rod had the idea he was gunna get a wildcard in the nationals. Threw a few sticks in the back of the van and hit the road:

You, Rod, Lisa.

Bas, snarly embittered bastard. One night on the road he found your dope and tried to eat it all. You got the bag in the nick of.

You never remembered nothing much of that trip cept packing C-1s, punching C-1s, passing out in the back, waking up when Rod found a wave. Then more C-1s.

He was keen to get out and hit a wave. Him and you, leave Lisa on shore.

Nice waves.

Rod surfed on smack. He kept pushing it at you but you wouldn't touch the stuff.

Rod took your wave. You got the next one, a bigger one, and you was deep inside the barrel. It still had a way to run but you saw Rod paddling out so you fell back and slingshotted your stick straight at his head.

Just missed.

Rod cacking himself when you paddled back out.

Can't believe you were inside a barrel but still had to kick your board at me, he cackled.

Priorities, you said.

Rod paddled off, laughing, shaking his head that you give up a barrel to try to hurt him.

He didn't take no more of your waves.

You camped. Lisa cooked: fried eggs on the open fire, toasted marshmallows, billy tea. After dinner, Rod take a shot and you and Lisa smoked C-1s. Bas passed out in the crook of Rod's arm. Lisa slung on her guitar and played you her sweet tunes. The brother and the dog snoring, the girl singing.

She brought you a big hessian sack which she filled with your muesli. In case you couldn't get it in New South.

You wrote postcards to Mo. Yous were living that Life eh.

Sydney, early summer '72:

Rod driving and hooting, stoned. You with your head out the window, stoned. Down the Pacific Highway, your first time in the big smoke: big houses, trees, hills and dales. Car yards and petrol stations like at home only bigger here, more English than American, that sort of thing

no words for it but

perfect day, sunny and a few clouds to stop the sky getting boring. Cooler than home and more geography here. You turned down the Mona Vale Road, big up-themself houses and big up-themself people, pale ones in European clothes, suits in summer, not like Queenslanders, where are all the shorts and sandals eh!

Then into the bush and glimpses of the sea.

You needed to stop and do a poo in the scrub. Your stomach buzzing loud no matter how many C-1s.

Then a last dip down the hill and you were there, that other Mecca: Sydney's northern beaches.

You stopped and looked at Mona Vale. Rod turned north. You stopped and looked at Bungan. You stopped and looked at Newport. You stopped and looked at Bilgola. You stopped and looked at Avalon. You stopped and looked at Whale. You stopped and looked at Palm. You stopped and looked at North Palm.

On the way back you stopped and looked at all of them again.

Worried: there was loads of beach breaks here, not a string of right-handed points like home. They was more like D-Bah, with peaky rights and lefts. Where the nationals were being held, North Narrabeen, had you worried enough already: a left-hander. Surfing with your back to the wave, you was never as comfortable. Sydney had more lefts than rights. All the locals down here, probably half of them goofy-footers, at home in the lefts, they'd have a good crack at you at North Narra.

You stopped and looked at Warriewood. You stopped and looked at Little Narra.

Then down between a caravan park and a big open paddock, over a little lagoon bridge, up the hump into the carpark, and there it was, most famous break in Sydney: Northy.

Four foot and clean and about thirty goofy-footers tearing it up. Mirror images of DK. No longboard cruisers here. They were surfing vertical: into the pit, up on the lip, turning their little toothpicks on a sixpence.

They'd caught up with you all right.

You went in the surf club and took another poo.

Lisa lined up your accommodation, a wooden house on the lagoon with one of the North Narra animals who been up the Goldie the last year. You dug them boys and they dug you. Of all the blow-ins up at Coolie, the Northy boys understood respect. They got out the water or sat in the channel while you DK was there. They wanted to look and learn.

As a show of mutual respect you paddled out and sit in the channel and give them a few waves.

Only a few mind.

That sort of thing.

This guy who had the wooden house, Brian Giblet, was one of the better surfers. Wore a Mexican wedding shirt like the one you seen Father A in. You'd have to start stocking them. And on his feet, Slaps with black velour straps. Nice. Loved his rum and whisky, Brian. Wouldn't touch your hooch, though he was cool with you punching C-1s on his balcony. He'd knock back rums all night and you and Lisa punch C-1s. Rod sneak to the downstairs toilet and have his fix, then come back up and dance while Lisa strummed.

Brian played along with her on his baby grand piano.

Reckon ya can beat us on our lefts? Brian said.

There was challenge in his voice. And rum. Something cocky about him: Sydney.

On home turf they was always different.

This was three am the night before the first round of the nationals.

You decided you didn't like Brian so much now.

You nudged him off the piano stool.

Ever played before? he said.

You shook your head and sit down. You been listening to Lisa for more than two years, you knew music, and like she always told you, you were pure natural genius. Mo said so too.

You pushed your aviators up the bridge of your nose (still there). Your moustache twitched.

You started playing. Just like that. Improv. Lisa picked up what you were doing and tuned in with her guitar and soon the pair of you were jamming like Cleo Laine and John Fricken Dankworth, Lisa even singing, making it up as she went, about how you were going to smash them next day at North Narra.

Finally you found a way to end it.

Brian, sitting pissed on his big brown beaten-up leather couch.

Yeah right, he said. A fresh rum and Coke in his hand. *Never played before.*

And he's hardly surfed no lefts either, said Rod, *but he's still gunna fuck yers all tomorrow.*

That night was special with you and Lisa. Her glazed eyes in yours as you lay on a cane lounge in Brian Giblet's sleepout. Mozzie mesh waving in the breeze. Offshores tomorrow, sweet.

Lisa didn't need to ask how you learnt to play piano just like that. She knew already:

Pure natural genius.

I want to stop time now, she said, curling up against you. *I want the world to end.*

And found a place between your arm and your rib.

Bigger money in this conness, about five grand all up. There'd been talk about the legends, Nat and Midget, making a comeback, but Nat pulled out on the morning saying he done his groin and Midget had to fly out to Hawaii. It still left Terry Fitzgerald, Paul Neilsen, FJ, Townend, Bartholomew, Peter Drouyn, some good surfers up from Victoria and WA, and about fifty goofies from Narra and Queenscliff and Maroubra. Surfing in Australia never been stronger than 1972.

Everyone talking about this new govt they had, Labor Party after twenty-three years. You didn't know about that. You weren't political or nothing.

Rod didn't get his wildcard but surfed the trials in six-footers, and cos it was big you went out as his caddy with his spare board. He was going all right. You sat there out the back, watched him ripping. He paddle back out, stoked. He might make it through to the conness proper.

But his leash was made out of a bike inner tube with a football sock as the ankle strap, you rigged it up for him, and it snapped and he lost his stick. He took ages to swim out the back to you, and when he got there, he was unlucky, very unlucky cos a huge beautiful set come in and you been sitting there for half an hour *dying*, watching them perfect waves, and you couldn't resist it no more, DK got on this massive left and was carving . . . then went down the beach and got a few more . . . and Roddy couldn't find you to give him his spare. Unlucky to get eliminated in the trials, he was.

You paddled out in your first heat of the main conness and ripped. Your back to the wave, you dropped in the pit, leant back and accelerated up on the lip. Tossed up big rooster tails of spray. Carved out big sheets on your bottom turns.

Then you pulled a swifty on them, something you only tried while you were putzing round in practice, never in a comp:

You switch-footed. You got up with your left foot at the tail, no leash, and your right foot forward. You carved the left-hander with your *face* to the wave, like a goofy-footer. You could hear yourself laughing in the middle of you. Nobody knew you could surf both feet, natural or goofy. Nobody ever seen such a thing in a national open.

Then, your next wave, just for fun, you moved your feet into a side-by-side parallel, like you were skiing. Crouched down like you had poles tucked under your arms. How hot were you, son . . .

Yeah . . .

Absolutely gutted the others in your heat. None of them'd surf any good in that comp after this.

Gutted the whole surfing world. Half the professionals out there decided to give up, in their hearts, that day.

The 'official area' was a nylon tent and a hamburger barbie up in the North Narra car park. A reporter was there, for Sydney radio, and bunged his microphone under your moustache and asked you a question, like, how had you done it, that type of thing.

Lisa handed you your aviators. You pushed them up on your nose.

I am the new govt, you said.

You were only just out of teenage, 22 years old, but you had deep lines horizontal across your forehead. You'd worn them in with the muscles in your forehead pulling your eyes open. *Keeping you awake are we?* You looked ten years older. Fifteen. Lisa said: *Like an incredibly hot 35-year-old*. She loved it. Made her feel grown-up.

The birds, the birds, the deep lines across your forehead.

The semifinals was later in the day in onshore mid-afternoon muck. You ripped again, straight in the final. Switch-footing, mesmerising them. Then the wind dropped and there was a new nor'-east swell. Perfecto for the final. You disappeared down Brian Giblet's place to smoke a C-1 with Lisa, so you didn't know what was going on up the beach.

When you walked back on cloud nine, everyone was crowded round watching the sea.

The swell had cleaned up and the lines marched in. It was about seven pm. Couple of guys out free surfing before the final.

One tall figure with arms out like a vase, smooth, gliding, silky.

Who they were watching:

So much for the groin strain.

He was too big for competition, too big for the nationals.

Just when your time had come.

Your day's over, Young!

He hadn't forgot. He was just here to pull his local crowd.

You ignored him when he come up the sand. You were putting your singlet on for the final. You and Lisa wandered down the beach and had a last little number. When you come back, Nat was being mobbed and the three others in the final walking past him with goggle eyes.

Except for this one dark, wiry figure leaping about Nat like a fricken blowfly. As you got closer you saw how this goblin was giving Nat an earful. Nat was trying to keep up his regal air, above it all.

Didn't have the hair! Didn't have the guts to take on DK!

The dark guy cackling his head off. He was wearing boardshorts with a big hairy scrotum painted on them.

Nat paused like he was going to nut this gremlin but thought better of it and moved on, up through the crowd.

Ta bro.

•

DK's surfing in the final was described as ferocious and mind-bending. With his back to the wave he disappeared into barrels and when they thought he been eaten by the foamball, he shot out onto the ramp.

. . . yeah . . .

Then you took off goofy and blew them away.

You cleared the water. Two of the other guys in the four-man final injured themselves trying impossible moves to match you. The only one with you by the end was FJ, your old mate, also surfing out of his skin with his back to the wave.

The last few minutes of the Australian Open final, you and FJ just sat there in the water, not saying much, few words about how good the waves had been, FJ saying Sydney wasn't as bad as he thought, you saying it was a good day to be a Queenslander . . .

. . . yeah . . .

Nice moment. You didn't bother to catch last waves. FJ had conceded the final.

On the beach they started pulling down the judging platform and the scoreboard. Everyone was going home and you weren't even finished! Then someone on the megaphone said, *Dennis Keith, you're the winner, if you want to collect your two hundred in prize money you can come to my place later.*

You and FJ bellied in together on foam.

You got your trophy. You had the bird.

Your press conference was some bloke from the radio ringing you up at Brian Giblet's for a live interview:

Dennis, any comments on becoming Australian champion?

Well, yeah. You pushed the aviators up on your nose. They were there. *But—nah!*

The cheque was two hundred bucks. You put aside half for buying new blanks for shaping, half for Mo, half for a blowout with Lisa, half for Rod for petrol and food for Bas, and half for savings.

Something like that.

THE THING PT II

Been a week and I haven't asked Mo to take me out in her car. No more surfing buddies.

She shouldn't of got me The Thing.

Can't touch it can't look at it.

The diagonals in the living rooms of retirement village units are all screwy. I go with Mo to watch her play bingo with her mates. I listen to the radio while she has arf-tea. She shows you off in the dining hall, like there's some part of the last thirty years that got skipped by the record needle of her brain and she thinks her old biddies are meeting the best surfer in the world, her pride and joy.

Instead of what they're seeing.

But retirement villages are all about magic.

Illusions.

I'm the rabbit in Mo's hat.

Then it's home up the rail (don't grab it) and in the living room where The Thing is waiting for me and I make for the bedroom and listen to me radio.

The things in my bedroom, I try to look at them and forget about the other Thing.

Shelves of books. I dig books. *Zen and the Art of Motorcycle Maintenance.* *The Fountainhead. The Dice Man. The Doors of Perception. Steppenwolf. The I Ching. Hopscotch. The Betsy. Van Loon's Lives. The Warrior's Way.*

Don't you call me an uneducated man. It come late, it come with a curse, but by hell and damnation it did come.

No tables or chairs, just throw pillows and throw rugs, Indian fabrics, incense stinkers, ratty seagrass mat on the floor.

Colour TV.

Clock radio.

Shortwave radio.

Stereophonic record turntable, Sennheiser headphones.

Me posters.

Me trophies.

Bear trap outside the window.

A portable motion-detector alarm aimed at the door.

Don't you call me an uneducated man.

Can't stop thinking about it.

It won't fit in the Sandman. Sorry Mo.

Roof racks?

Everyone'll know. They'll see DK's panel van with a Thing on the roof. Sorry Mo.

Trailer?

Ditto.

Walk it down to Rainbow Bay? It's nice for learners there.

Ha fricken ha.

But:

Can't stop thinking about it.

In the slop, down the secret spot, windiest mushiest dirtiest days, when nobody else will be anywhere, the only days I'm game to go:

The Thing's the only board that'll ride.

That's why they invented Things.

For fatsos and beginners.

Fatso beginners.

It's the only thing that'll go. Only thing that'll bear my weight. Only thing that'll give me a ride.

The Thing.

Must of cost Mo six pension cheques.

Them Things cost a thousand bucks and this one looks new.

Sorry, Mo.

HB

Mo organised for the Australian champ to get his passport. Took weeks, cos there wasn't no birth certificate. Mo scored him a suitcase.

Mo packed his suitcase.

Mo got him to the airport.

Then you're on your own, son.

He missed his plane. Phoned Mo, she come and picked him up.

In the car:

You had one job, Dennis. One job.

Eh?

To check the time of your flight.

Next day, reissued ticket, Mo packed his suitcase.

Mo got him to the airport.

Too early this time:

Got the day wrong.

Phoned Mo, she come and picked him up. Didn't say nothing.

But:

Next day, Mo got him to the airport. He was crying like a baby, full nervo in the parking lot. The stress of it and he didn't want to be let go and she didn't want to let him go.

Waited with him till he went through immigration.

Saw the jetliner take off.

Didn't want to let him go, and inside the plane:

He didn't want to let her stay behind.

Lisa was already over there, waiting for you in California. Nineteen seventy-three. US Open, Huntington.

Lisa trying to score a record contract. You didn't want to think about what she had to do for that.

You were gunna tear them apart.

The hell of the flight. You didn't know how to work your light. You didn't know how to work your window. You didn't know how to eat your food.

You, not drinking, not passing out, not sleeping, not able to work your window.

Not safe off the surface of the earth.

Just add water.

A wreck when you arrived in LAX. A wreck when they piled you in a hire car driven by a Californian surfer in boardies and a bearskin coat. A wreck as you looked out the window in the middle of Los Angeles looking at fields of—

Oil wells pumpjacks pumping pumping heads up heads down demented woodpeckers, like this kid at school you remembered who could do nothing but sit in his chair and rock forward and back, forward and back, forward and back into his own lap. You were the only one in the class who wouldn't bark him out.

A wreck when they helped you out in the lobby of the Huntington Beach Travelodge.

The lobby swarming with surfers. You could tell from their shoulders. Surfer shoulders.

Surfers with their shoulders whooping it up, hitting the big time, America, California, time of their lives. Meeting old buddies in the lobby.

You feeling sick.

Man in a business suit standing next to you at the reception desk, saying:
I'd like to check out.
The hotel staffer: *Sir, but I don't believe you've checked in yet?*
That's right, thank you, I'm leaving. Who are these people anyway?
Sir—welcome to the 1973 US Open Championship of Surfing.
You'd of checked out with him. You pushed your aviators up so many times you wore a red hole in the bridge of your nose. You crept to the lift, up three floors and bolt down the corridor to your room.

Never been in a hotel room before.

•

Minibar. Room service. Television of your own. Sharing with FJ. His gear all stacked neat by his bed, in the shelves, hanging on the hangers.

You feeling sick.

You wondered where Lisa was. You been meant to meet her at LAX. You'd forgot. Now you remembered but it was too late.

You'd forgot everything.

Inside your room looking in the cupboards, in the bathroom, in the minibar:

For *her.*

There was this opening-night party. The Australian national surfing team was waiting for you in the lobby in green and gold Australian blazers looking like the Olympic Games march-past.

Terry Fitzgerald, Ian Cairns, Mark Richards, Peter Townend, Glenn Tinkler, Col Smith, Simon Anderson.

And Dennis Keith.

You'd changed into a suit Lisa bought you before she left:

Velour. Deep purple.

Never a finer group of Australian surfers:

TF, Ian Cairns, MR, PT, Kinky Tinky, Smithy, Simon.

And Dennis Keith.

Three future world champions.

And Dennis Keith.

They were rolling round the lobby laughing at you. These monkeys, these zoo animals in green-and-gold blazers were laughing at *you.*

Where's the team suit? TF said.

You didn't know about no team suit. You didn't know about teams full stop. This was surfing not rugby.

Yeah, Smithy drawled, making like drug-fucked, *but nah!*

You had him up against the wall hand clawed round his throat before he'd drawn breath. The others pulling you off him. In your deep purple velour suit. In their national blazers. And gold slacks. And white Panama hats. All ready for the opening ceremony.

•

After the official function you raced to your room but couldn't sleep, parties everywhere, walls banging, boys, birds. Still no Lisa. Putting you out of your misery a knock on the door:

DK?

You opened up.

You sweet mate?

Since when had Kinky Tinky started calling you DK? What was wrong with Dennis? What now, the bloodnut want you to call him *GT*?

Still in your velour suit. Standing at your hotel room door. Parties everywhere, walls banging, boys, birds.

Tink held out his hand in a bunch.

Welcome to America, DK.

You looked at his fist. He cracked the bunch. You looked at him. Pushed your aviators up.

Guess we should just blow it now, Tink said and come in.

You and he watched TV.

First taste of Mexican, he said. *Acapulco Gold. Not the worst thing you've ever done eh.*

Fully blasted, watching TV. Welcome to America, DK.

You looked at Tink.

So where's the party?

The stats would be quoted back at you over the years like it was your wave-by-wave score. Even the BFO reels them off:

Hotel guests for US Open Championship of Surfing: 154

Hotel capacity: 120

Value of towels stolen: $1000

Value of other hotel items stolen: $5000

Value of unaccounted minibar purchases written off: $10,000

Value of unauthorised room service charges: $3000

Number of six-ton Ford trucks driven into the lobby, demolishing six indoor plants and the guest services desk: 1

Number of swimming pools emptied after guests found doing the business in water: 2

Number of rooms gutted by fire: 3

Number of times Huntington Beach Travelodge would host a surfing championship again: 0

•

These days, like when the BFO gets hold of them, these kinds of numbers get a laugh, like something heroic, the gold old days, the wild days. But in the gold old wild days it was no joke.

Yous were a disgrace. Surfing was trying to get serious, get professional, and you and 153 others had turned the official hotel into a bomb site, a tip.

California police in and out. Trying to get statements, they got sucked into the parties.

Here pal, cop this for a statement. You handing a California policeman a big bunger. All or nothing.

You were portrayed as the leader.

You were never the leader.

You were the king.

Each morning you opened your hotel room door to a pile of joints, bags of dope and pills, condoms and board wax. Tink said people been coming all night to donate, help you get through the open. Apparently you been telling people you couldn't surf without 'medication'.

They're Americans, Tink said. *They don't get our sense of humour.*

You were on your knees scooping it all up.

Who says I was joking?

FJ, who hoped to beat you in a surfing event once in his life, had got himself transferred out of your room, so you were sharing with Tink now.

The jammy redhead been in hotels before. Course he had. These blokes went to hotels and motels and even hotel-motels on holidays with their parents. Tink showed you how the stuff worked. The showers, the doors, the alarm clock, the television, the radio, the room service, the minibar.

He showed you the way down to the pool.

The problem was what the problem always was when there was a problem:

No surf.

You'd read about Huntington Beach, the famous HB, Surf City USA. You'd read about it and heard talk about it and for now that was all you were going to learn about it, cos when you were there there was nothing to see.

Flat.

Huntington had this big long pier with concrete and rotten wood pylons. South was a chunky right-hander which sometimes went left direct under the pier. Guys were known to ride heavy waves through the maze of pylons and out the other side. North was a channel to paddle out and another wave that was wonky and sometimes sizey both ways.

Not a bad wave. Not that you'd of known. Sometimes at night you rush out on your balcony cos you thought you heard a wave breaking, but it was only cars dragging on the highway.

But HB wasn't about the wave. When it was breaking, the wave was as okay as about three hundred waves in Queensland.

What HB was about was the scene. And in '73, HB had more surf clothing and surfboard shops and hangers-on than you thought could exist in one shopping centre, more of The Life here than any place on earth.

You went into none of it. You didn't like shops.

There wasn't just surf shops. There was beer bars, tiki bars, a bikie joint called Club Tahiti that pumped out Black Sabbath and The Who, heaps of second-hand junk stores. Everything was for sale no matter how crap. There was duplex unit blocks and a whole lot of industrial-looking buildings that didn't have signs or names. There was tatt parlours, auto-repair shops, two-storey motels, always two-storey in a kind of L-shape around a car park, coated in this sick yellow peanut-butter stucco like God had spewed on them and nobody could wash it off. There was weedy vacant lots and alleyways running off the Coast Highway into dark corners. Here and there a crippled palm tree as convincing as plastic palms on a birthday cake. This Surf City was a long way from the good old Goldie.

The only normal ones was the Mexican fishermen who hung at the bottom of the pier. You could of talked to them, but you didn't cos you didn't ever talk to strangers. Mo said never do that. HB also had hippies and dropouts and acid heads who would paddle out when it was flat and dream they were scoring ten-second barrels. Didn't matter about the size of the wave, man.

They didn't even know there was an international surfing scene.

They didn't even know there was anywhere.

You didn't like hippies even though your hair was long.

You kept getting woke up by sirens, police sirens day and night, ambulance sirens, motorbikes motorbikes motorbikes howling up and down the highway strung between the Travelodge and the beach like a ring of barbed wire. Up at the north end where the waves were said to be all right sometimes, nobody never surfed: these were the hangs of the gangs from the inland empire, and nobody dared to go up there, they shoot you in the water for a laugh and not even the cops pull them up.

HB had a murder a night. When guys dropped in on the locals at HB, they come in to shore not to find their tyres slashed, like they might on the Goldie, or the fins snapped out of their boards. When guys dropped in on HB locals they came in to knives. There was graffiti on the walls and heavy bikie dudes in dark clubs up against the grey highway.

Some locals reckoned they'd bought themselves an extra five years of peace with their war tactics. Defence is attack. Attack is defence. Five years they didn't get overrun yet.

If HB wasn't your local and you still went there for a surf, they said you had to park your car right up on the boardwalk so you could see when someone was swiping your radio.

All too heavy for you.

When there was no surf in HB the surfers got bored and went the bikies.

When there was surf in HB the bikies got bored and went the hippies.

The US Open was always at HB and it drew thirty thousand. If they didn't like a result they flip cars and torch the judges' tent and go on a spree and smash the windows of the shops and loot loot loot.

That was HB, a hot stinking ugly concrete dune rancid with hate and boredom and no waves.

Even the sea smelt bad outside your window, no medicine from King Neptune here: instead, tar and car smoke. Horizon lit up at night with oil rigs.

So apart from one quick walk on your second night, darting through the smeary yellow light dribbling out the tatt shops and beer bar windows, terrified the bikies sitting in the garages might say something to you, you never left the Travelodge in two weeks of waiting for waves.

Inside the walls of the Travelodge it was worse.

Them American surfers, they got ideas in their heads. They always had to tell themself stories. They talked too much. Yapping, always yapping. And when you was there, yapping big yarns about DK.

The shrine of dope, Quaaludes, mushies, angel dust, they turned it into a ritual, built it and left it outside your door every morning. They showed a Super 8 movie of you doing Big Kirra. They'd went down to Australia to shoot Nat, and ended up shooting you.

You'd never known they were there.

They built you out of stories what you did at the hotel: how many times you surfed the pool on a cut-down Mal, how many times you skateboarded the car park hanging on the back of someone's van, how many times you banged some groupies in the jacuzzi, how many trips you took in one night, how many this, how many that, competing with each other to make DK into the biggest craziest wackiest mother that ever come by and none of it was true, none of it was you.

Here's what they were like:

You sneaked wasabi into their food, and when they ate it and their heads blew off they were stoked, cos DK had done it.

You slammed your door in their faces, and they were stoked, cos DK had done it.

This night when half the world tour was in your room and there was a bang at the door.

Police! Police, open up!

The story went that one top surfer flushed out an ounce of coke down your toilet. The story went that one top surfer who wouldn't think of dumping his ounce climbed out along a six-inch ledge and nearly killed himself getting to the next balcony. The story went that one top surfing official tried to flush himself down the toilet.

When the door opened, it wasn't police. It was some junior pulling a prank. His penalty was he had to carry everyone's boards to and from the beach when the conness started, and pull out in favour of an alternate who was in the room, and pay a couple of individuals a sum of money.

You didn't remember none of that. You remembered being stoned in a corner of all the parties with a lemonade you were pretending was a vodka. That's all you remember being: a pylon.

Still no surf.

Still no Lisa.

You wrote Mo postcards.

It possible to fall for someone cos of the way her head sits on her neck? One of the things about Lisa

I mean

you couldn't get it out of your brain the way her head was poised on her neck, centre of her balance, when she walked. Everything else swayed side to side, swinging hair, swaggering hips, rolling arms, but her head was just so fricken still.

Couldn't get over that.

You didn't do nothing with them groupies.

You go off with them for an hour and listen to them gabbing and then when they took a breath and said, *You wanna bang now?* you go, *Love, I'll give you this bag of whiz if you go back to your friends and tell them I was the best root in your life eh.*

Dunno why you did that. Spreading rumours.

But like they say, there was one thing worse than people talking about DK all the time.

People not.

So that was your action with the birds. Spend an hour listening to them, pay them off to spread stories. Crazy sometimes.

But still no waves.

No Lisa.

The Australian team got in some practice in their green and gold boardies. They went down the coast to Trestles and jagged some waves. You didn't go. You couldn't leave your hotel room without being mobbed. Them Americans.

You decided you didn't like Americans.

The Australian team come back to Huntington. There were boredom riots outside the Travelodge and Bolivian marching bands inside. Not a wave in sight.

You wrote postcards to Mo but never got them out your door.

You had postcards piled up beneath the ashtrays, the roaches, the mirrors, the wallpaper art, the dead dreams in your hotel room.

You never been in a hotel before.

That was all you wanted to tell her.

Then Lisa showed. Big smiles: Hollywood style. She cut a deal. CBS, EMI, A&E, R&B, R&D, OMG, something like that, you didn't get all the letters involved. She leapt on your neck and sucked the tongue out of you and locked you in your room for three more days. Your shrine piled up outside the door. Lisa went and raided it. She hadn't done no gear in her month in LA, she was hanging out for a party.

You didn't tell her you'd kept yourself nice for her.

She heard about everything you were meant to have done.

She didn't care.

You wanted to tell her they weren't true, the stories. But they were good for your image.

Lisa cared about your image.

So you let the stories ride.

She didn't care.

She brought her guitar and played for you in the middle of the night.

Her songs were bad now.

American songs. New ones.

She'd picked something up.

In Hollywood.

She had this shine in her eyes. She was gunna make it big. She wasn't her anymore. She was *Lisa Exmire*. And you were *DK*.

She had a vision.

The way she showed her dimple, it didn't come out by itself no more.

She made it come out when she wanted it. Her dimple was her performing seal.

She was going American on you.

You didn't like America. Too full-on that joint.

The day Lisa turned up there was waves. But you were jack of this place. You hadn't surfed since you been there and felt like rubbish the morning of the first heats.

You crossed the Coast Highway and nearly got cleaned up by a crew of bikies and a Mack truck.

You walked down the broken concrete steps to the sand and nearly tripped over with your board.

The Australian team screwed up. Tink, Simon Anderson, Terry Fitzgerald, Mark Richards—what a team. They been in the Travelodge too long. They screwed up.

All except FJ, who moved to another hotel. To get away from you.

Blond FJ, the golden boy, the corporate man, the clean liver, the kid with the home swimming pool, the one who knew to keep it together, the future world champion. FJ kept it together. He surfed like DK.

DK surfed like, like you don't know what you surfed like. You sat out in the line-up and looked at the pier and wondered what it was all about. You watched the thirty thousand on the shore and got scared. You tried to swallow but you'd forgot how your swallowing-muscle worked. You panicked. Lumpy four-footers rolled in and you hadn't wanted a wave so badly since you were born, but you couldn't get down on your chest and paddle. You just sat there and let them go through and let the Americans take them, trim them, waste them. Meanwhile you DK was sitting there out the back trying to remember how to get his throat to swallow.

What a waste.

Your US championship.

Screwed.

You had nothing in your belly, no buzzing, no calm, just nothing. Like you'd died. You weren't tired. You were light-headed. Like you'd floated away from this.

The hooter sounded for the end of the heat.

You saw the dot painting of thirty thousand faces, quiet.

You hadn't paddled for one wave. Your competitors had caught six or seven each, wasted them all.

DK sat there, they wrote, *like Mahatma Gandhi in non-violent protest.* Nobody knew what you was up to.

Then, just as the hooter went, a bomb set come through. You been sitting further out than anyone and now you were on the spot.

You saw the set and you swallowed.

Wait for number three. Lucky number. You picked off the third of the set. You took off late and dropped in the pit. You hooked the board right and hung on the rail with your left hand. You went into a crouch on a high line.

It closed down around you: deep dark green gut.

Deep dark green gut.

Where they can't see you.

Time stopped. So quiet in there. Nobody to see you. No Americans.

Five, six, seven seconds in the green fricken cathedral. Nobody else rode a tube all that week.

Five, six, seven weeks . . .

It spat you out and you ripped up the rest of the wave: cutback, into the foamball, out again, up for a hack on the lip, down the drop again, and another barrel, power on, power off . . .

. . . yeah . . .

You got two barrels on the one wave.

Then you paddled in.

Thirty thousand going bananas.

Big stink among the judges.

It wasn't that they judged you as being too late. They were all as stoned as the surfers, the judges were. They scored your wave.

Big stink was, two judges scored you a 20 out of 20—enough to get you through to the next round, seeing the guys in your heat had got nothing better than 6s and 7s in their scoring waves.

And the other three judges scored you 3s and 4s. Not enough points.

Huge stink. How could some judge score you a 20 and the bloke next to him score you a 3?

No worries about you being after the hooter. There'd of been a riot if they hadn't scored your wave.

But the three judges who scored you 3s and 4s:

They hadn't seen the two barrels. They saw you drop down in the first barrel and disappear and they figured you'd wiped out . . . and then they looked down at their pads and wrote the scores while you were inside barrel one, barrel two . . .

Huge stink.

DK was eliminated. No television footage, no instant replays, no proof that what the two 20/20 judges had seen was for real. The other three didn't believe them.

So there was a riot anyway.

•

Lisa rode with you in a limo out of there: HB burning behind you. The bikies, the hippies and the surfers all united, joined forces in protest.

Lisa's eyes shining. The fires of HB shone in the glaze of her eyes.

DK's done for them what nothing's ever done before, she said. *Given them a common cause.*

You looked out the back window: the Travelodge in flames, the judges' tent in flames, columns of grey smoke piling high into the blue California sky. All because three judges hadn't seen DK in his two barrels.

Common cause.

Since she come out of Hollywood, Lisa didn't call you Dennis anymore. Didn't even call you you. Now you were third person. You were *DK*.

You drove to the airport with a suitcase full of dope and postcards for Mo. When you got to LAX, Lisa kissed you and said she was taking the dope.

You didn't understand.

I'm coming back soon, she said.

You didn't get it.

Off you go! She nudged you with a smile bright as a golden globe. She wheeled out her dimple.

Then you realised her guitar wasn't in the limo. Or her suitcase. Or nothing. Just *your* stuff.

You got out the car in a daze, hadn't been paying attention. Now Lisa waving through the back window blowing kisses at her mighty DK. Her dimple gone professional.

You pushed your aviators up the bridge of your nose.

The rest of the Australian team was on your flight, except for FJ. Little blond rich boy snuck under your guard. While the beach burnt, while the town went up in flames, Frank Johnson was still surfing for the judges.

The new judges.

While you was on a plane home, the kid from Coolie won himself a US Open title.

The future world champion.

You were going to mess somebody up.

That type of thing.

INCOMMUNICADO

When you was still DK, that's the word they used for you when you was a pylon in the corner of the party:

Incommunicado.

Like you was the fricken Latin Pope or something.

A rattle at the aluminium security grille. Bad diagonals shaking all over the shop.

You holed up in your room. Turning up the radio. BBC World Service, NPR, Deutsche Welle Radio.

Block her out.

Mo at the shopping centre or up the bingo hall or in the dining room having her lunch or playing cards with a mate.

The Thing in the corner of the living room, cruelling the diagonals.

The BFO smashing down the security grille.

You in your room, hands mashed against your ears.

Your radio on maximum.

The BFO showing her true colours.

'I know you're in there, Dennis!'

Like she's the cops.

Incommunicado.

FJ

You come home to Kirra and Snapper and D-Bah and Rainbow and Greenmount, *where the US Open champion surfed.*

You hand-delivered Mo her postcards.

Rod been looking after Keiths Surf Boards while you was away. Rod and his white mate, Harry with the baggie pants. And Basil, Rod's gnarly offsider.

They always said you was a homicidal maniac in the first comps back after the US Open. This lunatic charging out of the bushes eyes the colour of fire. This wild animal who went out to tear Frank Johnson limb from bloody limb.

They always said.

They always do say.

But you weren't that fussed at first. Out on Greenmount headland, on the park bench that replaced the one you and Rod had burnt down with a bong-making exercise went wrong. You had your morning surf and was watching FJ with his snowy mop, walking up and down his longboard, dancing on the waves like he was doing the fricken tango, that sort of thing. Arching his back. Soul surfing. Judges still loved that crap.

There never was any such thing as soul surfing, or not by the early seventies.

Don't listen to what they say.

There'd been pop-out surfboard factories and Surf-O-Rama and shaping machines and Gidget and magazines and wetsuit models since before you surfed and they'd already burnt out, sold out, soul surfing nothing but a myth. Surfing was spoilt by 1960 let alone '73. All wrecked. The only pure surfing left, innocent surfing, golden age surfing, was in *you*, back when you was too young to know about all that other crap. The golden age of surfing is when you're twelve years old and the days last for fifty hours and every day the surf is glassy and huge and nobody else is out and you catch a hundred perfect rides in a session. It's when you see someone else carrying a board and you stop and ask them which break they're going to, and you get talking and you walk off to that break together. See the golden age is always happening to some twelve-year-old, then he wises up and surfing's all went commercial, it's overcrowded and it's ruined and he has to live the rest of his life pining for the good old days.

And when he sees someone else on the way to the beach with a board under their arm, he hopes they get run over by a car first.

Golden age bulldust.

You were still a bit rusted-on and ratty after all that Mexican weed and hadn't surfed good since you been back. Part of you was watching FJ and almost admiring him.

But then you felt someone sit next to you. Plonk down so heavy it half tilted the seat up, seesaw mudgeridoor.

Reckons he's the ducks nuts.

You pushed your aviators up your nose. They were there.

So was Mo.

Ever since he's back, he's giving radio interviews and filling newspaper pages and the whole bloody star of the show eh. Nearly as bad as when he saved that tourist.

You didn't say nothing. You had a headache that your post-surf number hadn't put out. Local weed wasn't doing the trick after all that Acapulco G. Have to have some shipped in.

Look at him in them pink boardshorts. Who's he reckon he is?

You didn't say nothing. You didn't say, *US Open champion Mo that's who he is.*

Mo kept digging at FJ. Not going off her head. Just whining next to you like a mozzie in your ear.

Digging at you.

Saying:

How he collected his press clippings in a scrapbook.

How he had photographs of himself blown up into posters and sold them.

How he had his own brand of T-shirts.

How he talked about himself as a 'professional'.

How up themself his folks were.

How he whipped you at HB.

How he never beaten you in one comp in Australia.

She didn't want you to match FJ: like make more money or go professional or collect your own fricken scrapbooks.

She wanted you to get out in the water and thump him.

So you did.

They talked about that morning for years: how it was better and bigger and longer at Kirra, but instead DK went out at Greenmount just cos FJ was there. FJ already had a crowd to watch his sleek rollercoasters.

And DK humiliated him. While FJ painted curves and curls into the waves, DK demolished them. When you'd done with a wave it was cut to pieces, a mess of busted lips.

You made him look like a kook.

His hands behind his back.

His toes on the nose.

You smashed him and the local grass wasn't even working for you no more.

But that was Mo: if there was one human on the earth who hated losing more than you did, it was her.

You surfed angry that season. The place changing. Too many new faces. Old faces gone. Not that you ever talked to them, but now they weren't there you were missing them.

Some tragedies: blokes who had to move away from the waves. Sometimes they got called up for national service, Vietnam, and that was that. Vietnam was still round them days. Yous never got drafted cos somehow Mo got you and Rod an exemption. Flat feet or family providers or what have you. Mo could scam pretty good when she needed to.

Sometimes blokes went to Vietnam and never surfed again—got ironed out by Cong. Or there was draft dodgers like Wayne Lynch, best surfer in the world before you come along, his ball dropped in the ballot and he disappeared into deepest darkest Vicco where he lived in a humpy and hid from the police inside fifteen-foot Southern Ocean barrels. Vietnam took him out of the equation, out of the line-up.

But most of them was everyday tragedies: blokes had wives, kids, couldn't work out how to get their surfs in. You felt sorry for them. Like they been kicked out of paradise. Responsibilities. You couldn't imagine it. Be like dying. Sure you appreciated one less body in the water meaning more waves for you but you didn't like seeing the old school drift away. They never guessed it but you liked familiar faces. Father Aplin, Mr Paterson. Both got involved in other responsibilities and couldn't fit their surfs in so much. Stopped worrying about missing big swells. Big hole in their lives. Kind of a hole in yours. You felt sorry for them. If it happened to you you'd kill yourself.

The problem was—the problem always is—no surf. They'd pumped sand from the Tweed out to Kirra Point and it stopped breaking. When there was no surf the soul of the place went black. Kirra Point never broke now, so the heart of the town did.

The Queensland police was coming down on what they saw as the druggie surfing culture. You didn't know what they were on about. All the surfers you knew were workers. Plumbers, butchers, teachers, newsagents, a priest. One or two board shapers. Honest working men.

But the Queensland police had it in their heads that surfies were drug-dealing drongo hippie dole-bludging dropouts. There was this big theory that the end of Kirra created a vacuum and all the smack dealers moved in. Which was rubbish. You wouldn't of tolerated hippies or drongos. No time for them at all. Or blow-ins from Briso or New South selling their gear. You could of maintained order right through the Gold Coast the way you maintained it on your wave. No sweat. But would they listen to you?

You should of been the new govt but instead they made you a target. Cops followed you round, not the Black Maria but unmarked cars, behind corners, sneaky sneaky. Parked across the road from your shop. Never advertised themself or give it away but you know they're there. You knew. You knew. They never broke down your door at four am like they did the others but you knew they was watching. You knew everything. That's what they didn't understand. You were in a surveillance drone like an Airfix model on the breezes high above, you circled looking down, looking down. They thought they was following you on your chopper to Bob's milk bar to the waves to Bob's milk bar to the shop to Bob's milk bar to the waves . . . but really you were following them, from high in the sky, your all-seeing eye.

Pure natural genius.

So even though you was the biggest target in a town of big targets, you were never busted. Never once. Or not yet.

FJ was, but. Which was very strange!

Frank Johnson, golden boy in pink boardies, US Open champion, who never smoked any substance, sat on one schooner of shandy all night, never put a foot out of line, wasn't even in the Huntington Travelodge, clean Frank, the operator, the commercial brain, the US Open champion:

Busted with a piece of buddha stick and a gram of hash in his locker at Snapper.

He said he had no idea how it got there.

That's what they all say.

You raised your eyebrow and pushed up your aviators and told everybody you were shocked, *shocked*, that FJ was a dope fiend, and you were sure, *sure*, that the cops had framed him up. But then again, you said, success does funny things to some people and FJ was now the US Open champion, wasn't he, so maybe, well, you said, maybe no, maybe yes.

You led the 'surfing delegation' to the courthouse and got thrown out for booing during the police evidence.

FJ got a six-month suspended sentence and a fine of $500.

With a criminal conviction he wouldn't be able to go to the US Open the next year.

Wouldn't be able to go to overseas legs of the brand new world championship of surfing they were talking about, starting that year.

He wouldn't be able to go to Hawaii.

You DK was *shocked*.

IN THE AGAVES

Sitting on Greenmount Hill. This seat gets replaced every year. Some kid always burns it down.

This place like an arena: you look down into Rainbow Bay and it's the same as the first times when you was a kid, just the blue shape of that bay with the yellow beach and the black rocks how perfect it is, waves hitting it just the right angle, all set up, and it must be the same as when a conductor looks at the orchestra before the first note or the coach and crowd looking down on the glowing green rectangle of a football field: all you can feel is the things that are about to happen. You can handle yourself here. This is your view where your happiness is.

Bury me here, Mr J-man, burn me up like them old benches, then bury me here, please Lord, if you have a last miserable scrap of mercy please do this one thing for me.

In the agaves.

Thinking about The Thing.

No Things out today: it's four foot and offshore and lining up nice. Local kids out there. They respect me. A kid drops into a clean sandy barrel from behind the lava rock and smokes six cutbacks before he's halfway through Rainbow Bay, and the same kid, sponsored by Quiksilver and Rip Curl and Billabong and all them others, the kid who's already piled up dollars and points on the endorsements and the junior pro circuit, this same kid, he's the one who'll come up to me later and all shy ask me to autograph his board.

What would he make of The Thing?

Can't do it to him.

Sitting on Greenmount Hill these days it's like watching a whole history of surfing: there's old kooks on longboards, noseriders in Okanuis, longhairs, kneelos, what they call them mini-Mals and hybrids and fishes, single fins, twin fins, thrusters, quad fins, five fins . . . blokes riding with their hands behind their backs and scratching their balls and tandeming with their dog or their girlfriend right through to fluoro wetties and rippers and flyers and stylers and what have you, kids with shaved heads and tatts in comp singlets. It left nothing behind, surfing: no fad ever died. There's even stand-up paddleboards out there, Hawaiian antikis, handcarved from wiliwili trees with v-bottoms. All the fashions, one after the other, all staying in the water, forever.

And they all leave behind them:
Nothing.
Nothing more than a cough.
Like every wave's an Etch-a-Sketch. Here it is, there it was. See yas later.
You can rip through a tube, cut back into it, blast out off the shoulder, and you look behind you and there's nothing left but the next bloke on the next wave. That's surfing. Free as air, free as water, you can't take it home and it produces nothing.
Freedom. Nothing. Freedom. Nothing.
Same diff.

In them days when I had all that coin, Rod trying to borrow a few hundred to score some smack, he'd go:
Ya know Den, ya can't take it with ya.
And I'd go:
Then I ain't goin.

Plenty hot little rippers out there today. None as good as me. None revolutionising the sport. Turning it inside out, upside down. None defying gravity.
They don't want to disappear in the barrel too long. They spend as much time flipping round in the air as they do on the wave. What they call these moves . . . what you put on a car, for the radio:
. . . yeah no . . .
They want everybody to see them: photograph them, put them in a magazine, pay them dollars to be a fricken model . . .
Kooks like FJ left a longer mark on the sport than I did.
Hits me hard, that.

These kids, the good ones, all want to be seen.

They don't just want to surf.

They want showbiz.

That's it:

Aerials.

Yeah and there's this one I been scoping a while: ripping. Sort of slower on the wave than the others, but smooth and graceful almost like a girl. Big arse. Easy paddling. Cocks his wrists when he turns like MR, the wounded seagull himself.

Then when he bellies into the sand and gets out and takes a shower and tucks his board under his arm and walks up the path past me, I see he is a bird.

'How's it going?'

She stops like I've caught her in the act.

'Oh, hi, Dennis.'

She stands dripping.

'You can surf eh,' I go.

She stares at the grass between us like she wants it to open up and swallow her.

'No sweat,' I go.

'I'm sorry,' she says, 'I meant to tell you I was in town but the waves were good today and . . .'

'No apologies eh.'

Half a smile and she goes:

'To you of all people.'

Push the aviators up my nose (still there).

'Me of all people eh.'

And so then we're there, her with her fat fishy little shortboard under her arm, me with my ankles crossed in front of me and my arms spread across the back of the bench.

My bench.

Me of all people/Tall people/Tall poppy/Pop-top/Chupa-Chup/Putt-putt/Lap-lap/Chop-chop/Tuk-tuk/Plucka-Duck/Fuck-Truck/FUCKHEAD!/FUCKHEAD!!/FUCKHEAD!!!/FUUUUUCKHEEEAAAAADDDD!!!!!!!

'You all right, Dennis?'

I'm wheezing now, me mouth flapping about, that was a bad rut just there FUCKHEAD couldn't get out of it, just say something say something DK—

'You know how good this wave used to be, before the sand?'

She doesn't make a move. She's staring at her feet so hard it's like she thinks even taking a breath will cut me short.

'When you were paddling into it you'd hear the thunder behind you FUCKHEAD where it was peaking and smashing on them rocks. You'd look round and see this thing like a cyclone chasing you. You'd stall, and tuck yourself into that barrel for dear life. FUCKHEAD! Every second you think it's gunna close out in front of you and smash you, but it's so fast it spits you down the line like you're a pea in a pea shooter. And it keeps on going, keeps on going, you can see right down the line, a hundred yards or two hundred yards and you know you've got all that wave to play with, goes forever. You can't help smiling, cos you've ridden it this size and in this swell before and you know it's gunna be more fun and more life than you can ever fit in one wave. And it goes forever. It's that good there's no word for it, love. That good eh. It keeps firing you down and you're thinking, this time it's gunna close over and smash you, you're too deep. But it doesn't. And then at the end of the wave where it sucks up on the beach it still fires you along, it's scary fast now, and you're still in it. Finally you get spat out on the shoulder and you can't believe it, you look back to where you started and it's gunna take you five minutes to stroke your way back to where you started, not cos the sweep's so bad, it's cos the wave took you so far. It went forever.'

And I'm feeling good, magnanimous today, and so I let her off her hook where she's dangling like a side of beef waiting to be sliced into steaks:

'You don't have any secrets from me, love.'

Her hair's hanging over her face, dripping down. She doesn't look up. But see, I know how she's feeling. She's just caught eight ripping waves down Rainbow through Greenmount. She may be acting all sheepish and shy, but I know, I remember.

She's on top of the world.

She's high as a kite.

Down, down, come down to earth, little birdie.

. . . yeah . . .

She goes:

'But not forever.'

'Eh?'

'The barrel at Kirra,' she goes. 'It didn't go forever. You thought it would but it didn't.'

Maybe she's wrong on that. Maybe I could take it with me. Maybe I never went.

'Spose so. Wanna come have a Splice?'

She comes along but with a pout.

Half of her's over the moon cos she ripped and I saw her.

Other half of her's pissed off at me for the same reason. Like there's more to her.

But she's got me wrong on that too. I don't care whether she's a good surfer or not. It means nothing to me. Never did mean nothing.

Wanna know what else she's got.

Fuckhead.

MR PRESIDENT

So FJ was a spent force. He might of been US Open champion by default but everyone in Coolie knew who was boss, and Coolie was what mattered.

You never got beaten fair in a club conness on the Goldie. Other blokes got their names on the clubhouse honour board, but only when there was some kind of fix in with the judges. Judges had to keep them interested. So there was bribes, conspiracies, blackmailings, frame-ups, all sorts of dodgy dealings. They made a full-time occupation of stopping you winning.

So you got yourself elected president of Kirra Boardriders. It was meant to be a culture clash between the 'professionals', the clean-cut serious surfers à la FJ, and the 'animals', led by yours truly, but the so-called professionals were on the nose after FJ's drug bust: everyone knew they were hypocrites.

Landslide.

You met in the Grand Hotel and there were blues every night, people throwing chairs and glassing each other, you never knew what that was about, being a non-violent individual yourself. You just stayed in the corner behind your aviators and lemonade.

Order.

As president you brought in membership cards for admission to the surf. Roddy had them printed out and laminated and handed out. They doubled as parking passes if necessary. There had to be a hierarchy. Some of the boys would go up to strange faces in the waves and ask for their membership cards. There was fights. Some said the surf is free. All that rubbish. So they cop a board in the head. Simple. Surf isn't free. Surf needs order and civilisation and etiquette. A pecking order that everyone obeyed. With you at the top.

•

It fell apart cos Tink became club champion. Yeah Tink, Tink, Tink, somehow he sneaked a win. It went flat in the final at D-Bah and you never saw him over near the breakwater sneaking some tiddly rights.

Unlike FJ, Tink was a real surfer. The redhead had learnt at your knee. Every time you created a new move, a new type of turn, found a new take-off spot, Tink be out there practising it. You couldn't keep no secrets from Tink. Little Tink. Now one of the men.

When they announced the points—Tink first, you second, Tom Peterson third, Peter Townend fourth—you pushed the aviators right up your nose till they were stuck in your forehead and you jumped up on the podium and grabbed the trophy in your capacity as club president and said:

Little Tink's the winner, come on everybody, give him a cheer, little Tink, he's the best surfer in the club, yeah yeah yeah!

And the boys were all cacking themselves and but nervous, they didn't know what'll happen next, and Tink looking like he was dying, so to put them out of their misery you went:

Yeah and yous'll have to find yourselves a new president cos this one's retired! Gawd save the Queen!

And you chucked the trophy down at Tink and he dropped it on the sand and they still talk to this day about you ripping up D-Bah lefts that afternoon.

You only become president cos it meant you didn't have to pay annual club fees anyway.

Trying to fill your head with *not-her*.

So this was the first year of the world tour, cooked up between some self-promoters and clothes makers. You didn't give it much time till you saw fifteen hundred bucks a conness and so that might be worth a dip.

Liked coin.

Genius with numbers.

First world tour event was Bells in August. Mid-bloody-winter. You piled in the van with Rod and Bas and wrote out a big graph with all the moves and points on it. World tour had this new scoring system, *objective*, points per move, so you wouldn't get crimes like HB where one judge sat there with a three-paper bunger under his belt and he saw Rudolf Bloody Nureyev when the judge next to him is seeing Deputy

Dawg. Most of the time you were so much better than anybody else not even a blind judge could stop you winning. But now you had a world title to compete for, they had to get serious.

You sticky-taped the scoring code to the windscreen and memorised it on the drive. When you got to Bells Roddy invited blokes for a C-1 at the van. Made sure they all saw your chart on the windscreen. They left defeated. If DK was doing it this scientific, what hope did they have?

Not that it all went to plan. A storm swell gave you ten-foot onshore bumpy Antarctic lumps and the board you used was undergunned, too short. You were bounced around, board chattering and jittering, and couldn't work your turns. You were flying too fast, airborne. Meanwhile Midget Farrelly, who was coming back for the fifteen hundred smackers, was leading after two rounds.

On the Saturday night you got Rod to run you into Torquay. You broke into the shaping shed of a mate of Rod's and spent the whole night working on a new board: longer, a heavier big-wave gun.

Rod sat on the floor smacked out of his head. Bas next to him. Two of them breathing fibreglass dust.

Next day you took your gun out and it was even bigger and bumpier. Midget had come down with flu and you ripped them to shreds, nobody seen nothing like it at Bells.

It was freezing and grey and rainy and the opposite of the Goldie. You hated Vicco but had to show them you could do it away from home.

Show them all.

She might turn up. She did last time.

There was a food fight at the preso. You didn't throw food. You stashed a hamburger in your pocket, didn't find it for three days, ate it stoned when it was covered in mould and lint, then went down with food poisoning.

At Torquay you got a cheque for fifteen hundred bucks.

At the preso the interviewer asked you how you managed to pull off so many moves, and you went:

I zigged and zagged between my zigs and zags.
Cracked them up.

But this was Bells, this was Victoria, Easter '74, this was rainy and grey and squally and horrible and all you could think was:

No Lisa.

You looked through the crowd and you were the Australian champion and leading the race for the world title and you looked through the crowd and you looked through the crowd and:

Yeah still no Lisa—
    been there last time.

Wasn't just the way her head sat on her neck like it was perfectly happy right there where it was, didn't want to be nowhere else in the world. More than that
    it's just
    nah
    she liked you I mean yeah love in it too, but she *liked* you. Nobody else ever did. Cept maybe Mo.
    Could live with her, couldn't live without her.

Rod took an advance of one hundred, for petrol money and dog food he said, but went to St Kilda with Bas and you didn't see them again. You had to get the train all the way to Sydney then up the coast.

Still no Lisa.

The Pit got burnt down that year, nobody knew who done it.
    And nobody knew who replaced the old

BE PREPARED TO FIGHT

sign with:

DK RULES

•

But still no Lisa. Ranked world number one and your heart in pieces in your chest.

I KNOW YOU'RE NOT MY BFO

'I know you're not my BFO.'

'Your what?'

'My Bi Fricken Ographer.'

A hand to her mouth, stuffing her giggle back in.

'Sorry. That's funny.'

We're at Bob's milk bar. Kids walk past and when they see me they go, 'Yeeuuwww!' and flash the Hawaiian two-finger horn.

'When they see you it's like they've seen a massive set wave coming,' she goes.

'Filling up the horizon.'

'Yeah. Filling up the horizon.'

I take a bite of pine-lime Splice.

'You're a phony,' I go.

'What?' She's acting ashamed, but her shoulders are twitching, her legs are twitching, her mind's still out there in those slippery four-foot runners . . .

Fuckhead. But calm down, don't go back there.

Yeah . . .

'It's cos of the coin.'

'The coin?'

Now she's looking at me. Now she's forgot her last two hours of bliss. Now she knows she's been caught.

'How I know you're not my BFO.'

'I don't follow.'

'Yeah you do.'

Cagey now, she is. Her moonface and brown shoulders. Black halter-neck top, wraparound sarong skirt. She's having a Golden Gaytime.

'Biographers don't have hundreds of bucks to chuck around as bribes.'

'Yeah?'

'Yeah.'

We eat our ice creams. I sign an autograph. A bomb set comes in. All these kids, they're ripping these days. Not a wave goes unridden. Nothing gets wasted. I should be proud of them. They're me legacy: these masses of kids who could of shat all over FJ, Tink, Mark Richards, Terry Fitzgerald, Ian Cairns. Could of shat all over all of them bar one.

Bar DK.

'So what am I then?'

She reckons she's playing me. Flirting. But DK seen this before. DK been played before. Like a guitar.

'That's for you to know and me to find out.'

She laughs again. You know that laugh.

You watch the kids shredding every wave off Snapper Rocks down the Superbank. Super Bloody Bank.

Nothing wasted. The crowds! Be careful what you wish for.

'DK would have eaten them alive,' she says.

'Ya reckon ya can read me mind?' I poke a finger at her.

Then just as she's looking shaky DK flashes her half a grin and holds out the licked end of his pine-lime Splice stick.

'This what ya came for?' I go.

Her brow furrows.

'I knew ya from the start,' I go.

She looks at the wooden stick I'm holding out. She takes it in her fingers. In Coolangatta, you do what DK says. Even if you don't know what to do next.

'That's all they need these days eh?' I nod at the stick. 'I've heard all about these tests on the radio. DN Fricken A, that sort of thing.'

Fricken A right!

She looks at the stick like it's going to tell her, like a preg test stick.

'That's what you came for, isn't it love? What it's all about? DN fricken A right! Right?'

And she sits there staring at it and what's wrong with you you're feeling sorry for her you put her on the spot and so—

'Yeah you're right it doesn't mean nothing,' you go. 'All of it.' With half a heart you wave your hand at the ocean. Dismiss it.

She don't speak.

'Spend twenty years thinking you're surfing but really you're on your feet, on a wave, for what, add it all up, all them waves, years and years of them, and what do they add up to, one hour? Hour and a half? All that hoo-ha, all that life and purpose, for five seconds at a time? Ten seconds in a tube? Yeah you're right love, add it all up it boils down to nothing, and you try to tell someone about it and who cares eh. It's like telling them about a dream you had, it's got no story, no human interest, who cares. You're right. Waste of a life, yeah, and for what.'

She's staring at the Splice stick. A flashing line from her face. Spot of wet on her knee. No tears, love. Not for DK.

Shaking her head now.

'I never said that.'

Looks up at me.

—*yeah but you thought it.*

'I never said that, Dennis. Never even thought it.'

WORLD AT HOME

Nineteen seventy-four. Watergate: you didn't know much about that, thought it was some new kind of wave park.

The world surfing tour had nine rounds: three in Australia, three in California, three in Hawaii. After Bells, the next Australian leg was Margaret River.

You'd never been to the wild west. All you could think about when you flew to Perth with your prize money (most of the other boys were stretching the Nullarbor in kombi vans, so long, suckers) was *sharks*. Southern Indian Ocean was seventy percent sharks. You were so nervous you dropped a tab of acid to tide you over the five-hour flight. You got picked up by a world tour sponsor's car and driven the four hours south to Margs. You dropped another tab to make the drive interesting. You had the jitters. You had the boogie-woogies. Every time you glimpsed the water you saw a great white. It was whitecapping with whites. Freaked you out.

The swell at the river mouth was everything it was cracked up to be: twelve foot on a big meaty A-frame, faster on the right. You looked down on it from the embankment, saw sharks.

You'd shaped a board, a gift, for Tink. Poor little redhead, he copped it from you over the years. His eyes were teary when you handed it to him: a lightning-fast six-footer. You were on a much longer, heavier eight-footer and with a tab of acid to quiet your worries about the great whites, you smashed him in the first round.

In the semifinal you thought you were surfing waves *with* the sharks.

In the final you thought you *were* a shark.

Two rounds, two wins. The Americans, the Hawaiians were in awe. This was the DK they heard about. Forget Huntington. Tink was blueing over his board.

The lengths you go to.

Nobody listening to him.

DK two rounds, two wins.

Third round was back home, Kirra the week after Christmas. Cyclone season. After a year dormant the Big Groyne was breaking. It needed fifteen foot of nor'-east swell, but when them cyclones come it's massive, walling up vertical and tapering off into a beautiful fast shoulder. It was more Hawaiian than Snapper, bigger and gnarlier. When the swell dropped a little it worked as a left.

Who'da thought it. They got it right with the rocks and that.

Kirra was on.

You, King Keith I of Kirra.

World tour caravan parked in your backyard: sponsors, radio, journalists, surfers, groupies. Cyclones lined up in the Coral Sea like cows at milking time, and it was *home*, home your beloved Goldie, you had the collywobbles when you were anywhere else but sleeping in Saga with Mo round the corner and all the diagonals working just right for you, you were *safe*.

Heaven.

Hell.

No Lisa.

You hatched an idea to do some serious promotion of Keiths Surf Boards. But when you got back from Margaret River, Rod had turned the workshop into Dr Bloody Frankenstein's bloody lab. There was boards shaped like fish, like dinosaurs, like burritos, like bloody onions. Rod had let his imagination get the better of him. He'd glassed all manner of stuff into the decks: not just bugs, but pencils, picture hooks, notepads, chip packets, even human turds were glassed into surfboards. You couldn't tell what was purpose and what was accident. Bloody no accident the throttling you give him when you found him. And it wasn't just the boards he shaped. There was grot and mess and sheets of glass and hard piles of resin and catalyst and who knew what chemicals. A hot mix had burnt down one of the piles and maybe the whole house was about to fall in on it. There was rubbish and refuse and half-eaten meals and half-full bottles of soft drink, it was just disgusting and you'd had enough.

Rod, nowhere to be found.

According to Mo, he was off 'working'. More like scoring and selling, scoring and selling, running himself out of cash till he come back with his tail between his legs.

His 'friends' drop in all hours and sniff about the graveyard for something—buried treasures. You'd had enough of these skin-and-bone junkies, you chased them off the premises.

The shop was locked up, out of business.

And no money.

Keiths Surf Boards coin, gone gone gone.

Day before the comp started you get a key from the locksmith's and went to the shop.

You walked in and Rod was there, zonked out behind the counter. The lights were off, place covered in dust, and all there was for stock was a couple of dinged second-hand sticks, a few pairs of boardshorts and some cakes of wax. Ghost museum in a ghost town.

Rod looked up at you. Pinprick eyes.

Whatcha think of me shop then? he had the hair to say.

You looked round. KSB: this was all it was now. Your dream.

Looking like nobody had been in for donkey's. Crash pad for your junkie brother.

Well Rod, it's got potential.

Didn't have the spark to whale out on him. You just turned on your heel and left him there to stew in it.

Back at the shaping bay you done a full inventory check. Rod had destroyed Keith Surf Boards, decimated it, left nothing but a heap of monstrosities no-one could use for nothing cept table tops. Not a sausage could be ridden as a surfboard. You be better off riding a car door than them things he shaped.

He'd went mad.

Keiths Surf Boards. Defunct. Should of been Keith Surfs Boards. Only one Keith left as far as you were concerned.

And so yeah, while all this was going on they were gearing up for the third round of the world tour, in your backyard.

And . . . yeah . . . and then Lisa.

•

She showed up her usual way: swaggering along, straight hair swinging, walk like a bloke's. Her strong shoulders under denim cut-off sleeves. Her muso mates mooning along like they wanted to have a crack but didn't know where to start.

She rocked up at Sanga. Someone'd found the 'n' and put it back in. You were in what was left of the shaping bay. Heard voices upstairs. Mo and someone. The starch in Mo's voice: pleasant and hateful.

Mo: pleasant when hateful.

A creak in the stairs and you didn't look round cos even when you knew it was her you thought if you looked it turn out to be a hallucination.

Holey moley, DK, it's worse than I thought.

Back after half a year. LA, at the airport car park, under that weird spaceship thing. Restaurant.

You couldn't turn round to look at her. In case you made her disappear.

She sat on an upturned crate. You knew her legs were spread, like she wanted to rest her guitar on her knees and start playing to you.

Singing her songs in Sanga.

You couldn't look. In case she was a mirage.

You left your brother to look after the shop. Phew, man.

You still couldn't look. In case you were dreaming her.

Something I been wondering Den, she says all casual, starting up a new line of conversation.

You didn't look.

How old did you say you were when Mo adopted you?

You didn't look. She'd pestered you about this before. Had it in her head that you wanted her to find your real parents. At least their names. She reckoned it was important to you. Even if they was dead. Lisa said you can't know who you are if you don't know who you are.

I've been to the children's services registry, up in Briso, she goes. Still casual like we're discussing the swell forecast. *Trying to pick up the trail, you know? But nobody could find anything. I figured I must've got the year wrong.*

I know who I am. I am DK. I am The Man.

A long silence. You sweeping up Rod's crap. A destroyed sawhorse.

Okay, if that's the way it's gunna be. Have your sulk. I'm playing at The Patch tonight. Eight pm. Be there or be cubic eh.

The stairs creaking again. The pleasantness and hate in Mo's voice. The front door.

She come back and you made her disappear. She was a hallucination. You dreamt her.

You was at The Patch: two tabs of acid, a few doobs, glass of lemonade. Aviators on the nose. A smile other surfers took as being smug, mysto, superior. To you it was just the way your face was stretched when your teeth locked.

Watching Lisa. Her scoping herself in the mirrored lens of your aviators. Her eyes meeting her own across a crowded room.

Wheeling out her dimple.

Big night it was, few weirdos took too much acid and ended up running down the main street in the buff and getting took away by the Black Maria. You just hung at the back. Finally the crowd melted and no words was needed, you walked out The Patch and Lisa followed you up Greenmount.

Where it all started:

Where it all ended.

Giving you a pep talk.

How you never got too close to the surfing in-crowd anyway; how in HB you got too close to them and things spiralled out of control. How you should be thankful that the shaping operations had fallen in a heap. How you could make more money as a pro surfer now, how you could give more to Mo so she could stop the poo-carting and the prawn-peeling and the bingo-calling, the handing-out-change at Funland. How if you won the worlds, Mo'd own Sanga and pay her own medical bills. How KSB was never going to achieve that for her. How it was DK who'd do it, DK alone, DK in the waves. How you were a surfer, not a businessman. Not a shaper. You were a surfer. A professional surfer. The best in the world.

Then:

So you can't remember what year it was when Mo adopted you?

•

Not really listening to her. You was looking at her and wondering if you could possibly ever go to bed with her. Had you done it before? You weren't sure. Wild eh.

This happened a lot: you'd be with Lisa, and it's like you've never got off with her and you're wondering if you can, if you can get *that* lucky, and you're so nerved out but then you remind yourself yeah, we done it heaps, and that brings a great flood of relief, so you know you can do it. Amazing. But then the next minute it happens all over again: you're just in the car with her or sitting across a table sucking back smoothies and you wonder if you can ever strike it lucky enough to sleep with this amazing long-haired bird, you're no chance you think, cos you can't remember, that's the thing, being with her is like being on a wave, you know it's happened but *you can't remember it*, you know the facts and such around it, there's proof sort of, but you can't remember it, not the actual thing itself, you've lost it somewhere in there, and so what do you do when you can't remember this great thing you get off on—you do it again. And again. Like if you do it a million times, you might start to remember it. But each time you've written it on water and it won't come back.

She was something that Lisa. Had the entire crowd heaving at The Patch one minute, the next crowning you on Greenmount.
Where you and she had laid that first night.
By the park bench you and Rod burnt down.
On the whole headland you and Rod burnt down.
Where it all started:
Where it all ended.

The way she touched you that night, she packed in a whole lot of new moves.
Too many new moves.
Good moves, but too new.
Like she wasn't *her* no more; you was DK and she was Lisa Exmire, big stars the pair of yous.

She never said nothing never a word about what happened. Why she dumped you in LA. Why she never come home. Why you never heard from her till she just blew in like it was yesterday and started running your life again.

Said not a word.

You, too scared to ask.

She can talk about you not knowing who you are. Like knowing your mother's and father's names is more important than knowing what she was doing in LA.

She can talk.

You're you. But who was she?

Next morning you surfed with red eyes of fire. Keith Surfs Boards! Fuck Tink (you got in his face and nearly killed him before the first heat; you saw *fear* in his eyes; you never had to lay a hand on him). Fuck them all. There was another fifteen hundred bucks waiting at the end of that cyclone right-hander off the Big Groyne, it was Your Kirra, you were King, you were gunna take them apart.

That first day of heats they were all beaten before you even got out of the sack.

Christmastime, 1974. Cyclone Fricken Tracy. Darwin looking like Sanga after a big night. The second morning, Lisa kept you in bed past your up time, too late for your heat. You come to your senses, Mo rapping at the door shouting your heat's starting in five minutes. Lisa rolled you a doob as you piled in your muesli. You smoked together as you took a shortcut down Rainbow Bay, jumped in the water and paddled straight out north round the points. A half-mile paddle, but quicker than fighting your way through the tents and crowds. It was a sunny morning and if they looked out to sea they were blinded by the glare.

Your heat's already started when you arrive in the line-up, only fifteen minutes left. You paddle in the first set and bounce round like a pinball. You paddle back out and jag the last wave of the same set. Tear it to pieces.

In your heat, some of the top Americans and Hawaiians. You didn't know them real well yet. But it was the story, the legend, that's always the thing to them. When you paddled in at the end of the heat, the Americans were shaking like a tree in the tradewind.

He come out of nowhere.

We thought he wasn't gonna show.

One minute he wasn't there—and the next he was!

He's never more dangerous than when you don't know where he is.

You won the heat easy, even though you missed half of it. You was interviewed on the podium about 'the legend of DK'.

You pushed your aviators up your nose. Still there.

Well yeah . . . but no!

Lisa was blown away. She said you proved that the best warm-up was a sleep-in. She said you could mess with those guys' heads by hiding out, keeping them guessing. By exploiting their paranoia. By *not* showing up.

The enigma. The mystery. The genius.

You looked at her and thought: *Where were you.*

And but she

Lisa Exmire was harder than DK

your looks just bounced off her white smile.

Lisa was getting to enjoy stories too. For you it was all about the board you were riding and the next wave, but for her it was all about the 'Legend of DK' and the mind games. She was American, singing American, working for an American record label and selling to an American audience.

She was full of the buzz, Lisa. Filled the QUEENSLANDER with it.

Mo just stood back, all broad smiles and hate. She didn't care about stories. She wanted you to win. Nobody remembers who finishes second.

Mo bumped into Kinky Tinky at the Commonwealth Bank in Coolie. When she was near enough behind him in the queue, she started the Keith murmur, real low, almost sub-audible:

You're not good enough, Tink.

At first he didn't turn round.

Not up to it kid, never was.

Tink screwed his finger in his ear, like it was bugging him.

Your style's old hat, you're past it, may's well just quit now Tink.

Then he turned round.

Oh, hi, Mrs Keith.

Hello, Glenn, she said, all sweet. *How's your mum and dad?*

His mum and dad had divorced about a year before.

Tink still only twenty-two.

The swell dropped before the semis on December 30. You were about to paddle out but it wasn't the right board so you hopped on your chopper and cycled back home to the rat cellar and pulled out your sander and worked in a frenzy a fricken frenzy your rails were too thick and rounded and your board wasn't loose enough for these waves. You planed and sanded and glassed and hopped back on the chopper.

Again, late for your heat.

Again, the other competitors spinning when you hadn't shown up.

Again, you tore it up. You'd won. Into the final.

That night Lisa played The Patch again but said you'd psyche everyone out if you didn't show. *Standing in the corner chilling on dope's one thing*, she said, *but not being there at all will really have them worried.*

Fair enough so you stayed home watched TV with Mo went to bed.

Lay there bugs under your skin. Night before the final and you couldn't sleep.

No Lisa.

You lay awake. Bugs under skin.

Nearly dawn and no Lisa.

Then: Lisa. Bumbling her way through the door, drunk, stoned, whatever. Gone out with a few of the Hawaiians.

So drunk she told you she screwed one of them. One of the big names. *Yeah yeah, but my darling, it was cool . . .*

You heard your heart fall on the floor.

She snuggled in your side, bare toes rubbing the tops of your cold feet. This was 1974. *Everything cool . . .*

Yeah . . .

And you lay there and lay there and it was cool, you were cool.

Cool and groovy.

Wanting to tell her.

Wanting to tell her, Sure, you've heard them stories about DK and all the birds, DK the chick magnet, DK who snakes his mates' birds, DK who jumps in bedroom windows, DK who all the chickies are lining up for, DK who just has to push his aviators up his nose and that's his chat-up line, DK who doesn't have to try . . . But all lies see, all bull. DK sits with birds and listens to them talk for a couple of hours then sends them home. DK asks them to tell all what a stud he is. DK has to keep up the legend. But DK doesn't touch them. DK wouldn't know what to do with them. DK hasn't touched a bird since you, Lisa. None since you.

Only you.

and but

yeah

and you're the same eh. Telling me these yarns about Hawaiians for Lisa Exmire's image.

Right.

Wanting to say

lying frozen beside her her toes trying to thaw yours out.

Wanting to say

but didn't say nothing

never said a word.

You be letting her down. You couldn't tell her. You got a legend to maintain.

So: not a word.

But you couldn't touch her neither. Frozen.

She said you must be nervous about the final, couple of hours away.

Did it have to be a Hawaiian?

Did she have to tell you?

Burnt.

You couldn't lie beside her. You wanted her to do some whiz and get you to thump her on all the places where she hurt. You'd do it this time no fear. A Hawaiian. In Coolangatta. Your bird, your backyard, with a Hawaiian.

Right there and then she killed you.

Stone dead.

You weren't saying or doing nothing, so she did try to wrestle you a bit and hit you, she clouted your ear and chomped your arm and snarled at you—get a reaction. She went hard, like this time she was gunna make you really go ape on her, and yeah you really wanted to but—

But you wasn't doing it. It was all too messed up eh you

you just wasn't going down that road
nah but
you weren't gunna do it
and she was the first one to fall asleep.
That did it
far as DK was concerned.

You get up early and cycled down the conness area. Sat in the tent among the in-crowd while you waited for the final. Filled in the forms and done an interview and behaved exactly how the organisers asked. Weirded everyone out: they thought it was another DK mind game.

But you was frozen solid.

Which of the Hawaiians?

Which one had it been? Ha-why-he?

Why? Why? Whywhywhywhywhy?

She done you stone dead.

You paddled out with everyone in the final round. Six surfers. Tink was there, and Kanga Cairns, three of them Hawaiians.

You paddled into waves, then haired out of them.

You give waves to the others, give up your priority.

You got nothing in your arms, nothing in your legs.

You copped a penalty for baulking a drop-in.

You were acting like you was on gear when it was the first surf in memory when you *hadn't* been on gear.

You come sixth in the final.

Everyone talking about it, on the beach. Their theories. You were sick, you were mentally unbalanced, you were having some kind of bug-out. Nobody ever seen you hair out of a wave. Something was off with you, but then again something always seemed off with you. So what would they know?

Tink won. Nobody remembered who came second but everyone would talk about who came sixth.

You walked home. Forgot you left the chopper down the comp area. Went in your room and smoked a doob. It didn't do nothing. Put on some music. Didn't do nothing.

Lay on your back with your hands behind your head.

For hours, till night-time.

And no Lisa. Her stuff gone.

Late at night you went out.

You come back, back to bed.

Some time, a shape at the door.

Big pale green house dress. Grey hair. Spider veins. Teary blue eyes.

Every time you opened your eyes Mo was there.

For hours.

In your door.

You fell asleep.

And woke up some time in the middle of the night, another ghost touching your hair. You nearly screamed:

Rod.

Den.

Been a while.

Yeah . . .

You sweet?

I'm sweet.

Rod sitting on the side of your bed. In the moonlight you can see the lines across his forehead, down the sides of his mouth. Bas at his feet, panting. Bas looked like an old dog. Rod looked like an old man. He looked like you. Never looked more like you than in the silver light with lines carved in his stone face.

Sorry about the boards, bro.

Cool, Rod.

Sorry about the shop.

Cool Rod. Eh you got any gear?

Some mull hangin on the tree.

Nah, you went. You couldn't see the look on Rod's face. *The other shit.*

Rod didn't say nothing.

Cmon Roddy, how bout a taste?

Roddy didn't say nothing but you could hear him breathing faster and swearing, *fuckety fuck fuckedy*, wheeze under his breath.

Eh Rod?

He rammed his fist in your bed beside you, got up and walked out, slammed your door behind him.

You fell asleep.

You saw Mo in the doorway. Crying. End of '74. All a dream.

Eh sorry I didn't win. Christ Mo, sorry.

She tore off like that was the worst thing you could of said. Her sobs shaking the kitchen.

You fell asleep again.

You were sorry.

You woke up.

Rod, again, side of your bed. Daylight now. You didn't know which day.

You all right?

I'm all right.

Den?

I'm sweet Rod.

I saw her down The Patch. With one of them Hawaiian cunts. I saw her, Den. I was there.

I'm sweet, Rod.

I saw her go off with a bunch of them. Your bird.

I'm sweet, Rod.

I saw her, Den.

I'm sweet, Rodney.

Sitting on the side of your bed. Bas panting by his feet. Mo still sobbing in the kitchen. House swimming on sobs.

She cruelled you.

I'm sweet, Rod.

She won't let you down again.

I'm sweet, Rod.

She made you lose the final.

I'm sweet, ya cunt.

And Den.

Yeah?

Ya don't want any of that shit. Believe me ya don't.

Whatever you say Rod.

And Den.

Yeah?

Don't let me or Mo hear you take the Lord's name again, right?

There was ghosts in that house. Shangrila. Sanga. You felt their hands on your hair while you slept.

It was a week later you got up. Bottles of pills by your bedside. Greens, whites, blues. You didn't remember nothing of that.

Nobody was there. No Mo, no Rod. Nobody. It was daytime outside, quiet. You couldn't hear nothing breaking down on the shore. Flat.

You must of dreamt it. No way could you have finished sixth in your own backyard.

PATERNITY

She smiles no thanks to the Splice stick. Everything so out in the open, not her style. Not mine neither. Guess she sees it more as a matter of trust, of *souls*. She wants to find some spiritual proof. Not chemical. She wants to find herself in you. Not in a DNA test.

Wants you to find yourself in her.

'So why all the put-on?' you ask. 'Why the pretending to write my bi fricken ography?'

Shakes her head.

'Who says I'm not?'

'Not gunna bite you, am I?'

'Spose not. But your mother—'

'Your grandmother ya reckon?'

She grimaces. 'Yeah, nah, guess she could be eh.'

You watch the waves a bit. There's always the waves. No matter what. Here at Greenmount. They can spoil it a million different ways but they can't stop the ocean.

'I never knew she'd had a kid.'

She gives a sniff. You don't look at her to see what kind of sniff it is. The image of her mother. Face, shoulders, all the mannerisms. You knew it from the start. You knew it. She was never no BFO. She's the ghost. She's Lisa back. Jesus what must Mo be making of it. Hallucinating eh. Lisa had a nipper eh. Wild.

'Did you ever ask, Dennis?'

'None of my business.'

'That was the basis of your . . . relationship?'

'That was the basis of the 1970s.'

'So. You never knew. She'd had me in America. She'd went away and . . . had me.'

Makes it sound like it was an operation. Childbirth, abortion—what birds went away to get done. All the same. Long as she kept it from you. Long as you never found out. What Lisa wanted.

'She didn't tell me nothing.'

'You never knew anything about her cos you never asked her.'

'You don't look that old. I thought you was about twenty-five.'

She winces, like I'm trying to flatter her to throw her off the scent.

'And you never asked what she'd been up to, what was in her life, what were her dreams, what she was made of. You were so far up your own . . .'

'Didn't need to ask her. We understood each other.'

'Dennis.' She puts a hand on my thigh, gives it a squeeze. 'You only needed to open your mouth.'

And I don't look at her and she's getting up and pulling her arms into her wetsuit arms and pulling her tag up her back and stretching and picking up her board, and she wants me to sit here and watch her snag some of them right-handers, and this is it, this is my chance, this is my only chance, only chance, only chance . . .

And but it's gone. She's walked off into the bay. It's gone.

Didn't have the heart to tell her.

What I know.

CALIFORNICATE

By the time you come to, you had a first, a first and a sixth and you DK was still leading the world championship by a thousand points. A zombie now, but zombie world leader, Mo and Rod didn't give a rats. Nor you. Just wanted to kill them all.

January the somethingth, '75.

This time you went on your own. You didn't care for the hoopla you just wanted to sneak out for a quiet surf, rip a few waves then go back to your hotel room and watch TV.

Only yours didn't have no TV. Since the Travelodge in '73, no Huntington Beach hotel would leave their TVs in the room while a surfing championship was on. Drove you spare not having TV.

As it turned out a big Thorn set was the first prize for the HB conness and you talked them into letting you have it on loan. Americans dig that kind of thing: cheek, gall, confidence, whatever. You said to one of the head honchos, *I'm gunna win it anyway and I'm goin spare with no TV in my room so what say I borrow it?*

They let you borrow it. They told everyone about it.

In America they wanted to interview you, the magazine journos and whatnot. You invited them to your room and sat watching *Lost in Space* and they laughed and high-fived every time you come out with some half-arsed grunt. They thought you was a comedian. They smoked weed with you to relax you but really were relaxing themself.

Stuff that. What was in it for you? They wouldn't pay. You give them words by the dollar. They stump up the dollars, you tell them whatever they wanted to hear.

Commerce.

America.

No Lisa.

She had to be in LA. Based there now you heard. She hadn't made a peep since the day you lost the event at Kirra. Some kind of a barney between her and Rod at home while you were passed out for them lost days, but the details were sketchy and you weren't one for asking questions.

She'd show up. Always did like a bad penny.

You kept looking for her at Huntington. Kept clocking lookalikes.

Amazing how many American birds were looking like Lisa now.

The swagger had caught on. All them strolling along the promenade like blokes.

You found some Mexican takeaway you liked, little shack in a car park near the airport. You kept taking taxis to this place to pig out on the chocolate chicken. You couldn't believe there was food like this. Chicken in chocolate sauce. You went there three meals a day.

Soon they started following you.

Surfers, journos, whoever.

They weren't seeing you in the hotel or round the comp, so they decided to tail you.

Everywhere.

Caught up with you at that Mexican joint. You told them the truth: this was the best fuel there was. But you made them swear to keep it a secret or you'd have to kill them.

They laughed.

Americans always thought you were joking.

Someone wrote you were that competitive, you'd turn nose-picking into a sport if you could.

Well yeah. You had to win. And once you won you had to win again.

Kill them all.

Kill.

Still no Lisa.

First event was at HB Pier in front of thirty thousand. Whole of Surf City USA close enough to hear your heavy breathing. Just like last time you freaked sitting in the line-up. It was five foot and lumpy. Breaking both ways, away from the pier and in under it. The right-hander, going away, would of been your choice, but you couldn't jag one. In your heat there was locals who got wildcards. You couldn't believe it: they hassled and paddled as hard as you at Coolie. They were the biggest hasslers on the planet these blokes. You couldn't buy a wave. The crowd, so close, was giving you the heebie-jeebies. It was a hot smoggy day and they all had their shirts off and went bananas whenever one of their locals got a decent ride. Locals cutting you off. Locals paddling round in front and behind you. Locals snaking you.

Only one thing to do.

You hassled harder. You dropped in and lost penalty points for interference, but it showed you were prepared to smash your board to get a wave.

It would be called the roughest heat in surfing history. These guys ganged up and shook their fists at you in front of thirty thousand cheering and all hated you, thirty thousand of them.

Then a big set come and you paddled like hell. You were going for the right, but two locals paddled in a screen to stop you. You angled left. Jeez. They pushed you into a six-foot back-hander going into the concrete pylons. But you had no option. Stop paddling and you go over the falls and get smashed. Your only way through was on your feet.

. . . yeah . . .

So you charged, got up, pulled a big back-side turn, stalled halfway up the face and you were in the green cathedral . . .

. . . ooh yeah . . .

You disappeared behind the solid curtain of seawater and the crowd went, the pier went, America went away.

They lost sight of you.

The barrel went in under the pier.

You closed your eyes and tucked in your arms. Fate. The wave was gunna decide if you got took out by a twenty-foot pylon or not. You were in the barrel.

What a way to go.

And then it spat you out into the light on the north side of the pier. Crowds rushed over to see how many pieces you come out in. Like Apollo 13 you'd went to the dark side. Under HB Pier in a six-foot barrel.

And lived.

You pulled a last cutback on the shoulder and hang-tenned it all the way in. Scored a few extra points by hanging your toes in the whitewater. Yeah why not eh.

You run round and paddled out again under the pier, into the line-up for the last minutes of the heat.

Locals wouldn't surf no more. They just wanted to paddle over and give you high-fives. They were dry in the mouth, shaking their heads. These were the scabbiest locals on the globe and you done what none of them had the hair for. Outrageous. They stopped surfing to honour that wave of DK's.

But you only got one scoring wave, and even if it was a 20 out of 20 you probably be knocked out the conness. Some argy-bargy about had you gone outside the conness area.

Then a bunch of locals stormed the judging tent and threatened to wrench the judges' arms out their sockets if they didn't send you through to the next round.

Didn't matter what the scores were. You got the greatest wave in the history of the biggest surf break in California. Instant legend. DK.

Thirty thousand chanting:

DK! DK! DK! DK!

You done interviews. They asked if you thought you were the best surfer in the world. This was the year of Ali and Bobby Fischer. You said:

Yes I believe I am.

No crap. That was DK. They ate it up.

So you've just won the HB Pro with what's being called the wave that was heard around the world. Where to from here?

Win next week at Trestles.

No bull. DK.

There were guys waiting for you on the beach with fence palings cos you'd been hassling so hard. By the end of the event they were carrying you out of the water on their shoulders. How did you turn it around?

You saw. People recognise greatness.

DK, DK, DK.

You DK was famous. People who you didn't know waltz up on HB promenade and chatted like you're their best mate. Full-on. You were a movie star. Americans knew how to treat their stars: blitzed you with their love.

A continent full of love but no Lisa.

•

In the hotel surfers want to play you: table tennis, chess, pool, Monopoly. They just want to beat you at *something*. But you got an authority to maintain.

They give you joints, trips, ludes, mushies, to dull your edge.

You beat them at table tennis.

Beat them at chess.

At pool.

Monopoly.

Somebody had to keep the world in order. Your belief system: a pyramid, with DK at the top. In all things.

All things.

At Trestles, a nice A-frame beach break, you disappeared in the sandhills and let them wonder were you in the country, in the state, in an altered state, on the moon . . . They talk about you and talk about you some more and lie awake all night wondering. Then their heats start and you aren't there. They get confident. Till they look out the back when a bomb set come in, and they paddle out like crazy to scratch their way over the top of the wall of water, and on the inside, deep in the wave, in the barrel, the Scream in Blue clearing the water.

They were gone baby gone. They loved you or hated you, they didn't want to surf against you. Either they were grovelling at your feet like you were the Second Coming or conspiring to get you kicked off the tour. They niggled the judges about technicalities: find something illegal you done. They wanted the scoring system changed back again to reward flouncy slow trimmers instead of the zigs and zags within the zigs and the zags. Michael Peterson said he'd never want to surf cynical like you surfed, and he pulled the plug. Weak. *Cynical!* You don't even know what that means. Petersons and their big words.

Nobody could handle DK.

You won at Trestles but they got in the judges' heads in the third Californian leg, at Churches. By now they had to keep some interest in the world title cos you were running away with the thing. Lot of coin changing hands. You saw it all from behind your aviators. The beginning of corruption. Sponsors. Beginning of the end.

But you finished the sixth event of the tour with four wins under your belt and six grand in earnings. You sent orders home for a velvet lounge suite bought for Mo. Apparently when the delivery men bring it to Sanga, she said it wasn't hers. They assured her it was, care of Dennis Keith. She unblocked the doorway and let them in.

Took her a while to sit in it.

Didn't approve of luxuries for herself, your Mo.

You been away from home six weeks. Before that, you been away three of five weeks for Bells and Margs. You were missing the Gold Coast so bad you were wasting away. Had diarrhoea. Had no friends on the tour. They loved you too much. They hated you too much. No room for friendship when you are a living legend. No risk to the winning edge.

No mates.

No Mo.

No Lisa.

Nineteen seventy-five still. More or less, you thought. You holed up in your hotel in your aviators and watched TV comedies, documentaries, news. No movies. You never liked movies. But comedies, yeah, and news. Surfing documentaries, for sure. Animals. Africa. Yeah.

All on your tod.

Going spare.

Thinking about the next stop.

The three legs, the Triple Crown:

Haleiwa, Sunset, Pipe.

Couldn't stop thinking.

About Hawaii.

The three legs, the Triple Crown:

Haleiwa, Sunset, Pipe.

Couldn't stop.

Going in the posters on the walls of your bedroom in Sanga.

You made a call home.

HOSPITAL

Mo has to go to hospital again, she does it more now, I dunno. She won't tell me what she has to go in for and I won't ask her in case I don't like the answer. She says it's only for a couple of nights
 and but
 but her spidery maroon veins her lovely face.
 Her eyes looking away from me all the time so hard they feel like they're boring straight through me.
 Whatever's wrong with her must be bad. But my Mo she's not worried about herself. She's worried about me fending for meself a couple of nights.
 'It's sweet Mo. I got some muesli. I'll go down to Bob's for lunch. I can do it.'
 She holds me hands. We're sitting at the melamine table. My feet are in the air cos I can't handle the diagonals. I want to go home. I want to sleep in Shangrila.
 'I'll be right Mo. I'll come visit you.'
 But I won't. I won't have no-one to take me.
 Half the fricken Gold Coast would give their right ball to drive Dennis Keith to the hospital to see his sick mother.
 But I won't. No-one will know about me and my Mo and what I need and what she needs.

BFO's gone. Shot through.
 I didn't tell Mo about the conversation, me twigging who the BFO was. Or thought she was.
 But no she
 Mo hasn't mentioned the BFO and neither will I.
 I won't either.

She gets the village minibus to the hospital. I see it through the metal security grille. My fingers white on the aluminium. Grabbing the rails.

Into the bedroom, under the covers, up with the radio.
It's only two nights. Sweet.

Dennis, you only needed to open your mouth.
She didn't have the heart to tell me.
What she knew.

Halfway through the first night I get up and go to the hallway closet.
The one that falls open with the old junk. The one that holds all of
Shangrila.
You get in there and find what you was looking for.
Get some blu-tak.
Go to work.

Darkness before dawn, time I used to get up to ride my chopper down
The Other Side, the hour when cops raid, I sit on my bed.
Feet up. Not touching these bad diagonals:
My work is done.

DAD V

He must of been Hawaiian. Rod spread a rumour round Kirra that your dad was Duke Kahanamoku—though the Duke would of been pretty long in the tooth by 1950, the year you were made. And probably not that type of man. A gentleman and a Duke. Royalty. Wouldn't of done that.

But the point was, Rod said, a surfing god must of made you.

A Hawaiian.

It was in the way you shaped your spine for your famous cutback. The way you chopped your right hand behind you to make the wave go as fast as your mind. The courage to take on the big monsters:

You had to have some Hawaiian in you. It stood to reason. You *felt* Hawaiian. You even liked their slack key music.

No idea who they were. Never heard of Hawaiians coming to Queensland in 1950. But there had to be. Brothers. Big-wave riders. Stood looking at five-foot Greenmount one day, shrugged their shoulders, too small for them, so went off looking for sport on land. Ladies would of loved them in Queensland. Take their pick.

Hawaiian big-wave gods.

One of them him.

WHILE YOU WERE WAITING IN YOUR HOTEL

You flew from America to Hawaii on your own. Feb '75.

LAX:

You kept your eyes on the floor.

Nobody hassled you.

Nobody knew you.

World's greatest surfer. World champion waiting for his crown: in a plane to Hawaii.

Hawaii.

The posters on your bedroom wall.

Hawaii:

Land of legends.

Hawaii.

Honolulu Airport:

Man mountains of customs officials smiling and waving you through . . .

Women in grass skirts and coconut bras singing and hula-ing . . .

A big half-pineapple full of juice and a straw shoved in your hand . . .

A necklace of frangipanis slung round your neck . . .

You'd died and went to heaven . . .

Aloha, DK.

Reporters grabbed you. Microphones.

Your press conference:

DK, they say you're the best in the world now, tell us straight up, man, what do you think about that?

Well I am.

Laughter.

You're brave, man, talking like that here.

You said tell you straight up.

Sweating pellets all the way in from the airport in the official car. Already paranoid about what you said. The coconut wireless be carrying your words round the islands.

Your heart playing tom-toms while the world tour's official driver this beefy Hawaiian with a kombi took you to the North Shore.

North Shore: Sunset, Pipe, Laniakea, Haleiwa. The place called Waimea which only the headcases surfed.

Hawaii.

The Rock.

You checked in.

You turned on the TV.

You didn't leave your room.

You could hear onshores mucking up the surf but you didn't look. Couldn't.

You couldn't handle Hawaii on your own.

While you was waiting in your hotel waiting for the onshores to drop and the surf to clean itself up, these things happened to Rod.

He took a call at home at the QUEENSLANDER.

He packed his bags.

He packed his mull.

He packed his harry.

He got Mo to drive him to Brisbane airport.

He kissed her goodbye.

He found out he couldn't get through immigration cos he didn't have a passport.

He called Mo.

He got her to drive him to the post office.

He went home for two days.

He got his passport.

He packed his bags.

He packed his mull.

He packed his harry.

He got Mo to drive him to Brisbane airport.

He kissed her goodbye.

He sparked up in the toilet in the airport.

He shot up in the toilet in the plane.

He had a few drinks.

He arrived at Honolulu airport and got took in by the police for suspected vagrancy and terrorism.

Sniffer dogs had sussed something out.

He got searched.

They found his full ding-repair kit: glass, resin, hardener, catalyst. Stink of acetone.

They analysed it. Thought he was making bombs but it was his ding-repair kit.

The smell of acetone was so strong, dogs found *nothing else*.

He got interrogated.

He said nothing.

Wouldn't even confirm the name they read on his passport.

Sat in the lock-up at Honolulu airport for six hours.

Told them nothing. Wouldn't even open his mouth.

They searched him again. Found nothing. He reeked of it: acetone, fibreglass, surfboards.

Kicked him out.

He got a taxi to Rocky Point. Fabled but inconsistent break: eight to twelve foot, occasional sets up to one foot. You knew this. You'd read about Rocky Point all your life.

He had no coin.

With his board and his bag, he done a runner.

Taxi driver was too fat to run after him.

Taxi driver shot at him.

He got away, slept in a cave at Rocky Point.

He'd forgot where you were staying.

Next morning, he took a shot and slept in, then thought bugger you, he's going for a surf.

He got some four-foot runners at Rocky Point.

He thought, bugger you, he's staying here.

He slept under the palm trees three nights.

He got four-foot, five-foot, six-foot runners at Rocky Point.

Just about on his own. Locals hooting him, buying him cocktails at night, bringing him ice cream. Coolest place on earth. Hardly anyone out. He could of stayed there forever. Heaven.

Hell.

Next day the surf jacked up to twelve foot and he went out again.

Crowded.

Heavy.

Rod didn't know. He thought he was in heaven. Dropped into waves and got smashed on the reef. Cut himself up.

Paddled back out.

Got hassled. Got threatened. Got told to get the fuck out of the water.

Rod took them on but wasn't good enough.

Got smashed.

Smashed.

Smashed again.

On the reef.

In his head.

Coconut wireless—

A group of them followed him in to the beach. Circled him. Said they were gunna smash him so hard the nailing he got from the reef'll feel like a Thai massage.

Closed in on him.

Rod in a noose of Hawaiian meat.

What Rod did next:

Started gagging on his own tongue.

Frothing at the mouth.

Babbling strange languages.

Sucking back screams.

Spinning in circles.

Blood drained out of his head.

Fell over, donutted more circles.

Babbling.

Frothing.

Spinning.

They thought he was having an epileptic fit.

Was what he wanted them to think.

Then they figured he was having them on.

Some laughed.

Some called him an asshole. Ass-*haole*.

But they couldn't beat crap out of him now. Not on the sand. He was too low down.

·

After that day he decided he come and find you over at Haleiwa. He been told you were in your resort hotel, waiting for him in your room.

Lost in Space was on.

Rod's favourite.

You didn't say nothing when he showed on your balcony. Cuts all over his face, chest, legs. Big deep black-red gashes.

You pushed the aviators up your nose (still there). You turned back to *Lost in Space*.

Rod: *Warning! Warning! Danger! Danger!*

He sit down beside you and got his works out.

He rolled you a doob. You said no eh.

He took a shot. He smoked his mull. You tried not to watch him.

Lost in Space.

When he was real stoned and staggering round the room, he caught you by surprise: come up to you, grabbed your ears and pushed his face up into yours.

You thought:

Rod don't choose this moment to turn queer on me—

But he wasn't kissing you. He was rubbing his nose against yours. Your aviators jumping round all over the shop.

What the f—

Rod fell back on the bed, laughing to break the mouth.

Aloha, DK.

Eh?

Alo means face, ha means breath. Aloha is us sharing the essence of our breath, our life, DK.

Ya didn't get any of my breath ya homo bastard.

He sighed and lay back: *Aloha Den.*

Put his arms behind his head on the pillow like he was settling in for the night.

Get off me bed Rodney.

But—

You watched more TV.

Conness was starting the next morning, and you had your bro.

Not alone no more. You were right to call him, buy his ticket.

The conness.

Hawaii.

You hadn't been game to look at a wave till your bro got there.
You needed your bro. Rodney Keith Keith.

Not alone no more.

He offered you a doob for the fifteenth time in fifteen minutes.

You shook your head.

Whasup DK?

You shook your head.

Here!

You put a hand up to the side of your face like a blinker, keep him away.

C'mon D, it's not a microphone!

You get up and went to the toilet.

You weren't smoking. You were going turkey on him. This was Hawaii. You was going to pay due respects. You were bugging out. You couldn't sleep. You were having nightmares. Your thoughts were inside out and upside down. You were choking down tears in the bathroom. Couldn't look at yourself in the mirror.

Couldn't look out your balcony door at the waves.

Hawaii.

No Smoking.

You didn't have the hair to tell Rod. He wouldn't of known what to make of it.

Of you.

You went back in the room and here's Rod, on the nod.

Next morning, Mecca had switched on. Winds turned offshore overnight and dropped by dawn. Perfect groomed eight-footers rolling into Haleiwa, jacking up straight over the reef, peeling out silky.

Least that was what Rod told you from the balcony. Going off his head with excitement. Pulling on his boardies even before he got yesterday's undies off. Smoking a joint. Amped as hell.

Mecca.

You, buried under your bedsheets feeling the ground shake and the bed squeak.

It's on.

It's on.

Twenty-four hours till they'll start the first heat of the first conness, your first wave in Hawaii.

February somethingth, 1975.

Greatest surfer in the world, buried under his bedsheets.

You asked Rod he got any of his stash left.

Yeah Den eh, knew you'd come round, you want some?

Nothing. Nah.

Rod went out and free surfed with all the best boardriders in the world: Tink, Nat, Fitzgerald, Simon Anderson, Ian Cairns, Mark Richards, all the mainland Americans. Perfect eight-foot A-frames. Perfecto. He said the walls of the waves were so high and clean that when his board held a turn in them he felt like he was walking in space, zero gravity. You could see him reliving them waves.

But no Hawaiians out, not a one.

And the greatest surfer in the world, buried under his bedsheets. Crying. Rod's stash on the other side of the room, sitting on the study table, last fricken temptation of Christ.

Don't do it, DK.

This is Hawaii.

Posters on your bedroom wall.

Mecca. Respects.

Twelve hours to go.

Rod come back in, muscles twitching like a Melbourne Cup racehorse getting hosed down. Eyes popping.

Best session ever, bro. I mean, ever!

You got any that stash left?

Eh Den, thought you'd never ask . . .

You buried yourself deeper.

Rod told you there'd been no Hawaiians out there. Like they were messing with his head. No Hawaiians on a day like this.

Lost in Space come on. Will, Penny, Dr Smith, the Robot. Only thing could calm you down.

You loved the Robot. Rod thought you must of smoked some of his weed, you were cacking so mad.

When he figured you hadn't, you were dead straight, he didn't know to be more worried or less.

Rod shot up, nodded off. You ate your fifth room-service club sandwich of the day.

Six hours to go, you woke up from the sleep you weren't having.

Boom boom boom.

Boom boom boom.

Like there was skyscrapers being demolished, being dynamited.

Boom boom boom.

The floor shaking.

Like a volcano was going off in five or six bursts, every few minutes.

Boom boom boom boom boom boom.

A war.

You woke Rod up and asked he got any of his stash left.

Yeah Den, let's have a smoke eh.

Nah, nothing, nah.

Two hours to go, you hadn't slept a wink. Today: your first wave in Hawaii.

The coconut wireless had sent the word out:

DK's coming, git out the way.

Every surf photographer snapping you, every surf writer writing about you, every surfer watching you. On earth: every surfer on earth. Tomorrow, your Mo reads about you in the papers. The most keenly awaited meeting between man and wave since the ancient days, since the Duke.

DK, meet Hawaii.

Hawaii, meet DK.

This was the winter that'd change surfing forever. The winter that'd kill off the Hawaiian relaxed style and replace it with:

You.

All the moves you done on them big waves, they be trying to repeat them for thirty years.

You'd bust down the door. You, and behind you Tink, Kanga Cairns, Rabbit, MR, the others. Mainly:

You.

Feb '75—

You stood on the balcony.

Boom boom boom boom boom.

Sets of five waves. Feathering mountains, and more mountains behind those mountains.

The Himalayas in every set. The most massive thing you ever dreamt.

Stood on the balcony in your sleeping boardies.

It had took five nights but you worked out that this room had diagonals, some safe, some unsafe. You felt good. You'd found the safe ones. Realised all rooms and all places had diagonals, good and evil, you just had to find the right ones. Was like church. You stretched your arms above your head, knitted your fingers up high.

The posters on your bedroom wall.

Hawaii.

Rod groaned behind you, waking up.

Eh bro, what the fuck . . . ?

Rod'd just started hearing it, seeing it. It's went from eight foot up to twelve, fourteen, eighteen, twenty, overnight.

Real Hawaii. The real Rock.

Fark, Rod said, standing beside you. His arm round your shoulder. Trembling. *Too big for me, they oughta call it off.*

Just as well you're not in the comp then eh? you said.

Rod just shook his head.

Just hope they don't call it off, you said.

Fark, Rod said again.

Rodney, I'm gunna blitz em.

Rod just kept shaking his head. Yesterday had been the biggest cleanest waves he'd ever surfed, and now it was twice as big and a bit bumpy. The tiniest lump would be like a chicane in the middle of a 200mph straight.

I get it now, he said, like he was talking to himself.

Get what?

He give a nervous laugh.

Why there was no Hawaiians out yesterday.

Yeah right.

You watched it for a long time. The comp was getting started. The first heats were paddling out in the channel. All four in the first heat, Californians and Australians, got hammered, two of them come in with boards in half, the other two with bits of leg rope dangling from their ankles, no boards.

Gunna be Hawaiians out today, Rod said.

Rod sit down the study table and took a shot.

Just before you went out the door, Rod told you something.

Bas had died, shop been closed for good.

You just looked at Rod and saw in his eyes the way Bas looked back at you, like Bas was reincarnated inside Rod and all the hate. You never been so gutted since the day you were born.

What happened to the shop? you said.

Lease run out. They locked us out for unpaid bills.

Where's the stock?

Flogged it all.

For gear?

Good gear but.

You scratched your nose. You didn't care so much about the shop. It had been already dead. Now it was gone, it was a weight off your shoulders. You weren't a businessman. You were a surfer.

Like Lisa said.

How bout Bas?

He ate me stash, Rod said. Looking at the floor.

Eh but dope was all right for him, you said. *It didn't kill him, just made him trip.* Your blood was starting to boil now. It was like whatever you felt about the shop would of stayed under if it was just the shop, but now it was Bas as well, it was like two things became greater than one plus one and you were getting wild under your skin.

Rod shook his head. *Me stash of this stuff.* Nodding at the bag. *We found him under the house in the shaping bay. He'd went off there with his sweet dreams.*

He OD'd on that, you said.

What a way to go. Went out doing what he loved. Fark.

Rod nodded but he was nodding off.

You nodded and felt like killing him. Yous were in Hawaii. Land of your fathers.

Never been so gutted.

Rod?

    Yeah?

    I'm ready.

    Yeah I bet you are, DK. I bet you are.

    Rod?

    Yeah?

    What's it like?

    What's what like?

    That.

    That? Ar, that.

    Yeah. What's it like?

    It's like . . . you're there. You've finally arrived.

    Arrived where?

    There. On the other side.

    The other side.

    Like you can put your feet up now.

    Relaxing?

    Den, when I take my first shot you know what I think? I only think one thing.

    What's that?

    I think: Thank Christ. Thank fucking Christ I'm here.

    Rod?

    Ar Den, I dunno.

    Rod?

    What time's yer heat?

    Soon.

    Ar Den, you done so good. You got The Life, y'know? Travelling the world, making coin, world number one. This—it's The Life. What more could you want?

    Rod?

    Nah Den.

You remember that night?

Rod remembered. Didn't need to say nothing.

You wouldn't give me none that night, and you done the right thing. Saved me bacon.

Fuck Den no.

I'm ready Rodney. This is the time.

Fuck Den, ya bloody idiot.

Rod bent over his works. Started cooking. Done it all slow motion, creaking along, hoping this wasn't happening and the clock'd save him.

Rod?

Yeah bro? Ya changed yer dumbfuck mind?

Couldn't look up at you. This wasn't that night at home. This was after that night.

Better put your skates on Rodney. Me heat's already started.

MECCA

Thank Christ I'm here.

   . . . yeah . . .

Rod was deadset. Them small Hawaiian days, eight foot, or when it was windblown junk, they called them 'Aussie Days'. Meaning, those were the days when the frothing Australians would race out and surf on their own and the Hawaiians wouldn't bother.

You hadn't bothered on the Aussie Days. You were in your room. AN HONORARY HAWAIIAN ALREADY.

February 26, 1975, you fell out your room with your big-wave stick under your arm, stubbed your toe black on the hotel step, paddled out into twelve-foot Haleiwa in a heat with one Australian and two Hawaiians, every surf photographer in the world snapping you, every writer writing about you, every surfer watching you, every judge judging you, and you gone cold turkey on mull for five days and just took your first handshake with Rod's buddy.

And thinking,

Thank Christ.

You could put your feet up.

Your work was done.

DK, meet Hawaii.

The other Australian in your heat, Brian Giblet from North Narra, got took to hospital after he went over the falls and separated his head from his neck. It went back in but he'd never surf The Rock again. These things were mountains.

Way they sounded, when you was sitting out there in the line-up, was like nothing you heard before. The big tearing crash of a wave come from behind you as well as in front of you, like the one wave had you covered both sides. You never heard waves *surround* you with their noise.

You had two Hawaiians, da boyz, in your heat. They weren't sitting on the inside like every other heat surfer. They paddled out, and out, and further out, to where the mountains were forming up, to where the sky went dark: blue North Pacific in every wave. Pulses running from Japan with nothing to stop them but a reef on the North Shore of Oahu.

The posters on your bedroom wall.

This was it.

On.

You followed the Hawaiians. The crowds and judges must of thought you're nuts, the three of you, go to those outside ones. As a heat strategy it didn't look smart: less waves, less chances to score. But as a heat strategy, sitting inside and leaving the beach in an ambulance Brian Giblet style wasn't so smart either. You had no idea what you were doing: you just followed the locals.

The three of you sit out there. You hear them talking to each other. You hear them spitting the word 'haole'.

Foreigner.

Whitey.

Blow-in.

You were no whitey.

Mountain after mountain these locals let them through. You done what they done. Then you started nodding off a little, sitting on your board. After a while you lay down on your belly and put your head on the side. They look at you like you was taking the mickey. But you were so tired, and thank Christ, you thought, you're here, you're here, in the posters on your bedroom wall, you can die happy, you can die *now*.

Then it hit you, paranoia, these two Hawaiians are sacrificing themself. Sit out here and sucker you into waiting, waiting, waiting, and miss everything so you end up with a zero score. They end up with zero too but it don't matter to them. They didn't care if they didn't qualify so long as DK didn't.

You thought all this in a blinding flash as this outside set lumbered up blocking the horizon like a city. You thought, if you paddle for the first wave and miss it, you'll have four tsunamis smashing you on the head. Smarter to wait for the last wave in the set. But if you done that, *they* might do the same. And they were deeper than you, in better position.

So you paddled.

Your bucket hands.

Your flipper feet.

You paddled like a shark was after you.

You didn't breathe.

Your teeth hard down on your tongue.

You weren't gunna make it.

You'll be with Brian Giblet in hospital.

You paddled.

You leapt up and still thought you wouldn't make it.

You threw everything forward: almost threw your board down the wave, your body after it.

You threw everything . . .

You were on it.

You were on it.

Someone paddling out on the shoulder: you give him the Scream:

He cleared off . . .

. . . The posters on your bedroom wall.

Thank Christ I'm here.

Surfer and *Surfing* both shot it: DK's first-ever wave in Hawaii.

You flew down the face and ripped a bottom turn, right-hander scooping you up into the walling section. You tucked in. You rode it. In the pictures, you're not in the barrel, you're not cutting back, you're not doing anything with it: you're just riding it.

DK's first wave in Hawaii.

The posters on your bedroom wall.

Thank Christ.

It didn't matter that you just rode the wave, didn't pull any of your zigs and zags.

They called off the conness for the day after that wave. It was too big.

You were the only one all day to get into a wave, to ride it all the way through.

Them two Hawaiians behind you got smashed by that same set. One of them come in with his teeth sticking out a hole in the side of his cheek.

Hawaii, meet DK.

You didn't hang round the comp area.

You ran as hard as you paddled:

Ran back to the hotel room.

To Rod and his little haole mate.

To Rod and your mate.

No more Bas.

And what Rod had also said, quieter, but sure as if he knew it for sure, finality, just slipped inside wrapped up in the greasy paper that was the end of the shop, the end of the dog, all that stuff wrapping round the thing you hadn't tried to think about, what made you say yes to the white man:

No more Lisa.

MO

One day you'll quiz her.

One day you'll sit down and face up, face to face with her, your face in her face, and it'll be the toughest thing yet.

How sitting and holding your own Mo's eyes in your eyes is tougher than throwing yourself down a four-storey building on a sliding glass surface with nothing below you but twelve inches of water and a reef with teeth like razors.

How sitting down and asking your own Mo a simple question is asking more than paddling out at ice-cold ten-foot Bells Beach monsters needing the wave of the day to win an Australian title.

All that's nothing compared to sitting. Down. With Mo. At the melamine table. Safe.

Fifty-eight years old and still not sure if you have the hair.

Why's she so fricken scary? Your own Mo?

Why's she so angry she could strangle you with her bare hands?

What did you do to make her so wild?

What?

One night when you was about eight, yous were walking along Hill Street. You were carrying the groceries in a wood box. She was carrying prawn heads in a bucket. Yous got bailed up by some drunk. Only wanted money, that's all. Shaking like a leaf, dumb prick. And this was the

yeah you couldn't believe

Mo picked up on his fear and before he knew it she kicked him in the nuts and dropped him to the ground like a sack of spuds. Then she started ripping into him with her gumboots. Then she poured all her prawn heads on him. No seafood stock for yous tonight. You just stood there and watched your Mo put this so-called mugger in tears.

She stood on his chest and when some locals come out to see the ruckus she told them to call the cops. She stood on him till they come.

Your Mo. That tough.

And so

yeah

THAT WORLD THERE

Weird thing about Hawaiians in the surf was, when it got big they started shouting each other into the waves. '*Go, Kenny!*' or '*Yours, Jeff!*' Helping each other. You couldn't work it out in a competitive situation why they done that. It confused you. Were they against each other or all against you?

But then at Haleiwa they started calling you in. '*Go, DK, GO!!*' And you didn't even need to look at the wave, if they were calling you in it was yours.

Too weird, threw you out. When they called you into a wave you fell off. Just fell off for no reason. Weirded out.

You didn't win Haleiwa, deserved to but. You won your second heat after you run late. You and Rod been picking mushies in some cow paddock, scarf them as you went, when you realised your heat was on. You raced down to eight-foot rights and the mushies come on last ten minutes of your heat, but you got enough waves before the water begin turning purple on you.

You won your third heat after you spent the morning at the cop shop. Rod been bailed up for whaling into yank tanks parked outside the Turtle Bay Hilton with a yellow-and-white roadblock marker as a cricket bat. You been bombed at the hotel and hadn't known. Next morning he's bailed up again at the post office, this time for trying to send some Hawaiian buds home to himself.

Anyway the postal workers seen it all before and shook their heads. You got him out of that mess when the cops recognised you and asked for an autograph.

Chief postal officer nodded at Rod who was weaving round the place in budgie smugglers and a puka shell necklace.

What you done to him, brah?

Dunno mate but he don't look real good does he?

You get down to Haleiwa in time for the second half of your quarter-final and get hit on the head by a four-wave set paddling out, but one of the other guys lost his fin, you didn't know how, and another had to change his board after a big chunk got bitten out of it by something or other, and so your two decent left-handers was enough to qualify you for the semis.

There was a weird vibe round the comp venue. Aussies were doing this 'Bronzed Aussie' gimmick where they made themselves look like models out of an ad. Mark Warren, Simon Anderson, Michael Peterson, Peter Townend, these guys thought they were in a swimwear advert. They give you and Rod a real wide berth and pretend they don't know you. They never wanted to share your joint or mushie omelette with you. So much for surfing as an alternative lifestyle. These guys were gone corporate. And the organisers, the Hawaiians, were itching to rub you out, but now they had objective judging they couldn't steal this one from you. They couldn't pretend your waves hadn't happened.

So even though you was late for your heats and high on mushies or dope or acid or smack, even though Rod was in the lock-up half the time, even though you were not one of the Bronzed Aussies, you were still winning cos *DK was the best surfer in the world and this was Hawaii, land of the legends.* Which nobody could deny. Which nobody could deny.

The coconut wireless. The posters on your bedroom wall.

You lost the semis but. Got wiped out by a no-show.

Story had it you were passed out in front of *Lost in Space* with Rod. Not true.

You were clear as a bell that morning. Straight as a die. Sober as a judge. Only thing was, you couldn't find your aviators.

The aviators.

Ones you'd had since . . . you couldn't remember . . .

. . . yeah, the aviators.

Couldn't find them.

They was always by your bedside, last thing you did at night was take them off and lay them down safe by your side.

First thing you did in the morning was put them back on.

Now this morning they wasn't there.

You turned your room upside down.

Piled up the bedclothes.

Unloaded the mattress.

Emptied the pillows.
Moved the furniture.
Searched the bags.
Through all the drawers.
All the cupboards.
Moved the TV.
Moved the boards.
Moved the gear.
Smoked a joint.
Took a shot.
Sat in the corner watched some TV.
Went through the whole room again.
And again.
Rod, from the couch: *Den, your heat's about to start.*
You went through the whole room again.
Everything on hold while you found your aviators.
You went through the drawers, the cupboards, everything. You kept scratching the top of your head, like you must of left them there.
Rod: *Den, your heat's starting!*
Piled up the bedclothes.
Unloaded the mattress.
Emptied the pillows.
Moved the furniture.
Searched the bags.
Through all the drawers.
All the cupboards.
Moved the TV.
Moved the boards.
Moved the gear.
Rod: *Fuck, man, your heat's already started!*
Through all the drawers.
All the cupboards.
Moved the TV.
Moved the boards.
Moved the gear.
Rod: *Oi, shitforbrains, your heat's about to finish!*
The drawers.
The cupboards.

The TV.

The boards.

The gear.

Rod: *Den, take another shot. Your heat's finished.*

You took another shot.

You found the aviators. On the balcony. Sitting happy on the chair on the balcony. You hadn't looked on the balcony. You'd forgot you had a balcony.

You took another shot.

Thank Christ I'm here.

Even though you hadn't made the final of Haleiwa you were that far ahead on the points table you only had to show up at Sunset and Pipe, probably not even that, to be world champion of surfing. Which you deserved. Which they couldn't steal off you. Even though you had so many odds stacked against you. You were gunna be world champ and you were the new world tour's worst nightmare. A world champion who was DK. And everything that brought with it.

There was a few days to kill at Sunset before the conness. The hammer, Rod's buddy, was good for your surfing. Like mull: others get wiped out by it, but with you it slowed you down enough to make you clear about things for once. You got a little tired but you never been one for long surfs. An hour max then take a break—that was your rule. So if smack made you a little tired after your hour, that was natural, that was a signal to come in.

Free surfing Sunset.

The posters on your bedroom wall.

World champion in waiting.

Nice day, eight foot, offshore, barrelling.

You paddled into a line-up that included most of the pro surfers in the world and half the population of the North Shore. Coconut wireless had put the word out—

DK is here. Be prepared to—

You couldn't get a wave. So much pressure. So many swarming.

They were paddling away from you, the Aussies. Didn't want to be seen with you. Jealousy.

The Hawaiians closed in. Not the pros, but da boyz. The locals who didn't stoop to surfing in comps.

The owners of this wave.

They closed in.

You couldn't get a wave.

They snake you, drop in on you, shut down your paddling line.

Closed in.

All vibing you.

Eight foot, offshore, barrelling and you couldn't get a wave.

Heavy scene.

Vibing you out.

They didn't go much on your Scream in Blue.

Ancient Hawaiian curses muttered under their breath.

Big boys: Polynesians.

Big boards.

Heavy.

Haole!

Someone shouting at you. Others laughing. Or growling. Vibing you out. They wasn't shouting to attract your attention. They was shouting to tell you to piss off.

Haole!

They was doing what you'd of done to them at Kirra. They was hassling, dropping in, snaking.

You had one card to play:

You hassled back.

You faded, you dropped in, you snaked, you cut them off. You took the initiative. You attacked.

Haole!

You hassled, you faded, you dropped in, you snaked, you cut them off. You still couldn't get a wave.

Haole!

You went right inside, way deeper than anybody, where the sea collected into a vertical pitch on top of the reef. A set come, and you paddled. But your arms were tired from all the hassling, all the no-waves, all the snaking, all the smack. You weren't fast enough and you pulled out of it. It come down on the bare reef like a ton of bricks. But then you look round and the next wave's onto you. You paddled out to the right, to the shoulder, but now there were local guys blocking.

You were tired and your arms were heavy and you just wanted to get one in, and so you turned and paddled into the wave anyway, even though there was this bloke, Barry Kalahu, built like a block of flats, biggest of the big men on the North Shore, already on it, and you went down the face and your board punched a hole in his and yous both come off and you lost your board and Barry Kalahu come in on it, and you bodysurfed in and saw him waiting on the beach.

Block of flats.

Half your board in his hand.

His board floating in the shorie.

The other half of your board in his other hand.

You walked up.

Peace brother.

Held out your hand.

Barry Kalahu's fists like soccer balls.

Yeah bruddah, my fault, you went. *Aloha.*

Kept your hand out there.

One of Barry Kalahu's soccer balls unfolded. Like it was coming out to accept your apology.

Never apologised in your life.

First time for everything.

Didn't mean to start nothing eh, you said. *Sorry brah.*

Shitting your boardies.

Barry Kalahu's soccer-ball hand come in slow mo. You saw it from the outside: its line through the air, like a charger on a good wave, accelerating as it got to the critical zone.

Your head warped sideways.

You went down.

Your head the shape of a banana.

Barry Kalahu said:

We don't like you here.

You mumbled through your broken head:

Peace, brah.

Barry Kalahu said:

Not your brah.

He didn't walk off. Having clobbered you into next week he just stood there, both halves of your DK board in the sand beside him. His soccer-ball hands hanging by his hips.

A tourist bus pulls up and they start taking pictures—
The only reason Barry Kalahu didn't finish you off—
DK, saved by a Japanese tourist bus.

The posters on your bedroom wall.
You stumbled off with your head in your armpit. Wanting Rod.
Feb '75—
Whole of the line-up saw you. Stumbling off Sunset.
Shamed.
Sheepish.
Paper tiger.
The best surfer in the world.
Done.

A passing hippie tour guide took pity on you.
Put you on his pony help you up the hell
—the hill.
You was slumped across the pony's back. As you were crossing the road the pony reared at something and threw you off.
On the tar.
You heard someone laugh.
A Japanese tourist.
Pointing.
Laughing at you.
Taking a photo.

THE ROAD

Two nights, I'm done. I'm hungry, I can't find no coin, I got no food or nothing in the house, I'm afraid to go out, The Thing staring at me from its corner. An untouched surfboard has a bad vibe: malignant.

The Thing. Yellow, white and black. Colours of pain looking at me.

And then she's back:
The BFO.
She who was formerly known as the BFO.

'Mo's at the hospital,' I go, like she's come here to visit Mo and I'm not wanting her to stay a minute longer than she has to. Be wasting her time with me whichever way.

She just shakes her head. Hands on hips in the doorway of the living room. Evil security grille behind her, framing her. I get my feet off the ground. Curl up like a Buddha on the armchair.

'How many years has she been going to the hospital, Dennis?'

'Dunno.' Like, what's it to her?

'Does she always go to the hospital for two nights, Dennis?'

I keep my feet off the ground.

'Does she go once every four months, Dennis? Is it a regular thing, Dennis?'

Push the aviators up the bridge of my nose (still there).

'Does she ever have anything wrong with her, Dennis? Health-wise? I mean, does she ever seem sick before she goes to the hospital?'

The BFO's standing there interrogating me, like she's angry with me, like I've disappointed her, like she has a right to be disappointed with me. With DK. I don't know about this. I don't know about this.

'You don't have a clue, do you, Dennis? Don't have a clue. Just another woman in your life you haven't bothered to ask.'

All too heavy for me. Get up and make a run for me bedroom. But the BFO's quicker than DK, faster on the draw, and she's got a claw round me upper arm and she's stopped me there, right there, and she's making another grab at me, at the face, at the aviators, she's wanting to swipe them off and I'm freaking and back away so sudden I bang my head against the doorframe and I'm rubbing it and almost crying it hurts so much, and she sees how I'm hurting and she lets go.

Taking pity on The Great Man.

'You don't know where she goes, do you?' she says.

I don't say nothing.

'Well yeah,' she says. 'But no!' Putting on the DK stink-eye. Enigmatic. Mysto man in the shadows.

But when she's doing it she knows how stupid she's making it look: the DK stink-eye. The favourite line.

Stupid stupid idiot. Don't know a thing. Yeah, but no, but don't know a fricken thing.

She nods. Full of piss and triumph. Got me now.

'She goes to the Road, Dennis. She goes to the Road for visits.'

I shake my head, or not really, my head shakes itself, like it's got Parko's, that type of thing. I back into me bedroom and slam the door on her. I jump in me bed and she's outside the door still.

Like she does think she's my girl.

Like she reckons she has rights.

Like she's entitled to be disappointed in me.

'She goes to the Road, Dennis! Not the hospital!'

The Road/The Rod/The God/The FUCKHEAD!/FUCKHEAD!!!!!

I turn my radio up so I can't hear her ranting and raving, but:

'And Dennis! When are you gunna ride this fucken thing? Eh? When are you gunna have the hair to ride a surfboard you *can* ride?'

Radio, right up to tops.

'Ar, fuckya, Dennis!'

An envelope like a snake under my bedroom door.

The security grille slamming behind her.

Must be some coin in it. Direct to me.

For my story.

I'll go for that.

Just me and her envelope and me radio now.

PIPE

Two days after Barry Kalahu, Rod figured if they turned on DK he lost his protection. He'd got this idea of saving energy by burying his boards down the beach, in a hole he dug in the sand. Save him carrying his two big-wave sticks to and from. Great idea, Rod. Next morning the sand-grooming tractor come along and minced up both his boards. Rod didn't take it as a sign of his own stupidity. Took it as a sign that Hawaii was angry with him and he had to get out.

He wasn't in your room.

His gear gone.

His clothes gone.

DK, alone again.

Hawaii against the paper tiger.

The coconut wireless: how Barry Kalahu had ironed you out. The way you drug yourself away. Saved by a Japanese tourist bus. Fallen off a pony.

Your coin gone.

Your name.

DK was sick and didn't front for Sunset. Jeff Hakman, king of Sunset, Mr Sunset, won it. In your absence.

Lying awake thinking they're gunna come and burn your hotel down—

In your dreams there was ten times Barry Kalahu and he or they got you in the water, shoved your face under your board and pounded you against the fins—

Drowning—

Then you got washed inshore and another ten times Barry Kalahu was on the beach with soccer-ball fists—

•

The last comp was Pipeline, the third one, the big one, but your Hawaiian trip had went from triumph into defeat, echo round the world. Sure you got barrelled at Haleiwa better than anyone had ever surfed it in a thousand years, sure you was definitely gunna be world champ, sure you stayed out of jail but

but you been ironed out at Sunset and hadn't shown your face since.

The disappearing man.

The ghost who surfs.

Ghost who don't surf.

Your insides tearing you apart.

You phoned Mo and asked for money.

She sent you an air ticket home.

You always loved her when you needed something (she said).

You go and cash in the air ticket and score some dope. Not smack, just grass to even you out. You didn't want to shoot smack with Rod not here.

You spent the week of Sunset stoned on Hawaiian grass.

Wondering what they were saying about you.

The world champion elect.

When you had to get something to eat, starving to death, you snuck out and ran across Kammie's Market in a crouch hoping none of the heavies seen you. You was like a commando. You pinched fruit from a stall and made a run for it.

When you come back you heard the hotel desk staff talking about you.

Saying they'd have to ask you to leave your room cos there was people threatening to burn the whole place down.

That's what you heard anyway.

You was so freaked you heard someone in your room middle of one night, jumped out of bed and threw a wild punch at what turned out to be the air-con unit.

Nearly busted your wrist.

Put the TV in front of the broken unit so the staff wouldn't see it.

First day of Pipe, you made your comeback.

Pinned on the sea wall a Keith surfboard snapped clean in half. Someone been busy the night before. Back half of the board spraypainted:

Good luck

Front half spraypainted:

DK

A message for you: *Good luck DK*. On a snapped Keith board. All talking about you.

Paddled into the line-up for your first heat. Heaviest wave in the world, most famous wave on your bedroom wall, and you hadn't even went out for a practice sesh. Not even a free surf.

Pipe getting solid that day. Fifteen, eighteen foot. There was blokes piking out of the conness all over the place. Best surfers in the world taking a look at it and fighting themself. When in doubt, don't go out.

You gone out.

In your first-round heat: Ian Cairns, Jeff Hakman . . . and Tink.

Tink hadn't even meant to be in the event. Tink wasn't invited. Tink was on the alternates list.

But when Eddie Aikau had pulled out with an injury, Tink's name been pulled out of the hat.

'Glenn Tinkler, you're in, come up, entry fee's $150.'

The rule was, alternates had to put up their entry money right there and then or else they were out and the next alternate got called up.

Tink had no cash on him.

The next alternate was Mark Richards.

And you know what MR did? Instead of rubbing out the scungy little bastard, MR, future world champion, *gave Tink his own $150*.

You were freaked by the whole thing. It went against everything Tink stood for.

He just stood there gobsmacked. MR said, *Go on, surf well*. Almost had to push Tink up there.

So that was the only reason Tink was in your head.

In your heat.

MR, gutless eh. Still a young kid he was. Tried to look like a terrific bloke by giving Tink his coin. Everyone knew he did it cos he was shitting his camouflage brown boardies.

•

So little Tink, one of the Bronzed Aussies now, red hair cut short back and sides, swimwear model, surfboard model, your little Coolie kid who you hadn't talked to since you both been here in Hawaii.

Hawaii.

Living The Life.

The posters on your bedroom walls. Both of yous.

Out in the line-up Tink paddled away from you. You wanted to talk to him. He was ignoring you.

Big set come and yous were both nowhere near it.

You paddled after him. Little Tink.

Fuck off, Den!

You didn't say nothing. Just wanted to sit out there on your boards together, not speaking, just taking it all in:

Hawaii, us. Come a long way eh? Who'da thought it?

But Tink was scared of you.

Thought you was gunna kill him.

He paddled into a mid-size wave, dropped down the face, pulled up, stalled under the lip, and rode this heavy dark barrel right into the channel, kicked off. The look on his face.

Nice one Tink.

Running second to you in the world championship points.

When he paddled back out you still hadn't got one.

Only wanted to sit on your board beside him, feeling the swell under your stick.

Here:

Hawaii.

But Tink kept paddling away from you.

So, action: you get a barrel better than his one.

You lost sight of the little bugger. Next set you paddled hard, got into position A. Just as you were taking off you looked down and there he was, little rinky Tink himself—he got inside you in the deeper part of the wave, somehow. He outpaddled you, outpositioned you.

But you DK was committed. You gave a last thrust and got up and your wrist nearly killed you, aching from where you TKO'd the air-con unit, so you were up a little slower than normal and dropped straight down the face in front of him, cutting him off. You dug your rail and pulled up the face in your bottom turn. Shocking drop-in, it cost you an interference penalty, but you had no choice. You were committed.

Amazing bit was, Tink hadn't eaten it inside you. Hadn't fallen off. You were firing down the line, hanging on for dear life, and you could hear his board chattering behind.

Must of wanted to nut you.

He had the better take-off so he had more speed. You heard his board right up your back.

You felt a hand between your shoulder blades.

The noise deafening, the barrel smashing behind you.

Tink with his hand on your back.

The lip about to smash down on top of yous both. Yous get smeared on the reef and it was your fault.

Must of wanted to kill you.

But he didn't kill you, didn't push you off your board. Instead he give you a firm forward nudge. He pushed you hard enough to get you through into the next section, past that falling lip, onto a beautiful twelve-foot ramp.

Behind you, he got buttered. On the reef.

The barrel spat you out, ages later. You raised an arm in the air, claiming the wave. Heard cheering on the shore.

But they wasn't cheering you. They hated you.

They was cheering Tink, who was up on his board and paddling back out.

Cheering him for what he done.

You were knocked round worse than him. Didn't know what to make of it. Felt like you were gunna spew out there. Physically ill.

Why'd he done that?

Tink still wouldn't come near you.

Best thing he ever done for you in ten years.

Why? What was all this 'sportsmanship' about, first MR and now Tink?

But he wouldn't let you come near him.

You only wanted to say thanks. Nicest thing anyone ever done for you.

He wouldn't let you.

Why do it then?

•

The sets were still coming, the heat still hot. You had to keep surfing. But no spark. You didn't want to beat your little mate, not this time.

You didn't know it yet but you felt it:

He just turned the present into the past.

Massive Hima fricken Layas rolling in from the west. There was a north swell too in the water and sometimes the west ones and the north ones doubled up into one warped wonky peak splitting the clouds. You never seen walls of water so tall and deep, like someone was rolling skyscrapers down a slope at you. One set was so big and you were so far inside you had to turn round and scratch that hard to get out and over the crest that you felt the panic rising—you weren't gunna make it. You were scratching your way up the crowning lip and a gust of wind come with it, flicking you up in the air, vertical—

You lost your purchase, you were gunna come down the face backwards, sucked down the falls—

But the gust died as you were up in the air and when you come down, the wave had went past you.

Off the hook.

Heart thump. They said you knew if you really wanted big waves by did your heart rate go up or down when you were out in this. With Hawaiian gods their hearts beat slower in thirty-footers. But you, your heart was going like a drag racer and you didn't want a wave, you wanted to cry. Not liking it out here. At home, even if the waves got up to eight foot, which was big big, you wiped out you might get a sand poo in your boardies and a razz from the boys. Here, if you wipe out you've caught your last wave. Too much for you. Too big. You didn't like it here in this—

Hawaii—

But DK the best surfer in the world so—

Paddled hard or pretended to for the first wave of the next set. It pitched up over the reef, all hollow inside—

—like your stomach. You pressed up with your sore wrist, got to your feet, drove through your bottom turn, come up to stall under the lip and tuck in—

Where nobody can see you—

Empty inside—

And the lip got you on the head as it come over.

You hadn't fitted into the tube—

Wrong size, Dennis—

Next thing you know you're head first flying—

Empty inside—

—in the black sea, black with reef rock and seaweed—

—still down, your leg pulled down by your leash—

—stick caught in the reef, holding you down?—

The wave holding you down—

There was boulders down there big as cars, and the sea rolling them round like marbles—

Then it let you go and you come up, dig yourself an escape tunnel up through the foam—

Then it suck you back down again with it—

No more air—

It come to you: that one was the third one in the third set. The ninth wave. You forgot to keep count. Served you right.

Your leash sucking you down in the reef. Reef licks skin off your legs, clean red sheets.

Like a movie when it gets to:

The End.

No: you float up the top and time for one breath before:

Another—

And another—

Colours of all pain: red, yellow, blue, black.

Red, yellow, blue, black.

For a second you blacked out. Then—

You were in the underwater night. Already dead.

Arms thrashing round the air pockets. Hands grip nothing.

You had your eyes open but it's all black down there. Dead. No way up, no way down. A dream.

Tears in your chest.

Dry tears in your gut.

Pressure in your ears squeaking like a pair of knives—

Empty inside. Didn't care—

So this is how it ends:

Hawaii.

They'd go: *DK eh he died doing what he loved.*

But you didn't love this. No love here in the black pain.

You weren't using your Scream in Blue here, not since Barry Kalahu.

Nobody could hear you anyway. None of those ones out there, walking the earth, swimming, sleeping, flying, those ones all of them with enough air to breathe, more air than they knew what to do with and none for you.

You just went ragdoll, empty inside. All done.

It's mind over matter they say.

But sometimes there's too much matter.

Ya've seen the last of her, Den.

She won't be giving ya no more troubles.

Ya can focus on what matters, Den. World tour and that.

Nah, forget her eh.

Roddy's Triple Crown: the shop, the dog, the bird.

Those last waves you saw, those big blue sets turned white against the big blue sky, big beautiful coffins wrapping you up and rolling you down:

Beauty. The last thing you saw on earth:

The beauty of a giant wave. How it filled up your screen on a scale you never seen before. Boils halfway up the face from sucky reef outcrops. You'd stopped paddling. Give yourself up to them. So much bigger and more beautiful than anything, filled up all your vision, no edges to it, just all blue. Blue. Blew your head open.

You loved them.

And now so happy—

—you gave yourself to them—

Never so stoked. You thought:

Far out—

You decided you'd do the Rolf Aurness now and

yeah and

the Lisa Exmire and

yeah and walk away from it all—

Thank Gawd I'm here.

BACK 1

Mo's back. Lets herself in the door. Didn't need no lift, no village minibus. Got back under her own steam.

From—

From—

I'm dying in me room. Kitchen like a bomb's hit it. Me, starving to death. Must be down to about sixteen and a half stone. Puffed up like a cooking sausage. About to burst.

Dying of hunger.

Nothing in that envelope kept me fed.

Bloody BFO.

Mo's in my room beside me on the bed, stroking my arm. Like she's caring for me, thinking about me, worried about me, but she's not really. Not here at all. She's back where she's been.

The not hospital.

The Road/The Rod/The Toad/The God/—

My Mo don't tell me where she been.

I don't know what to do.

I don't know what to do.

She's not back.

BACK II

It was Tink and Barry Kalahu fished you out.

Alive? Sort of. Depends what you—

Mixed blessing.

Tink and Barry brang you in. Without your board. Coral and sand sticking to your skinned legs.

They said you looked even worse than when Barry had ironed you out.

All laughs.

Barry Kalahu said, laughing but solemn too:

What we say here is, you were touched by the Finger, DK, but the Hand moved on.

But he was wrong, you was dead:

Red, yellow, blue, black.

You went to the sick bay.

Broken jaw.

From Barry Kalahu.

Gashes in your knee, your back, the back of your head. Cuts down your ribs and feet. Legs done over by the giant apple-peeler of Banzai reef.

Love from Hawaii.

Dear DK—

Love, Pipeline.

You were sob city. Bursting in tears at the drop of a hat.

Tink got the boys out of there so nobody'd see you. But some of them had and that's how the story started:

The Great DK left Pipe shaking, crying like a baby . . .

You DK was out.

Of the Pipe Masters.

Of Hawaii.

You died inside the posters on your bedroom wall.

Mo, Brisbane Airport. March '75. The Sandman panel van sprayed purple and orange in the No Standing zone.

Twenty years fell on her face when she laid eyes on you.

In you, the black pain all on again.

Mo.

Salright love, yer alright.

Shook your head over and over.

Here comes the waterworks, sob city:

Mo.

Salright love, yer alright.

You weren't all right

nah

you died and went to hell.

In the posters on your bedroom wall.

You come back from Hawaii strung out and covered in cuts and bruises and stitched up and sick in your stomach and wired in your jaw and choking down the shame, the shame, the shame, the shame.

And the champion of the world.

Inaugural champion of the World Professional Surfing Tour.

You.

Nobody at the airport to meet you but Mo.

You won, Den love. You won.

Her flabby arms wobbling round you.

Nobody remembers who come second, eh Mo? you mumbled.

That's the truth, Den love. Don't you ever forget that.

Her flabby arms. Her gold-coloured floral house dress. Her hair gone white while you was away.

And then people start spotting DK in the terminal, running towards him with their cameras, their banners, their autograph books, their microphones, their tape recorders, their love and their love.

The Kirra Boardriders set up a podium and presented you with your world champion's trophy, the dinkiest cheap little gold-painted plastic surfer you ever seen in a lifetime of dinky cheap gold-painted plastic surfers.

Yeah thanks a lot, was your speech. And in case they didn't realise how much it meant to you, you added: *And thanks.*

They went wild. You brought the house down. World champion. You could fart and they'd of went berserk.

Middle of '75. Spent in pain. Rod was back home and he nursed you. Him and you didn't talk much. Didn't have to. Him and you had a mutual friend.

In pain, Hawaii. Tink had bombed out at Pipeline, leaving you with the most accumulated points in the nine-leg world tour, from your wins in Australia, months earlier, the wins nobody remembered now cos all they remembered, all they talked about, was *Hawaii.*

The posters on your bedroom wall.

The TV, the newspapers, the punters in Coolie were all on about how you was world champion.

The surfers, the ones who knew what meant what, were all on about how you been ironed out by Barry Kalahu first and Pipeline second. How Hawaii had beat you. The big one-two. How you had no respect for the home of surfing, how you'd went in there like a dumb vandal, and how Hawaii had paid you back for your disrespect. How your world title rings like an empty glass. Ding ding ding.

Empty: you filled up on Rod's friend.

The world champion. The Hawaii kook who couldn't handle big waves and big men. Small-wave bully, champion of the dribble. In the big waves, a scaredy-cat.

Your behaviour that next cyclone season wasn't the best to be honest. You and Rod went out and swiped cars and Rod drive them down the wrong side of the highway. Sometimes you even drove, just to get a feel for it. You be cranking on whiz and smack and grass and flying down wrong side of the highway but Rod had complete trust in you and you had complete trust in DK and you always managed to pull out the way of the oncoming car on the blind corner

but yeah but I just can't

you weren't only nicking cars and driving them. You be smoking cigarettes as you sped along. That weirded Rod out cos you never smoked fags. You dropped acid and thought two-foot Snapper was six to eight Pipe. You pinched blokes' birds. Not that you were up to doing anything with them, but you had to keep pinching them. Had to keep breaking into their bedrooms. Their bathrooms. Not that you did nothing. Most of the time to stop them screaming out you had to tell them you made a mistake, got the wrong address, and if they kept on screaming you run away. Not that it mattered. You only did it for the PR. Had a name to keep up.

World champion DK.

The greatest DK in the world.

And still the only world trophy you got was the plastic one from Kirra Boardriders. Nobody from outside the Gold Coast turned up to interview you or give you your fricken crown or whatever it was—

Till you went through your old mail:

Letter from that World Surfing Federation

yeah but nah

some technicality over Sunset

sent months ago

Xerox copy of the rules saying

nah

entry in all events as a condition of

you couldn't

We know how much adverse publicity this is likely to attract but

nah they fucken

We would appreciate if you

they fucken

null and void

they

as a consequence the championship is declared vacant

they—nah

by way of compensation and goodwill we offer you entry and top seeding into the next

they

we do hope you understand the nature

The nature? The fricken nature?

You had to burn that one so Mo'd never

they must of wanted to kill her.

No other reason for doing that.

Kill your old Mo. After everything she done. They done this.

That's it.

The End.

THAT THING AGAIN

Mo's back from the not hospital but not really.

'Mo?'

At the melamine table. Fat feet in the air. Can't get any diagonals working in this place.

Mo's eyes look up. Her red rims like hammocks. Her eyes not comfortable enough to lie back in them and relax.

Push the aviators up me nose. They're still there.

'Yeah love?'

I nod at the other room. Even though I'm nodding at the doorway we know what I'm nodding at:

Yellow black and white.

Standing in its corner. Making new diagonals.

'What is it love?'

'I want to go again in the morning.'

I nod at the—

Through the doorway—

I want Mo happy with this but she is not happy. She looks sadder. The eyes sadder than the rest of her. Sadder and sadder. Every breath a sigh. She walks round *sighing*. Like it's all catching up with her. Like I'm catching up with her.

Her hands open and close on themselves, but weak.

'I'm glad you give it to me,' I go.

After all them things I give her when I had the coin, after all them things she give me when I didn't, after all the things she give, all the things we give, all the things she give and give and give and give and give, I never said I'm glad before. But I want to now because it's too late

before it's too late.

Mo just shakes her head.

'Den love.'

Sigh. Her bloodshot nose whistling.

I push the aviators up and look away from her. Don't want her happiness now. I've said what I have to.

'Den love. I didn't get it for ya.'

DEVIL WIND

Seventy-five, the year they said the devil come to Snapper. Junk dealers rocked up and stood on Greenmount Hill, give a whistle, surfers in.

They come like trained puppies they come.

Be perfect mornings, four foot and offshore, and the waves empty. Instead the boys lined up outside some fibro shack at Point Danger.

Junk dealers in trench coats.

You didn't mind. You surfed on smack while everyone else zoned out on couches. Anyone watched you surf junked-up, they figured this stuff had to be good for the surfing. Then they go off and shoot up and zone out.

You get a lot of waves to yourself that year.

Roddy's good mate eliminated the competition.

Final victory.

Yeah nah, you didn't behave your best. Nineteen seventy-five. You was free surfing three-foot D–Bah and Tink tried to fade you. You took him out with a rugby tackle, leap from your board got him round the ankles. Under the water you tried to throttle him. Saw him turn green before you let him go.

First time you seen him since he fished you up the steep sand at Pipe.

Your surfing was blitzing but you were empty of every drop but anger and hunger. On smack you won the Queensland title on eight-foot Burleigh. FJ was back for that one, back from his break, blondie in the heat before yours. He'd went even more corporate if that was possible and had his own shops up and down the Goldie. Riding a shocking pink FJ stick, piece of crap, and paddling for the last wave of his heat. Well you were in the next heat after him so you paddled in the wave. FJ screamed, *Get off, DK, it's still my heat!* First words exchanged between the pair of you since '74. You drop straight down the face, cut him off, sent him smash on the rocks, brand-spanking-new stick and all.

Your stick got washed in too so you swum over and grabbed FJ's. He yelled out:

Gimme me stick back, ya dickhead!

You blanked him.

You didn't get penalised cos you weren't technically surfing a heat yet. But FJ was out of the comp.

Welcome back son. Welcome to surfing the same water as the champion of the world—

well come on nah—

you nodded up to the three thousand mugs on the point and said to FJ:

They come to see me, not you eh.

You surfed your heat on FJ's board while he had to swim against the rip to get back to shore. He got a point-blank view of you winning.

Winning yeah.

You was able to mess with their heads even more. You done your disappearing acts before a heat, but this time, before the final, when the swell had jacked up to cyclone strength and everyone getting a bit nervy (cept you), you paddled out half an hour *before* the final and freaked out all them cos that was the one place they hadn't expected to see you. As it turned out they got hammered by a set at the beginning of the final, all them washed in at points up the coast, and you DK was the only one left in the water. You only had to catch one leftover wave to win the title but instead you put on a big show in the close-out sets, barrel after barrel. For the fans. Going where they couldn't see you.

You won again at Bells, smashed the South African wonder kid Shaun Tomson in the final. Being champ you were attracting television cameras like flies to dog poo so you weren't too keen to show your face.

Rod's car broke down before the preso so you couldn't make it. They put on a second preso at the pub the next night and you made your longest speech of your life, you acknowledged all the other surfers you beat except for that little show pony FJ. It was a class act and brang the house down. Then you disappeared again—off with Rod to meet a blind date.

•

But something wasn't working right.

Wasn't working right.

Wasn't working.

With you.

No Lisa?

Rod: *Forget her. Gone. Buried.*

Something else.

Didn't help you were doing smack every day, chain-smoking joints like ciggies, a little acid or goey on special occasions. When you go down to Sydney for the Surfabout at North Narra it was Disneyland: smack on tap. You had no idea how good the gear could be and how cheap. You spent your $2500 from winning Bells and really needed the $3500 from winning Surfabout, so you went out, greatest surfer in the world, DK himself, all the mind games and the freakouts—

And bombed. Fell off your board. Dug a rail. Nosedived. Got clobbered trying a barrel.

You shut your eyes under the water and saw:

Hawaii.

Posters on your bedroom wall.

Barry Kalahu.

Pipe.

Then you were in a third-round repechage heat with FJ and you almost faded him but pulled out, you didn't need an interference, put you out of the event . . .

FJ was hassling and hassling and zigging and zagging between his zigs and his zags. Your legacy. They all copied you. Including the mind games. It was savage you was hassling each other so bad neither of you was getting a wave.

Then:

Eh DK, ya hear that on the beach?

FJ. You blanked him.

Nah seriously, ya hear that?

Your hearing was never that good during a heat. All you could hear was the megaphone announcer saying, *Keith Keith Johnson Johnson Keith Keith . . .*

Deadset, FJ said. *They're saying we been DQ'd for a double intoe. Bastards!*

No way.

·

You listened hard. You were bombed out of your gourd. But he was right. They were saying *Keith and Johnson have both been disqualified from the heat*. Far out, if that was right you was out of Surfabout.

FJ started paddling in got his last wave on his belly.

You followed.

When you come on the beach here's FJ and a bunch of his new Bronzed Aussie mates shitting their pants laughing so hard at you. Pointing.

Turned out you hadn't been DQ'd at all. FJ been pulling your leg rope.

But you was out of the Surfabout.

FJ had enough points from earlier rounds to stay in it.

But you, out.

Of the conness.

No money left.

Out of it.

Walked off without lifting your head.

Left your stick on the beach.

Been pulling your leg rope.

Just then Tink walked past, on the way to his heat. He looked sad at you. Pity. You couldn't take that.

Eh Dennis, Tink said. *What goes round comes round, eh?*

The worst thing was he wasn't having a go at you. He was sad for you.

You needed to get back to Rod and Rod's mate eh.

Eliminated.

Nice one.

No money. Have to call Mo get her to send some down.

You met Rod in the van in the car park.

We gotta call Mo, you said.

What'll we do before the money arrives?

Dunno, you said. *Surf?*

You weren't planning to surf. You were planning to score. This was Sydney—

Disneyland.

You told Rod you purposely lost your heat cos the tax dept was going to audit you if you won.

That's right Dennis, deadset, Rod said.

Sitting in the van—
Crossing the bridge at Narrabeen Lagoon—
Cops.
Pulled over, searched:
Champion of the world.
Luckiest day of your life cos you hadn't scored yet, hadn't got any coin.
Nothing in the car but a few stems and seeds.
Cops didn't book yous.
Wanted an autograph:
Champion of the world.

Australian titles were in South Oz that year.
Late '75:
South Oz:
Sharkland.
You weren't behaving your best—
Since Hawaii.
You and Rod got lost on the road and front late for your first heat.
As usual. Stoned out of your bonce. As usual.
But they wouldn't let you in.
The national titles, with you as defending champ.
Champion of the world.
And they wouldn't let you in.
Be buggered.
You and Rod got in the van drove straight back out. Got lost again, in the desert.
Old days yous'd of cacked your brains out.
These days nothing much was funny. Yous got down to business, the works, the van, you and Rod.
A nap on the roadside.
Heading north again.
Queensland.

The edge:
Gone.
Something caught up with you.
Something from behind.
You didn't see it.

You felt it, you heard it.

Didn't see it.

Like another guy had took off even deeper on the wave and for the first time you been shocked, hadn't seen him coming . . .

. . . yeah . . .

You DK was champion of the world and started losing events in Australia. Unprecedented.

As they reminded you.

Tink was winning.

FJ was winning.

You giving the most interviews you'd ever given. Mile a minute.

You told the reporters you was bored with winning.

You told the reporters the scoring system hadn't caught up with you yet.

You told the reporters you hadn't reached your peak yet.

You told the reporters they'd lose interest in the sport if you won everything, so you were losing on purpose to get them into it again.

You told the reporters you felt sorry for your fellow pros and wanted to give them a turn.

You told the reporters there was conspiracies against you.

You told the reporters you was turning away from the backstabbing on that world tour, the politics and that.

You told the reporters you was sick of the other reporters.

You told the reporters you was gunna retire at twenty-six and put yourself through college. Business degree. That sort of thing.

You told the reporters you was only properly respected in Hawaii. In Hawaii.

They didn't ask you about Barry Kalahu.

They didn't ask you about Pipeline.

They didn't ask cos they all knew.

They let you go on about how you were bored with winning and if you didn't want to win you didn't want to surf.

That kind of thing.

(Still no Lisa.)

You decided to stay in Coolie that next season, sit out the '75–76 world tour. Sponsors couldn't believe it. Organisers couldn't believe it.

Nobody couldn't believe it. But you had enough of comp surfing. Let them wait for you. What Lisa would of said: let them catch up to you.

And Hawaii hadn't invited you.

Kept that to yourself and it didn't get out:

To the reporters.

But Hawaii hadn't invited you.

You had a call from Fred Hemmings, organiser of the big Hawaiian events.

Sorry, Dennis, there's no place for you this year.

But I'm world fricken champion!

Sorry, Dennis, there's no place for you this year.

You can't leave out the world fricken champion!

Sorry, Dennis. You're not world champion in Hawaii.

Hawaii.

You took down them posters off your bedroom wall.

But you was spending a lot more time in there.

With Rod and his mate.

With Rod's mate

yeah but

Rod was out a lot, with Sydney blokes. Sydney blokes brought it up. Queensland police had weeded the town, Gold Coast was a weed-free zone, and so but now all yous had to have fun on was the old Harry Hammerhead, and why wouldn't yous. Why wouldn't yous. The odd bloke clocked out with an OD, but you were careful. Mixed your own mix. Pure.

Pure natural genius.

You and Rod, that year yous were closer than you ever been. On the same flight path, same common interests in life. You woke up in the morning, you knew what you were gunna do that day and the best thing was, Rod was doing it too. Yous had a purpose. Brothers with business to do. Mo sort of shrugged and left yous to your own devices. Something changed in her since Hawaii too. She was nicer to Rod for a start, and a bit harder on you. Her and Rod, you'd often come in the kitchen and find them talking quietly together over a cup of tea, Rod stoned out of his bone, Mo not caring. Mo give you a growl, tell you to get back out surfing. There was peace in Sanga eh. Only now it'd lost another letter. On the front of the house, now: anga.

Rod when he was stoned once give his theory on it all. Like drugs had been the best thing for us. *Me problem me whole life*, he said in this big open-heart moment, *was that I had this chip on me shoulder cos you was always Mo's favourite, y'always got the preferential treatment, and it shitted me royal cos she was my mum but she put you first. So I was like better than you, had to tell meself that, I was better than you and you'd get yer comeuppance soon. And but so now, since we're on the gear eh, it's like, nah, I'm not better than you and you're not better than me, nothin makes no difference, we're just two junkie cunts and that's all there is to it and we're just as bad as each other. Makes me feel good eh.*

And made me feel good too, long as I kept me ears shut to what he wasn't telling me. The bit they left out.

Seventy-five, seventy-six. There was funerals, busts, blues, barneys and cops. Friends there one day gone the next. Some doing harry, some not. Cops watching you. Cops. Cops cops cops. Been watching you all your life.

Not all them wanting an autograph now.

No invitation from Hawaii.
Hawaii.
Barry Kalahu.
Pipe.
Smack.

The world tour on again, and FJ, Peter Townend, Mark Warren, Kanga Cairns leading the Bronzed Aussies:
Media.
Stunts.
Coaching clinics.
TV.
Gold jumpsuits.
Coin. Loads more coin.
Sponsors.
The world tour.
Moved on without you.

The world tour somewhere, and you in Coolie:

And the waves were empty.

And the waves were empty.

And the waves were being wasted.

And you were wasted, wasting the wasted waves.

Where'd all them blokes went?

What happened to Coolie?

Smack!

Funerals, funerals, funerals.

Courts, courts, courts.

Cops, cops, cops.

And you DK was not in them wasted waves. You was in your room, in Anga, with Roddy and Roddy's mate. Brotherly love, thicker than water.

No Roddy, just Roddy's mate. Your mate now.

Wasted, wasting the wasted waves.

The waves never stopped in Coolie.

Surfing did.

And the cops never stopped—

And the cops—

And the cops at your door—

The knock you been waiting for.

Smack!

Dennis Keith?

You pushed the aviators up your nose. Four in the morning. You been on the couch, dreaming Pipeline.

Dennis Keith? Are you Dennis—?

Shut up, mate, course he's Dennis Keith.

It's the other cop. Strange he's not wearing a police uniform. He's wearing plainclothes.

Mr Keith, we would like to ask you to come down to Coolangatta police station with us for an interview.

You arresting me?

No, Mr Keith, we're not arresting you. We want to talk to you.

What's he done, ya pig bastards?

Screech of Mo at your shoulder. But something about the police pushed her back in her box. She backed away, hand to her mouth like she's gunna scream.

We just want to talk to you—
In connection with—
In connection with—
In connection with—
Dennis?
Den love?

The world tour's somewhere in Brazil, or South Africa, or California—
    And you in Coolie cop shop.
    In connection with—
    A body.

BFO AGAIN

And but so yeah nah I don't touch The Thing again after that conversation with Mo.

I been as far as I can humanly go. Far as a man can go. So it's back to safety: radio at night, muesli in the morning, pine-lime Splice at Bob's, hang out Snapper and Greenmount while kids on the dream tour come up and chew the fat and tell stories about Tahiti, Maldives, Chile, all the weird places they go now, all the coin that's in it, all the gear, all The Life, but most of all talking about waves, and they wanna know about waves from way back; then roast chicken and potatoes with chicken salt for lunch, TV afternoon, chops and chips for tea. Wasn't for the gnarly lines inside that retirement unit I say I'm living like a king.

. . . yeah . . .

Mo getting edgy but.

Dunno why.

She won't move The Thing out of the living room and either will I.

And so yeah, it's out of the blue when this mother ship of a fricken people mover pulls up out the front door, for a second I think I'm seeing the Chariot from *Lost in Space*, it's like a bus but with surfing logos all over it and out jumps me old mate, she who was formerly known as the BFO. She come across the forecourt with her dish face and her muscly swagger, boy in a chick's body. In a black singlet and flowery boardies and thongs. I wonder does she got any friends or is she like me and Mo. Don't believe in friends. None of us do.

'C'mon, DK, we're outta here.'

Strides in the door like she owns the joint and picks up The Thing in both hands, walks it out and down the steps like it's one them corpses they find in this place every few weeks, loads it in the Chariot. There's other boards in there, a whole quiver. Serious surfer it turns out this bird.

And Mo sitting with her hands flat down on the kitchen table in her own world, like none of us is even there.

Mo freaking me:

The Road.

And so but yeah, nah, like a zombie I come out, follow the BFO to her Chariot and in the passenger seat.

'You need me to belt you up?'

She's standing by the door and I jump, mistook what she said.

'Nah I'm right.' I pull the seatbelt on.

And we're off.

It's that easy.

Didn't wash me hands before eating today.

Through the toy roundabouts, up the road out of Coolie, over the causeway to The Other Side, down the highway into New South. Not much said. What there is is one-sided, her asking questions of herself, yapping away typical surfer. Till I drop in:

'Favour?'

'Eh?' She looks at me across the cabin.

'Don't wanna go the same spot.'

'Where you've been trying to get back on the board?'

'Nah, that spot isn't being good to me.'

'I don't blame it.' Savage little laugh.

She knows the spot. Knows I've been going there. I look out the window, push the aviators up my nose.

'I saw you one day when you were with Mo,' she says, not looking at me. 'Trying to get up on a gun in one-foot onshore slop. It was either the definition of optimism, or . . .'

Shakes her head, chuckles.

No humour there.

'Or I didn't want to be seen.'

'Except you were.'

'I was?'

'Seen. By me.'

'Right. Yeah. You got nothin better to do?'

She grins to herself.

'Nice of you to ask me a question for once, DK.'

I say nothing.

I tell no-one.

'I like the quiet spots too,' she goes. 'If you can't get inside a barrel, the only place no-one can see you is the place where nobody surfs.'

Lying.

Make sure I'm looking out the window and she can't see my eyes. Not even the aviators. Can't have her seeing the eyes.

We drive past the turnoff. Going further south. If anyone sees me in this Chariot, The Thing in the back, I'm deadset gunna die on the spot. Hope she knows that. I will die. Deadset. Promise.

Maybe she does know. Could be she does want to kill me.

'You haven't read my letter, have you, Dennis.'

Don't say nothing.

'You haven't even opened it, have you.'

'Yeah nah, I did open it. Thought it might of had some coin for me.'

She nearly laughs.

'But you wouldn't read it, would you. Don't have the hair.'

She thinks I'm an uneducated man. Rather die than read her writings.

Wrong again.

THE OTHER SIDE

Coolangatta police station, July 19, 1975:

Pissing down rain, winter on the beach, no sadder place on the night of the earth. Coolie cop shop, they built it in sight of the waves. Used to be a debate in The Pit about did the cops do it on purpose—lock-up was bad enough, but lock-up while you can see hollow six-foot barrels in a winter offshore was sheer hell. If they did it to torment you. You reckoned, from a night or two of experience, the view kept you sane. Can still surf them in your head.

Interview room out the back, fibro shed rattling in the wind and rain.
Three coppers: one plainclothes, two Queensland. And you.
Two uniforms, one plainclothes.
The uniforms standing, the plainclothes sitting:
In front of you.

You know them two uniform ones. Tall one asked for your autograph when he pulled you over the other week. Plainclothes is an old-time regular longboarder from Snapper and Greenmount:
Butchers, plumbers, schoolteachers, priests, newsagents—
And cops.
Cops among the boardriders. Foxes in the henhouse.
Always had it in for you, them longboard riders you chased off the points.
Big fans of FJ and the Graceful Style. The clean-cut pros, the soul surfers, the bearers of the flame.

So, DK, plainclothes goes, with this smirk like he already knows you. You're famous. People know you who you don't know.
He got a big mo, even bigger than yours, droopier handlebars.
How's the dope trade going?

You push the aviators up your nose. Still there. Thank Christ.

Doing much dealing still?

He's smirking. Like we're all in on the joke.

But this isn't what we're here for.

In connection with:

A body.

Heard you got Mr Sunset hooked on the hammer when he was out here from Hawaii. Really fucked him up.

Plainclothes spent too much time in the sun. Heavy freckles. Chasing him off the points, you probably saved him from dying of skin cancer. He should be thanking you.

Lot of surfers buy gear from DK, that's what we've heard, says the tall uniform. *Big-time. They say you smuggle it round the place in hollowed-out surfboards. They say you smuggle it round in the door panels in cars. They say your brother smuggled it inside a fake plaster cast on his leg. They say you bring it in from South America. From Thailand. Stuffed inside hollow surfboards. Stuffed inside the panels of cars. Stuffed inside a so-called broken leg.*

They say, they say.

Well, longboard kook plainclothes goes, *man's gotta make a living somehow. Not like surfing's gunna do it for him. Even if he's the 'world champ' he's only making about ten grand a year max. Just a professional deadbeat.*

This isn't what they called me in for. So I keep me trap shut. Just like Rod done in that American airport.

Don't say nothing.

Say nothing.

Don't tell no-one.

Tell no-one.

So, Dennis, cat got your tongue? goes cheap suit.

Ar, DK never has much to say, goes uniform. *Do ya, Dennis? Well yeah . . . but nar!*

They're all cacking themselves at how he's drawled it out, like he's some zonked-out banana-bender drongo.

By the time they've finished wiping their eyes and appreciating a good joke in these tough times, good medicine laughter is, the mean cheap suit looks at you and goes:

So when did you last see Lisa Exmire, Dennis?

In connection with—

In connection with—

In connection with—

In connection with—

No.

Nah. Definitely no way.

You push the aviators up your nose. Still there.

When did you last see Lisa Marie Exmire, Dennis?

What I don't get is what they're on about. Aside from that I'm doing fine.

Dunno. Few months ago. Last year.

It speaks! Cheap suit gives a clap.

(What she said once—that Greenmount—inside you—is she still?— how would they know what she said?)

Am I under arrest? I say.

Dunno. Should you be?

I shrug and fold my arms and lean back. Not gunna crap on with this crap no longer. I'll answer their questions if there's a question to answer and that's that.

So when did you last see her?

Weren't you her boyfriend? They smirk at each other, like the joke's going on.

Spose so. Gotta answer that. Matter of record.

So why don't you know where you last saw her? Funny way of breaking up, eh Dennis? Nah, you were with her on New Year's Eve, weren't you, like all good boyfriends are with their girlfriends, eh Dennis?

Shrug. Push the aviators up the nose. Still there.

I go:

She more or less did her own thing. I wasn't gunna stand in her way. She had her band and stuff. She went off and did her own thing, then come back, then went off again.

They both nod, like they know all this already.

An independent woman, eh Dennis? What they're all like these days, goes the longboarder in the shiny elbows. He's taking over now. His freckles are getting big on me.

Had her own trip going, I shrug.

Do you like that in women, Dennis? Independence?

I dunno what he's getting at so I keep my lip buttoned.

She had a few other boyfriends as well, didn't she? Did her own thing there too?

I don't say nothing.

Which you didn't really like? She sort of humiliated you, didn't she?

Nothing.

Put it out here, there and everywhere, eh Dennis? Wasn't really edifying for a big-time he-man like you, was it? Not very nice to have a girlfriend like that? Eh Den?

I say nothing.

I mean, it's okay for a bloke, but when it comes to chicks it's not really the done thing, eh Den?

I say nothing.

She made your blood race, didn't she, Dennis?

I say nothing.

She made your blood boil, didn't she, Dennis?

They all just let that hang there, grinning at me stone-cold. I push the aviators up me nose and keep me arms crossed. Don't tell them nothing. Like Rod in the airport.

She's got your blood right through her, eh Den?

Got your muck in her.

Right through her.

Doesn't look good, Den.

Doesn't look good.

What I don't get, I say, to break the silence, *is why I'm here.*

And what I don't get, the narky cheap suit pushes his mo right in my face, and now it's no joke, now he's mighty pissed off, *is why you haven't asked us any questions.*

Now they're trying to get me talking more. I say nothing.

Like, we're telling you that your ex-girlfriend has been found dead—

You hadn't told me that.

Your ex-girlfriend has been found dead in a place that looks very, very bad for you, Dennis, very bad indeed, and not only dead, my friend, she's been absolutely slaughtered, and you know what they thought they had when they found her body? They thought they'd found a very fat, huge black man. That's what it looked like. So decomposed and bloated, Dennis, that's what became of your girlfriend, and it's sickening, you know, sickening, turns the stomach of any decent human being it does, and this is your ex-girlfriend, yours Dennis, someone you're supposed to have cared for, 'loved' even, and she's been savagely

*and brutally murdered and dumped at this spot that, well, only a few people
know about, don't they, and you'd be one of them, and you're her ex-boyfriend,
mate, and here we are, this is why you're here, mate, and, mate, you were her
ex-boyfriend and join the dots, right, and what's more, what's more, my friend,
her body has been tested and her skin's full of* fibreglass, *pickled in it, and
it's pretty obvious she's been done in in a place where there's a lot of fibreglass,
right, get it, itchy stuff, drives you mad if you get it in your clothes and in your
skin, would've driven her mad if she hadn't had other problems to deal with, eh
Dennis, fibreglass fibres, fibres of glass, mate, like you get in a* shaping bay,
*and she disappeared last New Year's Eve, mate, and who do you think she'd
be with on New Year's Eve but her boyfriend, right, so we've brought you in
here to ask you a few basic questions and you haven't shown a glimmer, not
the barest glimmer of surprise or curiosity about why we've brought you here,
and now I'm telling you this, you're not showing me anything either, you're just
sitting there like a department-store dummy, mate, and that to be honest fills
me with suspicion it does, it makes me ask a few questions myself as to why
you are sitting there so cool and calm when we're telling you this, and not the
least bit surprised, well that's a red flag to me, mate, that's a red fucking flag,
and I don't know about you but I want to ask you a lot more questions because
you've got me very interested now, and I suggest, and I don't suggest this very
often but I think it's the responsible thing to do, and it goes against my better
instincts but I'm going to make the suggestion, Dennis, I'm going to suggest that
you get straight on the phone and call your solicitor if you have one, or if you
don't have one you should call someone who does know a good solicitor for you,
because you might find yourself in a lot of trouble by the end of tonight and I
don't want anybody to be able to say that you were not given a fair go, because
before too long you're going to find yourself in such hot water that being beaten
to a pulp by Barry Kalahu and a three-wave hold down at Pipeline is gunna
seem like a picnic in the park, eh Dennis, a picnic in the park, right, so I'd get
on the blower quick bloody smart if I were you, eh Dennis?*

That was below the belt.

That was real mean.

How they knew about Barry Kalahu and Pipe.

That riled me up.

But I say nothing.

You gunna call a lawyer? goes shiny elbows.

I say nothing.

You gunna make a statement?

He's like this all the time, goes the tall uniform. *That bit he said before, about his girl doing her own thing, that was the biggest speech anyone's ever heard him make.*

Quiet achiever, eh? goes shiny suit.

Might need to go Plan B.

He nods to the tall uniform who goes outside. That leaves plainclothes and the other uniform, short, dark, no-neck, head like a thumb. I ain't seen him before. He ain't said a word.

Sitting in a fibro shed—the 'interview room'. It has diagonal metal security grilles on the windows, and fly screens. I got my feet up in the air. All the lines in this room are way too confused, way wrong for me.

You know she had a kid, don't you.

Cheap suit says it as a statement.

Little girl. Year old now. Living with her grandparents. How does that make you feel, Dennis? Orphaned girl? No mum for her? Or dad? How does that make you feel? She yours? Course she isn't. Course she bloody well isn't. How did that make you feel when you found out about it? Eh Den?

Always had it in for me. I burnt him off the points. Longboard kook. Trimmer. Wasted too many waves. I only had to bring some order to the place, some hierarchy, some respect. These blokes never forgive me for that.

But you knew about the girl, didn't you. You knew about her and you knew she wasn't yours, right?

Don't say nothing. I say nothing.

Don't tell no-one.

Tell no-one.

The first kick gets me in the shin.

I look up at thumb-head who's standing over me, to the side of the desk, like he must of made some kind of mistake here.

The second kick gets me in the other shin.

A stomp down on the arch of my right foot. My back foot. My power foot.

A crow-peck on the top of my head, a knuckle right into the bone, while I'm looking down at my foot.

A jab with a cheap shiny elbow into my nose, knocks me aviators off. I get down on the floor to pick them up again and now there's a boot in the ribs and a crunch as I go down in a ball. Got the aviators in me hand, that's sweet.

Then a kick in the ribs again.

Then a stomp on the neck.

Then a real hard kick up my arse, right up the clacker.

Then a stomp on me thigh.

Then they pick me up and sit me down and punch me in the eye.

Then I'm down and a stomp on me back.

Then they pick me up and sit me down and punch me in the throat.

Then I'm down and a stomp on me back.

Then they pick me up and sit me down and punch me in the stomach.

Then I'm down and a stomp on me back.

And that's where I stop remembering it.

Except the colours:

Red, blue, yellow.

Black.

New ones:

Purple:

Green:

Orange:

Gold shimmers.

Brown pain.

The whole fricken rainbow, new discoveries, all I see is them colours.

Then they pick me up and sit me down. Both of them in me bruised battered face, talking soft now, like they're sorry they had to do what they done but it was tough love, deep down they're my mates.

You did it, didn't you, Den?

Your own girlfriend, slutting about, had a kid on you, slutting everywhere, making a fool of you.

You did it. Eh DK?

You'd had enough.

You had a reputation to keep up.

She was humiliating you.

You took a knife to her.

You took her to a place nobody'd know about.

Lonely place to finish dying. She bled to death in that place, you know that, Dennis?

You didn't even finish the job off.

Not really a man, eh Dennis? But that was the problem all along, right?

Had a gutful. Eh Dennis?

Slutting around, women's lib eh? Not for you, eh Dennis?

Going having kids on you. No good, that slut.

Slut, eh Dennis?

You did it, right?

Just give us a nod and we're done.

Eh Dennis?

Eh Dennis?

I say nothing. I see:

Red, blue, yellow.

Black.

New ones:

Purple:

Green:

Orange:

Gold shimmers.

Brown pain.

The whole fricken rainbow now, new discoveries, all I see is them colours.

Don't say nothing.

Don't tell no-one.

Tell no-one.

Then they're into it again: the bit they dig.

The first kick gets me in the shin.

The second kick gets me in the other shin.

A stomp down on the arch of me right foot. Me back foot. Me power foot.

A crow-peck on the top of me head, a knuckle right into the bone, while I'm looking down at me power foot.

A jab with a cheap shiny elbow into me nose.

Kick in the ribs again.

Then a stomp on the neck.

Then a real hard kick up me arse, right up the clacker.

Then a stomp on me thigh.

Then they pick me up and sit me down and punch me in the eye.

Then I'm down and a stomp on me back.

Then they pick me up and sit me down and punch me in the throat.

Then I'm down and a stomp on me back.

Then they pick me up and sit me down and punch me in the stomach.

Then I'm down and a stomp on me back.

You can end all this, Dennis.

Like he's my best mate. Fucken police detectives, winter '75.

Just tell us you did it and you'll be right.

Barry Kalahu, Dennis. Pipeline. You're finished. Everyone knows you don't have the hair for Hawaiian waves. Real waves.

They want to make me mad.

Need a shot, Dennis? We can give you a shot in five secs if you do the right thing by us. That what you need?

They want to make me hungry.

No speak, no shot.

They want to make me sick.

Well yeah . . . but nar!

Pissing themself. Wiping their hands down.

Pissing themself laughing, now pissing.

Pissing on me.

On and on.

Red, blue, yellow.

Black.

New ones:

Purple:

Green:

Orange:

Gold shimmers.

Brown pain.

No Lisa.

Lying there now and it's sunk in:

Rod wasn't bullshitting.

You know she made a complaint? cheap suit goes. *Couple of years ago? She said that when she slept in the Keith family home, she believed one time she was assaulted. She came here to the Coolie cop shop and put it on the record. You didn't know that, Dennis? There was a lot about Lisa you didn't know. She laid the trail though. She made sure that if anything happened to her, we'd know where the trail led. But there was a lot about Lisa you did know, right*

Dennis? Like the baby. Your baby, someone else's—same diff, eh Dennis? Not what you wanted. Not part of your grand plan.

This bloke. Last time I saw him I burnt him on five-foot Kirra. Faded him and forced him down the pocket where he couldn't turn his longboard and he got smashed. Totally smashed.

Always had it in for me them types.

But no Lisa.

Lisa in fibreglass.

A big fat black man.

They shouldn't of said that.

In fibreglass.

I want a lawyer, I go.

Aha! Civil liberties!

A lawyer . . . I go through broken teeth, busted lip, fat mouse on my eyes.

Fuck off, DK.

Too late now.

Missed your chance, Dennis.

Then so I say nothing. Tell no-one.

No Lisa.

They say nothing neither.

We got ourselves a Mexican standoff, eh Dennis?

MEGAN

Yeah nah I sort of started reading it she wouldn't know that but.

Surfer magazine DK exclusive first draft: for Dennis's eyes only
'Me and DK'
By Megan Exmire

The conversation I wanted to have with Dennis Keith is the conversation we were never going to have. I spent several weeks interviewing the reclusive former Queensland champion. I ended up with fourteen and a half hours of recordings. Almost totally unusable.

On the recordings there are long, long questions. That's me. Now and then you hear a grunt or what sounds like a cough. That's the legend. Then: silence. In the silence you can hear me waiting for more. But there's nothing. In the silence you can hear me filling up with hate.

DK's reticence is as legendary as his surfing. To say he is a man of few words is to say the moon is not the easiest place to get to. But it's not just a pose. It's him. To think of all this man has been through, all the life he has lived. And now it's down to a bowl of muesli, an ice block, a piece of roast chicken, a chop at night. That's how much all that life has left him with.

Everyone in the surfing world reckons DK deserves your sympathy, or your respect.
Wrong.
He deserves something. But what? That was the question I was here to ask.

Jesus Mary and Joseph. Can't keep reading this when it never changes no matter how many times.

GONE

I can take silence longer than them. Drift in and out. Sleep. They don't need to give me a shot. I am shot.

So, Dennis.

This is after hours. Sun's almost down. Blazing through the window. The diagonal security grille. Sun's right there, standing guard outside.

I can hear it. New swell. Thumping down on Rainbow.

So, Dennis.

I open me eyes which have been glued shut by blood. Me eyelashes get ripped out. Me lids busted.

Put on the aviators. Still there!

No Lisa.

Nononononononononononono.

A kid.

So, Dennis.

It's old flyshit face. The longboarder who give up. The trimmer. The waster of God's gift.

So, Dennis, when was the last time you saw Rod?

Rod? What's Rod got to do with it?

Ar bugger him! goes tall uniform, who's back. *Rod's off doing his own thing. That what it's all about in DK's world. Everyone's off on their own trip. He can't remember.*

Convenient.

Yeah, convenient.

Last you saw Rod was a week or so back. Yous had a blue. He gone off and sold the panel van he'd been borrowing for a grand to score some hammer. Or was that the week before? Whenever, nothing out of the ordinary. Typical blue. What he didn't know was you had gear—some hammer, some speed, some dope—stashed in the back of the van, in your secret spot. One of your secret spots. Rod had got a grand but lost about five grand's worth of gear. We had a fricken fist fight. Overdue that one. Been years since yous'd had a good blue. Most of the time in your life when yous want to fight, yous're sitting on surfboards in the water and yous can't really go each other, yous just splash and snarl and spit like a pair of statues in a fountain. Can't even touch each other, no purchase. But this time I got mad at him on land and I nailed him. Pure natural genius. He walked out.

Not telling them that.

Not telling them nothing.

Just colours:

On and on.

Red, blue, yellow.

Black.

New ones:

Purple:

Green:

Orange:

Gold shimmers.

Brown pain.

And no Lisa.

They're wrong.

They're wrong.

They kept you in a few nights, patched you up—and released you. First you didn't know why. They drove you home to the Queenslander and dumped you like a bag of rubbish. You went inside and went to your room and took a shot and took more shots and passed out for a week.

You didn't see Mo.

Didn't talk to no-one.

Only get up to eat cereal and go to the toilet.

Then back to bed.

Another secret stash.

No Lisa.

Then, all hell:

Rod arrested and charged for the murder of Lisa Marie Exmire.

Rodney Keith confessed to murdering Lisa Marie Exmire on December 31, 1974.

Your world champion season.

They knew it all along.

They knew it before they interviewed you.

They knew it was Rod.

They already had Rod.

When they interviewed you.

They already had him.

They knew it wasn't you.

They done it for fun.

And cos they were sure Rod must of needed some help to do the job.

But Rod confessed.

Rod confessed to doing it alone.

Done it cos he hated her.

Done it cos her and him been having it off, behind yer back. She come onto him for whiz, he said, and smack, while you was away. Roddy and Lisa. No way. You didn't believe it till they told you he said he done it when they was on whiz and smack and she started belting him in the head and he hit her back and then, he said, they said, *it got out of hand.*

What he confessed to.

Rod had done Lisa. Then he'd gone her. Then he'd done her in.

Done it cos he hated her.

Done it cos she was humiliating you.

The Great DK.

Rod confessed.

Rod.

Showed them the spot in the shaping bay where he done it.

Told them before they interviewed you.

You never visited Rod.

Mo wouldn't let you.

He confessed so there was no trial, only sentencing.

Got thirty-five years. Discount cos he confessed.

Horrible brutal murder.

All over the Goldie:

Surf Champion Murder Scandal.

The Girl in the Fibreglass Grave.

Surf Champ Brother Killer.

Mo wouldn't let you see Rod.

You couldn't go yourself.

Half a year, first half of '75, you and Rod knocked round together and he'd known it he'd already done it.

Half a year:

Hawaii.

Together in Hawaii.

Back at home you'd been best mates again. You and Roddy and the hammer.

No surfing.

No Lisa.

He already done it.

WRONG WAY GO BACK

'So but yeah,' I go after a long few clicks down the highway. Scrub on both sides. Aussie coastal scrub: nothing uglier in the whole fricken world.

'It's okay, Dennis. I know.'

'Right,' I go. 'Right, sweet then.'

And she puts a big vacuum of no-talk between us, she puts it there and waits for it to suck me down, a big hold-down for me to fall down down down under . . .

Pissed off that I haven't read her so-called article.

So she thinks.

She's taking me almost to Brunswick Heads. Right down in the deep dead dark heart of New South. Almost as far as Byron. Man, that's one joint I never surfed. Only ever went there to score. And sell. Byron: scoring and selling, selling or scoring. Commercial affairs not surfing.

I don't say nothing. That's it. That's the end of this conversation.

But she's kept on thinking.

'Man, you are deadset lucky, all I can say.'

She turns off the highway. I am not liking the look of this not one bit.

Down this bush track eh. Some secret spot? Yeah nah this is not good it always seemed bad and this is worse than it seemed. Bushes close in so tight they're scraping the sides of the chariot. Grey branches arch overhead, joining on top of us. Darkness, tunnel. She's

yeah now it makes

I just

can't *see*

FUCKHEAD!

Chariot bounces, you go for the door handle. Locked! Fricken brought me here and so

yeah . . .

'Dennis, don't even try, central locking's on my side.'

You can't get the door open, she's brang you here and locked you in and you glance up at her and she's looming, she's big, see, she's tough and tan and powerful, much bigger than you she can snap you with her surfer shoulders she's fricken stopped the chariot and this is the spot, her secret spot to end all secret spots, this is where she's brang you to do the business and them green eyes is full of hate and she's coming at ya now and yer curled in a ball against that fricken door that won't fricken open Mo, Mo, *where are ya Mo!*

'Yer fucken psycho the lotta yers!'

She got that same cruel laugh you used to hear in The Patch. Same couldn't give a rats.

You're blubbering down into the floor, where the feet go.

She's just sitting there, enjoying it to the end.

'This was yer plan eh, track me down and do me in,' DK snivelling away. 'I never done nothing but yer so fricken psycho ya don't care, yers're all the fricken same.'

Great DK's face is in his hands, waiting for the last fin chop. Crazy fricken chicks, this was what it was always coming to eh. Revenge. She reckons you done Lisa. Not Roddy, not her own dad. Roddy took the rap to protect you. Someone's told her he done the real killer's time and so now she's got you where she wanted all along yeah she was never no BFO she's yer Ass Fricken Assin, it's in her blood, look at it three fricken generations down the line, the only way their lot know how to settle things is

yeah only ever makes sense when it's too fricken late so

come on

fricken psychos the lotta yers . . .

'The Great DK, look at him.' Her voice is full, like she's wiping her lips after a big meal. Satisfied, happy. 'Bet you're glad you're adopted now eh!'

UNDERGROUND

Lisa been found where nobody ever looked for her. Everyone went walkabout time to time, sometimes turned up, sometimes not, it just wasn't worth it to keep on looking for some whiz-head rock chick probably gone off chasing her dream.

So no-one ever looked in the obvious place.

It was this Chinese family found her. Said the big fat dead black man in the bone house of the Chinese cemetery wasn't their dead grandfather's bones. And there was hair and clothes.

And fibreglass dust.

Shoved in the Chinese bone house.

Not too many people knew their way in there, and it wasn't gunna be some old Chinese takeaway family put her in there, right.

They got him, and he confessed—

A confession, so:

No trial.

Rod.

Rod.

Lisa.

Rod.

Rod.

You:

Gone.

All over the news it was, all over the Coast, all over the country, round the world to Hawaii . . .

World Champion Murder Scandal.

Nahnahnahnahnah—

The girl in the fibreglass grave.

Mo went AWOL a few weeks, wouldn't talk to you after Rod's sentencing. Told you she had to go to hospital. You was on your own.

Sink or swim, DK.

Everyone talking about you. Couldn't step out the front door still less walk down Kirra or Greenmount.

DK, DK, DK . . .

Gone.

Painted on the rock at The Pit:

DK KILLS

Only one thing could save you:

Only one thing you loved:

All your loves killed off, burnt back:

Down to the last one:

The thing you needed:

The thing that would save you:

Your redeemer:

Rod's mate.

There goes the seventies. Jimmy Carter, hostages, ayatollahs, test-tube babies, disco, punk, petrol rationing, Afghanistan—you pretty much missed it all.

Most of the eighties too, turned out.

Your last mate on this earth put his jaws round your leg and took you down with him, down down down down down—

It wasn't you done so much of it. There was others done much more, bigger hell men, and they died. Lot of them died. Lot of funerals you didn't get to, you'd be seen and it'd turn into a circus, that kind of thing, but there was a lot of funerals. Ones got left on the street, in the car, in the shower by their own mates too busy doing a rail or a shot to notice their buddy dying. Just neglect. Just too much going on to think of mates.

You were lucky: a one-shot screamer. You never built tolerance. Small amounts done the trick. Piss-weak. Probably what saved your skin.

•

Cops cops cops. Always following always watching. But now Rod was away, now they had their way with you they didn't seem interested in nabbing you. They just wanted to scope who you hung with who you met where the gear was coming from. You were their canary down the mineshaft.

Bad bad shit.

You wouldn't let them take you inside again.

They talked to you about people.

You too scared not to talk back.

It was said you grassed up.

There was a lot that was said.

You never let them take you in again, the cops. Never again.

Bad bad bad.

No more Kirra Boardriders Club: talent was either in jail or dead or something in between, like you. In jail *and* dead.

Meanwhile Frank Johnson become world champion in '76, slayed them in Hawaii. World champion in a points system of his own devising.

Meanwhile Glenn Tinkler become world champion in '77, slayed them in Hawaii and California and Brazil. They said Tink was so aggro these days, there was stories about him jumping up and down shadow-boxing before his heats, psyche the other bloke out.

Meanwhile the Aussies were 'bustin down the door' in Hawaii. Whoever did good in a conness, they shout all the others the ten-dollar smorgasbord at the Kuilima Resort. They was a team, they was mates, they was Aussies together . . .

Ian Cairns slayed them at twenty-foot Waimea Bay. Tink got accepted like one of da boyz. Even started beating outsiders up. Like, now that you were gone, Tink could finally be the big man he always wanted.

Well bully for him eh.

Loved telling stories about themself that crew.

You weren't interested.

Meanwhile the new crop, Mark Richards, Cheyne Horan, little South African prick Shaun Tomson, Martin Potter, you didn't keep up with the names you lost interest in that world tour rubbish. Surfing sold out. Too much coin in it. Kids on thousands of bucks a month from these new companies, these Quiksilvers and whatnot.

Simon Anderson put three fins on a board and everyone said he changed the face of the sport.

You tried a three-fin board back in '71. No future. You didn't give a rats anyway.

But they was still out there trying to beat you. Still trying to be better surfers than DK. You felt sorry for them to be honest.

You travelled, saw the world:

Got on buses to Newcastle, Sydney. You disappeared, went for walks and met new ones in pubs. You crashed at mates' houses and tried to climb into bed with their missuses. You crashed at mates' houses and flogged their boards for coin. You crashed at mates' houses and used their gear. You crashed at mates' houses and brought strangers with you in the middle of the night to party.

Cronulla, Dee Why, North Narra—
The good tough breaks—
The good tough ones—
Sydney: Disneyland.

Cronulla, Dee Why, North Narra: rows of red-brick and yellow-brick flats marching back off the beach, plain box houses, workers' cottages, auto shops and board factories and petrol refineries. Blue collars in the waves. Drop in on a wave, get back to your car it's got no windscreen. Blokes likely as not to get finished off in a pub fight. Smack and coke ripped through these places like the great fire, like the black fricken death.

You said you were surfing but you weren't.

Most of the surfing inside your own head.

You got into coke, in Sydney. That was good for you. Brightened you up. Went for more surfs. Sometimes five-minute micro surfs: one power wave then back to someone's flat, someone's car.

You had friends everywhere.

Good tough ones—
Nothing wasted cept the waves—
Too much wasted.

•

You got another dog, not a beagle this time just a wiry mongrel bitzer this, bitzer that, which you called Dave. You liked to have a dog with a name that wasn't a dog's name. Dave sat with you and talked to you and kept you company and was your alarm clock. You got to keep feeding Dave even if you don't feed yourself much. Dave give you a reason to drop into country supermarkets to buy Pal. Dave was a smiler, a grinner, like he was the world's luckiest dog and figured the world ought to agree with him. When you had Dave people thought you couldn't be all bad.

After a while but the good tough ones didn't want you and Dave crashing in their places no more, and you went down to Melbourne—
    Where it all come from—
    Rod's mates—
    Good tough ones from Collingwood, Richmond, St Kilda—
    And you didn't have to worry about waves you might be missing. Waves was where you weren't going—
    Where they talked about Rod.
    Lisa.
    You.
    Rod.
    Lisa.
    You.

Meanwhile golden boy FJ was starring in Hollywood movies. Meanwhile Tink was world champ and had his own clothing line: fluorescent wetsuits, checked boardshorts. They was carving out The Life, only surfing when the lighting was studio quality, surf the Kodak reefs where they get snapped and get paid for it but
    but I don't know it's
    this was what they meant by 'living off' surfing. Like a tick lives off a cow. Logos on their boards and surfers' hotels and surf tours and put their faces on board wax and leg ropes and all this was meant to be good, or good for someone anyway, good for someone. You even heard FJ was back on the Goldie talking about Being A Professional Surfer at the careers day at your old school yeah
    good for someone

meanwhile surfers was saving the earth from sewage, nuclear weapons, development, themself . . .

Meanwhile Aussies ruled it . . .

Meanwhile the world's greatest surfer was underground like a badger, like a wombat, like a worm.

In Melbourne with good tough ones—

Where no one could see you—

Win win.

And all them travelling days and years you never once thought about Lisa.

And all them days you never once thought about Rodney.

Never wrote postcards to Mo.

Not that you didn't want to think about them, but see there had to be order. Pecking order. Had to be civilisation and hierarchy even inside your head. Most of all inside your head. A head is like a surf break. There must be civilisation in it or else every good thing gets wasted.

You been in a three-wave hold down at Pipe—after you done this, it's easy not to think about what you're not meant to think about.

So all them nights and days and silver mornings you never once thought about:

Lisa—

Rod—

Mo—

—and you never went surfing no more. And never done nothing that might ask you to think about them people them days and

and this was when the diagonals started to burn—

when them words started to dance together like brothers and sisters and sons and mothers, they all start to sound the same—

when you got into radio at night—

when your hands always tingled with dirt and you couldn't remember if you done them already or not

or what

KING KOOK

'Anyway, we're here,' she says, swinging into a car park. It's fricken one of them Byron beaches—Taragos, Wallows, some crap like that. I can't believe it. She's fricken let me down bad. She does want to kill me. From embarrassment.

It's offshore and fat and one foot and *crowded*.

'The most perfect little longboard beginner's wave you're ever gunna see, Dennis. So good you could eat it.'

The sun crisp and not too low.

The water the colour of Lisa's eyes.

Jam-packed with kooks and spazzes and grommets and starters and families.

Jam-packed with big soft Things.

'It's all about hiding in plain view,' she goes, coming round and opening my side of the Chariot. 'Nobody'll suspect it for a second. Nobody here's even heard of you. These aren't surfers. These are families. These are fifty-year-old grommets on holidays. C'mon, Den, this is the safest place in the world for you.'

I let her help me out.

Stomach cartwheeling.

Fricken . . .

Big fifty-eight-year-old gibberer in boardies with his ten-foot soft-top. You'll fit right in here, DK.

She pulls The Thing out, and a glass longboard for herself.

'Be a gentleman and carry your own board, will ya?'

Watch her go down on the sand in front of me. Hell. Pure blinding burning hell.

Death of DK. This is. This really is.

Do a poo in the bushes . . .

•

Drag The Thing down the sand behind me.

King of the Kooks.

'And Dennis?' she tosses over her shoulder. Waits for me to catch up to her.

Most perfect afternoon since the early seventies and you got sand between your toes.

'Dennis? I always knew you weren't.'

'Eh?'

She puts a finger to her lips.

We get to the edge of the water.

She's right. Fat old guys on soft-tops. One foot and peeling. Holiday central. I'll fit right in.

'So—yeah, nah—but so then, how come you?'

But she hasn't heard me. She's paddling out.

Follow her out through the tiny sweet peelers and even my eighteen stones doesn't put The Thing underwater no matter how hard it wants to.

Get out the back which is only twenty yards from shore and water's like a bath and full of kids and their dads wearing surf hats and surf gloves and surf goggles and every brand of wetty and rashie there is, all the gear that made Tink and FJ millionaires, it's brand city out here, and you DK is the King of the Kooks and you can even sit on this Thing without falling off

but I mean it's just

you wait out there King of the Kooks but you dunno what for. One of the dads or the kids gives a thrash and two-armed pull-along and they're chesting onto a wave and ten minutes getting on their feet but they do, they do, a knee then a foot they stumble up eventually and by this time the wave's just a dribble of white froth but they're still moving cos these Things are like boats can move on anything and they've got their arms in the air, arms in the air, like they're claiming a fifteen-foot Pipe barrel

how stoked they are

punching the air and whooing and their kids whoo-Dadding them too and everyone's got a fricken smile on their face.

And her sitting out there with you and sees you scoping:

The smiles on their faces.

The dimple on hers.

'Oi. Oi!'

You keep at her till she looks. Sitting on her glass board a few ripples away.

'Ya know, serious, birds aren't meant to surf.'

Cheeky thing splashes water at me, makes me duck.

'That right, Dennis? So what are you doing out here then?'

Before you can think up anything to say her head snaps round, out to sea.

'Whoo! Here's one, Dennis—it's got your name on it.'

You see what she's looking at and it's what might be called a set wave. The water thickens dark in the wall. Might be one foot. Maybe one-and-a-half-foot face.

You drop on your belly and thrash.

The way the kooks do.

Your fat legs swinging wide apart.

Your arms go dead.

The wave lifts you.

You look down.

It looks like four foot.

You push up.

You're going down the wave.

Your belly's still on the board, your arms are propping you up:

You push up . . .

You push up . . .

But nothing in them. You got noodle arms.

Surfing always good for your weight: kept you away from the fridge for hours at a time.

The wave collapses and pulls The Thing away, the rug from under your belly.

Not even your feet.

You stand up on the sand.

Water to your hips.

Thing floats round with the toddlers on the sandbank.

You turn round and here comes the BFO, legs flexed trimming a clean little peeler straight past you like you're a marker buoy.

She whoos herself. An arm in the air.
Patronising.
Like this is all the stoke there is in the world.
And you're out of there.
Out of there:
Gone all over again.

Now you remember: you were a kook once, when you was little. There was these times you come down to Rainbow not know for sure if today you can stand up or not. Worried you won't catch a wave. Might have a no-wave surf, most depressing thing in the world. You stand on the sand and think how maybe you won't be able to do it today.

Then you paddled out into the water and surfed.

Eventually it went away.

Now it come back.

In the Chariot:

'Nah Den, it's not you I'm gunna kill.'

TILL YOU HEARD

Ar bad years, bad bad, heavy years, heavy heavy . . .

Years . . .

No Rod, no Lisa, you took off up and down the road. Your boltholes. Your safe houses. Christmases as a guest. Your hot turkeys and your cold turkeys.

Seventies dribbling away in bad surf and onshore winds, dribble dribble.

You:

A man is an island.

With a dog on it.

If you need a friend, they say, *get a dog.*

Dave kept you going. You couldn't let him go same way Bas went.

Up and down the coast, always the coast, your boltholes and your safe houses: to where there were waves and nobody knew you except your good solid tough ones with a friendly stash and music. Up and down the coast for the end of the seventies: seventies surf towns, hard core only: Crescent, Scotts Head, Old Bar, Nobbys, Sandon, Dolphin, Green Island.

You surfed but didn't really surf. Could only surf when you were so bombed you couldn't remember you weren't meant to surf. Dave sit on the beach and watched. Good judge of a wave, Dave. Sometimes you walk out and hop on a six-footer with a no-paddle take-off and blow them all away, and that does you.

Out the water, in your bolthole, your safe house, with your good tough solid ones.

You shaped where you shaped. Shaping: barter for hammer. Shapers offered you jobs cos of your name. They brag to their mates they had The DK shaping for them. *Remember DK? Yeah! Retro boards? Whatever.* But shapers had to follow directions and you couldn't do that wouldn't do that you shape perfect boards for yourself but nobody else can ride them and then you take off with the finished boards and flog them for coin or nick some blanks and flog them for coin, or take buckets of glass and resin and hardener and flog them for coin . . .

Up and down between Thailand and Queensland, happier on planes now cept for the rocks in your shoes and the rocks in your arm and the rocks in your head—

Man had to put bread on the table somehow.

You would be the rich, like FJ and Tink were now the rich:

Thailand—

You parked Dave with your Melbourne connections.

You survived till the trip when you flew back after putting 28 grams of smack in 28 frangers and swallow them all with Coca-Cola. You caught the flight with a stomach full of heroin and Durex rubber and The Real Thing.

You got off the flight and sat on the pot and shit out 26.

You unpacked them and piled it up. By the time you were ready to on-sell it in your boltholes, your safe houses, your seventies hard-core surf towns, you was doubled over and yellow with hep.

Hep A, B or C, never worked that out. Multiple choice eh.

Three weeks in hospital with hep.

Weight from thirteen stone down to nine.

You went home to Mo a scarecrow, cold turkey in your bedroom at Anga.

Hot turkey, cold turkey.

You lived on lollies and muesli and walked with a walking stick. Dave thought he died and woken up in hell as a guide dog.

Soon as you were well enough to walk you were back on it.

Nobody wrote about you in surf mags now except to ask where you were. Or report a sighting. Someone seen you rip up ten-foot Angourie doing switch-footers. If it was you it was you it was you was it you. But nobody could find you to ask, for you to reply:

Well yeah . . . but nah!

You'd of needed sponsors' invites to go in comps.

The invites came and went unanswered

what else am

in them first years they thought you'd still turn up, even in Hawaii they waited on the edge of their seats thought you DK was gunna materialise out of the never-never and clean them up—

Still spooked by The Great Man—

You were never more dangerous than when you weren't there—

But you *weren't* there.

Invites stopped coming.

Cops, cops, cops. Tailing you up and down the coast. Poisoning your water. Putting electronic satellite surveillance on you. The full James Bond trip. Cops cops cops. Bad cops. Bad you. You carried a wig, blond as Frank Johnson, white-blond, and if you saw a cop make a mistake— let you see him—you pop on the blond wig and stroll along in safety.

You bought a bear trap.

You measured diagonals all day long.

You didn't surf and didn't think.

When you looked round your head, you saw that order was well and truly established, couldn't have been more orderly in there if the Queensland police was running it:

No Lisa nowhere.

The end of the seventies:

You owed coin to the underworld.

You nodded off in your muesli.

You walked past old surfing mates in the streets of Coolie and didn't know them.

You walked past Mo in the streets of Coolie and didn't know her.

Then you went off again, nobody knew where or how long.

Least of all you.

You lived in your boltholes, your safe houses.

You lived in Greyhound buses. Packed Dave into cages in the luggage hold.

Your tough solid good ones up and down the coast.

Seventies surf towns, strictly locals only. They worshipped DK and opened their doors to him, but soon they found you, *you*, inside their houses instead, scarfing their macrobiotic food, smackies were all into the health food diets, only organic vegies and no food combining and no toxins, and shooting their junk and hocking their stuff.

Hard core.

Then you be kicked out and onto the next in your mobile home, the Hound of Grey.

To the next hard-core bolthole.

Start out fresh behave yourself this time.

But still couldn't hang on to friends.

First night in any new place you sit up talking with them all night and you show a snap of Mo you carry round with you and a snap of Basil. The women fell for you. The blokes already had.

You cook for them, but you don't really know how to clean. Back home Mo or Rod always cleaned up for you. You cook but burn food onto the bottom of their pans and hide them in a cupboard cos you didn't know how to scrub it off. Or you set their kitchens on fire or leave their fridges open and the macrobiotic health food rot all night and that wasn't the problem, the problem was you were so embarrassed and ashamed about what you done that you cover it up you lie about it blame someone else for it, you always had to cover it up and make it worse, till things blow up and complicate and they have to ask you to go now, please just go.

No good out of water . . .

Or sometimes, they knew how freaky you was about germs, they cry out they seen a cockroach, just pretending, but you don't know that, you're out the door, out of there, onto the next place . . .

Meanwhile:

FJ world champion—
Tink world champion:
The rich.
The end of the seventies.

December 31, 1979:

Somewhere down the south coast of New South. Far South New South. Bucketing down. You and Dave living in a caravan with a tough old friend and his wife and twin babies:

Heavy.

Good hammer but.

And they kicked you out the day of New Year's Eve.

You took your board and walked out and surfed two-foot onshore grovellers.

You fell off your board. You couldn't cut back. There was other guys in the water and you thought they might know you. You didn't want to try cutting back in case you fell off again.

You got scared of making a move.

You just stood up on them waves and trimmed along.

Like a kook.

Like a longboarder.

Like a beginner.

You couldn't turn your board no more. Too heavy or too light, one or the other or both.

You got going on a set wave and tried to turn back into it:

Couldn't.

Could but wouldn't?

Nah. But yeah.

Couldn't.

And you been kicked out of your good tough solid mate's caravan and don't even know what his surname was to ring him up when you got out the water, he was just Doghead to you and his missus was Mrs Doghead, and so you don't know what you were gunna do and you're broke and it was New Year's Eve and

still: not the first NYE you spent on your own

but the first in Far South New South and couldn't do a simple cutback.

Couldn't turn your board.

You might fall off.

Frozen solid.

Gone.

No Rod.

Rod.

Rod.

Lisa.

Rod.

You.

Mo.

•

You waited in the surf till dark. Waves were crap. But you were scared to go back on land cos you didn't know where you'd go then.

And Mary Mother of God be praised there was an *Oi* from the water.

Dennis Keith?

You squinted in the direction of the voice. Old crusty sitting up floating on his longboard in the dark.

Dennis?

He's paddling over.

A cop, a cop, a cop—

They're everywhere—

A plumber—

A butcher—

A newsagent—

A teacher—

A priest.

Dennis, is that you? Jesus Christ, you look shockin mate.

And he looks familiar but not really.

You couldn't clock him.

You look like the fricken Grim Reaper, DK. What's gone on?

You start to paddle away.

Knew you shouldn't of gone surfing again. Too dangerous!

Don't tell no-one.

Say nothing.

Eh Dennis!

Longboarder after you—

Familiar face—

A cop, a cop, a cop—

They're everywhere—

A plumber—

A butcher—

A newsagent—

A teacher—

A priest.

You stop paddling. Buggered. Bloke's faster than you. About thirty years older, late fifties, still faster than you.

The end of the seventies.

End of the world.

You don't recognise me, do you! He laughed like he was pleased with this.

Father A?

You squinted at him. Couldn't help yourself.

Ex-Father A, he said. *One of the great unwashed now.*

You said nothing.

Eh, what you doing tonight, Dennis? Who you celebrating with? A bevy of local beauties you wanna bring over to my place?

Tell no-one.

Son, I can't believe I ran into you here of all places. Kept shaking his head.

What freaked you was that he was burnt now. Father Aplin, who never got burnt no matter how long he spent in the sun. Now that he was in Far South New South, all that Queensland had finally caught up with him. Even in the semi-dark you could see lumpy moles on his forehead, pink burnt-off patches on his cheeks, white bits and grey bits and even greenish bits falling off him. He looked like a poster in a skin doctor's room.

His burnt head. Shaking it.

And he'd cut off his comb-over. That was what spun you out as much as the skin bits. No more comb-over. Just a shaved head. And somehow now he'd lost the comb-over he didn't look so bald no more.

Lucky I still believe in miracles, eh Dennis? Well let me tell you something. Why don't you come and see in the new year with me and my old lady.

Not me, you go. *Not me.*

Yes, Dennis, he said. *You.*

But you and Dave was walking up the dunes with him. Eight in the evening, New Year's Eve, you didn't know where else to go. Father A yammering away.

Spose you're down here in training for the Straight Talk Tyres.
Eh?

He laughed. *Don't stress, your secret's safe with me.*
Eh, Father A?
Ex-father, Dennis.
Eh right. You got any smack?

He laughed again. Always laughing whether he was Father or ex, this one.

Dennis we gotta sit down and have a long talk, son.

The Straight Talk Tyres—
The eighties.

BACK FROM THE OTHER SIDE

In the Chariot she drove me.

Didn't hassle me about it.

Didn't cheer me up.

Didn't say we'd try again.

Didn't take the mickey.

Didn't change the subject.

Didn't make light.

Didn't play mind games.

Back over the causeway. Through the toy roundabouts. In the car space behind the Sandman panel van sprayed purple and orange.

Salt water drying on me. Crusting up and crackling on my face. Haven't felt this for a while and I'm unbelting myself and ready for her to come in the unit but I don't hear nothing from her side of the car and look across and there's this shine on her cheeks. Her chin's crinkled up like a rip current pulling through it.

The moment's sitting there and I dunno what to do with it.

It goes on a while.

She takes some breaths, wipes the snot off her nose with the back of her arm. Won't look at me.

Then:

'Of course you didn't do it, Dennis.'

'Eh?'

'It happened on New Year's Eve. Somewhere round midnight. That's how I know it wasn't you.'

'Not me?'

She looks across the cabin of the Chariot and hits you with:

The dimple. She got it. Just she doesn't bring it out much not with you anyway.

'You were out surfing in the dark, right Dennis? New Year's Eve?'
Your head shakes.

Girl smiles through the tears. 'I look at you today on that board and I think about, fuck it, Dennis, it's so fucked. Made me think about what you were.' Wipes her nose again, it's streaming, probably salt water trapped in her sinuses. 'You were so beautiful.'

Now she tries looking at me but can't.

'Yeah,' I go. 'But nah.' What I mean is, I got to be in my room now.

'Dennis—'

'Ta for the lift.'

Out of there, up the stairs.

Grab the rail.

In the kitchen.

In me room.

Turn on the news radio.

Sit down for some reading.

It took me a long time to find out anything about my mother. I was raised by my grandparents, Lionel and Maureen Exmire, who Dennis Keith met once. They were always nice to me but it was a very quiet and sad house we lived in. Very ordered, very clean. Cold. I was a difficult kid and must have been a handful, especially as a teenager. I wasn't very warm or loving, and that must have been tough for them. They put a lot in without getting much back.

I went to school in Brisbane, where they'd moved when I was little. They sent me to an all-girls school and fell over themselves to 'protect' me. Which meant that to this day I've never had a serious boyfriend. I've been in love a few times but it hasn't worked out yet. I wonder why?!?!?! Maybe next time.

I was close to my Auntie Jodie. She told me she stayed at the Keiths' house at Rainbow Bay and thought it was haunted at the time, but later she figured out that it was probably Rodney Keith creeping around in the dark. She told me just recently that she believes it could just as easily have been her, not Lisa, who

Psycho birds eh. Enough.

MR AND MRS FATHER

Father Aplin wanted you to call him John now, insisted on it but you couldn't really come at it. He hadn't stopped believing in miracles, he just stopped believing in celibacy. He met this bird Julie and she was *the miracle that was irreconcilable with the priesthood*. He quit, got married, moved down to Far South New South, earnt his bread shaping boards for locals. Holy Smoke Surfboards.

You been in the town in a caravan shooting hammer for four weeks and never heard of him.

And he hadn't heard of you:

That was worse:

He hadn't heard about you.

But he had you now.

Still a fisher of men, Dennis. Never lose that.

Had a laugh like a kookaburra.

He'd had a new surfing accident, Father A. In a nothing wave bellying into the shore, he speared his shortboard off the sand and into his face. The impact pushed his lower teeth through his lower lip. Tore himself a second mouth. Once they had the painkillers in it he stuck his tongue through it to give a fright to his missus Julie and the nurses. Now he had a friendly pink scar. It was always smiling.

He had you for New Year's Eve and a few spliffs and by midnight a big grand plan, how he was gunna put Holy Smoke on the world map.

I could do with a reliable hand.

Nah not me.

We're gunna make you a board to ride in the Straight Talk Tyres.

Nah not me.

Dennis, you want to do it the easy way or the hard way? You're gunna say yes eventually. Why fight?

He lived with his missus Julie and their dogs, a chihuahua and a dachshund, and a million mozzies in a fricken fibro dump on the edge of this lagoon.

Dave got on well with the toy dogs. First time in his life Dave felt big and tough.

Father A sit you down across the upturned packing crate that was his outdoor card table.

Yous were playing poker.

The Straight Talk Tyres, he said. *Biggest prize-money event in surfing history. Twenty grand for the winner. This autumn at Snapper.*

You lost interest. You didn't do surf comps no more. You couldn't do a cutback in two-foot dribblers. You was done.

I know you're not interested, he went on, *but just in case you are, let me tell you some reasons you should reconsider. One, it's twenty grand. Two, it's twenty grand. Three, it's twenty grand. Other reasons? It's twenty grand. And it's up in your own backyard, Dennis, your home break. I don't care what shape you're in, or not in, you can ride Snapper right-hand barrels in your sleep. If there's no waves they'll move it to D-Bah. You've got it tied up, Dennis. Twenty grand!*

You wanted him to play his cards. You were gunna win fifty cents off him with a pair of nines and that was the biggest punt you were prepared to take. Then you'd up the bets till you won fifty bucks off him and then you find what other coin they had in their fibro shack while they were asleep and in the morning you nick off with it and be gone before they can kick you out . . .

All the world tour guys there, Dennis. FJ, Tink, Mark Richards, Rabbit, Peterson, the Hawaiians, the South Africans, the Americans. All wondering where you are. All worried about you. And you know what? It's a unique new format they're trying out. It's different from every other surf comp anyone's ever been in. They're making history.

What you got, Father?

He had a pair of eights. He laughed to break the mouth. You raked in your fifty cents.

It's man on man, Dennis.

What's man on man? You stopped raking.

The heats. They're man on man—one on one. None of this compulsory six-man heats accumulating points. It's one on one, you against the other bloke, nobody else in the water and the winner goes through to the next round. It's personal.

So . . . just one bloke against the other bloke?

And everyone can see what's happening, you take the waves you get. There may as well not be judges. It's that easy to score. Just one bloke against another bloke.

Not the old points system?

Dennis, it's made for you. Made for you.

He was working some kind of God fix on you, beading into your eyes. You pushed your aviators up your nose.

They weren't there.

They weren't there.

Dennis, I can see you want to do it. And you know what? You're gunna do it on a board we design and shape together. We've got two months to work on the board and get you fit and fed and on the road up to the Goldie. I'll organise the sponsor's invite. Holy Smoke'll pay up to be an event sponsor, and we'll make sure you get in. It's that easy. This is the new era of surfing, Dennis, and you're gunna go up there in triumph and you're gunna absolutely nail it.

Where's me aviators, Father?

Dennis, bugger the aviators. Just tell me you're in it. Made for you, it is. On our board.

Where's me aviators???

Dennis, say you're in it.

Sweet, sweet, I'm in it Father, but where's me fricken aviators???

They're here, Dennis.

Had them behind his back the whole time.

What you want them on for in the night-time anyway?

You didn't say nothing. Clapped them straight on.

After a while you thought about it again:

You heard about Roddy, Father.

He was dealing the cards.

I heard, son. I'm sorry. He was the sweetest little altar boy we ever had. The bishop's favourite.

They won't let me back in there. The pro tour. Since Roddy and that. Pointless.

But it wasn't you that . . . Have you ever asked?

Why would I ask? They'd only say . . . they're all cleaned up, their image and that, they don't want me. Not since Roddy and that.

He looked at his cards.

You looked at yours. Rubbish. Slapped them down. Start again.

But you didn't do anything wrong, son.

Doesn't matter, Father. Guilt by association and that.

But you haven't asked for an invite, have you.

No point.

But you haven't asked.

Your deal, Father.

He dealt. Crappy old Qantas cards. You'd already memorised what was what by the stains and folds and foxing on the backs of them.

He called his missus out the fibro shack. She was blonde and well-built, type of bird you used to get to help you keep up your name round the traps. You liked her even though you couldn't look at her when she was looking at you which was a lot of the time. She come out and stood there with her hands on her hips. In nothing but a dirty white sarong.

Jules, see this? Dennis and I are going up to the Goldie next month to win twenty grand in the Straight Talk Tyres on a Holy Smoke surfboard—a type of board nobody's ever seen before.

She put an arm loose round his shoulder and smiled at him like he was her kid. You hooked your head hard away. Only seen this kind of 'love' a couple of times before. Weirding you out that it was the priest of St Barnabas. Mo'd have a fit.

He looks at you deep into you.

Yeah. Dennis . . . yeah. It'll be the Second Coming. You bet, babe, it's the Second Coming. Christ! Dennis?

Your eyes glanced off him and his poxy sunburnt mug. But he could wait longer than you. And you wanted to play for another fifty cents. You were on a run now.

Not a priest anymore, his missus said, *but he still believes in miracles.*

With her talking, you couldn't look up.

When you looked up again, Father A went:

Dennis? Reckon I can phone your mum to tell her where you are?

Father, you can tell Mo what I'm doing, sweet. Just as long as you don't tell her what you're *doing.*

WOMEN

Won't have a bar of it I won't.

Mind games, mind games. Treat me nice treat me bad. Give me food give me none. Take me for walks leave me at home.

Won't have a bar of it.

No matter how many times I read it it still won't change:

It was Auntie Jodie who eventually answered my questions about my mother. I'd always known who she was—Lisa Exmire, the folk-rock singer—but my grandparents told me she'd died in childbirth. I know why they did this. When's a little girl old enough to know the truth? Never, in their eyes. As for my father, they said he was someone they didn't know, and my mother hadn't really known him either, so best not to ask. Move on with your life, the new life your grandparents have constructed for you.

As a kid and a teenager, at this nice all-girls school I went to, I was good at sports—hockey, netball, cricket, swimming, running—but on a holiday to the Sunshine Coast I discovered surfing and got hooked. I went with girlfriends to the Gold Coast and Sunshine Coast every weekend and every holiday. My grandparents freaked and tried their best to discourage me. But the more they stood in my way, the more determined I was. I actually thought I was good enough to be a pro, even though there was no money or opportunities in it for girls. I lived and breathed it.

My grandparents must have been terrified. They wanted me to stop going to the Gold Coast. But I had blinkers on. I wasn't interested in finding out about my mother, even less my father. I was satisfied with the story I'd been told. I only cared about surfing.

After I left school, I went in a few contests but soon realised I wasn't good enough to go further. No-one tried harder but I just didn't have the talent.

Still, all I wanted to do with my life was surf and be around the surf, so I worked in surf shops and volunteered when the big contests came and worked in event management and sponsorship and marketing, all the fringe stuff you do, and started doing a bit of writing.

Because I was writing for the mags, I read them too. I came across mentions of Dennis Keith, the reclusive legend and all that. I was quite curious but not too much. It kind of grew on me, the curiosity. He seemed such a sad case, and there was all this tragedy in his past. I wonder why he was so fascinating to me—maybe it was a message I could hear but not yet understand.

Soon I was reading everything I could about him. In his old interviews he was all bluster and bragging but you could tell it was a show. What was behind it?

Once I thought I saw some insight from him, in an interview in Surfer. *The interview was titled 'I Blame Myself'. Now that caught my eye. You never hear a male surfer saying he blames himself. Never! Let alone one who'd been as arrogant as DK. So I thought, here we go, some humility at last, some humanity. I read on:*

'I blame myself,' DK said. 'I wrecked surfing. Single-handed.'

'How?' the interviewer asked.

'Made it look too easy,' DK said. 'People came to the coast and saw me surf the way I did, and I was so natural they all thought it must be pretty easy. Next thing, every man and his dog's doing it. I'd have been better off surfing like a kook. Fall off my board. Make it look hard. Nobody would have took it up. So yeah, I blame myself for why it got so popular.'

Aarrrrgh! I wanted to scream at him. But then I came across the story that brought my whole world crashing down.

Yeah no matter how many times you read it it's still the fricken—

Yeah, nah, my words exactly: *Aaarrrrgh!*

SHAPING UP

Father Aplin's shithole in Far South New South deserved the name, you even had to shit in a hole. He'd went o-naturale with his missus, stomping round in the buff half the time, both of them to and from the creek they used as a bath and the surf they used as a shower. Father A was surfing a lot trying out these boards he was shaping and you spent a lot of time alone with Mrs Father A. You tried cracking onto her after one long session over the campfire that they used as an oven but she just brushed you off with a laugh and said, *Dennis, I guess I should be flattered but I know you're not up to it.*

Like, if you were, she might give you a shot. But not really. More like, she never be interested in a billion years and she was trying to think of the nice way of saying thanks but no thanks.

You could of been kicked out for a stack of other crimes and misdemeanours. Sometimes you shaped boards so hard and got so lost in the planing, planing, planing that you had them down to communion wafers and Father Aplin had to chuck them. Blanks cost fifty bucks and you couldn't be costing him each time you had a bright idea, but he didn't say nothing or do his block at you.

All he cared about was what he called the Skywalker, this idea he had to shape a board with flares and jagged flanges down this cut-in tail. Father A was fixated on it, raved day and night how it'll cut through the Gold Coast right-hand point breaks, and he even had new moves in his head, this thing where you jump the board up onto the close-out and ride it down straight, he called it a Big Dipper, and another where you actually take the board into the air.

All science fiction to you. Father Aplin had went bats down here, bats in the belfry. You nodded along and looked at the Skywalker sketches and wished they could cast the same spell on you they cast on Father Aplin. He was dreaming twenty years into the future and all you could see was tricky planing and a stack of wasted blanks.

Not that you cared. You had a roof over your head and some food in your belly for a few nights. What would be would be. You got into reading books now, hard core, whatever he had you'd read. Even the fricken Bible, that's how much you were into reading. It all come back from confirmation classes, you liked the Old Testy most. You had to get some words in you. You didn't have your heart as set on the Straight Talk Tyres as Father Aplin and there was times you wished he'd just enter it on his Skywalker himself. And leave you down here to cuddle with Mrs Father A:

All you were ever up for, cuddling—

But he was on and on and on getting you out of bed every day and sometimes in the waves, you going one day at a time.

Dave was in his element with the toy mutts and you owed it to him to stay a few days longer.

You were off the Harry Hammerhead down there you couldn't find no one to score off and if you left the shaping bay for half an hour Father or Mrs Father be on you like a ton of bricks and hurl your stuff in the creek, they were that nuts. You was a bit scared of them to be honest. They were on some religion trip but without the religion, all nature and storms and God is in this tree and God is in this rock and God is in this hole here, look down you can see him with all your turds getting steamy in the sun.

You tried to steer clear of most of it. One time you had a go at them, told them they were mad as cut snakes and totally psycho, and Mrs Father A shot back:

You're a drying-out washed-up junkie with no friends and no money and a big chip on your shoulder because of what happened with your brother and fair enough, but we're *not judging you, man, and you're here sleeping on a patch of dirt dreaming about waves you caught five years ago and you're saying* we're *fucked up, you're doing the judging?*

Thing was she had this way with a big smile and a line down the middle of her forehead so even when she was heaping crap on you you couldn't help feeling she wanted the best for you.

You went quiet, then:

Ya reckon I should give it a go?

She couldn't stop laughing, for a minute or two.

What's so funny?

You, Dennis—give religion a go?

What, yers reckon yers can find God in a fricken seashell but yers can't find it in me?

I was peed off at her so didn't say nothing more.

She wiped her eyes and felt sorry for you again.

Dennis, it's not that I think your soul isn't open to a higher plane. It is. Of course it is.

She went soft and serious again.

It takes work, that's all. Spirituality takes discipline and belief but most of all it takes work. And there's one thing all you surfers have in common: you wouldn't work in an iron lung. Even Aplin. None of you can stand the sight of hard work.

Kind of true it was but. True about surfers true about you. You never thought of it before. You never known a decent surfer who worked, not since the early seventies anyway, not since your mob.

All you'll ever commit yourselves to working for, she said, *is a half-decent wave.*

The Aplins did acupuncture: needles, matches, flame, candle wax.

Eased the pain.

She taught you how to do it to yourself.

Shove in them needles.

Mrs Father A caught you reading your books. You tried to hide them but she got you.

Doesn't surprise me, she said, leaning against her tree watching you pretending to fumble with your gear. *That's the tragedy about you, Dennis. You've been starved of intellectual company. The only conversation you ever knew up there was if it's high tide or low tide or east or south or offshore or whatever. You let yourself go dry, man. You needed more than that, didn't you? That's why you needed dope. So you could have someone to talk to. Pity the only person who was up to talking with you was you yourself.*

She knew too much and not enough, Mrs Father A.

With no smack you got by on Far South New South grass, which Father A handed out in strict rations three times a day. It was like some kind of methadone program: you lined up at the kitchen table, he hand you your morning spliff and shoo you off to the shaping bay.

MALCOLM KNOX

Then you're back again after lunch for the afternoon's work and back again after dinner to get buzzed for cards and reading.

Three spliffs a day handed out at the kitchen table. He was making it boring for you.

And down Far South New South, loads of onshores blowing all day. Waves got split into pieces: you see the lines forming and but then they disappear. Currents, chop. You try to paddle for a wave but it's here now gone the next.

Confused waves, no clear mechanical lines.

It wasn't making sense.

Some days them waves got so confused, you got confused too and before you knew it you were sitting there on your board bawling your eyes out.

You couldn't make sense of it. Gibberish waves.

And they these people these waves cracked you open and night-times you'd start to think:

A very big fat black man—

Baby Face—

Betting at cards to be the one to get out of washing Basil—

Hell.

RIGHT HERE

They're in the kitchen as usual do women talk anywhere else? The way they're facing each other like two parts of a mirror makes me think maybe Mo could be the BFO's nan, which is what she would be if

yeah

and why is it they spend so long talking? What can there be to talk about?

And so but yeah I go in the kitchen and push my aviators up my nose and clear my throat and they look at me with this identical irritated face, like I'm some kid they been lumped with, some invalid, and you take about eight stone and fifty years off my Mo and it's in the eyes, in the eyes, the pair of them, and it's making me want to puke and making me want to pike so I'm so nervous I just spit it out:

'I wanna go see him. I want yers to take me to the Road.'

And nothing, I swear, not a skerrick, changes in either of their expressions. The pair of them. Just gawking at stupid fat old Den.

'Took your time, didn't ya?' says Mo.

'Famous for your timing,' goes the BFO.

I look at them angry now, like *Didn't yous two hear what I said? I said I want to go see my brother at Boggo Road! He's in danger! I gotta warn him!*

But Mo just shakes her head.

'It's too late, Den.'

'Eh?'

'It's too late,' says Little Miss Echo.

'Come again?'

All them years Mo been seeing him and not telling me and letting me think we're never talking to him again and me finally waking up to it and it's too late, too late she cried, too late she cried—

But she's not crying. She's kind of grimacing. Both of them. Same face.

'Yeah.' It's left to the BFO. Mo's got her big meaty face down between her big sausage fingers, her big inflatable elbows on the melamine table. 'Yeah, Dennis,' the bird goes. 'Too late for going to the Road. Rodney's being let out tomorrow. You can see him right here.'

Back to me room and shut door hard as it goes.

It took a long time for me to digest, and I still don't know if I have. I spent weeks in libraries and government archives, finding out what I could.

I'd sit with the old stories in front of me, staring into space for hours. Dead numb, or bursting into tears, never in the middle, one extreme chasing the other.

The bombshell sort of exploded in my head and kept exploding for months. I was often in tears. I kept it all to myself for as long as I could, but eventually told my Auntie Jodie, who of course went totally spare. She sat us all down, me and my grandparents, and it came out. Or sort of, bit by bit. They told me how they had lost contact with my mother in the early seventies. They'd had a big falling-out when they'd met Dennis Keith and demanded she break up with him. She refused, and they became estranged from her. That was their biggest regret.

My grandparents—they were parents, too.

They'd heard how her music career was going well, in America and around Australia, and she was putting records out, and she was still with that Dennis Keith character. They heard rumours of drugs but this was the seventies and they were bewildered and sad and possibly angry but felt there was nothing they could do.

In 1974, they thought she was still travelling around doing her music and hanging out on the surf scene. They heard she'd been in America. Then she turned up, literally on their doorstep, with a baby—a baby girl. She wouldn't tell them who the father was. They assumed it was Dennis Keith. Lisa, they were sure, was high on drugs. She was, in their words, 'off with the fairies' and didn't make any sense. She stayed with them a few days over Christmas, then said she was going off on a tour, and asked them to look after the baby for a couple of weeks.

This was how I came to be raised by my grandparents. They never saw Lisa again. It was Christmas, 1974.

Lisa hadn't been reported as a missing person until the middle of 1975. This is one of the things that gets me most. I guess my grandparents were at their wits' end. It was just like Lisa to go off, do her own thing, leave her baby with them. They had their hands full with me. Maybe also I was better off with them anyway, so the longer my mum stayed away, the better for me.

The Keiths never reported her missing either.

I guess the seventies were different.

All of this threw me off the rails for a long time. Who was I? Who was my mother? Nothing like I'd been brought up to think. And who was my father? Who? I had a lot of problems adjusting. But I believe the world has a purpose. It sends you messages. It had been trying to send me a message for a long time, through my fascination with Dennis Keith. And then, I received another message. I don't believe in coincidence. There's always a reason.

I got a letter, care of a magazine I write for. The editor handed it to me like it was a telegram from the Queen. It was from the famous Mo Keith. My God, I couldn't believe it. My hands were shaking. Terror, anger, excitement, and a lot more—there's a fine line, and at that moment there was no line at all. This formidable force, this woman who'd been picking up the pieces of her family for thirty-plus years. One son gone to jail and the other gone to ruin— what a life. I'd had a lot of sympathy for her. I used to.

My hands still shake when I remember sitting at my desk to open her letter. Her tone was quite formal and distant. Like she was an informant writing to a journalist. She seemed to need us to play these roles, her and me. The essence of it was, she wanted to offer me a world exclusive. She wrote that nobody knew the truth about what had happened with the Keith brothers all those years ago. She said that what was said and printed was all lies. She was prepared to tell me the true story, if I came to Coolangatta and met with her. And with Dennis. I would be allowed to write the story if, after hearing it, I still wanted to.

Mrs Keith's letter made no specific reference to why she'd singled me out, after so many years when they slammed the door on journalists. But I wasn't naïve enough to think it was because she'd read my fantastic articles. She saw my name. No coincidences.

For weeks, I didn't reply. I knew how much it would hurt my grandparents if I even considered going to meet the Keiths. Nobody can imagine how devastated my grandparents still are. Thirty-odd years, it never fades. It casts a shadow on every day. They'd moved me from the Gold Coast, tried to raise me away from that shadow, and kept the truth from me. Because there was no trial, and DK had disappeared into obscurity, not a lot had been written about the death of Lisa. The community—the surf community, the Gold Coast—looked after its own, and closed ranks around DK and his mother. He was obviously in a bad way, and they let him be. The world might have known about Lisa's death, *and who went to jail for it, but the world forgot too. When I was growing up it just wasn't news anymore. Honest, I'd never heard about it. I led a carefully sheltered life, I guess.*

But there's no shelter really. We'd lived in a sad house. Now I knew why.

That's it. I got to tell Mo. Me and her got to take steps to protect our boy.

STRAIGHT TALK TYRES

Father A didn't have no car. Mrs Father didn't believe in them. The end of the earth will come and you got to know how to get yourself A to B without modern technology. So she said. So he said too. They agreed on everything that pair.

So: the Hound of Grey. The smackie's chauffeur. You and Father A in your trench coats keep yous warm. You left Dave with his new best mates down in Far South New South. The bus smelling of puke and nylon, hot chips and chocky milk. Skywalker snug in newspaper and blankets in the hold downstairs. So secret yous didn't even want the bus driver to see it.

North north north north north north north north.

March 1980:

And got out at Central Station in Sydney late night went looking for some hamburger for yourself Father stayed at the bus stop eating scroggin.

And scored some of Rod's old mate from someone you used to know in one of them squats on Regent Street.

Not for use: for insurance.

North north north north north north north north.

And got out at Nambucca Heads middle of the next day went looking for some hamburger for yourself while Father stayed at the bus stop eating scroggin.

And scored some weed from a good tough man you used to know over the oyster leases.

Not for insurance: for immediate use.

North north north north north north north north.

And got out at Lismore late that day went looking for some hamburger for yourself while Father stayed at the bus stop eating scroggin.

And scored some goey from a good tough man you used to know over the marshes.

Some for immediate use and enough for insurance.

You missed bus reconnects. You slept in bus stations huddled round the Skywalker. You read books. *The Magic Mountain. Catch-22.* Father never said a word, just shared your weed to stop you overdoing it. A saint, he called himself.

You never said a word.

Raining for a week on the Gold Coast before the Straight Talk Tyres. There was warm-up events. Father A had caused a stir by entering DK on the start list, as a sponsor's invite from Holy Smoke Surfboards.

Course they wanted you. You was the greatest surfer in the world. How could they not? You DK was all they talked about and then you freaked everyone out by not being there, by them thinking you were being there, by your ghost being there.

After all these years . . .

All their talk like a drumbeat: DK, DK, DK, DK . . .

March 1980.

They didn't believe.

While you were still down south. South south south south.

It kept raining, spinning verge of a cyclone.

East east east east. Swell rolling in from the Coral Sea and the cyclone. Rain always a good sign.

Rained for a week right through them warm-up events.

They talked about you and talked about you. Talked your ghost into solid lifesize. All the Hawaiians was there, all the Americans, some South Africans, Brazilians, Mexicans, more Hawaiians.

All the Australians: Mark Richards, Ian Cairns, Peter Drouyn, Paul Neilsen, Cheyne Horan, Wayne Lynch, Mark Warren, Michael Peterson, Peter Townend, Wayne Bartholomew. Lot of blokes come out of retirement, or hibernation, that kind of thing, for the twenty grand.

Yeah and the two Coolie locals who been world champions.

FJ. The Blond Bombshell—

Tink. Billy Bloodnut Kinky Tinky—
Yeah.

Straight Talk Tyres started on time, you wouldn't of been in it. You missed that many buses with Father Aplin and the Skywalker you might as well been going in the '81 event. But it rained so hard they put it off. Official explanation was they couldn't erect the grandstands and TV towers at Snapper in the rain.

Competitors all said they were waiting for you. Couldn't put on the world's richest event, the first one-on-one conness, without DK

after all these years

couldn't wouldn't shouldn't.

It pelt down for a week. You were late by a week. The draw was in The Patch, club where she used to sing.

You weren't there.

Rod wasn't there.

She wasn't there.

The draw they said was all Vegas glitz and showgirls and bikini girls and promo girls. America America welcome to the Gold Coast. It was 1980, yeah.

The new era of surfing.

One on one.

Made for you said Father A.

Made for you said everyone who was waiting.

You drew a Hawaiian in the first round, Derek Ho.

You was in the same half of the draw as FJ. You couldn't meet him in the final. Have to beat him first.

Tink was in the other half. You have to beat him in the final. You wanted to take your time with him, do him slow.

Not that you knew that. You were wired up in Murwillumbah running round the streets with Father A thinking you'd left the Skywalker at a bloke's place, or the place of a bloke before that.

You left it in the bus station, in a locker room.

Meanwhile, biggest surfing event in history the start of the new era the revolution

starting without you.

The rain stopped.

They'd had enough of waiting.

First morning you were drawn with Derek Ho at nine fifteen am. Thursday March 20, 1980.

You rocked up at Anga with Father A and the Skywalker.

Mo nearly falling off her velvet lounge suite.

Too tough to cry.

Tough old possum.

Just come up and gave you a punch under the chin and:

Make sure you win it eh.

All she said.

Done a lot of talking with Father, catching up on church gossip and whatnot and

and you sat there watching her how big she was how huge and you just wanted to get inside her house dress and hide there, hide, watching her as she fussed round the kitchen

and made you this massive bowl of muesli.

Cloudy and cold that morning and by the time you got down the beach they said it was like a vision come down off Point Danger.

Easter fricken Monday.

With Father A, spiritual counsellor. And Skywalker. Still in newspaper and blankets and masking tape.

In your trench coats.

Down the beach, through the crowds, fifteen thousand they said, twenty thousand they said, thirty thousand they said . . .

Hell . . .

Father A on his knees taking the wraps off the Skywalker.

You in your trench coat and aviators:

The living dead come down from the graveyard.

(Still no Lisa.)

Walked up to Tink and flashed him, opened up the trench coat with all its pockets stuffed.

He said you looked like the full pharmaceutical factory in there. Insurance.

And half a cold piece of battered fish sticking out of one pocket.

•

Derek Ho was waiting in the water.

Father A busted out the Skywalker. Only give it the full spray job after you tested it out.

Stars, dark purple galaxy, swirling nebula. In the centre, a gold cross: a Jesus cross with little bits of shine coming off it. Beautiful.

God is in the galaxies.

God in the Skywalker.

Father A sit you down in the dunny block give you a pep talk.

Dennis, the place where the ocean meets the earth is the point of greatest untapped energy on the planet.

Dennis, go tap it.

Dennis, you will be aware of every ripple, every bump, every pulse of energy no matter how big or how small in that ocean.

Dennis, the greatest surfers can actually make a wave change its shape so that it will form itself around your next move.

Dennis, the greatest surfers can keep the lip of a wave holding up. Keep the barrel going.

Dennis, the greatest surfers can bend nature to their will.

Dennis. You know the line-up spot. Sit there. Wait. Wait for your wave. It will come. You will make it come. You will paddle in, three decisive strokes, and you will enter the tunnel that sucks up every drop of water from beneath it and throws it down again with a thunderous roar aiming to bury you, plant you in the ocean floor, destroy you, but it will not, you will destroy it, you will be totally calm and have all the time in the world and you will never forget this moment.

Dennis—you got any of that smoke left?

Somewhere you began to nod off. I had Father A figured now. He was lying.

He never given up God.

But Dennis—

Dennis?

Dennis, wake up!

Dennis? You know, Hawaii . . . Pipe . . .

Dennis?

Mate, listen. It's no shame that you were scared of the waves in Hawaii. They scare anyone.

Dennis?

It's no shame.

I wasn't saying nothing.

But Father A, he was wrong, right? Somewhere deep down, or not even that deep, I knew he was wrong. God may be in the waves, surfing may be the highest religion in the world, the waves may be the be-all and end-all, but he was wrong you know, because a girl got done in, and all because they love and hate each other and they're brother and mother and son and they love DK, they do all that cos they love DK too much and he loves the waves too much and it's all too much and it's not worth it, Father, it's not worth it, it's none of it's worth it and but—

You start with a no-paddle take-off on a seven-footer and get creamed. The Skywalker lucky to be in one piece.

Ho got a couple and you got mad.

You paddled behind the black granite lava rock. Ho too scared to follow.

Thought you'd get creamed again.

You paddled into a big one, took the drop. Made the bottom turn behind the black granite. Spat out in the bay. Wrote poetry with that Skywalker.

Crowd going bananas. Fifteen thousand at daybreak, up to thirty thousand since the coconut wireless put it out that DK

from the water you could see it: the Roman Amphitheatre. Camera towers, towers for music speakers, the Marlboro scoreboard, the grandstands, the dots of faces and behind them the new unit blocks, Coolangatta gone skywards, the eighties, Den, this is the eighties, this is the end of the world. Above it a loudspeaker going on and on with this one pair of words:

Unfinished business—

. . . yeah . . .

Derek Ho shook your hand. You disappear. Nobody could find you.

You couldn't find yourself.

Second round you beat Mark Warren, one of the Bronzed Aussies. Third round you beat another Hawaiian, kid called Something Something-Ha.

Hawaii, meet Queensland . . .

Unfinished business.

    Man on man.

    New era.

    One on one.

    Made in Queensland.

    Made for DK.

That was it for the Thursday. You gone home and Mo done chops. You decided to go vego like Father A. You and Father went in your room. Mo said nothing. Mo loved Father. She never been this proud since your confirmation. Nothing like a priest to look after her little boy.

In your room you done your own acupuncture. Burnt it in yourself. Needles in your arm ease the pain.

Did some reading. Old Testy.

Took the edge off.

Friday there was only one heat before the onshores blew in. You and Cheyne Horan. Before it you were laying cable in the dunnies. He saw you come out the cubicle and his jaw drop and what he saw was murder. He ran like roadrunner. Thought you was gunna kill him.

In the heat he hardly took a wave. By the end he could of scored a perfect ten and he still wouldn't of won. They called that a 'combo'. DK did the first combo ever, on Cheyne Horan.

Saturday blown out. You come home and Mo done lentils. She looked so sad you asked her to go buy some chops.

You and Father A went in your room. Mo said nothing. Mo loved Father A. Nothing like a priest to look after her little boy.

In your room you done your own acupuncture. Burnt it into yourself. Needles eased the pain.

Blown-out Saturday:

    Father A went off to see some people.

    Hell.

    No Rod.

    No Lisa.

When Father A wasn't there you and Mo didn't speak. You got a good look at her now.

Mo rattling round Anga, ten years older than when you last seen her two years ago.

You and Mo couldn't talk no more. You looked at her and saw this hard woman did hard things when she had to.

Anything for you, she would.

You couldn't talk to her.

Not a word.

No-wave Saturday:

Hell.

No surf no comp just you in your room.

Turned on your radio but it didn't work.

Smoked weed but it didn't work.

Snorted rails of whiz but it didn't work, or worked too well.

Tried acupuncture but it didn't work:

Hell.

You had an insurance policy against *Hell*.

Rod wasn't here no more.

Rod's mate was but.

Father A woke you Sunday morning. Your works lying all over the bedroom. Skywalker on its nose out in the hallway, one fin busted. Dunno how that

Father A spinning out:

Dennis, it's eight foot and offshore and you have a semifinal coming up and Dennis, and Dennis, oh what've you done to the Skywalker, my Skywalker, our beautiful Skywalker . . .

But he was a good one Father A, a good tough hard-core man and he saw the state you were in, he took you in his arms and Mo come in and saw you and thought it was the passion of Christ . . .

It's only a busted fin, Mrs Keith, Father A breathed heavy, talk himself down from the ledge. *It's not the end of the world.*

Yeah just think if he'd of snapped off the nose.

You and Father A went down the rat cellar and glassed the fin in again.

He walked you down Snapper. Late for your semi.

The semi:

In their quarter-final Frank Johnson had beat Mark Richards.

Your semi against blondie:

Thirty thousand, forty thousand.

Cameras, TV towers, grandstands.

The Marlboro scoreboard.

Easter Sunday on the Goldie.

Eight foot and offshore.

Nonononononono.

You give Father A the Skywalker and had to go to the dunny for a poo.

Your works and your gear, tucked down your boardies . . .

As the hooter blew for your semi they found you on the nod in your cubicle.

Had to kick the door down—

Dennis Dennis Dennis . . .

Father A with you in his arms.

Dennis, we couldn't find you . . .

He found you.

You and FJ out there in eight-foot Snapper. All-time. You lost you got one grand. You won, but lost in the final, you got three grand. You won this and the final, you won twenty grand. Lot of coin. Lot of coin.

FJ looked at yous sitting out there on your boards, and you knew you knew you knew that white-blond corporate pretty boy, that *ex-world champion*, that *convicted drug felon*, was shitting his boardies. His lower downs letting go.

Letting go.

Couldn't look at DK.

So scared of you he didn't dare paddle for a wave while you were in the line-up. He only went for waves after you got one, while you were paddling back out.

You kept paddling back out.

You waited for last wave each set.

You knew FJ only get rubbish waves at best.

•

Thank Christ I'm here.

Rod's best mate taking care of you
yeah caramel
the relief—
Rod—
Sunday March 23, 1980, Straight Talk Tyres, forty thousand faces.
But a nice three in that date—

Unfinished business/unfurnished witness/untarnished bigness/unvarnished
wigless/—

It was starting and you can't stop it—

You took Frank Johnson apart master class, they said. All them crowd
and competitors on their feet. Awe. They talked about a barrel you
caught was all sand, not even no water just a shocking ugly five-foot
dredger by the ocean baths. A barrel so dark it was night in there.

Where they couldn't see you.

Father A in tears. Mo breaking through the back of the Marlboro
scoreboard to give the judges an earful you

yeah you never found out what for.

Five scoring waves: You beat FJ 43 points to 15.

But now they could see you, were all round you, people people too
many people.

You asked Father A for your works and gear.

You give him the Skywalker.

He give you your works and gear. It's Sunday. Church day.

You went in the dunny block, the old clubhouse. Reek of piss in
there. Surfers was animals. You never liked none of them.

Locked yourself in a cubicle.

Thank Christ . . .

SHANGRILA

He is due but he is not here yet.

My Mo has made her mind up. She wipes her hands on a tea towel and loops it over the rail of the oven. She is wearing her best pale yellow floral house dress.

She got me on me own. Her big old meaty face with its square jaw and its blue eyes slouched in their shiny red hammocks: the vertical line down her brow: the grooves from the corners of her mouth to the line of her jaw:

Father Aplin said only the truth sets us free, eh love?

In her face I can count the lines I cut.

And she has me backed in a corner and my feet in the air to miss the bad diagonals and I cannot move.

Push my aviators up my nose (still there, still there).

She sighs. Breath whistle through her nose.

She leans close and starts a whisper in my ear. She is careful and deliberate with every breath and every word.

My aviators fall on the floor. Right across a bad diagonal.

My Mo:

Do anything for me.

Did anything for me.

Rod:

Do anything for us.

Did everything for us.

So I could be the champion of the world.

THE THING PT III

. . . the dark the light you do it in the dark, nobody watching, nobody listening, the light so dark you DK is the only one who can see and even then I can't . . .

. . . Hawaii . . .

Still no Lisa.

Rod back today. Last night you snuck into Mo's room. BFO was sleeping over, on the couch. You waited till you heard her snoring. Got into Mo's and:

Told her.

BFO's grand plan.

'She's not my BFO. She's a AFA!' You whispering so hard your voice's cracking, you're shivering.

'Eh love?'

'She's the Ass Fricken Assin. She's waiting for Roddy to get out and then she . . . you know, get him back for all that . . .'

In the lamplight Moey looked at you for a long long while, the longest long while yet. Her hands drier than the rest of her.

'Ya having a nightmare, love. Hop in.'

Me Mo. Take care of everything.

You slept like her baby.

. . . radio on all night while I'm waking while I'm sleeping, your dreams are the dreams of important events where it's light, where you're dark, eyes are closed . . .

. . . yeah . . .

Markets, terrorists, killers, earthquakes, tidal waves, numbers, sentences, waves of words.

You like the radio.

I fish out my up time, three am, swing my legs, knee-free tubes, hairy calves, lard arse, over the edge of Mo's bed and plant the feet—yeah!

... standing up straight I can't see my thongs, can't see nothing beyond the peak of my stomach, *too fat and full, too fat, too full* . . .

A Thing . . .

Don't listen to what they say, I know where I am and when I am and what I am, that is me genius . . .

. . . yeah . . .

Don't! listen to what they say.

Don't!

Up out the room, seventy-five-year-old ladies don't sleep well, they sleep with their eyes open, their ears open, probably knows and hears but is turning a blind eye.

Turning a blind eye: her genius.

BFO's gone. To paradise. Where'd she go? You thought she was here last night to sleep over but—

This nightmare unit:

Rails aren't even metal, they're white plastic. Wouldn't hold me up not if I grabbed them on the way down. Them diagonals all wrong.

Not sure I've even woke up.

Out into the dark, has to be the dark, not a light not a sausage.

Walking morning.

Thing under the arm. Then on the head.

Walking.

Fat legs, kneeless tubes out, busted free, legs pump down past the shops, past Greenmount Hill, down Rainbow Bay, the inside section, Little Mali, sandbank for kids and their dads, fifty-eight-year-old groms, it's darker than dark, the darkest dark where nobody won't see

yeah this is

lights of town glowing on the water, I don't throw a shadow in the shadows, a big blob in sleeping T-shirt and sleeping boardies and he's off, home free . . .

Moonlight on The Thing.

A bird scatters.

But I don't see: lapping of tomorrow's swell, across the open stretch, up the channel . . .

I'm here. On Rainbow. Where everyone comes. Why wouldn't you?

Only way I can

only way I can get up.

Easiest wave in the world.

The way it has to be, has to be, whatever will be, no, not whatever—
DK will make it what it will be.

Step in the ink.

Got the hair for it?

Just like them New Year's Eves:

Creatures blindness fear.

Nah:

Memories.

Paddle into memories.

Beneath his fat gut The Thing floats.

Put me fat hands under me fat boosies and push meself up into a
seat and for a second I've got it, got it at last, but nah, not this time
buster, over we go a wobble and a correction and an over-correction
and over we go . . .

Wade over to get it, bung it under chest and paddle back into the
one-foot peelers . . .

That shallow . . .

Paddling leaky bucket hands . . .

Kicking mouldy flipper feet . . .

And this kook, flap and fall and embarrass meself and invite all
them regrets back in, open the door, all the terrible things and the
waste, the waste, the waste, the waste . . .

I am you are DK is waste . . .

. . . and the magnet is that seventy-five-year-old lady back there the
only one who knows, right now lying awake in bed wondering if she
can still pretend . . . pretending she isn't the only one who knows . . .

. . . yeah . . .

She knows.

She's the magnet.

Mo.

I do it.

Up.

In the night air.

I am flying.

Not long.
Long enough.
Rod'll see.
Mo'll see.
The bird'll see.
I can do it, see. *Fly.*

There's one not wasted.
Yeah.

Back in bed well before muesli.
Rod today.

Some light reading.

By Megan Exmire.

THE FINAL

And so the final. Eleven am Sunday March 23, 1980. Year of Ronald Reagan. You'd heard of him. Liked him. Was on your page:

Kill them all.

Yeah.

At the keyhole you was waiting for a lull and up come your little mate, fresh from spanking Shaun bloody Tomson in his semi.

Two local kids, two Coolie kids, two Goldie boys, but when he was coming through the crowd they was telling Tink to fuck off back to Kirra, they was spitting at him hissing that he beat DK he's a dead man, and DK was gunna kill him kill him kill.

Tink shaking like a redhead autumn leaf behind me at the keyhole:

Me and Tink standing there with our sticks:

Me and Tink fourteen years old, standing here with our sticks:

Me and Tink, all them times, all them times:

Not a word from DK:

Tell them nothing:

Give them nothing:

Tell no-one.

DK thinking about Rod:

Lisa.

Mo.

And me and Tink there.

Unfinished business.

Kill.

Forty, up to fifty thousand now. Hanging out the windows them brand new unit blocks smashing up the skyline of the coast of gold:

Thank Christ I'm here . . .

The Skywalker tight under me arm:

•

And Tink:

And Tink:

Good luck, Dennis. Hope the best surfing wins.

Half dropped the Skywalker on the rock.

Half lost it in the wash.

Eh?

I said good luck.

He caught me looking at him.

I pushed the aviators up my nose:

Not there.

No aviators in the surf.

Left them with the works with the gear with Father A.

Looked away but he caught me and he knew he had me.

Gone Gone Gone.

Hawaii—

Barry Kalahu—

Pipe.

It was when he said good luck that the penny dropped and you saw what Tink saw. Coolest kid in the schoolyard, best-looking, best surfer, the one all the chicks wanted, the bravest, the funniest, the hardest, the street-corner Messiah all the boys would of give their left nut to be, you were their general, the commander of their army, best wave rider in the world but it

but it was only a moment, only a wink, when you were that kid, when you were the bright and shiny DK what Tink and everyone else wanted to be, and now in 1980 the way he's looking at you is like you DK was stuck back there, still hadn't outlived that kid, still stuck in DK the boy wonder, and you being still that now was just plain sad, all the other boy wonders grew out of it, you were stuck still, still stuck, hadn't of evolved, and what was even sadder was you couldn't tell it was better to grow up and do what Tink done, and Tink found a life, not The Life but a life, and you hadn't, and the upshot was, he was just standing on them jump-off rocks at that keyhole feeling sorry for you . . .

Yeah, good luck, Den . . .

•

The lull come and yous were in, Tink paddling away from you.

Yous sat out there few feet apart and didn't talk. Music on the loudspeakers like this full rock concert. The announcer talking old mates and unfinished business and local derby and twenty thousands of dollars . . .

Tink—

I paddled over to him.

He ignored me, looking out to sea, thinks I come over to psyche him. Another ploy.

Tink—

He paddled away from me.

Hawaii . . .

He paddled away and in the first wave of the first set.

I watched him. He took a big drop, bottom-turned, come up the face and stalled. In a big sucky barrel that spat him out five seconds later. On the shoulder, cut back. Arms swinging like George of the Jungle. Stayed on it. Bottom-turned, stalled in another barrel, two on the one wave. Best wave I ever saw a man surf.

Something missing in your arms when you paddled into the first one. Got on it all right but speed's gone. Something inside you, gone. Didn't make the barrel. Got knocked off by the lip.

Next wave Tink took the drop, bottom-turned and it didn't barrel but he did three or four cutbacks and reos. Second-best wave I ever saw a man surf.

I paddled into a big one. Took the drop, bottom-turned, stalled under the lip but overcooked it got knocked over by the falls.

That's how it went. Tink smashed me. Tink killed me. I see him get six, seven, eight great rides. He even pulled one of Father A's moves, what he called a Floater. Better name than Big Dipper. You tried a couple of Big Dippers and a High Flyer but they didn't come off. You felt the noise in the crowd go down, then rise again like it wasn't happy it was angry:

The eighties.

●

You surfed all right for a smack addict who been on the nod in the dunnies just before the final but

just see it's

but Tink killed you.

Father A tears in his eyes, taking the Skywalker back, his baby, thinking how was he gunna tell his missus they hadn't got the coin . . .

Mo with a hard cold face and a square jaw:

Nobody remembers who come second.

You with the aviators back on.

You prop yourself against the stucco wall, junked out, taking a shower. Thousands in a mob crowded round you. Cheering, taking photos. Like you DK was some kind of monkey. Like your whole life been sideshow alley heroism and athleticism and madness and exploitation and tragedy and love and hate and life and death and humanity and nature, all a big show for them. Like you were *for them*.

Except you weren't doing that. You weren't no work of art. You weren't that. You hadn't done nothing. You just been getting through the days. You weren't any them things. You was just you.

Why can't they leave me alone?

Somebody turned the shower off for you.

Then:

All the Gold Coast and the whole circus, Sunday lunchtime, fifty thousand in Coolangatta, the unit blocks, the skyscrapers, the eighties, all round you while you stood on the Marlboro scoreboard beside Tink waiting for the judges' votes to be tallied.

Tink downcast, not looking you in the face. Far as you knew. May the best surfing win.

Then the scores go up and

and uproar, bedlam, pandemonium.

You don't remember much more the bloody

the screams

pushing Mo away rough like you don't want her ever come near you again

someone trying to put a lei on you

Tink's freckly back climbing down off the Marlboro

Father A on his knees with the Skywalker

the ugliness of the crowd, the fear, the anger, the triumph:

Got one back.

The good tough hard-core ones had got one back.

You remember Tink's freckly back.

You remember Mo swallowed by the crowd.

You remember:

No Rod.

No Lisa.

Give you an oversize cheque and a cup. Ask if you were allowed to take this cheque to the bank now and cash it.

The chanting the cheering the ocean of waves of faces

chanting your name your initials:

You remember your speech:

Yeah thanks a lot . . . and you thought that wasn't enough so you come back to the microphone and went: *And thanks.*

Wild they went. Like animals. All on your side. One back for the hard core.

The eighties.

Twenty thousands of dollars.

And last you remember, before you got your works and gear back and went into your bedroom for a month, the last thing you remember was:

Never surf ever again.

And:

None of it's worth that much Lisa.

And:

Thank Christ it's

DEAR DENNIS

I'm in me room shaking like a fricken leaf. She's gone and I don't know what Mo done with her. I sit on me bed and turn on the radio real loud and it still won't block it all out and but so when I pull me hand away from the set I see a envelope under it.

Me name on the front.

This time no fart-arsing about. Fall back on the bed and tear it open, only breaking to wipe the blur out of your eyes.

Dear Dennis

There have been a lot of times, in the months since I met you, I've felt that Mo has been playing a cruel joke on me. She never told me 'the truth'. She left me to work that out for myself, and like all of us Keiths I'm not the fastest thinker.

And where's my world exclusive, anyway?

She's been setting me up for something.

When she first contacted me, Rodney Keith's sentence was going to end within months. Before he got out, she wanted me to know what had happened. But she wasn't going to tell me. You can lead a horse to water . . .

I've fallen for her, that was my problem. Fallen for her . . .

A couple of weeks ago, I went back to the government archives, where I'd first gone to seek information about Lisa, before I ever heard from Mo. But this time I wasn't trying to find out about Lisa. I wanted to find out about the other half of me. Which meant finding out about you lot, Dennis. Without understanding you, I couldn't understand Mo.

And like I'd fallen for Mo, I'd fallen for you too. It's something in the blood, Den. We can't help falling for you. And you and I, we have too much in common. We both surf. We both don't know where we come from. We both don't exist.

I went after information about the Vietnam draft. You'd said Mo got you excused from the draft. It seemed strange to me that she could do something like that, in her position. Mothers can't just get their sons out of the draft. But when

I went into the records, there was nothing. Understand? Not just that Dennis Keith wasn't drafted. There was no Dennis Keith at all, either in the draft or out of it. Rodney's name was there, but he'd been exempted from the draft for unspecified medical reasons. Your name wasn't there at all.

I went into electoral rolls. Mo's name was there, and Rodney at the same address, but no Dennis.

I went to births deaths and marriages. And guess what . . .

I went to immigration and found out that the first time you left Australia, to go to the US Open, there were a lot of delays in getting your passport. Mo had handled it all, but had provided no birth certificates, no other identification. She had a great deal of trouble obtaining authorisation to act on your behalf. That would be strange, wouldn't it—the difficulty of a mother proving her son is hers?

But you were adopted, of course, so I went to the family services registry. I couldn't pin down exactly what year you'd been adopted, when Mo established that you were effectively a foundling and an orphan.

And you know what I found?

Well, you know I found nothing. You weren't there. Nothing. You don't exist. But I guess you know that.

What you mightn't know was that they keep records of whoever else has been searching the same files. It's not hard. These hadn't been touched since 1974. When they're looked at, they're stamped like library books.

The files I'm speaking of are where someone would go if they're trying to ascertain your existence—where you came from before Mo adopted you, how and when she adopted you, all the relevant documents. These archived government files, it's the only place to look.

The stamps on when the documents were last searched were dated December 1974. And the member of the public who was doing the searching had had to do what I'd done, and identify herself.

Yes, Dennis. You know who'd been running down the same dead end that I was?

Lisa Marie Exmire. Only time I've ever seen her signature. It's just like mine. Now that's weird.

She'd found out, Dennis, that you didn't exist. Or if you did exist, you'd been picked up and hidden from the state. In December 1974, when she was figuring out what to do with her baby—who she wanted to make your *baby— Lisa went to family services to get your birth certificate and details of your adoption, and she found nothing. You might as well have been made up.*

When Mo and Rod found you in the cemetery, Dennis, she never took you to family services. She never adopted you. She took you. And Lisa found out about it. Were there missing children nearby? None that I could find in the police records. None that fitted your age. Everyone has to come from somewhere, but you didn't, Dennis. It's like you say, you were born out of the ocean.

But Mo—she has a past all right.

I can see why she would want to keep that secret. You were world champion, or sort of. You were headed for the stars. You were hers. She didn't want any questions about that.

She loves you to death.

Rod too. God knows why, but we all do.

You're up and on the run.

'Mo! Moey!'

She's in the kitchen. Diagonals burn your feet but you don't—

'Calm down love, what is it?'

'Where is she?'

'Who?' All innocent, her pleasant smile. 'Who's that, love?'

'Mo? What've you done with her?'

'Ah Den, she's in a better place. And Rodney's home today, so why don't you calm down. Greens first, blues, whites, and I'll fix you some of your muesli.'

NOBODY EVER DOES

Father Aplin didn't want the twenty thousands of dollars you won for the Straight Talk Tyres. Couldn't of took tainted coin. He knew like you knew you didn't deserve it. Knew something gone badly wrong with the judging. Tink was better. Some ugly evil spirit come along and hijacked the event and stolen it for you.

Injustice, the curse of comp surfing.

Father A took his Skywalker and three grand for you winning the semifinal, cos that was the last one you deserved he said, and then he says he's gunna do his best down Far South New South. And he done his best, he did. His shapes went all right for a while till Mrs Father A got mixed up with some grommet and that was the last news you heard of them till a few years later when someone said he gone back to the priesthood but was still shaping Holy Smoke boards with a crucifix logo.

The skin cancer never got him, far as you knew anyway.

Dave stayed down there with Father A for his retirement. You never had another dog after the Straight Talk Tyres.

You give the seventeen grand left to Mo instead.

She quit her last job.

She took on her biggest job:

You.

Said it beat peeling prawns.

There was hospitals.

Coloured pills, electro shocko.

Invalid pension keep you ticking over.

Another two decades lost lost lost. Only bits remain.

Only hospitals and the legends of DK and the posters on your bedroom walls.

The books: you found the good stuff.

One good thing come of it:

Don't you call me an uneducated man.

Meanwhile Tink become head of an academy of junior surfers and head coach of Australian surfing

meanwhile FJ become head of the world professional surfing body.

A Sandman panel van sprayed purple and orange.

The aviators.

Your muesli, your diagonals.

You washed your hands; you stopped shaping; you stayed out the light. You live on chops and chicken and chips and muesli and pine-lime Splices from Bob's. No more trips, no more Harry Hammerhead, no more wanderings. Just home safe with Mo, radio, some books for education and a brain that remembered everything, the filter busted, the doors wide wide open . . .

Peace . . .

They wrote that you didn't surf no more cos all them poisons and whatnot caught up with you. They wrote that surfing was your keystone, and when the keystone got pulled out the whole arch come down. They wrote that you didn't surf no more cos you were too scared someone might see you getting old and wobbly and no good. They wrote that you didn't surf no more cos you wanted your surfing to die young and stay beautiful, beautiful corpse for everyone else to remember.

Like you was always doing things for everyone else, even spending twenty years not surfing for everyone else.

Went out on top in a blaze like some final act in a stage show.

When the truth was you didn't surf no more cos the thought of it made you sick. In all them lost years when you even thought of the idea of going surfing you started sweating and shaking and bugging out. The weirdest part of all them years of weird was life got easier for you and safer and more peaceful and happier when you stopped surfing.

The Straight Talk Tyres killed it for you: winning when you wasn't meant to win. And when you stopped surfing you were close to the fridge an extra five hours a day. And your greens and whites and blues.

And when you got big the thought of surfing made you even sicker. You thought of all them things you done when you DK was surfing and who you been in the water and you want to puke, you want to kill yourselves so

so everything nicer and safer when you was with Mo, where she knew where you was, on land stubbing your big toes.

You got your grand prize:

Diagnosis, names for what it was was wrong, names that come with pills, names telling you there's something skewiff about you all along.

They couldn't explain if it was the drugs that brought it on or a knock on the head from a surfboard or being drop-kicked into the sandbank at Rainbow Bay when you was fifteen, or anything, or Lisa, or Rod, or too much muesli, or some chemical in the shaping bay, or too much pine-lime flavouring, or anything what happened. Or if the disease was the bit what happened first and everything else followed in line, like the waves have to come first and everything else has to follow in a certain order and there's nothing you can do, nothing you ever could of did, it was all just there whether you DK was in it or not, like the waves which keep coming now you're dead.

They couldn't explain was it the sickness that made you good, the sickness that give you your genius.

Nobody really knew did they. Nobody ever does.

Then Mo and you both went in the retirement village.

Then you stopped taking your greens and whites and blues.

The colours of pain come back—

Red, yellow, black, blue, purple, brown pain—

But so did the waves.

Come back.

So did the waves.

And you plotted your comeback:

Waves and waves.

None wasted now.

YEAH, MO'S SENT HER TO A BETTER PLACE

If you ever had something to confess, you could of told my Mo. That's what I could never confess to Father A. Next to Mo, he was a rank amateur. She could keep a secret till judgment day. She would of been a ripper of a priest.

Three decades I never been past it. Rainbow Bay is a small place and it's hard to take walks for thirty years and avoid the same corner of the same street, but that was it, I couldn't bear seeing the QUEENS-LANDER, broke me heart when we left it, it'll break me heart to see it again. I never laid an eye on it since we moved out. It had a force field. I thought we'd sold it anyway, for my hospital bills and that. Turns out Mo wasn't telling me something.

And so yeah we park up the hill, past Bob's, up the road where they've filled in all the drains with crazy paving, the road I never walk up, to the top of Rainbow, where nearly every QUEENSLANDER's been ironed out and turned into a block of holiday units. We get out and Mo's holding me elbow for balance and puffing out another of her fricken secrets, one breath at a time.

And yeah but: this other secret:

She'd never sold it.

Eh?

Back then, 1980, after the Straight Talk Tyres, she'd owned it outright. All them prawns, all that poo, and a little help from DK's winnings. She didn't owe nothing on it.

With Roddy in but, she transferred the title to his name. It been his from then on. Still had renters in it, still has now.

'Least I could do,' Mo goes. 'Rent money from all them years, he's got something to start him up again.'

DK you are floating up that hill

and she

nah but

'And that's where you sent her?'

Mo sort of nods. She's shaking but. Shaking fit to fall over. Hanging onto me arm for dear life. Dunno why cos I'm shaking even more.

'Tenants have stepped out for the day. Very considerate, I thought.'

There it is and me heart goes over the falls, that instant of floating and then bam down she goes. A real QUEENSLANDER. Falling to pieces. Nobody's done a thing to it. Stilts holding it up like the way they chair a winning surfer out of the water. Victory! Cream-coloured slats, busted shutters, rusting red-painted corrugated iron roof. Steep cracked driveway going up. Black metal sign, fancy written: Shangrila. Banana trees without bananas, mango trees without mangoes. Cemetery still next door. All the tightness goes out of me, floods like blood into the grass under me feet. DK you are turning into a pool of salt water, ocean meet ocean.

QUEENSLANDER! All me diagonals. Can feel them right, good, right, from here on the footpath.

Yeah nah, they done one thing to it: the letters on the name, all back. Shangrila.

Up there, girl-shaped shadow moving away from the window.

Mo can't make it up the steps so we stay down near the bottom of the drive.

'Mo?'

'Yes love?'

'You really told her you did it?'

'I did love.'

'And Mo?'

'Yes love?'

'Did you?'

'I'd do anything for you, love. And so did your brother.'

'Did you?'

'That's what I told her, love. So now she can meet her dad.'

'But did you?'

'Course I did, love. She'll put it in black and white one day, and that'll make it true.'

•

So that's where we're at.

Mid-morning and we wait. Flies buzz round your face and you can count them as you swat:

Three of the bastards.

BFO doesn't come down. Mo wheezes like she wants to say something but can't bring herself to.

Understandable in the circumstances.

The tension.

Not quite a happy tension.

Not quite sad.

Not quite angry.

Tense tension.

Mo crushing my free hand.

'And so but we kept taking her coin?' I go.

Mo nods. 'Gotta eat, Den.'

His shadow first, creeps round the corner before he does.

Then him:

His shadow is bigger than him and healthier.

All them stones I put on in these thirty-odd years, Rod's lost. Like I stole them. He's a long smear of pigeon shit now. Him and me'll fit together like two pieces in a jigsaw puzzle and when we are put together we will be what we once were.

Stupid bugger. And the years we stole them too. Maybe we can put them back together.

A piece been missing from a jigsaw puzzle that long, there's nothing to say it can't still fit.

Yeah.

His legs don't seem to be moving but he's getting closer. Got a beaten-up leather carry-all in his right hand. Wearing this faded black singlet and skinny black jeans and GP boots. Still walks with the right-side limp from smashing his leg up all them years ago. Looks like he could be in surfing shape in no time.

Rod got a tight smile could be a grimace of pain. Mo's sniffing.

I can't see Rod's eyes, is he looking at his mother or me or up behind us, his daughter. Or whatever she is.

•

She's come down the drive, walks out ahead to meet him first. Blanks us like we're rubbish, pieces of garbage left out here on the kerb be picked up by the council trucks. We're nothing to her now.

Face like she's going to the gallows. As hangman or victim, what's the diff.

It's sunny, Queensland mid-morning sun, the hottest there is.

Rod's wearing aviators.

I am a surfer. I have ridden a wave in the darkness. I have flown.

Put that in Rod's pipe he can smoke it:

Rod, you been in the Road thirty-odd years, I been surfing.

He wanted to surf so bad, he tried to bust out a year before his head sentence finished. They bunged on a couple of years more.

He wanted to surf so bad he tried to escape again a year before his parole come up. They give him more.

Maybe he don't want to surf so bad no more.

He will when I tell him what I can do.

I sling an arm round my Mo. Strange, her shoulder: she's smaller than me now. Last time I put my arm round her she was bigger than me. Always bigger than me, my Mo was.

My Mo:

Do anything for me.

Did anything for me.

Done everything for us.

But not worth it, you know?

She leans in my side. Us two big people watching skinny Rod stop and face up to this tough little bundle of girl. They stop there on the street, right out where a car could knock them over.

Both sort of sway inwards. Hands hanging by their sides. Rod's carry-all on the ground. Look Mo, no arms. In the space between them I can see right down to Greenmount. It's offshore, low tide.

Rod and her, all along. Bloody dark horse he was but he

but he paid the price

he done the crime he served his time but

he yeah
he done *a* crime maybe not *the*
who's arguing anyway—

My voice crackles like all-night news radio turned low, in my Mo's ear.
I get it now, Mo. I get it.
She leans into me a little harder, pressing like her world's took a
tilt, like she's on water, a wave walling up, pulling into a critical turn.

AUTHOR'S NOTE

Anyone familiar with surfing in Australia over the last forty years may recognise a number of similarities with parts of the fictional character Dennis Keith and some of the personalities in Australian surfing over that period.

However, Lisa Exmire is a creature entirely of the author's imagining, as are Megan and other members of the Keith family. Most importantly, no part of this book alleges or infers that any real person committed any criminal act. The story of the murder of Lisa is totally fictional and has therefore no connection with any real person, whether still living or not.

Also, although a number of real people's names are thrown into this book, their participation is fictitious.

The author acknowledges the following books in the construction of Dennis Keith's story: *All for a Few Perfect Waves: Miki Dora* by David Rensin; *Bustin' Down the Door* by Wayne Bartholomew with Tim Baker; *Occy: The Rise and Fall and Rise of Mark Occhilupo* by Mark Occhilupo and Tim Baker; *Nat's Nat and That's That* by Nat Young; *Zero Break: An illustrated collection of surf writing 1777–2004* by Matt Warshaw (ed.); *Eddie Would Go: The story of Eddie Aikau, Hawaiian Hero* by Stuart Holmes Coleman; *Tapping the Source* by Kem Nunn; *The Dogs of Winter* by Kem Nunn; *Stealing the Wave* by Andy Martin; *Breath* by Tim Winton; *Some Days* by Will Swanton; *High Surf* by Tim Baker (ed.); *Layne Beachley: Beneath the waves* by Michael Gordon with Layne Beachley; *North Shore Chronicles: Big-wave surfing in Hawaii* by Bruce Jenkins; *Best of Surfer* by Steve Hawk, Chris Mauro and Dave Parmenter (eds); *Stoked: A history of surf culture* by Drew Kampion; *Pipe Dreams: A surfer's journey* by Kelly Slater with Jason Borte; *Gidget* by Frederick Kohner; *In Search of Captain Zero* by Allan Weisbecker; *The Tribes of Palos Verdes* by Joy Nicholson; *Caught Inside: A surfer's year on the California coast* by Daniel Duane; *Da Bull* by Greg Noll; *MP: The Life of Michael Peterson* by Sean Doherty (the best book on Australian surfing yet written, in this author's opinion).